I0764641

UPLAND ROAD

ALPHAR PUBLISHING
www.AlpharPublish.com

UPLAND ROAD

ALPHAR PUBLISHING, Burbank, CA, New York, NY.
www.AlpharPublish.com

LIBRARY OF CONGRESS CATALOGING IN PUBLICATION DATA
Moore, Thomas Dr.
UPLAND ROAD
A Journey Within
1 Title
ISBN 0-9786024-20
ISBN 978-0-9786024-20 (at 13 digits)

ACKNOWLEDGEMENTS:

I am grateful to the Campaign for Forgiveness Research which has funded 46 innovative research projects on the effects of forgiveness, including: Jennie Noll, Ph.D., professor of Social Work at the University of Southern California, Kenneth Hart, Ph.D., University of Windsor, Canada, "Forgiveness in Faith-based Groups" by Robert Wuthnow, Ph.D., A senior scholar at Princeton University, "The Causes and Effects of Forgiveness: A Twin Family Study" by Lindon Eaves, Ph.D., professor of psychiatry at Virginia Commonwealth University.

Thank you to my Whanau: Steven, Katie, Gabrielle, Heather, Michelle, Anthony, Murray, Neil, Jean and Bruce. Thank you to my mentors, especially Norman Bilbraugh, Diane Brown, Emma Neil, Chris Else, Stephen Stratford, Michael King, and Owen Marshall.

Thanks to my Village of support: especially Kathleen Spivack, Anthony Chaytor, Sue Hosiet, Tony lee, Rikki Lind, Andrew Jamieson, Pat Edwards and members of the California Writers Club, Paul Chapman and members of the Back Beach Writers Club, and Anna Paliser.

I acknowledge contributions by the following authors: Philip Roth, Toni Morrison, Michael Riddell, Ben Olson, Philip Temple, Brian Caldwell, Chuck Polahniuk, Drew Stepek, Nick Hornby, Chris Else, Owen Marshall, Henry Miller, Richard Powers, Chris Abani, Elizabeth Moon, Lloyd Jones, Witi Ihimaera, Vanessa de Oliveira, Arthur Blessitt, Curtis Sittenfeld, Janna Levin, Marianne Williamson, Ezeibieli Kingsley Chidi and Anne Desclos. See the bibliography for titles.

I gratefully acknowledge contributions to this text from journalists such as: Mark Magnier, Steve Geissinger, Chuck Plunkett, Anne Hulls, Dana Priest, Gene Weingarten, Thomas Curwen, Steven Pearlstein, Ann Hornaday, Carl Bernstein, Edward Klein, Gail Sheehy, Brian Williams, Seth Borenstein, Eric Zorn, Joel Stein, Seth Borenstein, Bill Morris, Jim Lehrer, Jim Hightower, Frank Rich and Maureen Dowd of *The New York Times*, Bob Woodward of *The Washington Post*, Seymour Hersh of *The New Yorker*, Michael Isikoff, Jonathan Alter, and Evan Thomas of *Newsweek*, Matt Cooper of Time, David Corn of *The Nation*, Richard Serrano and Ronald Brownstein of the *Los Angeles Times*, Brian Ross of *ABC News*, Chris Mathews, Greg Brouwer of *LA Weekly News,* James Walcott, Joe Scarbotough, Michael Savage, Sidney Blumenthal, Michael Moore, Brent Scowcroft, the following *Newsweek* staff: Richard Wolffe, Mark Hosenball, Holly Bailey, Debra Rosenberg, Jonathan Darman in Washington, Arian Campo-Flores, Catharine Skipp and Carmen Gentile in Florida and Lee Hudson Teslik in New York.

Editing by Andrew Jamieson.
Cover design and art by Mathew Tribuhovic of Third Eye, Dunedin.
Photography of author by Max Lowrey.

PROLOGUE: Year 2009

It was my cousin, Witi, who first tried to explain it all as he sat with my daughter, Natalie, and I on Ihimaera Hill overlooking the Marae. We had been watching albatrosses climb the thermals that rose above the cliffs in the distance when Natalie turned to me. She started asking the questions I knew would come one day. And yet I was not prepared for them.

"Where is my mom? What is wrong with me?"

Natalie stuck her chin out; stretching her skin over her jaw, the same way her mom did when debating something important. My daughter has her mom's jade eyes… and the big Hotta lips and teeth. I suddenly felt a manic burst of energy, like I could run to the end of Upland Road and be back before the next cloud crossed the sun. Yet all I could do with that phony energy was to grit my teeth and sit quietly beside her, my eyes searching hers for an explanation. How to tell her what happened, where to begin? Words didn't seem to have enough power.

The clouds, swirling through the sky, cast strange patterns like fleeting dragons with tongues of fire, marching, ever marching.

I will always be thankful to Witi, who winked at me and turned to Natalie, his voice shrill with excitement.

"Many families are like jungles. So it is with ours. Natalie, I want to tell you the creation story of the Maori as I was told it, down on the Marae.

I took my first breath down there at the Marae but, ara, I have eternity in me also. My life began even before the Stairway to Heaven was built. At our beginning was Te Kore, the Void. Within the Void, there came Te Po, the Night," Witi says.

"Then from Te Kore and Te Po arose the first gods, the primal parents, Rangi awatea and Papatuanuku, the Sky Father Above and the Earth Mother Below. The Sky Father began to create the Heavens but, during his labors, he thought to make love to Papatuanuku because she was so beautiful. They pressed together in a close embrace, so close that they shut out the light. So it was that when they had seven male children, who were gods themselves, the children were born into the darkness: Tane mahuta, god of Forests, and six other gods.

With the coming of the Light, that resulted when the children were finally able to separate the parents from their union, creation was resumed. The children of Rangi and Papatuanuku completed the building of the Heavens, of earth and the water, of all things in them, animate and inanimate. Then, because all the children of Earth and Sky were male, Woman was created. It was Tane mahuta, instructed by his sky mother, who fashioned the first woman from the red earth. Her name was Hine ahuone, and she began to live when Tane breathed life into her. Tane mated with her and--when his daughter was born, he mated with her also. His daughter's name was Hine Titama, Maid of the Flashing Dawn. It is she who fled to the underworld to become Hine nui te Po, the Great Lady of the Night with luminous jade eyes. She did this because of her shame that her husband was also her father.

None of our ancestors, the offspring of the gods, knew death. Thus they increased and multiplied upon the earth. Among them was Maui tikitiki a Taranga, who was aborted by his mother and cast into the sea."

Witi paused and looked deep within Natalie. You have much in common with the brave Maui, my dear little cousin, Natalie. Maui survived and became half man and half god. It was the aborted Maui who tamed the sun so that it would go slower across the sky, and it was he, Maui, who brought death into the world on his final mission—when he tried to destroy the goddess, Hine nui te Po.

Witi looked far out to the east, across the Pacific Ocean before continuing.

"Maui set off toward the red flashing light in the western sky where the goddess lived. He took the smallest birds of the forest with him as companions. His plan was to enter the goddess' body at her vagina, make his way through it and reappear at her mouth. *If I can pass right through her body I shall live*, he told his bird companions. Thus Maui began his mission. But a fantail broke into song as Maui entered Hine… and she awoke, opened her luminous eyes of jade and closed her thighs. Maui's body was crushed and he suffered the agonies of death.

Because Maui failed in this mission, all men became mortal—but before Maui died, he fished up the islands of New Zealand, of Aotearoa--our home, Natalie… fished our home up from the great ocean," Witi finished.

I turned to Natalie, hugged her and tried to explain the significance of the creation story without revealing too much to a twelve-year-old. "Your beginnings have elements in common with Maui because you are a powerful person who is unique, and your mother is also unique—like Hine. Your mother, Lillian, suffered the great shame of being coerced into lying naked with a male family member. That shame haunted her thereafter… so much so that she tried to deny her own pregnancy."

Natalie had listened intently to Witi and I saw her puzzled look when she contemplated Maui's origins. As I finished my efforts to respond to her curiosity, she turned to me, and the same puzzled look filled her face. I could see her trying to work it out, another question on her lips and in her eyes, eyes so much like those of her mother, Lillian.

CHAPTER 1: YEAR 1996

It wasn't always troubled between Natalie's mom, Lillian, and I. From the beginning, Lillian and I worshipped this thing between us. We looked at each other often, and it was safe to dwell. There was no reason to look away, no reason not to swim into her eyes. She was always a natural, with luminescent jade eyes. A sensitive quiver of her generous lower lip aroused a wish to protect. All men agreed that she was hugely attractive. Others would go beyond that, much further, and risk their fortunes for her. Desire wafted on her exhaled breath, fresh as gooseberry. Her eyes had subtle flecks in the green irises and would moisten when I stared. We inevitably reached for each other. Then our lips might barely touch. Often I lay at her feet and she stroked my hair. I was so in love with her, my lady of the night with the luminous eyes, that I could not imagine a future without her.

Mushrooms-on-toast became my convenient dinner when eating alone... which I always did on the troubled *D-Tox* days. Lillian's son, Paul, was home at dinner hour, but preferred to stay in his room, brooding. On *D-Tox* days I dressed in my best casual outfit; a beige jacket, dark trousers, and sandals--then drank a tall glass of milk while waiting for Lillian. She finally returned from her office and tooted at the curb. I stepped out into the sinking evening sunlight of San Francisco.

Lillian's face was normally lit with brilliant teeth and flashing eyes—but on that particular *D-Tox* day she looked gray and gaunt, like a man serving a long sentence. She drove Paul and I slowly down the hilly Janna-Levin Boulevard of San Gabriel and limped from the car like she had a shagged back. Her son and I followed, down the tidy pathway to the drug recovery program—ironically located in a converted bar... nicknamed *D-Tox* by the youthful patrons.

The door was green and had a lock box. Lillian punched in numbers. There was no receptionist. The meeting room had an unusual smell: not just a carpet glue smell--but something else that I thought must be onion rings and fermented hops. In the corner there was birthday cake and soda... to celebrate the milestone of Paul's new sobriety anniversary—he was about to receive his ninety-day pin for being clean from alcohol and drugs for three months.

There were ten sullen kids and fifteen nervous adults scattered around the perimeter of that familiar Kaiser rehab center at *D-Tox*. I stood before one of a pair of vacant chairs, taking Lillian's thirty-four-year-old hand as she waited patiently for her stiff knees to bend. We sat on the red chairs and I took her shaking hand again, sensing the pain behind Lillian's grief, pain reflected there in the caramel color of the walls. I also sensed the love for Paul behind Lillian's crisis, as I looked three hundred and sixty degrees around the room. Some people shone larger than others: Lillian's ex-husband, Larry, was there, wearing an eye-patch due to the invasion of an infection and sucking on his mints. The head counselor, Dr. Frank Gunter, put his phone down, sipped a lethal dose of caffeine, and settled himself with a brush of his tie.

There, in the caramel color of the walls, in the way Gunter's face perspired--even in his short-sleeved shirt… I came to the distracted realization that Lillian would never escape her mother's unjust condemnation for her choice in men, for choosing an addict as her first husband—and as much as I wished to help Lillian with her son, maybe I could not.

A built-in bar mirror trapped an image of our group in a circular chunk of animated glass. On a plain wooden chair, in a corner near the fireplace--almost camouflaged beside the green of a vinyl bar booth, sat Lillian's son. Paul was small for a thirteen-year old and wore a large baseball cap that hid his eyes and most of his freckles.

Frank Gunter stood and raised his hands. "Listen up! One of our group, Paul, finally did a urine test last night. Paul was eligible for a ninety-day sobriety pin… Unfortunately, the unfortunate has happened. Paul has been doing drugs. He is busted!"

Gunter paused for dramatic effect.

"We have watched Paul accept firstly his forty-eight hour pin, and then his one-week pin. We have all applauded loudly, watched his pride as he stood to accept his 30-day pin, and then last month, his sixty-day sobriety pin. But now Paul has tested positive for marijuana, has fallen off the wagon. Paul will be eligible for a twenty-four hour sobriety pin… tomorrow."

Lillian was sobbing silently, and the rest of us shuffled in our chairs. A sense of compassion and betrayal rippled around the group circle of the Kaiser Parents. The ensuing discussion was labored. I recall three months before that meeting, when Lillian told me that Paul was too shy to pee in the clinical environment of the weekly urine tests… at the age of thirteen! I had almost believed it!

Frank Gunter turned to me. "Dylan, why are you not surprised about Paul's relapse?"

"I could tell by Paul's behavior, the way he has been acting out with loud music, stacking dirty dishes on my desk, and lying to his mom about attending nightly AA meetings."

The counselor liked my response. "You've hit the heart of the program. Users lie… and hold resentments—about which more is always revealed later."

Paul didn't like my response. His scowl made it clear that I had overstepped the mark.

Frank asked us to step into his office at the end of the meeting. Paul reluctantly agreed to wait in the library.

It was a torrid discussion with Frank, about boundaries and tough love.

On the way home we stopped so the kid could get a burger. Paul gave his mom a choice. "This is America. Whose home is it? Dylan's or ours?"

When we were out of range of Paul, Lillian begged me. "What are we going to do? Should we send the kid to a military academy?"

"Maybe, but only if he refuses to accept boundaries and curfews."

"Bullshit! Your fanatical ideals only work for therapists! In the real world we support our children. I want you to move out! By tomorrow!"

I did not want us to kick Paul out of his home—I wanted the best for Paul, to give him a real shot at recovery. But I misspoke… I knew there was no way that Lillian could conceive of kicking Paul out of her home.

The next day I booked into a motel and sat in the TV chair to pull off yesterday's socks. I should have known. But just like that--I was homeless.

Should I try to make amends? Shit! Forget about it all that for the moment. Try and get some sleep and then go back. I worked hard to remember as close to nothing as possible. But my brain was devious…

PART II

CHAPTER 2: YEAR 1980

Gulls are gloating as they fly west, coming in from the Pacific Ocean. The township of Carey's Bay winks and glimmers across the water from our Elsinore, reflecting the late afternoon sun. Several dockside cranes at Port Chalmers are foraging like giant ants. My shoes echo from the concrete driveway leading up to the house of my neighbor, Professor Powers. A warm gust comes in suddenly from the west, off the hot earth of the hinterland. The noisy gust rattles the rusty iron roof of Professor Powers' barn--a reminder of horrors I can't escape. The suture of the driveway centerline draws me downward into the blackness of memory. I have to push the intrusion of that reminder away because I especially want to go to band practice today—to see the foreign girl. Long horizontal lines of balcony railing guard the Powers family. It is always about boundaries! I feel as if I have taken every wrong turn you can take in my short life… and from the wrong lane. Our driveway is longer than Professor Powers'--but his home dominates our bay, like a visiting cruise ship dominates the little port across the harbor from our Elsinore.

The Powers front door is faced with copper, and has a brass doorknocker shaped like a nose. I bang it, hard! A broken scream, then another… a plume of sea spray shoots through a flock of gulls below, wings beating, clean.

"Dylan Hotta? Well I never… Take your shoes off." Dr. Powers is wearing slippers that match the gray of his hair.

"Sorry I'm late." I shake his warm hand.

"I didn't recognize you all cleaned up. How are you?" Dr. Powers asks.

I don't like personal questions. "Good. Is the calf that was born last night feeding OK?"

"How'd *you* know about it?"

"I heard Nelly moaning—and got up. It was a breach birth." I was disturbed that such a young cow should have been put in calf. Poor girl!

"Thanks, Son. Come on over early next week… for a game of chess."

"Might do. Where are the boys?"

"In the basement… Come in." Dr. Powers ushers me downstairs to the band room.

"Your dad getting much gain on his new ewes?"

"Yeah, but they'll jump through any fence. Dumb bastards!" I say.

He twists the brass handle on the basement door. The boys are setting up the band gear. A girl--who must be the foreign exchange student, is standing beyond the doorway. Her intense expression startles me.

"You must be Dylan," she says. "I'm Lillian."

She is captured, motionless. A breeze blows in and slams the bedroom door behind her. She is carrying a backpack, and her expression is now expectant. Perhaps she assumes our band will play authentic blues… I wish we played better.

"Uh… carry on," Dr. Powers mutters as he leaves.

The first time I ever saw an expression of such arrogance as that now dawning was the most effeminate face pictured on the cover of the first *Stones* Album. "Christ, you look like Brian Jones—that guy from the *Stones* who overdosed."

Although my comparison is gawky, she grins. "Call me the resurrected One." Then she fusses in her backpack. "Excuse me. I forgot something."

She leaves the door open… and the wind slams it again. My mind jumps at the violence of the slam, irritated by the disturbance this must have created within Lillian—and the reminder of my pending punishment… for what I did secretly with Lomas in the Powers' barn.

When I feel sadness and lethargy rise, I usually play the blues to comfort myself--with messages of past grief, messages of suffering written by other tortured souls. This girl looks so pained that I know I have found an ally. But there is an echo—I also fear losing her.

Lillian returns, pulling a diary from her backpack. She senses me watching. I swallow and collect myself. She sees it on my face--recognizes what it is…

Band practice with Dr. Powers' two sons and my cousin Witi will surely relieve my anxiety--but I wish I had chosen to play lead guitar instead of bass, so I could turn the volume to ten without blowing a speaker.

Lillian shuffles to my corner of the room. She places the diary on the desk that supports my bass amp. Her eyes follow me as I fetch the tuner. I have to look away momentarily. She opens the diary, smiling at me with jade-green eyes.

"Hello, I'm Dylan." Shit! She already knows that.

"Lil Bjorn," she says. Her eyes flash.

"Anyone got spare gum?" she asks.

Her eyes are strangely luminous, and free of the gothic make-up that I have heard about from Witi… and she has brushed her hair. Her jeans and T-shirt cover the reported Californian tan, except I can see her naked feet.

"Lillian… interesting name."

She turns towards me and gives me the exact look I have always feared… she gives me a look of indifference, a look that wonders why this ridiculous boy is wasting her time.

"How are you liking New Zealand?" I ask.

"I'd feel better if I had a piece of your gum," she says.

Her expression remains arrogant as she turns back toward me. I try to smile, but can only produce an awkward grimace.

"A piece of gum?" She asks. "What do I have to do to get gum around here, Dylan?"

"What? Oh yeah. It's American gum… off a cruise ship."

I give her my last piece.

"You play originals?"

"Just starting out. We play a lot of blues, and a few originals."

I feel Lillian skinning my ass. "I'm more of a songwriter," I say.

She snorts. "What do you write about?"

"The blues..."

Witi starts on his guitar at this instant. Witi's voice and mine weave through each other, borne up by the band's curtain of noise, antiphony--a lost way of thought. Warwick is too loud on the drums... But we all finish together. That's Mat's thing: *Get the beginning and the ending tight and we're sweet.*

Lillian writes rapidly in her diary while the music batters away, until the band finally takes a break. This is my chance.

"Want to go for a walk later, after rehearsal?" I ask.

"That's OK if we can talk about homework," Lillian says.

"What subject are you struggling with?"

"Chemistry, mostly."

Perhaps she isn't interested in homework either.

"It's hard to imagine us having trouble with chemistry," I grin.

The boys come back into the practice room, taking the heat off.

Lillian and I meet up after dinner, and fall into step without feeling obliged to talk. Lil's face is almost pale, except for the sunburn on her nose. I look closely at her new eagerness; feel the stir of her energy, watch her wide jade-green eyes, thick blonde hair, and strong smooth-skinned body. Her eyes flick over me then away. They are restless and very bright. We end up along the top of the cliff, from where we watch a flock of gulls chasing dolphins. The sky is turning red and I can feel my face getting hot.

Lillian breaks the silence. "Chemistry's OK, except for the organic stuff."

"Yeah, C2H5OH takes the romance out of alcohol."

"Alcohol never did have any romance." She hasn't totally scoffed at my joke... but I change the subject.

"I'm going to California. What's it like?" Whatever I say sounds feeble.

"Too many people."

"Too few people here, and they know everyone else's business."

"You got a lot of secrets to hide?" she asks.

Secrets! My anger breathes out for a moment. I once considered exorcising my memory of Lomas with the technique of violent revenge—murder hidden from discovery by the sanctuary of the thick local bush. *Bush Justice*!

"It's not that... making mistakes is a huge sin in a small country."

"Why do you worry about what other people think?" she asks.

How do girls think? "My mom worries. I caught the bug from her I guess."

"How'd your mom catch the bug?" she asks.

I don't like these personal questions. "From Grandma. I reckon the pioneers had a tough time. Turn your back and the bush would jump your bloody fence."

"So the past's been tough?"

Tough's not the word. "My past's no tougher than for anyone else."

"California has fenced off nature with freeways and parking lots. You're better off to stay in New Zealand."

"Swap homes if you like it here so much."

Lillian's face snaps dark. "You wouldn't want my family, not my dad--not evil Eric… or my mom."

"Maybe. But it wasn't easy growing up here either."

"How come?"

This conversation is going too fast… I direct Lillian to look at an Albatross as it drops in with the dusk, settles on the opposite hillside, grazing for a few minutes. Then, at the sound of a distant milk tanker, the bird starts beating its wings. The neck stretches long; her legs lunge forward and push on. Her knees buckle with the effort, she is loping forward, tottering like an infant. Wings uncurl upwards, twice the length of a man… Spread like fingers, they tip the bird into the wind's grasp again. The royal head bows and the wings flap buckets full of air, exerting to gain lift.

"How come it wasn't easy?" she asks again, after the bird has merged with the darkening twilight.

"Only seven kids in my junior school class, and my parents from another planet."

"Your parents, too?"

Now I have to continue. She's cute, but she throws out questions faster than even my mother. "My little brother, Selwyn, can talk like equals with Mom and Dad. But it's like I've been adopted."

"I'm like an orphan too," Lillian says.

"Tell me about it."

"It's getting late," she says.

I know better than to push her.

Lillian walks close beside me. Our hands touch. She has it all… wet eyes, relaxed lips, and a throaty laugh. I forget all about my fact-finding mission. But Dr. Powers calls out, *Lillian*…. then turns the garage light on. She says goodnight with just a dart of her tongue.

CHAPTER 3:

Mealtime is my favorite. Mom is dressed like something out of a movie: half waitress, half meter maid. She has always been too young to be my mother.

Mom shakes her head. "Don't you need a license to be this happy before you've eaten your dinner?"

"It's in my wallet. A photo of Lillian Bjorn."

She serves lamb chops and eggs. "You did say spinach didn't you, Dear?"

I nod. I hadn't mentioned spinach as far as I can remember—but I am forgetful. Often times I pour a glass of milk right next to the one I have left half-drunk.

Through the kitchen window I see another three Albatrosses are finding their way back. The afternoon sun has cooked the air into rising thermal columns that the birds climb upon to scale the cliffs. The old scoutmaster, Lomas, had once encouraged me to study the Albatrosses as they performed their famous breeding dance. *When a bird first returns to the colony it will dance with many partners, until one partner is chosen. The pair will then proceed to perfect a custom dance. Albatrosses undertake these intricate dances to ensure that the appropriate partner has been chosen.*

The fledgling youths spend much time practicing the dances, and these mating skills are mastered more rapidly if the fledgling birds are around older, more experienced birds. Lomas claimed to know a lot.

Two weeks have unfolded, and I still meet Lillian almost every evening after dinner. I hurry over to the Powers home to see her now. Doctor Powers answers the door. "Mat and Warwick are in the study… but I know that you have someone else in mind." He signals for me to go down to Lillian's room.

"Hey, Dylan. Just who I want to see."

She peers at me. I wonder what those shiny green eyes are telling me. It's raining, so we stay in her room and write lyrics for a song and then do chemistry homework. After homework we sometimes do our own chemistry stuff. Anything goes as long as her clothes stay on. I like it when her face gets hot and she sighs those impure sounds. But tonight is different: She just strokes my knuckles with her thumb.

"The band is going nowhere. There's no rhythm!" I say.

She keeps a steady pressure on my knuckles and says nothing. Something in her perhaps shares my sense of inadequacy. Then her eyes reassure me. She changes the music to *Muddy Waters*, and stands, rotating her wrist in the air. "You guys will sound like Muddy in a year. Let's dance."

I shrink against the back of my chair, stunned. "I don't dance."

"What are you talking about? Everything alive dances." She laughs at my terror. "Just get out here and wiggle."

She pulls me out of my chair. I scramble to the center of the tiny room, waiting her instructions--but none are forthcoming. She stretches to full height. I kick my knees forward, shoulders flapping, and wave my hands to scoop buckets of air.

She laughs at me. "You look great!"

I feel like a clumsy fledgling. But my body is pulsing with the beat. The music suddenly stops, stranding us. I stand in a pool of light, needing to fill the emptiness. She looks up at me, desperate for connection. Her eyes are shiny. After we sit on the bed, Lillian opens up and talks about how she still has nightmares from her childhood. Her cryptic disclosures shed no light on the details of what haunts her. She talks about embarrassing things that happened back in California--like neighbors calling the police. But she doesn't tell me enough. I need more of the details, but she always rushes, never giving a context to her distress. I try to coax her into further explanation about her family, but she shuts down.

After I back off, she turns on me. "OK, if you insist on being invasive, I write my stuff down. You can read my diary one day, but not until I've known you longer."

I have pushed her too far. "Didn't mean to hit a sore spot."

Lillian changes the subject. "What's different about your brother? Why doesn't he feel like an orphan?" she demands.

I reluctantly shift gears. "I'm four years older. Home was normal during Selwyn's early years."

"What was Selwyn like as a kid?"

I don't want to talk about this, so I give Lillian a coin to dive for: "He never got bullied, never had the world fighting against him."

"What could possibly cause you to feel like that?"

She has me pinned--but I can't tell her about the Powers' barn. "When I was much younger, I often got ambushed walking home from school."

"How do you know that Selwyn isn't a rebel like you?"

"Because he's got no venom… Selwyn didn't dare pee in the bath water."

"What? Who'd pee in the bath?"

Oh shit! She has got me pedaling backwards again. "This has got to be our secret. OK? Mat Powers did! Warwick heard Mat peeing into the bath one day when Mat was mad at Warwick."

"So you never peed in the bathwater?" she asks.

"I always bathed last," I say cleverly.

I feel shitty about sharing Mat's secret, but I have to share something of my past. "Even though the Powers family is rich, the two boys share the same bath water because it doesn't rain on the Powers' roof any harder than it rains on the Hotta shack."

"So you collect the rain off the roof for your water supply?" she asks.

"Yeah, of course. I bathed last cause I was either caked in mud during the rugby season, or covered in sand during the beach season."

"So, you do have areas where you are vulnerable?"

"The bath is one of the few areas where I am vulnerable… because Selwyn could have peed in it. But Selwyn has never taken advantage of bathing first because he's afraid of trouble. He'd be waiting in the living room when I came home late, and would look enviously at my dirty knees and bruised thighs--and then draw the hot water for his and my bath dutifully."

I visit Lillian in her room every evening now, but when she's writing in her diary, she circles the book with her arm until she's finished. Today she has tears welling up. She looks fragile, and then her shoulders let go, shuddering. The tears spill over and crawl down.

"What's wrong, Lil?"

"I got a call from home. Family problems! I just need a good cry."

Mrs. Powers barely knocks, then crashes into the bedroom with a plate of cookies. I jump off the bed. She looks at Lillian's tears, then at me--like I have said something to hurt Lil. 'What's wrong Lillian?" she asks.

"Just a sad bit in the poem I was reading."

Mrs. Powers gives Lillian a peck on the cheek. "God, love you." She closes the door with a bang that makes Lillian jump.

I wonder why Lillian is so secretive. I'm not sure how to enter her world. Some days I don't want to hang out too long in her room. It is better to go walking, let nature do the talking. We often stroll, following Upland Road to the trails that have been surveyed naturally by sheep, along the top of the cliffs above the ocean where the Albatrosses fly. Chicks might be hatching because a stream of Albatrosses is flowing in the sky, all zeroing on the headland. We have been taking these hikes for months, never talking too much, but when she laughs the pleasure of it glows.

"The sight of the chicks makes me horny." Lil pulls me up and leads me off the trail.

We are soon making out in the woolshed… I like that her flesh is cool. I kiss the side of her neck as I slowly grind on her. She pulls away. I rest, and then grind some more--until she puts her arms back around my neck and pulls me tight to her. An important part of her wants more and she arches her back. When it is too late to take it slowly, she stares into me, her jade eyes wide. I pause, kissing her. She wants me to do it more, and I do. Her whole body begins to throb against me, and then she pushes me away and sits up.

"I'm ready to go all the way."

I watch each gesture of her undressing: the way she unbuttons the cuffs of her shirt, and then sits on a wool bale. I help her pull off her boots and unhook her bra. It is difficult to inhale as I slip off her panties. Our naked thighs touch. She likes it when I tease her--I can tell by her urgent whispers. She pulls me close. I pause, now that I am sure she will not change her mind. But perhaps Lil is a sex kitten. Perhaps she wants me to do it harder, because I do. Her head is banging into the wall. Then she gets a lot louder. I still don't stop. She calls out, over and over, trying to pull my hair back and bite my nipples.

"Oh God, That's just what I needed," she finishes.

Lil and I can do it all. The sun is warm, and I have a new packet of Trojans. She's always seems available for me, and never demanding. We don't do it every day because I feel shy about asking for condoms at the local pharmacy--another problem with living in a small town.

We toss our clothes aside, then jump into the flax bushes behind the long grass that lines the side of the road. The Tui birds scramble when our naked bums sink recklessly into the cool flax bushes. Her breasts are steep like a volcanic cone. Her lips feel swollen as her tongue runs inside my upper lip. I never wish for anything to be different, except that we put up with the fear of getting caught, or getting pregnant.

Lil unexpectedly prepares to fly back to California for three weeks, through the Easter holidays. She has tears at the airport. This time I kiss her in public. Lil gives me a photograph and whispers to me, begging me not to find another girlfriend, *and if you do I'll fuck every boy in Elsinore.*

I feel uncomfortable about her saying that, sort of unbalanced--and don't like watching her disappear into the sky to another land that might not be safe for her —But Elsinore has not been safe for me. My childhood was stolen by a scoutmaster, who used his respected position to trap me. And after this Lomas guy, everything was different. I remember how my school grades declined, and how I crashed my dad's car on the Elsinore Bridge. It could have been worse. Dad didn't say anything about me stealing his Ford Prefect. He found me bloody, in the gutter. His face was tight, skin stretched, eyes straining, relieved that I was not dead. I love my dad.

After the crash, my parents argued with my headmaster that, because of the decline of my grades, I should be held back. But the headmaster insisted that I needed the stimulation that came from being in the upper stream. I told my mother that she was ignorant and needed to take some child psychology classes. Mom called the headmaster for help; *Dylan has become angry and sullen… But at least he is still going to scouts.*

I fill in my waiting time by fishing and sailing, and am glad of some time alone to think. By half tide, the outgoing currents have swept away the surface silt around my boat, and the bed shines with blue-gray stones, shell pieces, and white compacted sand. It is difficult to remember what life was like before Lil--except her departing threat of betrayal has diminished my enthusiasm. My catch today is three blue cod. I fillet the fish in the kitchen, looking out on our rolling valley with its bluebells and stream to the sea. I can see that the smaller boats are marooned, dry on the beach. Through the telescope, the foreshore is flat and white, except for an invasion of sea lettuce at the water's edge, and the furrow from a boat that has been dragged out to the water's edge. Seals doze on the rocks, and ancient Kanuka trees rise into the hills. Upland Road is graveled and windy as it leads from Dunedin through Elsinore up to and past my home. It is dusty at this time of the year, except at the top end, where updrafts of wind from the cliffs vacuum the surface.

Finally, after the Easter holidays, when school has been back for a few days, Lil calls me from San Francisco. Her accent sounds more American than before. I can hear the ocean surging down the phone line. She says she misses me, is in love with me--and asks me to get a ride with Mrs. Powers and meet her at the airport tomorrow.

Lil steps down from the plane and hurries across the tarmac, returning at long last to Elsinore--with platform shoes, a psychedelic bag, and that dart of her tongue. I can hear my heart beating in my eardrums.

Mrs. Powers drives so Lil and I sit in the back. Lil holds my hand and we travel the winding road down the Peninsula, just a few feet above the kelp-strewn foreshore of the harbor that stretches from Dunedin to Elsinore. We lean against each other on the corners, kissing on the hairpins when I am confident that Mrs. Powers will have her eyes glued to the road.

There's a village every few miles along the coastal road. Elsinore is fifteen miles east from Dunedin, the last settlement before the Pacific Ocean, and the smallest. The Powers' house reigns at the head of our valley, just below the crest of the north-facing hill and overlooking the mouth of the long harbor and the Pacific beyond.

Lil and I stroll under the crescent moon, to the woolshed, and get comfortable among the wool bales--new bales; warm from when Dad and I shore the lambs early this morning. Lil says she can still smell sweat and sheep shit from the day's work, and requests that we go to the Powers hay-barn instead. I do not openly resist, even though the hay-barn has rancid memories. We make love, slowly at first, eyeball to eyeball. Then she tells me that I am fucking her good. She moans and arches her back, pushing against me with her shoulders jammed into a hay bale. That sets me off, which in turn sets her going for it.

Afterwards I ask her about her family, that edgy hole from the past. I am pushing her, but Lil seems like she might be more open than usual.

"Why do you want to know?" she asks.

I see an opening and jump in. "Because good friends share personal secrets."

"And you think you can be a good friend to me?"

"Yes, I think I am."

Lil bites her lip, then starts.

The smell of the hay is relaxing. I turn onto my side and face her, then hold her close so that her mouth is beside my ear. She talks for more than an hour. I hold her hand, and squeeze sometimes to acknowledge her stress.

It's late, I'm tired and Dr. Powers is starting to get suspicious. I want to be home--alone, so that I can begin to make some sense of the mystery that Lil is. I can relate to her more than she realizes.

CHAPTER 4:

As I climb into my lumpy bed I recall feeling her squeeze my hand in a death grip a few times during the telling. Lil talked for more than an hour. Her story was more than I had bargained for:

"I never did like my name, not the Bjorn part. My father, Eric drove my brother and I to school. My mother, Ruth, drove us home, and explained that the Bjorn name is from her side of the family, not from Eric. I would have preferred to make my own way home from school. Make my way home to what? My parents lived an endless cycle of dramas, silence, and drinking.

Eric's electric saw could be cutting firewood in the living room one minute, then Mom might threaten a heart attack, and the next minute they could be sitting in the living room, in silence, reading the newspaper. Soon they might get out a bottle of gin and watch a TV program, or go to their bedroom.

The best time I can remember was when I was ten and went to the mountains near Lake Tahoe on a school trip. I was playing in the snow out front of the cabin, alone with my teacher, before anyone else had got out of bed. Mrs. Stevens asked me if I had some Swedish blood, on account of my name.

I explained that my mom's family came from Norway and I got the Bjorn name from her; *I'm not sure that I like Bjorn. I'd like a normal name and a normal home.*

My teacher agreed with me too quickly. So I made my point again, explaining that my home felt unsafe.

Mrs. Stevens wanted to know what *unsafe* meant. She reached out to hold my hand. I pulled it away.

In that cold morning air my breath came out like smoke and my footsteps squeaked. While throwing snowballs with Mrs. Stevens I found a deep drift of snow, up to my thighs. I held my arms out horizontal, and then rolled back on my sinking heels, to fall safely on my back, making a coffin in the snow. A coffin with soft white sides formed around me. Snowflakes sprinkled on my nose and my cheeks. I felt like I was in another world there in the snow, where people were as sane as animals.

Mrs. Stevens smiled at me. The snow felt as cozy as my bed, and some of it was trickling under my jacket and around my neck.

Mrs. Stevens took a photograph of me laughing in the snow. I liked that Mrs. Stevens invited me into her office to teach me about the feeling words.

I didn't need words. *Fear is yellow. Anger is red. Shame is blue, like bruises.* It's always been hard for me to explain crazy. *Crazy is something like not knowing the right thing to do, a mixture of goofy and ugly.*

I felt that I could ask her about the things that I had always been wondering about, like… *Are there real angels who really love us, and protect us from bad things? There are in the bible, I know, but I mean in real life?*

Mrs. Stevens let out a long sigh. *Somewhere in the world, if you look deep enough, you'll find somebody that feels things just like you, your soul-mate.*

I longed to be away from all the fights, happily married to a prince who is good like my teacher. Not a man like Eric who doesn't even know he's bad.

Mrs. Stevens gave me the photograph of the laughing me. I keep it hidden in the drawer beside my bed, and still take it out to remember what happy is like.

One of the times when I really needed the photo was before Christmas seven years ago, while stacking dinner dishes, the night before my eleventh birthday: I heard Eric chopping firewood in the living room. The impact of the axe shook the house. My mom screamed, louder than usual. Mom had cut her finger on broken glass and blood was dripping on the carpet. Eric yelled at Mom: *You're a stupid bitch! You've wrecked our lives! Only a fuck-wit would buy a white carpet!*

I put my arms around my sobbing Mom. She refused to go to the hospital to get a stitch: *I'm too sick to drive. I don't trust Eric's drunken driving. And we Bjorns have more dignity than to ride in the bus.*

My mom glanced at me before turning back to stare into space. I pretended to go to the bathroom and snuck a look at the photo that Mrs. Stevens had captured of me laughing in the snow. That photo lifted me so that I could go back into the kitchen without feeling much at all. My mom didn't have a photo to rescue her.

Eric poured himself and my mom a gin. And soon he poured another, and another, until they went to their room. I cleared the table, loaded the dishwasher, baked a cake for my birthday the next day, and then watched TV. I was too panicky to take it in at first. But I did like the girl who shot the bad guy with a ray gun and made him invisible. It was a good episode.

I went to bed after that and kept the photo beside my pillow. When I heard them clinking bottles outside, then heard them looking in the garage for another bottle of gin, I got Eric's pistol from his bedroom closet, and put it under my pillow. I was waiting for just the right time to turn Eric invisible.

The next day got worse. I stayed in my room, staring at the chocolate cake with raspberry frosting, mounted on top of my dresser. The cake had turned out well, but I wished I could change my birthday, away from the Christmas fuss. I wish I could trade-in my insane parents for normal ones.

Eric yelled from the kitchen: *Birthday dinner's up! Get out here now!*

I yelled back, equally loudly: *NO! I'm not coming out until you stop fighting!* I reached under my pillow for the pistol.

That was the first time I had said *NO* to him. There would be violence any minute now. Eric hates disrespect, and especially mutiny. But enough was enough. I wanted to punish Eric, and also my mom… to punish them for bringing me into a hopeless world of panic that I had no part in making. I was born into the wrong family. I could shoot them both… No! Just shooting Eric would be sufficient, but that would cause more trouble. What to do? Run away? Nowhere to go! Then it had to be suicide. I sat on my bed and hugged Eric's pistol to my chest. I didn't feel right about doing it in such a hurry, a bit guilty. I needed a prayer.

Eric attacked my bedroom door with an axe. I slid the heavy gun back under my pillow.

Eric yelled at me: *I've had a gutful of your behavior! Mother's brat!* He grabbed a fistful of my birthday cake from my dresser and threw it. He missed. It splattered on the wall so he glared at me. I felt like I was trapped under water and my head was pounding. Mom crashed into my room, armed with a baseball bat. *Stop it! Get out now before I call the police!* I could tell Mom meant it… So could Eric. My dad edged out past Mom, past her cocked baseball bat, a strange smirk on his face. But would this signal the start of the heavy drinking, the drinking before the sex or violence?

My mom picked up a towel from the floor, wiped my bedroom wall, and promised me that she'd get the bastard.

Now I was alone in my bedroom. I had to scream. *Why don't you both just stop it? Don't buy into his violent games.*

Mom came back and softly closed my bedroom door. I heard bottles clinking. Any hope of a change in my parents had gone. I retrieved the gun, put the barrel in my mouth, and reached for the trigger. I lifted my head all the way back. My hand was shaking. There was a splattering of birthday cake on the ceiling. A Christmas carol was playing on the radio, *Silent Night.* My thinking raced like a bumblebee in a jar. This always happened when there was a pretense of normal in my home. Fights felt less crazy than the sham of peace. If I were to pull the trigger my mom would be scrubbing blood and brain from my bedroom walls for days, in between Eric yelling abuse, and maybe giving Mom an extra beating. Another drinking binge would surely follow. My dad hated fuss. Then I remembered the photo. I took the gun out of my mouth, carefully.

The photo was beautiful. It is still difficult for me to conceive of laughing, not like I laughed that time when photographed in the snow. On an impulse I put the gun into my laundry bag and walked out to the kitchen. My mom and Eric were reading the newspaper, sitting in front of the Christmas tree, pretending to be normal parents. My mom's knuckles were white, and Eric had blood on the back of his hand, probably from when he punched the wall. A bottle of gin sat between them. My parents didn't look up. I walked over behind Eric. He jumped when he felt the cold barrel of the gun against the back of his neck. *You are pathetic Eric! Get violent again and I'll blow your brains out!* I let the gun rest on the back of his chair. Suddenly Eric rocked the chair back. I grabbed his hair, tore it sideways. *Don't move!*

I've called the police! Eric sat very still. Dad was afraid, for the first time ever… then my brother, Kurt, walked in, and he seemed to be sane for a change, or… at least he wasn't stoned. I offered the gun to Mom if she would take it to the county disposal center. She said she would. Then Mom started to cry and it was more than self-pity. She sounded like a sad lady in a TV tragedy. Something had changed because Mom sounded almost real. I had saved my mom.

I felt strangely calm, in control even. I was tired of living in that crazy house but my new hope was that Mom had learned to stand up to sick Eric. Then Kurt told me that he had a present for me, outside. It was a Christmas tree. *Because your birthday is the day before Christmas, from now on I am going to get you a birthday tree every year, your very own tree.*

I told him that he was sweet, but that he should forget the extra tree next year. I kissed him on the cheek. His breath smelled of beer.

Kurt told me not to be so cheesy, and said, *That'll be the last time that you kiss me. I'm too old for that.*

Grandma Stephanie let me move in with her until things got better. And they did get better.

I moved back in with Mom and Dad when they hired a live-in referee: Uncle Ray helped for a while, but he turned out to be a sleazy bastard and left. Good riddance!

One morning my dad moved out. There was no final dramatic fight. Dad just started packing up on the evening he was served papers and left while I was in bed, suffering nightmares. Even three years after the crisis my dad was still quiet, almost kind. But my mom must have wanted to be free anyway. Mom explained to me that she was now legally separated from my father and getting a divorce, and that twenty years living with that brute was enough. *You and I can start a new life.*

Two nights later my mom came home so drunk that she tried to give me a hug to persuade me to cook dinner at midnight. She brought home a young hippie from a bar. I hate Mom drinking. My eyes stung from toxic tears as I lay in bed for hours listening, hearing the noise of clanking bottles and forced laughter. I woke early the next morning. I got up and went outdoors. A blue jay landed on the gutter behind me. I turned and caught sight of my mom standing inside her bedroom window, hair up high, putting on hippie earrings, preening. I tore into her, asked her why it took her twenty fucking years to dump Eric's butt--then leave me to do all the suffering alone, while she looked for another man to do the same fucking thing with?

I threw my hairbrush at Mom's bedroom window. The explosion of shattering glass sounded appropriate. Mom shrieked, stormed outside and hauled me by my hair into the kitchen. She slapped me and spat venomously: *You've got some bad blood; you're tainted with your father's blood.*

My anger hit red and I demanded to know what in hell *blood* had to do with it? I wrestled Mom to the ground and held her down, yelling that she cared nothing about my blood.

Mom ranted on that she'd had enough of me and planned to call a therapist.

I didn't care. She didn't know how to be a mother!

Then Mom made her big move: She told me that she was taking me out of school, sending me to boarding school. I sat at the kitchen table calmly, observing my mom cleaning and ordering, until she picked up the phone and called this guy John. *Hey John, Lillian's been having tantrums again, is struggling to deal with her dad's craziness. I do think your idea, the exchange student program in New Zealand, might be a good idea.*

Who in hell was John? Surely not that hippie she dragged home. Maybe he was the lawyer she was talking with at the tennis club barbecue the previous month. Must be! Mom wanted me out of the way. That was serious. The lawyer would be better for her than the young hippie. But a year in New Zealand could have been just the fix I needed, wherever New Zealand was.

The following week, Mom drove me down the main street in silence, to the little yellow building with the brown sign: *Mary Blake.* Mom didn't trust therapists. She must have been scheming. The therapist's smooth skin warned me that Mary was a woman younger than her gray hair indicated. I'd learned that medical people could be dishonest, especially when they assured me that I was loved. There were some kids in my school who were loved. I could tell which of the kids were loved because they believed any old lie that I told them.

Miss Blake sent Mom out of the room, and listened to me for a long time. I talked to her about my crazy father, about Uncle Ray, my father's brother--who turned out to be a pervert, and about my mom, Ruth, the bitter drama queen who didn't know how to say anything nice. Kurt had always escaped it all by checking out, out of the house, out of responsibility, out of his mind.

Mary Blake asked me to lie down. I reclined with my head on the armrest of the soft couch. The therapist's hands hovered over my head. I touched the piece of jade hanging from Mary's neck, stopped it from swaying. Those relaxed therapeutic hands held me, one on each side of my head. I felt a warm thick flow of blood seep through me, flowing out from my heart, down through my stomach, reaching my toes. My anxiety shrank to almost nothing. I felt myself separate from my body, from my self, scanning down on it, my dirty old blood transfused, replaced from a clean spring of hope.

Mary Blake explained that my mom felt that I needed help coming to terms with my father's violence, and that I should do a student exchange program. This would be a chance to live in a healthy family in a new country for a while. *Take a break in a new environment while your mom sorts out a new home for you here.*

That was fine with me. And that was that.

Later, during the afternoon, I sat in my familiar kitchen with the warm oak cabinets and crimson walls. My arms and legs no longer itched due to anxiety. Could this miracle last, I wondered? Mom looked at me without frowning for the first time in ages. I wondered if this new look of curiosity meant that Mom could now overcome whatever obstacles had prevented her from protecting me for all those years, and from neglecting to teach me about being a woman. But how could she intend to teach me anything while I was living in a foreign country… for a whole year?

I had to make the best of the situation so I did an investigation to learn more about my proposed host family: The man of the house would be Professor Richard Powers, a well-known neurologist who was in the news because of his new book, *The Echo Maker.*

I studied the author's photograph, a gentle gray-haired man in his fifties who looked like a writer. The thoughtful eyes gazed just alongside the lens. They seemed to find me out, almost half suspecting my story. I purchased the book and devoured it in three nights. For chapter after bewildering chapter, I could not stop reading; Dr. Powers' book provided a guided tour of every state that consciousness could enter. From his first words, I felt the shock of discovering a new frontier. *Now more than ever*, he wrote, *especially in the age of digital diagnosis, our combined well-being depends less on telling than on listening.*

I read about split brains fighting over their oblivious owners. Lives that had been changed because of emotional or physical trauma differ from the *normal people* only in degree. *Each of us have inhabited these baffling islands of addiction, low self-esteem, mental illness, and psychoses--if only briefly.*

The following month, Dr. Powers came over for a meeting in San Francisco—continuing on his journey after his medical conference at the downtown Hyatt. Dr. Powers took a liking to me—and then I knew for sure it was going to happen. I was going to live in New Zealand for a year, down under, beside Australia. I was going to live in an innocent place, a place that has too few people to be rich or corrupt.

Of course, crazy Eric just had to show up at the San Francisco meeting. He barged in, straight off the plane, wearing battle fatigues. Eric had joined some far-out militia in Arizona. He wanted to go to New Zealand with me. He said that he was not going to trust his daughter to be safe in the home of a foreign doctor. Mom called the police. Eric left. And now I'm here, safe in your arms."

I held Lil for a long time... She cried and told me that was the first time she had told her story to anyone.

Lil was my princess from California, but also a refugee from the dark side.

CHAPTER 5:

I have been toying with the idea of leaving my dinner uneaten. Something strikes the window of the dining nook with a sickening thump. I turn and see a bird struggling away across the lawn… with green and blue feathers mangled: a large female pigeon, a Kereru, which had been attacking her reflection in the nook window, thinking herself an intruder on her own territory.

"Do you boys want to put on the tea?" Mom breaks my focus.
"Not for me, Mom. Selwyn can do it." I say.
"You're not your self, Dylan," Mom says.
"I'm a bit distracted."
"What's up?"
"Can't get hold of Lil."
'She always liked the *War and Peace* series on TV," Selwyn says.

Lil's absence is needling into me. And these foreign dramas aren't Dad's cup of tea, *too highbrow and toffee-nosed.* But he watches them anyway.

"The male lead with the vodka-sounding name needs to get out of bed earlier. Do a bit of real work," Dad says.

"Are you trying to get up my nose Dad, for being a bookworm?"

"No, Son. I'm glad you're good at studies. I just wish Mom didn't have her eye on that foreign actor."

"He's not my type, Hotty. Not intellectual enough," laughs Mom.

Monday is a holiday, and Lil is still not back from her trip.

"Shit!" There are no pans on the burners, no smell of bacon or mushrooms this morning… Mom is crying in the bathroom. "What's wrong?" I ask.

"You have an Aunty Bridget. She died this morning, in a mental hospital."

"I'm sorry." I don't know any Bridget, but am concerned for Mom.

"…Grandma Olive has always insisted that we don't talk about Aunty Bridget. Grandma used to ride the Christchurch train to visit Bridget in the Cherry Farm asylum every week. Bridget's illness was incurable so we didn't let you kids know about it. There, now you know. Please be quiet today."

I dislike family secrets, but now is not the time to debate. "How did she get locked up?"

"Bridget was picked up for being a vagrant… after she lost her job at the age of sixteen. That was normal practice; not enough money in your pocket and you were assumed to be mentally ill. After a couple of days unclaimed in jail it was off to the asylum."

"Why didn't Dad get her out?"

Mom is tiring from my questions. "He was away at the war. When he got back home his sister Bridget had tuberculosis, was quarantined, then lost her mind."

"Wow! I didn't know it was that easy to go insane." I shudder.

I skip lunch and head for my boat down on the foreshore. I am haunted by a fear that I am being punished for all that I have done wrong. I untie the boat from the cabbage tree, and drag it out to the water. My course is set upstream toward Dunedin, to a sandbar not more than half a mile from Elsinore. The outgoing tidal currents are strong because there has been a springtide. It is slow progress with the oars.

I rake for cockles on the sandbar. The raw shellfish are thirst quenching.

A woman's scream pierces the offshore breeze. There is no movement across the hillside, apart from the rippling of crimson bed sheets on the clothesline at Witi's house. But the bush and sand dunes over there could easily hide a crime.

Lil's absence is churning me. Jeez, it's only been a month since Lil returned from her Easter trip home, and we had been seeing each other almost every night--either walking along the beach, to the end of Upland Road, or to the wool shed. This week could have been the right time to tell Lil that I might go to hell because of what happened in the Powers barn--that was four years ago, and I still haven't talked about it. Lomas nailed me shut: "Do you want me to tell your parents what you've been doing?"

No! The most important issue in my life is disguising the fact that there is something wrong with me. It hides inside my head, screaming, while the people around me hear and see… nothing!

I often stop into church for a secret confession—a temporary remedy. The church rector sometimes tries to engage me in conversation, but it is important to avoid clever people like him, people that might be able to read my mind.

Band practice is finished for the evening and Lil still hasn't shown up. I see that Dr. Powers is upstairs in his study. I knock on his door. "I haven't seen Lil for a week. Do you know what's up?"

Dr. Powers motions me to come in. "Let's have a chat… but wait a minute. Let me go to the kitchen and make some coffee."

I have always been in awe of the professor. Dr. Powers is respected—even by his students. Last semester, I asked him if I could sit in on his class at the University. I wanted to learn about how to erase my bad memories. Professor Powers stood before the rostrum in the ancient stone lecture theater. His voice came out, full of amplified authority.

Next to the brain, all human knowledge is like a lemon drop next to the sun. Today I want to tell the story of H.M., perhaps the most famous patient in the literature of neurology… And let us not make judgments because this is not about the reputation of the surgeon—Public judgment is nothing but shared schizophrenia. Now… One summer day half a century ago, an ignorant and overzealous surgeon, trying to cure H.M.'s worsening epilepsy, inserted a narrow silver pipette into H. M.'s hippocampus—this gray-pink area right here—and sucked it out, along with most of his parahippocampal gyrus, amygdala, and entorhinal and perirhinal cortexes—here, here, and here. The young man, roughly your age, was awake during the entire procedure.

The theater of students was completely silent.

Those of you with functioning hippocampi who attended last week's lecture will not be surprised to learn that, along with all the tissue evacuated through the pipette, came H.M.'s ability to remember his past…

Bingo! But how can I possibly persuade Dr. Powers to erase my memory in the same way… without surgery.

It is a week since that lecture and the wall clock in professor Powers' study now says 8.10pm. I can hear Dr. Powers still rattling in the kitchen so I trip clumsily across the threshold into his study.

Dr. Powers returns. "Ah, there you are." He ushers me through the stacks of books into the bowels of his sacred study--across the expensive carpet where we band boys are not allowed to tread.

"Lillian showed me a book you have written. You must have psychic powers?"

"The brain is a surprising place. You'd be shocked at what trauma it can recover from," Dr. Powers says. "But healing always takes many years… and rest."

I am definitely uncomfortable.

The professor continues by leading me through a sequence of formal questions: "How's your health, studies, cricket training? What're your future plans?"

"Good, fine, hard, do well at university, establish a professional career, marry an educated free-spirited woman, have witty spirited kids, make money, and then write really good poetry that people will read in a hundred years time, and... I don't need to do anything after that sir."

Dr. Powers nods, and then finally gets to the point. "I like you, young man, have known you since you were a toddler. But my wife and I are concerned for you."

This sounds serious. "What are you concerned about Professor?"

"Your well being."

"Is that all?" I laugh, relieved. "There's nothing to worry about."

He shakes his head while pressing two fingers into his neck. "You've an enthusiastic attitude. That'll get you ahead at university."

I turn to escape, but he clears his throat and continues. "I'm concerned because Lillian has problems at home. I know you two are attached, but she's not the right person for you. Do you know about Ashburn Hall?"

I'm nervous again. "No, sir. But Lil has told me about her alcoholic Dad, and her weird Mom."

"How sad that is… Ashburn Hall is a mental hospital, where Lillian has been a patient recently, twice in fact. She's highly strung, should never have been sent abroad. I'm afraid Lil's mental health is not improving. I need your help to encourage her to go home."

I swallow and try to collect my racing thoughts. "Maybe I could transfer my studies to California?"

"No. That's not practical, and too expensive. Give it up, Dylan." The doctor scrunches his lips.

He might as well have asked me to give up breathing.

"I like Lil a lot. If you could give me a loan of the airfare, I could pay you back, me being promising and all that, Sir."

"No, Son. I'll tell you why." The doctor speaks slowly, like my old school principal. "My professional opinion is that there's a danger that Lil's depression could ultimately infect you. She could make you vulnerable to states of mind like cynicism and apathy. She could move you on to perhaps a fascination with the sharing of nightmares, and God knows what other deviant behaviors. I have seen such a development with my own eyes."

My God! Talk about judgmental! Will he ever stop?

"I like Lillian. But my wife is convinced that she's dangerous for an innocent boy like you. You must call her when she gets back tomorrow. Tell her you can't see her anymore. Do I make myself clear, Son?"

"That's outrageous! Where is Lil now?"

"In Ashburn Hall again, for just a few days."

"What do you think is wrong with her?"

"Clinically it's called episodic psychosis, aligned with manic depression…"

"Whatever that means! What's the cure?" My fury can't resist sarcasm. The world has become obsessed with science and psychology.

"Lillian suffers as a result of her anxieties about her violent home and family relationships. When she entered a relationship with you, her anxiety was triggered further. She has secretly resorted to smoking cannabis to calm herself."

"Where would she possibly get cannabis from?"

"Some transient farm worker! Her breakdown has presented in the form of a delusion, a delusion that men are all predators. Such a delusion is the unmistakable symptom of a psychotic person."

"I can't believe that Mrs. Powers would go along with such an unlikely conclusion, Sir."

"Dylan… the devoted attention of a noble young man such as yourself can be an irresistible brew to a woman like Lillian."

"Now you are patronizing me. I'm not happy!"

"A doctor's duty is to beg for forgiveness from everyone he has inadvertently undermined that day. Forgive me."

"What's Lil so afraid about, afraid that I'm going to *do* to her?"

"Lillian assumes all men are akin to violent alcoholics or predators, and she is programmed to manipulate them--to get revenge for the cruelty of her past."

"So what does she really want?"

"Lillian is compelled to act out on her obsessive need for attention. I strongly suspect that Lillian has been sexually abused during her childhood... because of reactionary behaviors on her part that I am trained to recognize."

"Bullshit!" I am close to losing my marbles so I excuse myself and leave. I swallow my anger down because the most educated man in Elsinore cannot be wrong about Lil's mind. He is a doctor who teaches at the university, a professor!

I call Dr. Powers several times during the following week... and then have another meeting. I respect everything that Dr. Powers stands for: university, medicine, the upper class, but I don't want to dump Lil. I don't tell him about my Aunty Bridget dying alone in an insane asylum. I don't tell him about how I am even more vulnerable to contagious insanity than he realizes. Hell's teeth! I argue that I'd rather be insane and happy than sane and hopeless.

Dr. Powers has pointed to signals that indicate that Lil is burdened with an irrational fear of betrayal in relationships: *That explains her insecurity around you finding another girlfriend while she was away in San Francisco.* Dr. Powers surely knows what he is talking about--so I make an appointment to visit him again the following day. I am going to tell him about what happened in his barn.

I am nervously sipping coffee, "You must promise to tell no one, not even Mom or Dad."

Dr. Powers nods. "I promise. It's my ethical obligation."

I blow my nose angrily and walk in circles "It was November. I was thirteen years old. This stranger, Mr. Lomas, a scoutmaster, spotted me at the bus stop on the outskirts of Dunedin. I was also in my scout's uniform, going home after a troop meeting. I was a lanky boy with fat lips and teeth that were too big.

Want a ride son, where do you live?

Elsinore. Are you going all the way?

Yes, yes I am, jump in.

The car was an ancient Holden and smelled of cooked oil.

I work on the planning team to build the smelter at Aramoana.

He had an accent. I guessed he must have been from Southland or Canada.

The next week, he gave me a cigarette... and another cigarette the next trip if I would take a turn at holding the steering wheel while Lomas lit a match. He didn't smoke and told me that he should report me for smoking.

The following month, Lomas organized a camp for my scout troop up beyond your barn. He said he was managing your ranch for you while your family was away in London. Lomas marched in out of the dark in uniform, late, and sat beside our troop master with a parcel of hot sausages and lamb chops. Lomas ignored me... it would have been embarrassing if he had treated me as his favorite."

Dr. Powers interrupts me. "Had you seen him working my herd?"

"Please, Sir. It's hard to talk about this," I say.

"Sorry. No more questions," Dr. Powers promises.

"After a further month of riding home with Lomas on Thursday evenings, I came to rely on the little pleasures of a large coin or a cigarette. Lomas asked me personal questions about my girlfriend. My answers gradually grew longer:

I was embarrassed after they turned the lights out at a party. Everyone started kissing. Christine complained that I didn't know how to kiss, that I'd just buried my head in her breasts without even taking her bra off or anything.

His questions about Christine were cleverly diluted with questions and advice about my school, family life, sport, and scouts. Other adults didn't take as much interest in me. I wondered if perhaps this was part of growing up and becoming an adult. I wondered if perhaps Lomas was my personal coach, appointed to introduce me to the adult world.

It wasn't until after Christmas that Lomas started to brush his hand across my knee occasionally, like when he reached down to change gear. After a few weeks of 'accidental touching,' Lomas started talking about pretty Christine with the white legs and short skirt. *Do you think she loves you?*

I know she likes me more than the other boys, although she does flirt with my buddy a little.

What are you going to do about that?

I don't know.

Has she ever tried to touch your penis?

No! You shouldn't talk like that. Christine's a nice girl... Besides, nothing like that could happen.

Lomas laughed. *I can teach you about being a man. It's about time!*

Then the hand on my knee moved, just a little bit at a time, and started shaking, and his breathing got hoarse. He would take his hand back to the wheel as a corner approached.

I didn't like it, but I was in Lomas' car and he was driving. I couldn't jump out. And how could I explain this to my parents? There wasn't anything much to explain… just that I was scared.

The next time Lomas pulled up at the bus stop, I told him; *I'll catch the bus and ride with my friends.*

His lips got thin like fish lips, and his eyes squinted as he snorted through his nose; *Okay dokay, but I would rather you come with me, since Easter is coming up and I've got a gift for you.*

Too late to escape! He handed me a ten-pack of cigarettes, a five-dollar note and a bottle of beer.

He turned off the main road before we got to Elsinore. At the ridge, the Powers' barn peered at me around the distant hillside. I became one confused bastard, Dylan bloody Hotta, while hijacked, sitting on a hay bale in that barn! It is always out there, just three paddocks beyond the Powers' ranch house. Lomas drove straight into your hay barn. He opened my door. *I've got some news about your Christine.*

He walked me down the stairs and lit a candle. He showed me pictures of naked women in a magazine. *Christine wants to have sex with you, but she needs me to show you how to do it properly, in a way that is grown up and sexy.* Lomas was having so much fun being my advisor that he gave me another bottle of beer.

Lomas fucked me! I try not to remember the details, but the bastard molested me and abused me. He was a calculating experienced pervert who controlled me. *Do you want me to tell your parents what you have been doing?* I was his thirteen-year-old *victim* and I hate that word. I don't want to be a survivor either; I just want to be me. I thought I'd forgotten, but it keeps coming back."

Dr. Powers stands. "I'm sorry, Dylan. It's a memory that's always going to hurt. I'm sorry that I hired Lomas to mind the ranch while I was overseas... I'd like you to get the police onto him."

I jump up; "No! You fucking promised to keep my secret!"

"OK. If that's what you want…"

"Let me get back to the story!" I yell.

"OK."

"Afterwards, Lomas looked white and scared, his forehead was dripping with sweat; *This will have helped you hugely, Dylan… Just like the fledgling Albatrosses learn mating techniques from their elders. It will help you to be successful with your dream princess, and that is what you want most of all, isn't it?*

No! You're all wrong, I said.

You want to marry a princess… some upper class girl from America? You want to escape to the land of the rich? I know what you want. Don't I?

I begged him: *I just want to go home. Please. Let me go.*

You have to focus on what you want, Dylan. How can you know what it is like to be a woman if a man hasn't seduced you… to know how it feels to be under a man? I have done you a favor, given you the passport to understanding women. And don't you forget it, Son!"

Dr. Powers passes me my glass of water. "I'm sorry… What would you like to happen now?"

"The bastard said to me, *I hope this doesn't come back to bite me after everything I have done for you.*"

"So Lomas obviously knew that he was doing something terrible."

"Yes. He slunk off to the next town a week later. I hear people say, *Child abuse is all part of the tapestry of life. Get over it.* That makes me so angry I want to smash something!" I stand up and walk in circles again. "But I want to hear someone say… any of my family or teachers say, *Fucking children is the most evil crime!* That is what I want most of all. But nobody can!"

Dr. Powers stands again. I'm afraid he's going to hug me. He pauses... and then yells, "Child rape is evil! What a demented bastard Lomas is!" And then softly, "Why didn't you tell your parents?"

"My life depended upon no one finding out. Anyway, my parents had enough worries without being burdened with my problems."

"What was school like after that?"

"I was not a good person. I got drunk at the school dance the next weekend, the day after my granddad's funeral—fucked-up on port wine and the memory of Lomas. All the girls were screaming at my ugly face during the dance. The next morning, I drank the water out of the vase of flowers beside my bed. Dad said he could understand what I was going through. He offered me a beer. *I don't want it,* I said.

We both miss Granddad, just trust that goodness always prevails, reassured Dad."

"Did your schoolteachers pick up on anything?" Dr. Powers asks.

"High school got slowly better after a miracle happened. A new teacher gave me an "A" for an essay. I did my homework every day after that."

"I'm sorry. Not a single one of us adults picked up on what you had been through. What about your buddies? Your girlfriend?"

"Christine dumped me, a few months later. I wondered if she thought I was damaged goods—but I had told her nothing."

"Yes, she probably did sense something," Dr. Powers says.

"So, abuse is something else that Lil and I have in common. See, we belong together."

"No! But she can subconsciously detect that you are damaged like her, a victim of abuse, of betrayal. You were an irresistible target for her to practice her obsessive needs--like co-dependents are hugely attracted to alcoholics. Well… you wouldn't know about that stuff. Lillian will never spend more than a few weeks without a boyfriend during her entire life."

All through this tense week I get counseling from Dr. Powers on why my relationship with Lil is based on her obsessive needs. Dr. Powers assures me that his advice is based on professional experience: "You must call Lil. Now!"

I have to tell Lil in person, but it all spews out uncontrollably as soon as I see her. "It's over. I'm sorry -- Us. I'm breaking it up," I say.

"What's going on?" Lil asks. Her voice is hoarse.

I don't know what to say because I can't tell her about Dr. Powers' analysis. "It's to do with my progress at studies."

"Say you don't love me," she demands. Her face is taut and her eyes are wet.

"I can't say that."

"You must say it!" she demands.

I can't respond. Her sobbing is getting louder. I want to respond. Then I feel a fist crunch my guts. Lil runs home before I can get my tongue to move. I have hurt her badly. This is not right.

The following day, I catch sight of Lil on the main street after school, in a group. She is wearing a black sweater and skirt, and bright yellow stockings. I like the effect. She is talking with my brother Selwyn, her lips flickering. Lil has just seen me. She breaks away from the group, marches up to me, throws her head back, and lets me have it. Spittle grabs the side of my face, like a kiss from the devil. The spittle hangs from the flesh over my cheekbone, spreads nearer to my nose. It slowly creeps down toward my lips.

"You don't understand!" I yell back.

"I understand you dumped me for no reason," Lil says, "But good riddance!"

"I'm sorry. I can explain!"

Lil dismisses me with a finger gesture. I hurry away toward the music shop. Selwyn follows. "Why did you break up with her?" he asks accusingly. "You're a bastard!"

"You're too young to understand. Don't worry about it." I stare back at my brother. It's hard to breath.

"I'm fourteen. Did you dump her because she's been locked away?"

"Dr. Powers told me that Lil wasn't right for me. He should know!"

"You've got to question people's advice, especially adults!" Selwyn yells.

"It's not that simple." I wish my little brother could be mature enough to know what this is about. Mom likes Lil. Oh, what's the point? What's the use in raking over it? Lil is furious with me.

The day before Lil is due to fly out of Dunedin, I see her from my bedroom window, walking along the top of the hill above Upland Road. She is alone, and wearing a sleeveless white robe. An albatross is flying around her in big lazy circles. Her tanned arms are stretched up to the sky and her soul fires a challenge at me, burning her scars into me. This memory of her is etched on my mind: a white "Y" shaped robe on a blue backdrop, her image staying with me, on the top of that cliff, the last step before the sky.

CHAPTER 6:

Queer how nightmares have started again, about Lillian this time… a year later. I wake in the stormy night, cold, but covered in sweat. I continue to see Lil sneering at her dad while holding a gun to his head. My wrists and ankles ache from tension, and my bedding is on the floor. Heavy blood oozes in my veins, cold and lumpy like lead. My thoughts shrink away from the dense bubbling sounds of failure—of drowning in my own incompetence. The pain of losing Lillian throbs, and the agony is my only comfort. I am concerned that Lillian might be anxious about revealing the sick stuff about her family to me. I am concerned that maybe she thinks that is why I broke up with her.

My obsessive thoughts of Lil revolve around a fear of betrayal—perhaps provoked by the memory of my first girlfriend, Christine… not long after the Lomas affair… she and I had made love in the sand dunes. That was the first time for both of us, that dizzy and liberating time. But two older boys, out on a Sunday drive from the city, had unfortunately spied on our sex. The two older boys had been drinking beer in the bushes and now wanted a turn with Christine. *Fuck off home to your mother, little boy. It takes a man to finish this job.*

I would gladly have been slugged down in a pulpy mess of blood and snot. That is what a man is called to do--fight for his girl. But Christine begged me not to fight.

"Go home now or you'll never see me again. I don't want you getting killed."

I reluctantly left, but returned, armed with a log of driftwood. I peeked over the bushes. Shit! I saw Christine on her hands and knees and one of the bastards was fucking her from behind. And she was *loving* it! I slugged them anyway. They stopped screwing Christine and beat the shit out of me!

I have often been haunted by that memory of Christine's betrayal--but I suffered last night from the guilt of betraying Lil. How queer that my *bed* was the venue at which my mind was ploughed and pillaged.

Dr. Powers calls, "Bring your books over and I'll help you with your homework."

"I'm OK, but thanks anyway."

"Any evening that you wish," he says.

Dr. Powers calls again, a few days later, with a pep talk about how my rejection of Lillian was all his responsibility. The doctor promises that he will check up on Lil, and encourages me to talk to the police--*confidentially*, about Lomas.

My University grades start to improve, perhaps as a result of the doctor's support. I decide to include Political Studies as a second major in my degree--in order to better understand the conflicts in the world around me. I become the chairperson of the Dunedin branch of the Young Conservatives, a branch of the National Government. I vociferously support the U.S. Republican President, Ronald

Reagan, all the way from his election to his State of the Nation speech and beyond. Dad thinks I am just being reactionary to his socialist views, and mostly ignores my political interests.

Alone in my room is not a good place for me… I have tried everything—tried—unsuccessfully, to compose a letter of apology to Lil--for my being panicked about her hospitalization in Ashburn Hall.

Why is Dr. Powers knocking at my front door? Damn! Mom shows Dr. Powers to my bedroom. I am embarrassed that my room is so small, so narrow. He is about to give me another lecture—I just know it.

"How are you doing Son, now that Lillian's been gone for a few years?" He puts his brown paper parcel under one arm as he reaches out to shake my hand.

I look down. In the past, Mrs. Powers has visited Mom for a cup of tea occasionally… so I know that a visit from the professor is bound to be a formal occasion.

"It was a terrible mistake, dumping Lil," I say.

"Chin up, Dylan, you'll get over her." The wooden chair at the end of my bed creaks when the doctor sits down.

"I'll never forget her." Powers can be a pestering old cod. How can I make it up to Lillian?

"Lillian left a diary that she wants you to read," Dr. Powers says.

"Why would she do that?"

"I'm not sure, but I had to read it, Dylan. Otherwise there could have been a severe breach of medical confidentiality."

"It wasn't right for you to read her diary." The doctor stands up tall and swamps my little room.

"I know, but it was necessary. Lil was complex for her age… and I was concerned that her diary might contain material that could disturb a sensitive young man like yourself."

"Why do you say that?"

He coughs nervously as he hands me the brown parcel. "There's nothing for you to be ashamed of. It's our secret anyway. And she's OK now that her father is out of the picture."

"Thanks. I need to read it. Now!"

"OK, call me."

CHAPTER 7:

Lil has written inside the cover of the green diary:

DYLAN, I WANT YOU TO SAVE THIS DIARY FOR ME.

I CANNOT TAKE IT HOME AT THIS TIME BECAUSE I HAVE A CHANCE AT A NEW LIFE, PROVIDED I FORGET THE PAST.

DON'T CONTACT ME FOR AT LEAST A YEAR, PLEASE.

I WANT YOU TO READ THIS SO I CAN FEEL THAT PART OF ME IS IN NEW ZEALAND, SAFE, REMEMBERED, WITH YOU.

LOVE,

LILLIAN

I turn the page:

I used to be miserable. Today I feel peaceful. Why? Can this girl be happy for the rest of her days? That is too much to hope for. But, if I write about what is inside my head now while I'm feeling well, then it might act as a map for the lost girl inside me to find her way back to this peaceful place. So, here goes:

~~~~~~~~~~~~~~~~~~~~~~

August 29. I am too self-conscious to talk about myself. Not the private stuff. But I want to understand what is happening to Lillian Bjorn. The worst possible nightmare has already come true in my life, at my young age. It may be important that someone knows my story because something isn't right; I am bound to have a short life. Maybe someone can help prevent it happening to another person. According to Grandma Stephanie, a midwife delivered me late on Christmas Eve. My grandma told me dishonestly that I came into a happy world. I have lived a fast life and am still young. There are things I prefer not to remember... my job is to quickly forget. Sometimes, I ask myself if I started again, would I do everything different.

~~~~~~~~~~~~~~~~~~~~~~~~

September 8. The morning of my arrival in Dunedin began with a red sky. As I walked across the tarmac, I felt adults scrutinizing me from the terminal. Dr. Powers looked different from when he came over to California for the interviews... no white shirt and tie now. His denim shirt was unbuttoned enough to see he had a lot of curly hair on his chest, which was turning gray. Mrs. Powers wore minimal make up, and gave the impression that she could handle herself in any situation. The Dunedin air soothed my nostrils with the same salty tang as the sea air of San Francisco. From the car I smelled freshly mown lawn, and marooned seaweed next to the Elsinore pier where a collection of ancient boats was moored.

My first day at Otago Girl's High School was strict—with fierce teachers and such proper school uniforms. Yet the commute home on the crowded school bus was entirely informal, with cigarette smoking and snogging in the back seat. I saw Dylan Hotta get off the front of the bus, but he didn't see me… It was strange how guilty I felt about spying on such a beautiful man—he was as natural as a wild horse. That evening I found myself walking along Upland Road, past where dust covers the lower leaves of the purple foxgloves… to where Dylan lived. A gust of wind rattled the trees in front of his home, causing me to flee.

~~~~~~~~~~~~~~~~~~~~~~

September 15. I didn't know about the band rehearsal time in the Powers rumpus room; I just walked in on them setting up. I took up teasing Warwick--there wasn't a scratch on his new drum kit. Then Dylan arrived. He looked gorgeous in a rough way, but he didn't show interest in me. I turned my eyes to the long fingers around the bass guitar that he was tuning. His head jumped up by the time I was studying a scar on the back of his hand. I didn't look away. Dylan had that Kiwi accent. His hair was dark and oily. Sweat stains darkened the back of his shirt. His skin was an earthy orange color.

~~~~~~~~~~~~~~~~~~~~~~~~~~~~~~~~

November 23. During breaks at band practice, Dylan and I found it impossible to keep our hands off each other. One night, Dylan's family was out at Selwyn's confirmation at the local church so we went to Dylan's home. He lived in an enlarged fisherman's cottage, above the bay at Seal Point, with four hundred acres. The laundry and pantry were in two booths outside. His home was not a model of order. A slew of newspapers sat on the wooden kitchen table. Teacups, a lamb's bottle, and abalone shells were set out to dry on the stainless steel kitchen counter. A dog leash, a pile of finger-marked mail and bills were stacked on the coffee table. The bright light in the kitchen was the same florescent lighting used in hospitals. In the living room the furnishing was sparse: one armchair with wide wooden arms, a couple of beanbags scattered around a frayed rug and a room divider sloping on one side; broken. Beyond the divider was the hallway to the bedrooms. In the living room, under the window that looked out onto the Powers barn, stood a stack of albums and CDs. I was in the middle of the room, gyrating to *Not Fade Away*, clutching the album cover with a photo of Brian Jones and the *Stones* to my chest. Dylan walked in and took the album cover from my hands. But we didn't get to have sex—Dylan was an entirely different person in his own home—nervous and shy.

~~~~~~~~~~~~~~~~~~~~~

March 26. My Uncle Ray called me in New Zealand. I wanted to forget him because Uncle Ray woke me early one Saturday morning to take me on a ski trip to Lake Tahoe for the weekend. He had moved in a year earlier, after the gun episode. It was Grandma's idea for Ray to be a peacekeeper around the house. He is Eric's
~~~~~~~~~~~~~~~~~~~~~

brother. I took a liking to him back then and followed him everywhere, even to the garage. But just after my thirteenth birthday, when Eric had flown out on a work project, my mom said goodnight to me on the Friday evening and told me she was going to spend the weekend in bed--recovering from my birthday, and the Christmas party, and the New Year party. Eric drank the most alcohol at parties, but Mom suffered more.

Ray gave me sips from his vodka and cranberry juice during that four-hour drive to Lake Tahoe. We drove down from the summit of the mountain pass into the town of South Lake Tahoe. I started to shiver. Ray turned the car heater to high, and lit a cigarette for me. Ray insisted that I hold off from the cranberry vodka--*Until we get to our motel room, then you can drink as much as you want.* Tourists crowded the main street and the motel foyer. Ray put in an order for pizza before we undressed. The spa had powerful jets but became too hot and that made me thirsty. The motel had a good heater and cute bottles of shampoo in the bathroom.

After eating pizza I lay down, feeling woozy, very woozy. Ray came over and joined me on the bed. I remember his cologne, and his hands touching me in places that uncles don't touch their nieces. Anyway, Ray betrayed me; I could see him through the ceiling mirror. Ray was wearing nothing but long black socks, held up on his white thighs with hoop garters. When I opened my eyes I saw him again, doing it with a thirteen-year-old girl—her face was flushed and her eyes bulging. That girl must be a sex maniac. I have heard about sluts behaving like her, but this was the first time I had ever seen one. I don't ever want to meet another slut; they can drive a nice girl like me crazy… I saw Ray and the slut doing it in her motel room.

I woke the next morning in a fog. Uncle Ray was asleep in the single bed. That was the first time I had gotten drunk, and I didn't feel good. I didn't remember much and told myself that the sluttish images had been a dream, but there was blood.

Uncle Ray didn't stay with us for long after that; he packed up in the night and moved to San Francisco. When I finally got the courage to tell Mom about what Ray did, she refused to hear it. That denial was almost worse than the Ray nightmare.

~~~~~~~~~~~

March 28. Can't write today, maybe the diary wasn't such a great idea?

~~~~~~~~~~~~~~~~~~~~~~

March 31. I got a phone call from Uncle Ray again. He wanted to talk dirty with me, was slobbering down the phone. I hung up.

I brought another stash of cannabis from Selwyn, from Dylan's brother. The weed was not too strong this time.

~~~~~~~~~~~~~~~~~~~~

April 7. I had a psychotic episode several days ago, after Mom called and disciplined me for being rude to Uncle Ray on the phone. That set me off! During dinner with the Powers family, I was ranting… about psycho men who were *stalking* me! I screamed at the bang of a door being blown shut by the wind. Dr. Powers sedated me and drove me to the psychiatric hospital in Dunedin, up the hill from my new school.

The doctor said I was there for five days, but you can't always trust men. The nurses were OK, except they did freak when I painted a half-eaten Christ, laid out over a psychedelic cross along a banquet table… being kept warm by a row of gas jets. It was supposed to be an art therapy program. The cooked Christ was served to the eleven disciples, who were engaged in polite conversation. My painting was real enough for me to know that Christ suffered betrayal in a horrific way. That comforted me… made me feel less weird.

I had to go home for a few weeks, supposedly because my mom demanded that I visit her—but actually because I was pregnant. I'm afraid that Mom wouldn't hold it together if she were told about my psychotic episode… (I didn't need to tell her that I was pregnant—my doctor would eliminate the need.) The Dunedin psychiatrists thought my episode might have been caused by manic depression at first, but ruled that out--*Probably just a short-term episode of psychosis, initiated by your violent alcoholic father and controlling mother, catalyzed by your new relationship with Dylan,* they said. Dr. Powers promised me that his wife and he were the only people outside the hospital who knew about my psychotic mishap. I didn't tell Dr. Powers or Dylan or the psychiatrists at Ashburn Hall about Uncle Ray—or about my pregnancy. It was best to keep quiet about that.

~~~~~~~~~~~~~~

April 12. I had space to think more about Dunedin as I flew home to San Francisco during Easter vacation. My grades were OK, and being away from my mom had taken the pressure off. But the episode in Ashburn Hall was unfortunate, had tarnished my reputation.

Mr. And Mrs. Powers, despite their strictness, were considerate… but foolishly trusted me to tell my mom the details about my hospital visit.

My new school friends were from a different planet, but a happy crew. And Dylan--well, he was a gift. My thoughts stayed on him. I remember the time he put pansy flowers in my armpits and navel, while we were lying in the sun in the Queen's gardens, waiting for the school bus. He rocked out that night on the beach after dinner.

~~~~~~~~~~~~~~
~~~~~~~~~~~~~~

April 13. The San Francisco airport was crowded and impersonal. My mom kissed me on the cheek, and told me I looked radiant. I thanked her, returned the compliment, and asked about Kurt--who hadn't shown up, again. Mom was mostly silent, until she was driving us home in her new Daimler. Then she explained about Kurt's latest episode on the bottle--when he ended up in jail. *It is just as well you've been away. Could have been trouble otherwise.*

Ruth had been going out with her boyfriend, John, for almost a year, and had sold her house, given half the money to Eric--and moved in with John, into his apartment in the city. Ruth and John were hoping to buy a ranch together.

~~~~~~~~~~~~~~~~~~~~~~~

April 15. My official American home was now a sparsely furnished apartment in the Italian district of San Francisco. John was the lawyer who arranged for the exchange student program in New Zealand. He seemed quiet. John and Ruth invited me to join them at their favorite restaurant. Between courses of Caesar Salad, served by Italian looking Mexicans, and Chili Rellenos, cooked by Mexican looking Italians, Ruth and John talked about their first date, the reason for my selection as an exchange student by Otago Girls High and their wish for me to finally enjoy a stable home life in New Zealand… *until things get sorted out in California.* I hoped, but didn't rely upon things getting sorted.

I was restless, so planned to stay a few days with Grandma Stephanie the following week. After three more dinners with Mom and John, and three breakfasts alone with the newspaper and a nauseous stomach, I rode an evening bus over to Yucca.

~~~~~~~~~~~~~~~~~~~~~~~~~~~~~~

April 20. Grandma Stephanie's house hadn't changed--except that the lawns were overgrown, and there was a bed of pine needles on the shake roof… A pile of Kurt's beer bottles was stacked beside the garage door. Grandma and I sat in the kitchen, talking about almost anything, but not about the important stuff, like what was going on with my boyfriend Dylan.

~~~~~~~~~~~~~~~~~~~

April 23. After staying in Yucca for two days and kissing Grandma goodbye several hours before the evening bus, there was time to visit my doctor. I answered the doctor's many questions and then waited at the pharmacy, for a prescription for the pill.

~~~~~~~~~~~~~~~~~~

APRIL 24. It was almost 9pm by the time I was well enough to explore the living room. The ocean fog that often haunts San Francisco was in again, and I felt cold. John and Mom were out, as I had hoped. I took one of the new birth control pills and went back to bed--taken over by a new and more tormenting depression that attacked any possibility of me being a worthwhile citizen. I spent a lot of time in my bedroom at John's apartment, looking over the San Francisco Bay, waiting to go back to New Zealand. I searched my backpack for Dylan's letter. The letter was in a side pocket. It didn't mean as much to me at this time. I had thought I might like to have Dylan's baby one day, but today I was not feeling well enough to have any baby, not ever.

~~~~~~~~~~~~~~~~~

April 25. My girlfriend, the girl with a name that rhymes with Bill, had got pregnant—and just had to have an abortion the day before yesterday: An abortion has taken place in my circle… one of many that occurred in the world that horrid day. But unlike a normal abortion, this one sneaked through a B-grade dream to reveal the existence of a dwelling place for the souls of aborted children, a Limbo place beyond Purgatory, a place that delayed the dead fetus on its passage into heaven, delayed it until after another visit to Planet Earth. Limbo is a place in which my baby boy must stay until an opportunity eventually arises for him to travel back via a new surrogate birth.

~~~~~~~~~~~~~~~~~~~~~~~~~~~~~~

April 27. I was in the lounge waiting for Ruth to dress for my farewell dinner. We were going to be late so I called the restaurant. John calmed me down and told me that he appreciated the way I was able to encourage Mom to dress more youthfully. I really didn't have much influence over Ruth. She changed from that floral dress into jeans, from dowdy black-heeled shoes to open sandals.

John had a warm smile, except he was missing a tooth on the left side. John was able to persuade Ruth to dine at a trendy restaurant, a significant achievement because Mom preferred country club gatherings--with starched table clothes and elderly waiters.

During our farewell dinner at the Mongolian restaurant, Ruth whispered; "John and I would have broken up six months ago, after the fight about Kurt's drinking problem."

John had no sympathy for Kurt's problems. But Ruth will never give up on her only son, not entirely.

I liked John's attitude: The upright posture, the confident hand gestures (that fizzled when he sat down) and the way he looked at me, like he was interested in my mind. John teased me about my laugh being somewhere between a miracle and the devil's work. He didn't seem like he was ever going to make a pass at me, which was a relief. But neither did he pick a bunch of flowers from the side of the road to give to Ruth, not like Dylan did for me.

~~~~~~~~~~~~~~~~~~~~
~~~~~~~~~~~~~~~~~~~~

April 28. I only slept for a few hours on the flight back to New Zealand. When I arrived in Dunedin, both Mrs. Powers and Dylan were waiting for me at the airport; Dylan didn't have a driver license because his dad wouldn't trust their Ford Prefect with a teenager. The Hotta family had a four-hundred-acre ranch but they had only one tiny car and a tiny house.

During dinner, I asked Richard and Jean Powers if I could meet with Dylan after our meal. Dr. Powers reckoned I was jet lagged, and had better not get overwrought and end up in hospital again. Mrs. Powers reminded Richard that Dylan and I were sweethearts, and reminded Richard of what they were like at our age.

I ached for Dylan all through dinner. We went for a walk, under the crescent moon, as far as the wool shed. The pre-lamb shearing has not long been completed. The perfume of sweaty labor and sheep shit wafted among the bales of wool. That smell turned my stomach, so we opted for the Powers' hay barn.

My birth control pills were now fully vested, so the latex barrier that Dylan insisted upon frustrated me. I had been anticipating unsheathed sex for weeks, but had relied on Dylan being so hot and anxious that he wouldn't think about condoms. I didn't want to tell him that I had got a prescription for the pill… that I wanted sex as much as a man does, even if not quite as often. Maybe that was because of Uncle Ray, or are all women like me?

~~~~~~~~~~~~~~~~~~~~~~~

MAY 7. I was listening to the Tui birds singing what was possibly their last song of the darkening day when my mom telephoned. Shit! I was due to meet Dylan… Mom tried to persuade me that my father was an unfaithful man who often left his wife and children to chase after other women. I did not believe that Eric ever had sufficient gumption to have an affair… he worried so much about what everyone thought of him that he was always at home drinking, or working overtime to please a boss whom he imagined might care. No! Mom and John were not getting along. That's what the call was really about.

The following afternoon, I got another phone call from Mom. She started calling me *Sweetheart*, and boasting that she would soon be worth millions. Mom's voice was horribly slurred. She promised to take care of me and advised me to marry a rich man--*So we can pool our fortunes and go to the Riviera together.* I hung up on her and at first felt a loathing for Mom. But that loathing transformed, unexpectedly, into envy for her freedom—freedom to do whatever she wished without undue concern for consequences.

The following morning, I sat a physics test and aced it. That gave me a boost, but it was short-lived because Mom rang me again in the afternoon, gloating over her conquest. I paced my room, sucking in what consolation I could gather from cigarettes. Ruth with money would be unbearable! It seemed like I would have no choice but to go back to California--the easiest place in the world to get wealthy, if
~~~~~~~~~~~~~~~~~~~~~~~

you can beat the local plague of depression and deviants. Or, could I live permanently in New Zealand, never having to deal with my family again?

~~~~~~~~~~~~~~~~~~~~~~

Fucking May. I was going through a dark spell, beating on myself, because I didn't resist uncle Ray with screaming, punching and kicking. One night, I started to cry during dinner, in front of my host family. The more Dr. Powers tried to help, the angrier I became. Why did it always happen at dinner? It had only happened occasionally at first, but then it seemed to occur every other night.

Could I handle the pressures of dealing with Mom, dealing with the ghost of Uncle Ray, and dealing with Dr. Powers' relentless questioning? It was getting to be too much. And Mom's drinking didn't help.

Next thing, I was coming home after another stay in Ashburn Hall. The house was darker now. And Dr. Powers had become a mind reader… but he didn't fuss over me that time.

~~~~~~~~~~~~~~

May 23. A few days after I got out of Ashburn hall--with a purse full of anti-psychotic pills and anti-depressants… I got a call from Dylan who asked to meet at the end of Upland Road.

"What's up?" I asked amidst the squawking of seagulls.

There was a long silence. Then he said, "It's over." He couldn't explain.

I asked him if he was sure, and told him that I loved him. There was more silence because Dylan couldn't deny that he loved me. Then he ran!

He dumped me out of the blue. Dr. Powers must have told him about my breakdowns! How to deal with such a crisis? Dissociate. Numb out! I lit a joint and didn't even open the bedroom window. There was a glimpse of Dylan's face in the smoke ring. *Don't let it make you hate yourself. Start off your life again. Be different. Lil, you're no worse than anybody else. Be like that psychiatrist at Ashburn Hall. Be detached!*

~~~~~~~~~~~~~~~~~~

May 31. I almost didn't take Mom's phone call last weekend. She started off all remorseful and newsy--with the Sweetheart stuff, and telling me that she was sorry that she drank so much last time she called. John had just told Mom that he wanted to marry her--so she went over the top. Then she said that she and John had got married, yesterday, at Nepenthe, above the ocean near Big Sur. I wanted to know who was there. Did Henry Miller go? Mom knew that Henry lived at Big Sur and was my favorite author.

"Yes," she lied.

I felt left out, not that I wanted to be there, but not to be invited was a snub. Mom wove a speech about wanting to get married alone, and that Kurt was too drunk to leave Yucca. He stayed at Grandma Stephanie's house.
~~~~~~~~~~~~~~~~~~

I congratulated Mom, telling her that I hoped she'd be happy… I felt the conversation drag. Perhaps Ruth was right… perhaps wealth was the only protection against perverts and psychoses.

Mom asked me if I was all right--as if Mom could change anything.

I said I was fine.

Mom promised to send me a thousand dollars and a ticket home… I would have been buying her the gift if we were a real family. Then Mom pleaded for me to help her to start building a new family. That was what I responded to. I took up her offer and rode a plane out of Dylan's world.

I tried writing in my diary early in the morning, but invariably some crisis interrupted me, or I simply could not bear living the rest of the day ahead with fresh memories of the persistent past. At least I tried… and my school grades were good.

~~~~~~~~~~~~~~~~~~~~~~~~
~~~~~~~~~~~~~~~~~~~~~~~~

CHAPTER 8: DYLAN, 1984

This is the morning that exam results are to be posted at the University. I will move from Dunedin to the capitol city of New Zealand after I complete my degree... Wellington is even more like San Francisco than Dunedin; has cable cars, ferries, and a flourishing gay district. But San Francisco is my ultimate destination!

Dad drives with me to check out the exam results.

Hotta, Dylan... A+

There it is! Dad looks up at the sky and beams.

"Thank you Lord."

I have a Masters degree. And I got an "A" in Psychology as well as in my major, Forensic Investigation. My dad doesn't say anything further, just grins. I walk in circles. Yes... but what now?

"Your mother is worried whether there'll be enough chairs to seat everyone in the garden after the graduation. Congratulations anyway," Dad says. "A good degree. No one can take that away from you."

My exam results haven't made me feel any better… I still feel shitty about Lomas and Lillian… So, I decide to take Dad's yacht out for some fishing…get away from people. There isn't enough wind to sail out, but it might come up later. In the meantime, I'll putter out through the mouth of the harbor and do some twilight fishing where the ocean currents meet near Cape Saunders.

As I march down the hill toward the mooring at Sandy Beach, I discover Dad's boat buoyant on the glimmer of flat water just before sunset. Even at this distance I can see that the hull is freshly painted, cream colored. As I approach the turn in the bay, the deck of the drifting boat appears to be squirming, like maggots on a dead sheep. I put my binoculars over my sunburned nose. An army of seagulls is sitting on the freshly polished deck. And they've been shitting.

An urge overcomes me and I sneak down to the Powers' boathouse where a gun is kept. Fuck! There's shit everywhere! I wait for a bird to take off from the once pristine boat deck, and shoot the bastard in flight. I fire one additional shot into the mass of gulls that are now running for cover in the hostile sky. One dead gull lands on the deck of the boat. The other corpse plunges into the bronze-green channel. The sky darkens as a thousand white gulls squawk in on the last rays of the sun. The gulls wheel over Dad's boat and shit again, splattering phosphate in bombing patterns on the deck. A large gull, a Molly Mawk, circles above me and drops a load. The flock swirls then continues outwards.

I can hear a heavy hum from the wings of the flock, below their falsetto squawk. The sound of the massed gulls rises smoothly in volume to a crescendo, and after an extended chord in unison, the finale ends abruptly: Waves of echoes bounce off the cliff, then silence.

The sky is empty of sound and gulls. New stars come to life, close, as the full moon rises above the ocean horizon. As I walk home I scan the bay. The boat is engulfed again with birds. Shit! How futile!

On graduation day, Mom complains. "Son, you *slunk* across the stage to meet the chancellor with your head bowed, your shoulders hunched, and your posture lopsided."

I don't like criticism. All those thousands of hours of study--and now I've got a posture problem. Mom ribs me at the party; "Time to find another girlfriend again eh, Son, get over Lillian. I know she was lovely, but you have to move on."

"She was good to me!"

"I know. It must have been hard for her too," says Mom, with the same emotion that people indulge in at a funeral, adoring the dead person after it's too late.

"I am thinking of moving to San Francisco, soon." I say.

"Are you sure that's wise?"

"Yes!"

Lil was my almost-perfect lover, whose pleasures included mind-blowing erotic sex, a type of sex that maybe was a by-product of her molestation. When we ate lunch together, at the Windsor milk bar, she behaved like a loose kid. Maybe that also was a by-product of the molestation. I was in the company of a dirty-eyed sex kitten. She said, *You know when a woman who really likes sex walks into a room… and a man knows it? Well, the same thing happens the other way round. With certain men, no matter how outwardly proper, all women instinctively know what delights a certain type of man is capable of enchanting them with.*

She only talked loosely when we ate out at the Windsor, when she and I were sitting beside the long mirror slurping vanilla milk shakes and crunching mushrooms on toast. That was the only facet of the girl that was left within her… and she was my gift. But I didn't send her a letter. I didn't give her that, so I failed her.

This evening at the graduation party, Dr. Powers drags me aside. "Any life you choose to pursue will have nuances, agonies, and victories. Go teach. Go learn. How much more flavor do you want? How much bigger can you hope to make yourself?

"I'm moving to San Francisco, instead of Wellington," I say.

"But first it's time to tell the police about Lomas. Then you won't be an exile from your own home town."

"Imagine me going to a police station. Who would understand?"

"Promise me you'll try, for yourself?"

"I'll try."

At the reception area of the Dunedin Police Station, a bald man in a sergeant's uniform says, "How can I help you, Sir?" He asks me this in front of all these hard-core looking blokes waiting in line behind me! Idiot!

"Yes, you! You're next. What can I do for you?"

"A scout master molested me when I was a kid."

The sergeant whispers directions to a third floor office, "Room 314."

The door at 314 is open. Sergeant Doreen listens, and then she explains that the police cannot prosecute Mr. Lomas. "It's your word against his, you need a witness, another victim to corroborate your story."

"Why?"

"There are three Lomas' on the electoral roll--up north, in Wellington. Why don't you ask your high school and scouting buddies if they have any further evidence that might enable us to prosecute?"

I can't believe what I am hearing. Is she asking me to go around my friends--and ask if they have been fucked by Lomas? "I'm not focused on prosecution, revenge, or anything… just healing."

"Healing is not the business of the police. Talk to a therapist."

"I have! Dr. Powers sent me here!"

"Try a different therapist, I do wish you well, and wish I could be of more help."

"Bugger me! I'm the victim here. I'm entitled to some help!"

"Dylan, I'm sorry. Our system is clumsy. I didn't mean to sound cold. We're just not equipped to deal with suffering. I personally wish you all the best. Child rape is a horrid crime. You're taking the right steps."

"OK, Sergeant Doreen. See you around."

Sergeant Doreen escorts me down the hallway to the elevator and makes eye contact as I leave.

I step out from the police station into bright sunlight reflecting from the marble entrance tiles. The road home meanders flat beside the harbor, toward the ocean. I grin. The highway here is like a miniature freeway in a child's toy set, two lanes wide with the edge defined by a solid white line, the boundary between asphalt and the sea wall. It is comforting that my community has set up boundaries and pathways along geometric curves for people to ride.

The water of the harbor vibrates, thick, moving like a plain of sand in the wind. The waves are not marching in straight rows, but are concave, bending toward me, away from the ocean. The incoming tide funnels by the island, rips and bubbles bronze on the briny surface. An albatross flies out east, beyond Elsinore, to the Pacific, in the direction of California.

PART III:

CHAPTER 9:

Coming in to land at San Francisco, the details of the eastern Pacific ocean are clearly visible on the Californian coast; white cap waves pepper the ocean randomly. The forensic investigation of tank failures and toxic explosions had occupied me in Wellington for a year after graduation… but a year was enough. The plane drops me into a noisy concrete puzzle built hurriedly in grays and pastels, with armies of paper people stalking success, staunchly dressed in grays and pastels. The New Zealand Department of Industrial Research had treated me adequately but lacked ambition and drive. But not me. I am immigrating to San Francisco for the purpose of achieving financial security and career recognition—more than for the purpose of escaping the failures associated with Lomas and Lillian.

I have to rely upon public transport in San Francisco because I must use all my frugal savings to fund the start-up of my new consulting business… operating out of my rental apartment--doing forensic investigations for several insurance companies located around the San Francisco Bay. The typical insurance adjustor wants his consultant to produce a report that is constructive, reasonable, and readable. I produce the goods. Clients and money flow in so it is necessary to hire staff. Projects arrive from other States beyond California--and a sought after Federal Government job is awarded on the recommendation of my first client. The job requires an investigation of an explosion near an Air-Force base in the Philippines.

I fly down to the Philippines, confident that our services are in demand and therefore confidently on my way to financial independence, secure, with a staff of three.

The investigation involves eight humid days examining the accident site at an automobile assembly plant adjacent to the small Quson Air-force Station. The nights involve washing of shirts and underclothes in my hotel room, followed by examination of engineering drawings, photographs of the accident site, and reviews of my interview notes. Two other companies have also been assigned to investigate this accident: one is a local company, and the other is from Japan. Only one building was entirely wrecked, but fifteen people have died. The dead bodies were not removed until the second day of my investigation, and even after that, there are still armed guards patrolling the blackened concrete hallways and rooms. They bring their weapons to shoulder at any sudden movement. My job is to ferret out what came first, the fire or the explosion. The accident was probably caused by an electrical fault, but terrorism can't be ruled out, not yet, not until the lab results are in.

My evening flight home, the first leg from the Philippines to Hong Kong, is delayed until 11pm. I have to wait for a civilian plane out of Quson. It is a hot evening, with smells of chili and rotting fruit, and the screeching of the parrots as glaring as their plumage. The trees beyond the wire perimeter-fence are so dense that in the dusk I can't distinguish a thing. All military planes are on standby. Then the sun is down and it is silent, apart from humming from the emergency generator.

The flight home is further delayed until 6am, and the only local hotel is full. The lights in the civilian airport terminal dim again. I go to the bar and read a book.

I take one more look at the barman watching TV, and at the sleeping businessman. I don't want company. I stand stiffly and stroll outside of the airport terminal to the parking lot--which is almost deserted.

I sit on a bench in the garden, adjacent to the aging stucco wall at the side of the airport. The quiet continues until a small plane comes in over the horizon. The shrieking of parrots breaks the resonant humming of the plane engine with the generator. Everything seems tangled: creepers growing up branches, lianas hanging down, and white and yellow orchids that are latched into crannies in the tree trunks.

There is a blackout of the Quson electrical supply. The terminal has only minimal lighting, powered by the humming generators. It is dim and humid. I stroll around the airport parking lot yet again, to relieve my numb butt, waiting for dawn.

Sometime around 5am I look up. A landscape of misty tropical forest drips beyond the narrow airfield after a gush of rain. But I am dry. Then I see an image of Lillian Bjorn in a white nightdress, walking on a lonely road flanked with gnarled trees and withered mangroves. A breeze ruffles her nightdress. A peal of thunder echoes as flashes of lightning illuminate the road. Lil cups her mouth, hugs herself and shivers. Her jade eyes shine left and then right, luminescent. A distant parrot curses. She bites her lower lip and walks on. Her calls grow louder, demanding my protection! I am frozen. Then Lil pulls her nightdress tight around her shoulders and runs into the darkness...

I still love Lil. But I have avoided looking her up... not until I am successful. I never drink more than one glass of wine with dinner, but I would drink a bottle now if the airport wasn't so industrial and sleepy--anything to distract me from the memories. I am cold so go back into the terminal lounge. I lean against the wall and drift into a moment of sleep again, before coming back. The businessman has gone. I'm almost alone, except the barman is still watching TV, and a couple are chatting in the lounge… they must have come in on the small plane. A wallet had been left beside a newspaper. It feels like expensive leather. According to the driver license, the owner is a male with big hair and straight teeth. There are also several credit cards and an ID card: *Greg Cunningham, Special Projects Director for the State Department.*

I call the phone number listed on the ID card and get a bleary response, then; "Thank you. You've saved me a lot of trouble. Perhaps I can help you? No one is flying out of there. Where are you headed?"

"Home, to San Francisco."

“Me, too. Want a ride? All flights have been cancelled out of there, could be days before electricity is restored. So, I’ve chartered a plane, leaving at eleven.”

Greg picks me up in a limousine. He looks younger than his fifty-one years, stands five-eleven, matching me. He has big eyeballs, a light cotton suit, and a dry white shirt. My sweaty paw shakes his manicured hand and I pass over his wallet. We share our stories on the flight.

It is getting dark by the time we exit the San Francisco terminal. Greg invites me over for a meal. By the time we reach his apartment, Greg has checked out every aspect of my background and asks a lot of questions about Angela Pratt… even though I only recently began dating her. Greg lives by himself in a high-rise apartment complex on the Embarcadero, with a view of the city lights reflecting on the water below, and of the Bay Bridge and its head-lamped cargo.

Greg is a powerful and influential man. I notice a photograph of a naked man beside his bed, but do not mention it--confident that I can handle myself if the need arises. Greg frequently employs sexual innuendo, but has kept his hands to himself. Our conversation touches on my home country, with questions about security in New Zealand, and the government's anti-nuclear policy.

Greg’s fridge is empty apart from a roll of salami, a loaf of bread, and a quart of tequila. We get drunk while he asks questions.

“Now, about the explosion. It couldn’t possibly be terrorism, could it?”

“I doubt it. It might be due to an electrical design flaw. Or it could be that an intentional fire triggered the explosions… tests are being done.”

Greg is having problems with China pushing at him in the aftermath of the Middle East wars. He says he is making progress at countering the Chinese. He boasts of besting the director of the CIA, *an associated organization to mine with a similar mandate to collect intelligence.*

“Fascinating,” I say.

“No vein of American government, business, or culture is independent of intelligence… not finance, media, economic production, labor-management relations, statistical analysis, fringe groups, or pedophiles. There is no natural end to topics that the CIA can legitimately interest itself in!”

“Yes,” I say.

Greg continues, “I’m more focused on the psychological aspects of intelligence, such as personality profiling of foreign leaders and terrorists.”

“Why are you in a better position than the director of the CIA?” I ask.

“Because the CIA depends on secrecy to develop its contacts, and because the CIA puts a premium on the exclusivity of its information. It has no organization chart! No one can be certain who does belong, and who does not--all except for my lovely friend, the director. But then I never saw him wear a gun to work, or get any mail addressed to *CIA Director*,” Greg says.

“Fascinating.”

I am interested in politics, but not in this much detail.

"The director, for his own protection, surely does not know about all the cells, the *enclaves* that operate within the organization. Try tracing the CIA's use of funds... a futile enterprise because there are compartments within compartments--set up like Chinese boxes…"

"Want some salami?" I ask.

"No! Imagine the hoards of wealth that might be diverted to Swiss bank accounts by project leaders who are active on covert operations that don't exist, except for a budget entry in an anonymous account. All receipts must be shredded…"

I am finally able to interrupt Greg. "I have heard that the CIA doesn't recruit agents who are homosexual. How do you know who is gay and who is not, who is a double agent and who is not?"

Greg laughs. "Certain CIA agents have been rumored to have discovered the boundaries of their personal identities to be clouded, and I can relate with that confusion. Given the double agents and moles, the proliferation of scenarios, what is a young man to believe? How can he know for certain the CIA Agency has not had a part in the assassinations of the 1960s and 70s?"

"Want some bread?" I ask.

"No! Don't interrupt," Greg says. "The Director of the CIA is rumored to be gay. There are also rumors that the gays have infiltrated my agency, attracted to male conviviality. In such a mysterious situation the personality divides like the two halves of the brain, a lobe, so to speak, for each plot and counterplot, for the various shifts of identity and cover stories required of all agents and their family members."

Greg's shiny skin is sweating out as fast as he is drinking in.

"Very confusing."

"Yes! The CIA is a mammoth of shuffled identities, and America's history may indeed be unknowable, and the same with the identity of the director, myself, and therefore yourself."

"I like the idea of becoming invisible. Identity is arbitrary and confused. So, why all your anxiety about China?" I ask.

"Their goal was never independence for Malaysia, Korea, or Vietnam, but to extend China's control in the East!"

He raises his eyebrow toward me. "Right?"

Greg pauses until I make eye contact. "Will you grant me that it is appropriate for our people to endeavor to secure the prominence of America?"

I reply with a crisp "Too bloody right," and follow up by nodding affirmatively as he prompts me with his wagging head.

"Then will you entertain the possibility that some of us are dedicated to preventing China from beating us in an economic or military conflict?"

I can't argue with that because my throat dries. Greg goes on drunkenly, oblivious to my spinning head. "I'm sharing this with you because I want to recruit you into our think tank! You have that British perspective that has experience with the PR of colonization. What's more, you have studied Political Science and Psychology."

"Yes, but I am not an expert at PR."

"OK. Let's agree! You work your company wherever you want--all you have to do is lease your brain. We don't need your allegiance, just your intelligence."

"Fair enough," I say.

"Do a professional job of offering your objective opinion during our discussion groups, and you'll be serving the planet--by exploring the options in the biggest game of power poker that civilization has ever seen. The Chinese are smart, very damn smart, and fully intend to beat us at our own game!"

"This sounds fine. And what do you want me to do?"

Greg smiles at last, although his right fist is still clenched. "To be a part-time agent who provides counter-arguments to our plans. Your native intelligence isn't muddled by local prejudices. Are you in!"

"How much?"

"We'll steer a client your way who'll pay you generously enough. The client will also pay for your travel to foreign locations to do research."

"That's the standard compensation package?"

"There's a retirement package, after ten years service. Done deal?"

I nod.

"You're on board. Best decision you ever made!"

This begins a series of meetings in Greg's office every other Monday afternoon for several years—most are a waste of time, but I have to support Greg. He's become a good friend who has fed me a lot of interesting projects. Greg also kindly comforted and advised me when my ex, Angela Pratt, unexpectedly got pregnant with our daughter, Kathy, and flipped out. A few years later, Greg mentored me through my painful split-up with Angela. Apart from the Pratt family and a few workmates, Greg is the only friend that I have made in my adopted country, the U.S. of America—and with him I can talk about anything.

CHAPTER 10:

I wish I could talk with my parents—the Lomas affair seems to have created a wedge. Maybe I should try and chat with Mom about it. God knows how she'll take it. But that's the good thing about living in a second country—all your eggs are not in one basket.

I wake up a thousand feet above New Zealand. The landscape around Dunedin looks like a child's toy set, a quilt of geometric fields planted with red roofs, white sheep and brown cows. Sparse and meandering roads reach out to serve isolated farmhouses. During the approach to land, when the plane bobbles in the wind just a few feet above the ground, I give thanks for a safe flight—but consider the possibility that my recent spate of good fortune might be interrupted.

At the small informal airport Mom kisses and hugs me while jostling my hair.

"We're coming over to visit you in San Francisco next year, before you return home to the ranch for good."

"That'll be great, Mom," I say.

"How is business?" Dad asks.

"Good. I'm busy on environmental damage claims."

"We don't like the American style of elections," Mom says.

The family ranch has a unique front gate at the start of the driveway: chest high but two feet off the ground like a swinging door, made of wood with an address plate, *1 Upland Rd*, above the mail slot. It swings beautifully back and forth on its hinges when dad nudges it open with the bumper of his Ford truck. It is good to be home, and nothing has changed.

Mom steers me away from Dad and into the kitchen for coffee.

"Sometimes I feel like an alien here. Did I have good self esteem as a kid?" I ask.

"Yes. But you have changed. Your divorce seems to have made you delicate," Mom says.

I am not comfortable talking about my failed marriage, or Lomas! But I did get abused by Lomas as a boy, I did recover and have a good business in San Francisco, I do have a child now, Kathy, and I did marry Angela Pratt--and I don't want to dwell on my failures. I have to change the subject, so tell Mom some details about my part-time job for Greg and his think-tank.

"Name it a *think-tank* if it helps your conscience, but it's just another name for a spy agency, and you're spying for a foreign government to boot."

Mom never went to University—but has educated herself by being careful in her selection of friends, reading material and television viewing.

"Oh, Mom. You could hardly call America a foreign country."

"It's a waste of all that good education that this country paid for. You should have studied medicine. Do some good for people… instead of dealing in fearful tattle."

I try to explain, wishing I had never shared my secret. "I took on a project teaching forensic investigation to a class of military cadets at Fort Bragg. Probably the most patriotic place on the planet."

Mom is never going to understand how the shiny faces and barrel chests of my military cadets represent the spunk of my new country's enthusiasm, where everything I see gives me hope of a fresh start… The sky, the skyscrapers, the freeways, the golden hills peppered with oak trees, old hills worn smooth.

In the face of Mom's disapproval, I realize that perhaps I have chosen to ally myself with the American intelligence community for a stupid reason—perhaps for the need to prove to myself that I am recovered from Lomas--and that I'm not homosexual… despite the way my sexual interest in Angela Pratt shrank.

Mom interrupts my thoughts; "There was always something about our family… and I don't just mean the lack of liquid cash—there was something about us that held you back. You think like a victim. You do, Dylan Hotta. You're as talented as my favorite authors, Philip Roth and Chris Else, put together. But you're burdened with shame."

It wouldn't be honest to disagree with her.

"I can tell you that you're running away from something… But for a young man like you, a handsome sensitive fellow with your enthusiasm? You think hiding secrets will bury your ghosts? Bullshit! And you feel bound to achieve your goals… but at what cost? I can hear your soul screaming out: I, Dylan Hotta, I have a secret that I can't tell my mom about. You can talk to your mom, Son."

I am gob smacked! Mom can read me like a book. But, I resist this opportunity to tell Mom about my fear that Lomas may have perverted my brain, and *that* may have driven Lillian Bjorn insane--which in turn may have impacted my failed relationship with Angela Pratt. There are other guys like me, who have been raped by a man, but they are probably not all as clever and secretive in the way that I am, living a shrewd part-time lifestyle in a gay intelligence community, proving that I *am* rid of the Lomas influence.

I must give up trying obsessively to please my parents, so I try imitating my little brother's more successful style: "Hey Dad, I'm off deer hunting. I've decided to borrow your truck. OK?"

"Of course it's OK. Don't be daft, Son."

My Dad follows up, "Time for you to take over the ranch, get yourself a better wife and build her a real home."

I look out the living room window. A breeze pushes the shadow of a cloud across the hill at the head of the valley, then along the top of the cliff over School Beach--where a new house might be built. Perfect! Then I hear the crowing of a rooster. I wonder if I have betrayed Lil. I shudder and shuffle my chair closer to the warmth of the empty fireplace.

"What about Selwyn?" I ask.

"You're the eldest. Besides! Selwyn's got a hankering to fix the world, by being a priest. He doesn't want a home."

"I just might take you up on that, but not for a while. First I need to stretch my legs with the big boys, see if I can make the grade on the international scene."

"Fair enough son, do what you've got to do--then find your peace."

Two days later, I tell Mom about the Lomas affair…

"I had no idea. I'm sorry. You must have suffered terribly," she says.

I tell Mom that I am pleased that she doesn't say what I most feared, *Why didn't you tell me about it back then?*

Time idles by. I spend it drinking tea with my parents and fishing from Dad's boat. The best fishing spot this year is out past Aramoana, through the mouth of the harbor, and around the lighthouse to Cape Saunders. I go fishing alone today, because my dad has a sore back from shearing fifteen hundred bloody sheep last week--with only one helper. Mom did the wool sorting. Selwyn is useless around the ranch, and best left with his books. My cousin Witi is away, fishing professionally. Otherwise he would have helped Dad.

The thermal currents bring a flow of nutrients here during the El Nino season. The green fishing line deviates under the surface of the ocean, bending away, the baited hooks invested deep in the fertile offshore canyon. An Albatross flies low over my head, and then circles the place where Lil had stood stretching out to the sky--the day before she flew back from Dunedin. A flock of gulls squawk above a school of mullet.

PART IV:

CHAPTER 11: YEAR 1996

Hell's teeth! It has been raining and blowing for three days. Trees have been toppling and now the electricity supply has gone down! Who would have thought California could be so fragile. It has taken me almost ten years of living here to discover that this sophisticated metropolis has a vulnerable underbelly—its infrastructure. The freeway is backed up so I must detour across city streets to get through Yucca. I'll be damned! Lillian Bjorn was raised here in suburban Yucca. There were probably only two traffic lights when she was a kid, but look at them all now. Yucca has grown too rapidly over the last decade, starting with the freeway and rapid transit stop, enabling commuters to reach their offices in San Francisco within forty minutes… except when the weather gets stormy.

Bloody Hell! I'm late for my speaking gig at tonight's Toastmaster meeting… and I left Greg's meeting early to allow for rain delays, but the electricity failure has screwed me. I hate being late! I crash through the side-door of the Toastmaster's hall shortly before the electricity comes back on. The master of ceremonies is standing beside a central candelabra, and hurriedly introduces me to a new attendee, Liz. She draws her shoulders back, offers her hand, and then moves to the rear of the room. This woman must be aware of her effect upon men. And there was something familiar about her; I recognize the style and uncomplicated assurance of a woman who wears the latest style of business suit. But it's not just that... she reminds me of Lillian Bjorn! She has those jade eyes, anatomically correct cheekbones and jaw, and the sculptured lips… but this woman is much too busty to be Lil.

Why haven't I looked up Lillian Bjorn now that I am living here? It is more than fifteen years since she was in Elsinore. Her mom was living in the downtown Italian district after a move from suburban Yucca. But was too discouraged to look her up… the San Francisco Bay area is huge, has a larger population than the entire country of New Zealand! Anyway, I have never felt quite brilliant enough to dazzle her.

When I glance across the audience I catch the expression on Liz's mouth. Grim! And her nose is stuck up--the look that my mom has warned me about. *Snobs are stuck up, and cynics hold their mouths sour.*

My speech expands upon concepts I have learned from the author Marianne Williamson:

"Adults who were abused as children often have difficulty in relationships because they can be too compliant, lacking sufficient boundaries to be effective in their relationships… They will seek to meet all the needs of their partner, without daring to ask for their own needs to be met. There is a high probability that, if you and I are not such victims, then we will get into a relationship with such a victim. How do we deal with this reality?

How do we deal with people who have not forgiven perpetrators of hurtful words or behaviors?

Before our soul berthed upon the planet, the soul entered into a sacred agreement with the Universe to accomplish a specific purpose, contractually, with full awareness.

An impaired personality cannot complete the task of its soul. It seeks to fill itself with external power over something or someone. But, eventually, that personality will hunger for the energy of its soul. Only when the personality learns to forgive, and then begins to walk the path that its soul has chosen--by becoming lovers, healers, creators, nurturers, or facilitators, will it satisfy its hunger. Then we become truly empowered."

The applause is encouraging so I invite the attendees to the party that I host at my home on Friday evenings; this party provides a regular stage for poets and musicians to jam.

It takes me an hour to set up the theater and art gallery with sound and lights. I am just finished as the first guests arrive. The regular guests know the routine, so it is virtually a no-host party. I play bass with the house band in the theater before reading poetry around the campfire.

A woman is approaching the outdoor fire pit, alone. Oh! It is Liz with the thick hair and the knockers. I didn't expect Liz of all people to take up my invitation. Her snobbish cynical look definitely turned me off, but now I cannot resist a second look. She has slipped into the circle of poets as they prepare to read around the fire pit. She is wearing a striped sweater. The unfortunate suggestion of sourpuss is gone. She must have had a tough Monday last week.

I stroll up close to her… but she is turning away.

I take her by the arm anyway and lead her into the theater. The lights are pulsing through the incense smoke, to the rhythm of the band.

"Shall we dance?"

She dances well and close, shimmering to a 12-8 blues number as the band does us proud. We dance in a way that assures me that we have a future… but the song ends too soon. She smiles and goes to the bathroom. I smell the bouquet of her essence, perhaps musk. She must be Lillian Bjorn! She had that same gift of melting into me.

I wait, and wait. She doesn't return. I enquire in every room. No one has seen her leave. I am in the art gallery. It has a door leading to the street. I catch the scent of her trail… skunk mixed with regret. I was certain that this woman would dance with me all night. I was wrong.

Three days later, I go to the regular Monday Toastmaster meeting… She isn't there. I copy her phone number from last week's file of new attendees: Liz Halifax 9357944. Not Lillian Bjorn. But it must be her. Damn! The phone number belongs to an elderly gentleman. "Have a good day young man, I know you'll find her."

There is compensation; I now know her current last name, Halifax. There are many listings for Halifax in the phone book. I am prepared to call them all…

"Hello, is this Liz?"

"Hi you… I wasn't feeling well, had to rush off, sorry. How did you get my number?"

So, she is aware that she left a false phone number. She must get a lot of interest from men.

"It took some detective work. May I take you out to dinner on Saturday evening?" I ask.

"But you don't know who I am?"

"I tried… "

She interrupts. "You still don't recognize me. I'm Lillian Bjorn."

She sounds on the verge of laughing at the end of each sentence, challenging me to be clever or funny. "Yes, I figured it out. What a miracle eh, to meet like this?"

"Or is it the devil's work? You were a bastard to me!"

"Sorry." I search for appropriate words—and am still stumbling over my tongue. "Shall I explain what went wrong?"

"No, it's gone, another world," she says.

"I have to say something."

"Sorry doesn't mean much. Just a word."

"I made a mistake." I won't discuss her time in Ashburn Hall. "Sorry, I was confused. I read your diary... powerful!"

"It's only actions that count now," she says.

"Can we go out Saturday night?"

"I've had enough of relationships for a while. We can have dinner and decide if we want to be friends."

"Agreed. I'll pick you up at 7.30pm." She gives me directions to her home in the hills of San Gabriel, nearby… and hangs up.

Lillian is more sophisticated than I had imagined she might turn out, and there is a determined purpose about her, like she might be a company director or a manager. I must be careful, and can understand her being cautious. I need to talk about Lillian, so call my parents in New Zealand.

My parent's answering machine says they are away, camping.

I call Selwyn, who is working as a parish priest back in Dunedin, and who has recently applied for a priest position in Mexico. Selwyn warns me to be careful. "Halifax might be her married name."

It is finally Saturday evening. I cruise slowly up Pebble Beach Drive, at sunset, to a compound of architecturally designed mansions--with massive hooded tile roofs, like Darth Vader helmets. The small faces of the houses that align below their massive roofs are lathered with stucco, in earth tones ranging from clay-gray to creamy ochre. The roofs dominate the hillside like an army of tanks. Her home is just five miles from my Victorian, but so different… opulent!

The front door of Lillian's house is solid hardwood, bleached, embellished with beveled glass and brass. She is wearing an olive-green pants suit with a gold zipper down the front—from throat to crotch. Her hairstyle is different, brushed aside from her forehead. Her face has that fresh apricot texture. A hint of a sunburned nose is a pretty blemish, a battle scar indicating fearless character. She wears no more than the perfect hint of lipstick above the raised collar of her blouse. I could live with that smile on a regular basis.

"Come in. Let's go to the family room."

It is a distance from the entrance foyer to our destination. Lillian walks with a cat's sense of rhythm. I follow her through the open entrance foyer, passing the formal lounge, passing the landing to the curved stairway which leads both up and down, and we pass the kitchen at amidships--where the ceiling is hung low, like the underside of a spacecraft, with circular lights. We stop in the living room, which has a gas-lit fireplace overhung with a sculpture of metal abstractions.

"Interesting art you have."

"Yes, I thought you might appreciate it. May I get you a glass of wine?" She does not pour wine for herself, but raises a glass of iced water. "God bless!"

Lillian introduces her daughter Barbara--who can be no younger than sixteen. Barbara stands at a distance. Her hand swipes at wavy blonde hair that frames hawk-eyes. Barbara has a perfect olive complexion. Lil could have been no more than eighteen when she gave birth to her daughter. Barbara remains in the family room and listens in to our stiff conversation: "Tell me about your Victorian home?" Lil asks.

"You've seen that I've added on the carriage house with multi-purpose rooms. The front house is now on the historical register."

Lil invites me to look around the garden before the sun goes down. "But first…" She takes down a photograph from the wall. "This is my son Paul, isn't he cute, he's twelve and is out in the city with friends. That's Barbara, and behind is my old boyfriend, big Bill… and I."

They are exiting a helicopter while on vacation in Israel. Paul has reddish hair, and freckles bunched in two clusters below his hazel eyes.

We go outdoors. The landscape is designed around a matching tiled pool and spa, located down at the lower terrace level. We walk around the upper terrace, drawn to a Kennedy sculpture of a couple, Romeo and Juliet, who have their arms flung high and wide, fingers outstretched. Their eyes are made from Abalone shell. The famous couple is smiling at us, reminding me of how good Lillian and I once had it. A wind sculpture whirls beyond the patio, and two sculptured sheep meditate on the plush lawn beside the steps leading to the lower terrace. The pool and spa whisper in Roman accents below.

I follow Lillian down a pathway between miniature orange trees. She leads me through an archway of wisteria, to a hidden fishpond, an approximate replica of the abstract shape of the swimming pool. Fermenting oak leaves lie on the gravel bed of the pond. A dozen green and yellow fish glide to and from the shady below the patch of water lilies.

Lillian beckons me on. She certainly doesn't need my money--my stash from Greg's projects and business profits… peanuts to her. I walk past her, and pause beside the swimming pool at the entrance to the gazebo. Lillian is studying me with a crease of lines on her brow… not the fresh faced trust she carried back in New Zealand, or the snobbish appraisal with which she dismissed the Toastmaster meeting in Yucca, nor the sexy woman who danced so well last Friday evening at my home. Her movements are precise.

"It's time to go to dinner," she says.

We drive in my new Honda, out of the complex of mansions, past the private tennis courts, down the hill to central San Gabriel, to dine at the California Café.

"An interesting home you have. Have you lived there long?" I ask.

"Two years. It belongs to my previous boyfriend, Bill."

"Ah, yes. The guy in the photograph on the living room wall?"

"Yes, the one in the kids' photograph. He died recently."

"Oh, I'm sorry. How long ago since you lost him?"

"Six months," Lillian says.

"It must be hard for you."

She grimaces.

We order our meal. Lillian prefers steak and lobster with a pinot noir, while I choose shellfish and iced water.

Lillian leads the conversation: "It's interesting timing the way I have met you again. I recently joined a gym and tennis club, got a boob job to get my spirits up and now I've decided to try out a Toastmasters meeting. I recognized you, but you just nodded casually at me. You had the same grin and dimples as the Dylan I knew in Dunedin. *What could Dylan Hotta possibly be doing here?* I thought."

"I have a business, doing forensic investigations of industrial accidents."

She nods approvingly. “I decided to bide my time at Toastmasters, watch the way you walked to the podium. Nice suit, Dylan. You said the word ‘mates’ in your fourth sentence with a definite accent. And went on to say:

I’ve learnt that many people from your community and mine were damaged by childhood abuse. Very few have healed. They are wounded, wound up, ticking, and perhaps thinking that they are normal. Nature is the most reliable method of healing available today…. healing away from human conflicts.

“That was awesome stuff, Dylan.”

“I’m surprised that you remember.”

“I went to a lecture that said, Couples wishing to date successfully should ask each other two most searching questions. Want to try the questions?” she asks.

“OK, sounds interesting.”

“What’s money to you?”

“Money is a license to use resources,” I say. “I don't balance my checkbook; just spend according to my needs.”

Lillian acknowledges my response with a cautious flash of a half-smile. “Yes, generosity is the inevitable product of a heart capable of true love.”

I could have felt trapped by the coupling of generosity with love, but Lillian is obviously well endowed financially. I’ve seen my parents struggle to build the ranch up to what it is today. I certainly won’t be buying anyone a new convertible. Frivolous expenditure is often mistaken for generosity.

“How do you feel about money?” I ask.

Lillian doesn’t flinch. “Much as you do. Fear is the biggest issue: Fear kills love, and it kills trust.”

“Yes, generosity is liberating. Do you use a budget?” I ask.

“Yes, I am a Financial Advisor. With faith we can afford whatever we need.”

“Yeah, faith is an essential ingredient to an abundant life.”

“Are you single?” Lillian asks.

“Yes. But I’ve a seven-year-old daughter, Kathy.”

“I bet she looks like you. Lucky girl.”

“How old is Paul?” I ask.

“Twelve. Paul and I are very close. Barbara is my ex-husband’s child from his first marriage, but I have custody of her. My ex-husband, Larry Halifax, is a musician. You know the type! Consequently, Barbara can be a handful.”

“Yeah, Kathy’s got a strong will too.”

“It’s important for children to be free of fear,” Lillian says.

“How did Bill get on with the children?”

“Both kids hated him! Barbara got mad when Bill didn't buy her a new car. He had done so for his other daughters. He was worth mega-millions, so the money was nothing to him. But he favored his birth children. I didn’t respect that!”

“How does Larry get along with Barbara?”

“He hasn’t seen her since the divorce. We don’t hear from him.”

"You've been through a lot," I say.

"Yes. Tell me about Kathy, and her mom?"

"Kathy's seven now, was born at Kaiser Hospital in San Gabriel; a little cherub smiling at me with a ruddy new layer of skin, wet black hair, and shiny gums. I've been hooked on her ever since."

"What about the marriage?"

"The wedding was a shotgun job. My mom cried miserably. My brother Selwyn tried to cheer Mom up, and they got drunk in the process. But I felt privileged to have a job that I like, co-workers that I like, and to be able to work with a wife that I loved, and furnish a nursery for the baby that we both wanted."

"So why did you get divorced?"

"After years of being just an un-oiled cog in the marriage, Angela pushed me too far. She tried to take over my business as well."

"Sorry, I didn't mean to hit a sore spot."

"I failed those I love... again. Kathy has a hearing disability, and will soon be fitted with a high-tech aid. But I'm teaching her to be a chess champion."

"That's great. I'm sure she'll make it."

We are walking toward my car. It is 10pm. I can't remember what I have eaten, or remember the faces adjacent to our table. I know there is a connection between us… and no time has passed at all in my heart since Elsinore.

Lillian breaks the silence, "What would you like to do now?"

"We could go to a movie across the road?"

"We can't talk there. I know of a new jazz club. Slates. Want to try it?"

"Yeah, I've heard of it. We can walk from here."

Lillian turns, "And the other question is, what do you want to ultimately be?"

"You start," I insist.

"I want happiness, to be safe and secure with my soul-mate, free of mistrust and fear. I want to be accepted just as I am."

I'm glad she doesn't want to be rich. That could be a problem, since Bill's estate owns her home. "I would like to live with my soul-mate forever, and to write poetry about our love, to die knowing I've shared myself with the planet."

Slates Club is a reproduction of Manhattan chic, with opera curtains over the tiny stage, soft lighting, under-employed models for waitresses, stoned jazz musicians playing with time to spare. We sit upstairs in a booth above the stage.

I order a 2007 Montana Sauvignon Blanc. Lillian drinks the same. We look at each other, and it is safe to dwell. There is no reason to look away, no reason not to swim into her eyes as the wine takes effect. She is a natural, with luminescent eyes and exquisitely shaped teeth. A sensitive quiver of her generous lower lip arouses a wish to protect. All men will agree that she is hugely attractive. Others will go beyond that, much further, and risk their fortunes for her. Desire wafts on her exhaled breath, fresh as gooseberry. Her eyes have subtle flecks in the jade irises.

Our fingertips touch. Warmth draws us in further. Her eyes moisten. I swallow. We reach for each other. Our lips barely touch.

"I promise to take this really slow."

Lil whispers the promise back, and adds; "I am falling for you, the man who will accept me just as I am." We stay in the trance.

A soft breeze rises and falls. We go downstairs to dance. The musicians pick up on our energy. We dance until we ache for each other.

CHAPTER 12:

Our table levitates in a soft corner away from the turning heads. Our waiter's presentation is impeccable, as is the escargot. Lil is wearing a string of pearls over a dark suit--with diamond earrings that flash when she talks.

"What do you want to happen with us?" she asks.

"I want to remain in love forever."

"With me?"

"Yes, and with the entire Universe. There will never be anyone but you."

She smiles stiffly. "I really do believe that you mean what you say."

When Lil is nervous, which is rare, I also get nervous.

"Of course I do. You are magnificent."

Lil leans forward, her elbows almost on the table.

I let the pause lengthen. I can feel her uncertainty, her discouragement beneath the mask of her social confidence.

"I'm hopeful," she says, "that we can work through our past."

"Whatever it takes. OK?"

"OK. If you think you're up for it?"

"Yes, I am. So tell me what you've been up to?" I ask.

Lil gets the conversation flowing. "My mom has married the lawyer, John. They live on a ranch at Garland, at the base of Mount Sierra, five hours drive north. My dad moved back to Phoenix after his stroke, where he limits himself to two cocktails at sunset under the cactus trees, with a new girlfriend whom he has never beaten up."

"So he's still a practicing alcoholic?"

"No! I haven't seen him drunk for sixteen years. But my brother Kurt is. He's still living in grandma Stephanie's house."

There is just the right amount of brandy in the shrimp bisque.

"A good choice of wine, Dylan. What's Selwyn up to?"

"He's a Catholic priest in Dunedin, and has become an activist for social justice. Not a commie, but damn close. He has been offered a job interview at Saint Mary's in Yucca. But he wants ultimately to work in Latin America. California is just a stepping stone to the front line."

"And how are Helen and Hotty?"

"They're still in love. Mom's taken up art. Dad is ranching of course, but has hired a local kid to help out. Mom and Dad both like to travel around in their motor home, and are at Aramoana at the moment."

"And Professor and Jean Powers?"

"They have become adult friends. Richard told me the details of your episode of psychosis. Have you had any other attack?"

"No. Never did have a psychosis. They figured it was just stress. I'm fine."

I wonder why she's in denial. "Tell me what you've been up to?"

"I've been back to New Zealand. Bill and I did Queenstown, and a ranch stay. Great skiing. The only other place I would like to live apart from California."

"Yeah, it's special."

"And so are you," she whispers. "Do you have any idea what you are in for with me?"

"You are accepted just as you are."

"Why? You don't know me fully."

"Of course. That will take many years. Love is a choice, a recognition of a common wavelength that ignites a profound connection."

"Perhaps we just have a high degree of sexual compatibility?" Lil suggests.

"We certainly have that. And I want to be your life partner."

"And I want to be your partner. No questions. You are accepted for whoever you are."

"It seems so simple," I say.

"It is. Your acceptance of me, unconditionally, conquers the doubts that I might otherwise have."

"And your love will never fade?" I foolishly ask.

"Not unless you have doubts. It is only fear and judgment that causes love to fade."

Lil's bedroom is L-shaped with a coffered ceiling. A desk and fireplace occupy one wall. Around the corner, separated by a slider, are double vanities, a spa bath and a tiled double shower. The walk-in closet is double loaded with summer clothes at the upper level.

I scan a book, *Creating Successful Relationships*, from her bedside while she finishes her work. It's early Monday evening but we have just an hour together because Lil is busy at work.

We lie on the royal bed, but Paul soon pokes his head around the door. "I'm not feeling well Mom, can I take the day off school tomorrow, please, pretty please Mommy? I love you." Then he smiles, with a version of his mom's charm.

Lil introduces me to Paul and says, "Yes."

Her way of looking at Paul and the tone of her voice radiates love.

Lil and I lie close. We travel through each other's eyes, patiently exploring, recognizing a friend, and then touching lips, feeling moisture but barely touching. Her breath caresses my cheek, then my eyes. The light softens as the sun kisses the horizon.

Lil invites me to join her for a family weekend at her parent's ranch. "I'm taking Paul because he loves to ski, and it's almost the end of the season."

"I'd like that, if you think its OK with your parents, not too premature?"

"Let's do it."

The next day, my push on Lil's doorbell provokes a trill of notes, like a line of dominoes falling. She pulls me in, leading me to the royal bed as she talks eagerly, "I woke up at 2am, from a dream that had us living happily ever after. I got up to my desk and wrote out my wedding vows to you."

Lil looks at me expectantly.

"We had agreed to take it slow. That was our promise."

Then I laugh at my fear. I feel a grin pour out from a warm lovely place and grow around my face like color on the horizon at first light.

Our agreement is acceptance of each other, for better or worse.

Lil smiles.

"I'm ready," I say.

"Dylan Hotta, I love you always."

Our legs twine together.

"You liked that red-head girl who was singing at the cabaret?" Lil asks.

"No." I say. "I used to go out with her, but we had the final talk the night after you and I danced at my home. She's not going to make any trouble."

"You like trouble?" Lil asks.

"No, but it can happen so quickly that it's best avoided."

"Good," she says. "Are you anyone else's lover?"

"No," I say. "Like I said, I've been married for six years, and now I'm busy establishing my own business."

"In that case…"

She wriggles out of her skirt then sits up and pulls off her sweater. Her neck gleams as she shakes her hair. A contrary breeze sends the vertical window blinds rattling. She hesitates, and then peels off her blouse.

"I want to touch you," I say. The jade of her eyes is not luminous tonight, only the whites.

"Of course," she says. "But we mustn't go all the way yet." Then she undoes my belt and pulls my Levis down. She is quickly over me and it is too late to protest. She rises over me like a mast, her face down toward me, but her eyes looking up, whites only visible, staring into the distance as she grinds herself. "We mustn't go all the way," she says. Her arms are taut, like stays, grasping for support from my hands as she rides and lurches down on me, shudders, and though this is premature, I ask her to marry me.

She pauses. "Do you want a wife?" she asks as she strokes me.

"Yes. We can make it work."

"Yes, I'm sure."

This is all she needs to say.

Paul has invited his friend James to join us for the family weekend at the Garland ranch… that is all he need say to confirm the arrangement. Barbara has declined to join us. The journey is not long started and the boys are calling for a stop at Jack in the Box for a hot pastrami sandwich and malt. They giggle in the back for the rest of the journey.

"Talk about your work, and tennis. Do not talk about politics, or religion," Lil says as we finally get to within fifty miles of Garland.

"But what does it matter? Shouldn't your mom get to accept the same man that you see?"

"It's about Mom, not you or I, Honey. Trust me. It's important that my mom likes you. Manners are important to her, and emotional stability and financial security. John is into science. He likes to talk about new technology."

"Why are you so... nervous around your mom?"

"I saved her marriage with John. Now she feels strong. And I have to support that strength."

"OK, I'll try."

"We'll have to sleep in different rooms. If you can ride a horse that will impress Mom."

"I've ridden horses back in New Zealand, but rarely with a saddle. We just plodded from one ranch to another."

"Bare-back is fine. I'll need to stop before we get there my darling, get a stiff drink at Sierra. Mom and Dad will have dinner ready, but we could pick up dessert."

We stop at the bar beside the shop and Lil gives Paul and James money before she goes in. I purchase an apple pie.

Lil and I reunite out front and hold each other, her breath is intoxicating, and then her swollen lips touch mine and turn inside out. The flesh of our inner lips mingles, melting my small doubts. We rush to the warmth of her Jeep Cherokee.

I catch the aroma of marijuana on the boys as they climb back into the vehicle. Paul offers me a choice of three flavors of potato chips, and then giggles. Lil grows quiet as we turn off the highway at Garland and approach the family ranch. The house has a silvery slate roof and dressed cedar siding that reflects in the moonlight. It is difficult to see much beyond, other than the outline of treetops in the dark, and snow-covered mountain peaks surrounding the valley.

Ruth and John look me in the eye, searching. Lil introduces us, "Mom and John, I would like you to meet my special friend. This is Dylan."

My understanding is that we have agreed not to tell her family about our engagement for several weeks. I look away, uncomfortable with this secret. They do not have strong handshakes. Ruth has an attractive face despite watery eyes, long shiny blonde-graying hair, and a slim angular frame. John holds the hint of a grin at the ready, dressed in moustache, plaid shirt, and leather slippers.

The kitchen has stainless steel appliances, a central serving counter and a view of the lighted spa. John's conversation is measured during dinner. "How do the potatoes taste? Have you had any more problems Lil--with dividing up Bill's estate?"

"Fine. No. I'm just having the usual problems. Dylan and I would like to ride tomorrow," Lil says.

"The nags can't be ridden at the moment. Something is wrong. Dylan could help me round up a couple of young bulls on Sunday. The neighbor is coming over to cut off their balls," John says.

"I'll be glad to help," I offer. "This food is great. Is this your own steak, off the ranch?"

"No. We don't do any killing around here," Ruth says. "There's plenty of food, so please, help yourself. A young one like you needs his food. The potatoes are grown locally."

"Thank you, Ruth. This is plenty. Besides, the boys ate on the way up. You have hardly touched your plate, Paul. Why don't I finish your steak?"

I accept Paul's outstretched plate.

Ruth kicks Lil under the table, pushes her lower lip out while rolling her eyes.

After dinner the boys go upstairs and we adults sit by the river-stone fireplace. Native American artifacts hang from the rafters, and woven rugs drape the wall opposite the fireplace. Lil pulls out two photo albums from the Hutch and passes them to me. They contain her baby photographs, wedding portraits--and one shot of Lil's huge naked belly while eight months pregnant with Paul.

Lil starts browsing my book of poetry, stroking my hand, and providing a commentary on the photo albums.

Ruth leans forward; "Lil, is that the book of Dylan's poetry you were talking about? May I look, since you're busy smooching like a love-sick teenager?"

"Is that OK with you, Honey?" Lil asks.

Ruth interrupts; "I'm surprised that he'd be interested in looking at baby photographs. Aren't you being a bit premature?"

John stands up abruptly; "I think it's our bedtime now, Dear. Let's leave these young things. We've errands to run tomorrow--so we'll see you for dinner in the evening. Good night." John looks at Ruth, stuck in her chair. He reaches out his hand. "Say good night, Ruth. Here, let me help you. Bring the poetry book with you."

I close the photo albums. Lil caresses the palm of my hand with her fingertips.

Ruth staggers to her feet noisily, and glances toward me, "Is that OK?"

"It's kind of personal…"

Ruth cuts me short and snatches the poetry book from Lil.

"Of course! Isn't all poetry personal? That's essential. Otherwise, it couldn't be interesting. Now, off we go. Goodnight, Liz. Good to see you're bouncing back from your delicate time. I hope you're not being taken advantage of in this time of travail. Will you milk the cows before dinner tomorrow, please?"

CHAPTER 13:

After John has bitten into marmalade on toast, I can see his tongue and hear his lips smack, and shudder at this reminder of my own appetites. "You shouldn't share personal stuff like your poetry with Ruth. Gets her too excited, Son."

Lil slips into my bedroom after breakfast and cuddles up. "Why don't we drop the boys off skiing and go to that lecture Ruth was talking about? Ruth and John are going to a wedding anniversary, so they can't use the tickets."

We spread the local newspaper and see the back page advertisement.

Saturday afternoon, 2pm. Marianne Williamson and John Bradshaw: renowned authors to give public lecture at the Sierra Public Library.

We nod at each other. "Let's do it."

The two gurus have been developing a following for their new-age ideas, which are getting the attention of many of our workmates.

The Sierra library conference room is almost full with environmentalists, new-age sages, and wounded ski buffs. We have to sit in the front row, or sit separately. The volume of the sitar music is turned down slowly as Marianne bounces onto the stage wearing slacks, tweed coat, and a yellow shirt. She bows, smiles, and looks around her audience with acknowledging eye contact. There is a silence before she begins: "Having been taught since we were children that we are separate, finite beings, love feels like a void that threatens to overwhelm us, and that's because, in a certain sense, it is and does. It overwhelms our small self, our lonely sense of separateness--our notion of ourselves as a completely unique autonomous separated-from-God self. This self-concept is a lie, which causes terrible anxiety, even neurosis. What needs to change is the frightened mind, so the love inside us can get a chance to breathe."

As she continues her speech, I find myself glancing at Lil, seeking to confirm our connection.

John Bradshaw advocates the importance of rebirthing our inner child:

"I wish for us to heal the innocent damaged child of our past, who is still inevitably inherent within all of us, the kernel within the evolving fruit of our lives. I wish to lead you through a process designed to help you with the critical process of revisiting your childhoods, and re-parenting yourself…"

Afterwards, we are invited to enjoy light refreshments in the adjacent cafeteria. A huddle of people is gathered around Marianne, so we stand back shyly and sip herbal tea. A woman smiles as she excuses herself from the huddle.

"I can feel a connection between you two, a special purpose. You are interested in healing the inner child? Yes?"

"Yes," I answer.

"Good, I look forward to seeing you at the next meeting."

We pick the boys up from the ski field, feed them at Jack in the Box, and return to the ranch. Lil's parents are still out. I clean up the kitchen, and then follow Lil down to the cowshed.

There are about forty cows filing along the race beside the river toward the three-bay milking shed. I can hear Lil from around the bend in the river, cajoling the cows to get along. The leading cows are already stepping up the concrete ramp into the holding pen. Lil has left the gate propped open, and the first three cows are so familiar with the daily routine that they step into the milking stations without prompting, waiting to be hooked up to the hospital-like equipment.

Lil acknowledges me with no more than a jerk of her chin. As I step closer I can hear the sterilizer whirring like a dishwasher. The floor of the holding pen is covered in a mixture of hay and shit. "Let's go, Sue, don't stop now. Give me a hard time would you, Phyllis. C'mon now Wroth, that's a big girl. Kyle! Move your ass away from the fence. Gladys, you old bitch."

Lil is grabbing them by the ear and herding them around the corner from the race, their feet clomping in green muck and then up the ramp to the concrete floor. Lil is shoving them until she can shut the gate on the last of them. Then she folds the holding bar over the three cows waiting calmly in the milking pens and secures them further with foot halters. She offers a handful of feed pellets to each of the cows, then takes disinfecting solution from a cupboard and wipes the teats of each cow clean before she starts the milk flow with a few strokes of her hand. She collects suction cups from the sterilizer and connects them to the pump. Relocating from cow to cow, down and up rapidly, she moves rhythmically, turning on the machines, watching the gauges that signal milk is pulsing through the pumps.

The udders deflate rapidly under the mechanical suction. Lil massages the udder to be certain each cow is milked out, removes the teat cups, and within the confines of the cow-pen, backing the cow up with a push, she steers the massive bulk of the milked cow by the ear, leading her to an empty holding field, leaving the gate open as she twists the ear of the next cow, confident that the previous beast will make its own way back through the mud of the lower field to the race leading to the alpine pasture through the gap in the trees. The suction noises continue throbbing, the soft deep breathing of the milk pump sucking the cows dry.

Everything that Lil does with the cows, the way she touches them and talks to them, is magnificent. Here we are now, in a cow shed in far north California, both of us concerned with making our mark in our own way. We walk back to the house, holding hands.

Ruth drives by with a sneer; She hates us being in love.

The kitchen is cold. Ruth confides to Lil; "I feel a little tipsy and need to go to bed early."

John follows Ruth. The boys hang out in their room after convincing Lil that we should all go skiing the next morning. Lil and I also go to bed early, separately. My room is dark and warm.

Ruth and John are still in bed when we pack up at 9am on Sunday morning to stop at the ski field for a few hours of play on the way home. We call our goodbyes along the hallway leading to Ruth's bedroom, and rush out through the cold air to the Cherokee. "Too bad about my offer to help with the steers," I say.

Paul chimes in, "Jeez, Mom. Grandma is weird, she gives me the spooks."

"Just focus on the skiing," Lil says.

A storm comes in and the boys snowboard through it. Lil and I only do a few runs down a less advanced slope, and then retreat to the bar and a blazing fire.

Later in the afternoon, the boys return and rush us to the car. They sleep most of the way home.

Lil and I recline in the spa for an hour and decide that I should stay the night. I lie close to Lil, reading a book. I have agreed to Lil's suggestion that we refrain from being fully sexual for one further week.

Lil snuggles into me and clears her throat; "Mom says that we are not destined to be together for long, certainly not permanently. Dylan, are you listening?

"Yes, I'm listening."

Lil rolls onto her back. "Mom's attitude is bothering me."

"Where does that come from?" I ask.

"Mom needs for me to have money and be respectable--to prove that my lousy choice of a first husband can be overcome by the application of her superior wisdom."

"Where do I fall short?"

"Ruth doesn't think you're wealthy or respectable enough. She threatened to take me out of her will if I don't dump you. How strange that Mom has turned hostile toward you so quickly."

I visit Lil two evenings later. Her house is silent apart from the chirping of her two finches. Then her two children bang through the front door and go directly to the pool. When Lil gets home from work she dumps her briefcase on the kitchen counter, sighs, kisses me, and takes me to her bedroom. As she removes her navy business suit and cream blouse, she tells me that another dream came to her about 4am this morning, and she hasn't slept since because of the excitement. She leads me to her bed. "I dreamed that we are going to have a little baby. It was as clear as day, our love child."

I lean my head into the gap between the pillows, scour a hollow for my hip, and squeeze my eyes shut as she nuzzles under my chin. How delightfully simple life has become. Love filters down our stomachs, between our legs, into our eyes, ears, noses, toes. I hug her while she entwines her legs with mine, pulling me closer, burying into me.

"That will be brilliant."

It is decided! Lil will buy a special thermometer to chart her fertile days--but we shall wait a few months before trying to conceive because we are still celibate. But we know that pregnancy is going to happen one day soon.

We are now ready to cook dinner; Lil prepares the steak and salad and I cook the mushrooms, corn, and mashed potatoes.

We eat in the living room, formal with candles, Grace, and Tarot cards. The steaks are rare, and the mushrooms are done in butter and soy sauce. Perfect. Lil shucks a cob of fresh corn cooked in its sheath: parting the hair to get to the tip; the edge of her fingernail just under, so as not to graze a single kernel. Then pulling down the tight sheath. As soon as one strip of husk is down, the rest obeys and the ear yields up to her its shy rows, exposed at last. How loose is the silk. How quick the jailed-up flavor runs free. I watch her kissing off the remaining kernels from the cob. She is bashful about the dribble down her chin--wipes it off with a napkin. No matter what your teeth and wet fingers anticipate, there is no accounting for the way that simple joy can lift you, prepare you to fall in love. The taste of tender corn with the best steak and mushrooms is my favorite. How loose is the silk. How fine and loose and free.

If success is about getting what we want, and if happiness is about wanting what we get, then I have both. And Lil's house is only five balmy miles from my home in Yucca--a different world of period furniture, ancient hardwood floors and a canopy bed. But I will probably stay with Lil again tonight. Ideas come at different times and places for me--on the tennis court, in the spa, while jogging, and especially in bed.

"Pass me the BBQ sauce, please Dylan?"

"…Oh. Oh, yes. I was in a daydream. Sorry."

The following weekend, while we are out shopping for Ruth's birthday gift, Lil pleads with me to visit a psychic. We climb the steep wooden stairs, and are beckoned to sit on a cane sofa by a short red-faced lady. She wears a woolen shawl around her shoulders. The room looks like a candle factory. Lil writes a check for eighty dollars and asks the lady directly, "How many children shall I have? I have two now!"

"Will you two please sit closer?" the psychic asks.

We shuffle to the center of the sofa.

"Yes, that's better. I can see you two have a future that is... complex. You'll give birth to one more child, more happy than the first."

We cruise home with our future contentedly resolved, and climb into bed with Chinese dinner. Lil has again invited me to stay the night.

CHAPTER 14:

Lil's hair is draped over the pillow, her face toward me. Her jade eyes flicker and look away.

"I think you should move in here," Lil says.

I'm barely awake. "I'd love to. But won't our children think us impulsive?"

"You have doubts?" she asks.

"My doubts are around our children."

"Why?"

"First, I've missed a scheduled visitation with Kathy, so Angela is all over my case."

"Angela is antagonistic no matter what," Lil says.

"Yes. But Paul is behind with his studies, and so discouraged. He doesn't need a housemate at this time."

"Paul has learning difficulties, he will always be behind," she says.

"Barbara will not be thrilled, and then there's Ruth."

Lil shrugs. "Both of my children are going to be difficult, no matter what. Accept it. Ruth's your future mother-in-law for God's sake! Conflict is inevitable!"

"Kathy will…"

"Yes, Kathy will be nervous, undermined by Angela. Kathy can come over here whenever she wishes." Lil sighs.

"OK. I'll start moving my things in tomorrow."

There is a nagging in my throat that tells me to resist Lil when she reduces important decisions to a three-minute rout of my legitimate concerns. But I'm driving to Lil's home anyway.

I'm hanging my clothes in her huge walk-in closet when she enters silently and hugs me from behind, placing her hands over my eyes.

"You're home early, let me kiss you," I say. Her fingers smell faintly of cigarette smoke--and her breath of gin.

"Yeah, but don't get used to it. We had a social before the tax-season rush."

She turns and I rush to kiss her, pinning her arms against the racks of clothes. Now, with my face nuzzled into her neck, I smell her natural fragrance. As I look at her I remember the sharp cry, the screams of love, the definite impression that she wanted me to impregnate her last night.

"What are you doing?" she laughs

"A rush on investments?"

"What? You want a quickie in the closet?"

"At work? Do you have a rush on investments?"

"Yeah, the tax-avoidance investments. But the cocktail party was mostly because one of the partners, Michael, is leaving. Had a horrible break-up with his wife."

"Oh?"

"Yeah. At the cocktail party at his home, Michael got suspicious when his wife left the table shortly after our boss, leaving only four people to imbibe in the rest of the drinks."

"What was going on?"

Lil laughs. "Fucking! Michael already suspected it was going on between his wife and the boss. He just didn't think the boss would throw it in his face like that."

"That's horrible."

"Yeah. I've got feelers out for another job. Hey, I need to chill out with a hot spa. OK?"

"Where do I turn it on?"

"I already have. Here's a robe. Grab the gin and olives."

Lil interrupts me in the kitchen. "Go back to the bedroom and put a robe on. You will not want to be scrambling for your knickers and shirt in the dark later. See you down there."

I am sitting in the bubbling warmth when Lil comes down the steps carrying two large gin martinis, a bowl of ice, and a pack of cigarettes.

We ride the jets, make out while the jets are stimulating her to the core, then up to the bedroom we go, light the gas fire and smoke a joint. Lil lies on a bearskin rug in front of the blazing fireplace, stoned to kingdom come. I massage her all over, slow and firm, then deep and soft. She knows we will see bliss, the full culmination, at some unpredictable time, some time before the candles burn out. Then we will sleep like teenagers, and this is important for Lil. Otherwise she will grind her teeth in her sleep, and get woken by a primal nightmare.

CHAPTER 15:

Lying in this huge bed with Lil sleeping beside me is as good as it gets, but it is also why am I not asleep at 4am. There is a full moon. Lil has talked a lot in the spa and around the patio table. I asked her what she had been doing since she left Dunedin. She threw her head back and laughed; "I cried for six months, and then got a life."

I thought she was going to stop there as she looked into the distance, but she refills our glasses with two inches of gin over three cubes of ice, and four green olives, and continues.

"I enrolled at the University of Santa Barbara, but had to quit college because Eric wouldn't pay the tuition costs. I sued Eric for 'Failure to Provide', and then moved back into the apartment in San Francisco with Mom and John. I was surprised when I lost the court case against Eric. Going to college was no longer an option. Ruth and John were under financial stress, something about a cash-flow crisis around a new business.

I started to party. My mom threatened to take me out of her will if I didn't straighten up.

What do you want me to do? I asked her.

Go down to the tennis courts before cocktail hour. Hit some balls with Louise, she knows the game. Ask her to play to your forehand, but stop before you start to perspire. Buy Louise a martini. Then make smart conversation with the sons of the wealthy. Show them you appreciate a nice home and are prepared to take risks to get to the very top. Be ambitious! A well-bred man will accumulate twenty million in ten years in this country. He can reach the top if he has a spunky wife who doesn't nag him, and makes his home life exotic. You can do it, Honey.

Are you sure about that, Mom?

Yes, of course I am."

Lil sips from her glass and then continues.

"It was November, summer was gone and the fall colors had started. John had been teasing me just before he left for a meeting with some lawyer associates. I got John with a jab: *You could be cute if you would get a decent hair cut and a dye job.* I did just enough stirring to make him laugh.

Ruth slammed the kitchen door shut. Ruth and John needed a time out. She was angry with us because we had laughed too loudly. My mom was probably revisiting her old resentments, about Eric's drinking and stuff, needed a few more Al-Anon meetings... and still does.

I spent a lot of time alone, feeling resentful… that my mom wasn't available to really talk. Not about my career choices, my boyfriends or the changes my body and emotions cycled through each moon. Mom never looked at me, not in the eye, not unless she was angry. My mom hadn't prepared me for school, boys, my period, dirty old men, real men, nothing. My first period came as a complete surprise. It was Uncle Ray who had explained the mess in his crazy way, when he was driving me to a tennis match. At first I had thought it was my stomach seeping out. I would have preferred not to be so regular, especially not every full moon. The full moon was not a convenient time for me, but at least I didn't get crabby like my mom.

I finally went to Mom's bedroom, sat in the armchair, watched Ruth fall asleep in the other armchair, and flipped through a magazine. Sleep was where my mom hid when she was depressed.

When Ruth finally woke, she still didn't talk to me. She stalked around her room with a fierce look on her face. I backed into the corner by the door. Mom seemed to forget I was in her room. She smoked the roach of a joint from the tray on her writing desk and looked vacantly out her window... for a long time.

She finally turned. *Is John back from his trip yet?*

No, I answered softly.

Good, Mom said. *That's a relief. You know him better than I do.*

John got back about 7pm. The three of us sat down to dinner, Szechwan beef and broccoli.

Feeling better now? I asked.

Ruth grunted.

Ruth and John shocked me a week later.

We've finally purchased the ranch near Sierra, Mom said.

What do you mean? I thought you already owned it?

No honey, we've been leasing it, Mom said. *Finally we are set. Paid cash. That's how you get a good deal. I own two hundred acres in Northern California, with a great house.*

I stayed at Grandma Stephanie's house for a month, because Ruth and John wanted to be alone at their ranch for a while. *Sort things out.* I didn't complain.

Mom visited me about once every two weeks. It didn't matter anymore. Ruth felt more like a rich aunt at that time, after all the partying Mom and I had done together during a recent vacation in Mexico. But there was still a sharp edge to her, an edge that I will never challenge lightly. I stayed at Grandma Stephanie's house for a further few weeks, kept out of the way of Ruth while my husband-to-be, Larry, was down in Mexico, on business… because I could smell craziness. Then, my new stepfather and Mom called to say they had finished moving into the ranch. *Two hundred acres, five hours north of Yucca. We'll be keeping the city apartment in the meantime.*

Sounds wonderful, I said.

Why don't you come up for the house warming? Ruth asked.

I'd love to.

Good. We'd like you to stay with Grandma Stephanie for a bit longer, till we are settled, but bring her with you.

I drove up with Grandma Stephanie, arriving late afternoon. The ranch house had knotted cedar siding, a slate roof, and tall river stone chimneys. A stream had been dammed to form a lake beyond the entrance. Blue jays pirouetted on the reeds and lily pads. The ranch felt like New Zealand, the hinterland from Dunedin, crisp dry air, but there were more birds at the ranch, and the sound of a distant stream. Not the huge sky and deafening silence of central New Zealand.

The hallway bathroom was cold, unfurnished. John left the toilet seat up in their new home already. The living room had neither curtains, nor linen on the table. The cathedral ceiling, with an open loft and interior balcony at one end gave the room the feel of a barn. The kitchen was stainless steel, institutional, a man's invention.

Through the bay windows I could see snow covering the barn and cows grazing on the brown parts of the piebald field. John came in from the barn and spent the rest of the day feeding the open fire, between reading a Science magazine and carving chess pieces.

The ranch is a different world from Grandma Stephanie's home in Yucca, the suburban bungalow that is always quiet. Grandma was too frail to travel more than an hour at a time between coffee breaks. I would rather stay with Grandma than in my stepfather's apartment in San Francisco. John's apartment is in the Italian district, with views of the bay, fog banks, and sounds of the big city.

While I was there in San Francisco's Italian district, I took for granted the convenience of shops and bars on the corner of each block. Although Yucca had unpleasant memories from my childhood, it is located in suburbia, within easy reach of a social life with a more professional class of people. I wasn't attracted to the fake machismo of the North Beach boys in the city, nor the gays in the Polk street district.

That night six of the neighboring ranchers drove up in pick-up trucks, wearing plaid shirts and jeans. Ruth and John looked out of place, liberals in a redneck enclave.

Grandma was drinking wine now. The party was getting noisy, drowning out the country music. A plate of mountain oysters was passed around. They were surprisingly good. The ladies tittered. Grandma Stephanie was less complex and stressed than Ruth, except that Grandma did freak-out whenever my brother came staggering to her home like a foal learning to walk, and vomited excess beer on the carpet. I have heard John thank Grandma for this arrangement. He said, *If Kurt wasn't living with you then he'd be here, victimizing Ruth.*

I spilt my margarita. Just as well there was no tablecloth. Otherwise, Ruth would have huffed. I wondered if my own behavior had become transparent, if my struggle with my demons was visible to other people, to my mom.

Mom was loose enough from drinking to confront her mother. *Goodness Stephanie, I'll be fifty-two on my next birthday. Don't you agree that I made a good match? John's generous, gets on with Lil, and Kurt doesn't intimidate him.*

Of course I do. Oh Ruth, it's time someone in our family had some peace and security. I just wish you'd drink less, and lay off those cannabis cigarettes.

Oh mother, don't be such a dunce. John smokes pot. Everyone does, Ruth said.

I must be more careful in conversation. Some people could pick up a lot of ammunition from an indiscreet tongue. As the party revved up, I moved away from Grandma and talked to the neighbor, who was wealthy and raised Black Angus cattle. He had been sneaking glances at me all evening, a boring man, but safe after a few drinks.

The morning was pretty. John had cleaned up the mess and gone out to the barn. Grandma Stephanie and I joked with Ruth at coffee time, trying to chip away at the tension between us. Now that Mom had allowed me slightly closer to her fragility, I could feel the level of my mom's fear rising around me, grabbing with cold hands like a San Francisco fog.

John and I spent the rest of the day in the study, drinking coffee and playing scrabble. I enjoyed teasing him, just enough to get him laughing and out of his shell. I like John. He could be a friend.

It was late afternoon at the ranch, a week before Christmas. John had won the game of scrabble and gone outdoors to the barn to check on a sick animal. I could feel my hands shake involuntarily. The smell of Mom's bath soap, the glint of sun on Mom's diamond wedding ring, the way that, in the Jacuzzi spa, our feet had sometimes inadvertently touched, anything like that was enough to make me panicky.

I sensed being watched by Mom across the dining table. We were as wary as enemies. Ruth picked absently at the food she had cooked, retching on whatever she tried to swallow. She ran to the bathroom, then, returning to the dining table, picked up her fork and herded a piece of corn around her dinner plate. Ruth's gorgon eyes shone like moonbeams then turned like traffic lights, from encouraging me to help, to pleading, to glowering.

Well into the New Year, Mom was still coming to my room every day. It didn't matter anymore. Ruth's behavior was less snobbish for me now… her having seen the other side of privilege while in India on her honeymoon. She even started telling jokes and laughing at sexy stuff on TV. There remained a sharp edge to Ruth. And I could tell that Ruth was still my rigid mother, the person in charge of resentment and propriety. I visited my grandma's house when the stress got too much.

The letters that my dad wrote from Arizona were stiff, formal, and unimaginative. They shared nothing of him, only how well his AA program was going, and how well his accounting practice was doing, advising me to choose the same career, not the physics and math stuff that I had been studying in Dunedin.

At the end of summer my mom pulled into Grandma's driveway, tooting her car horn, the only warning of her visit. After a half hour of formalities Ruth demanded that I should clarify the situation between us by going to her therapist's office the next day, in the same building as I had visited Mary Blake before. The single-story yellow box on Mount Diablo Boulevard would always be the same. Ruth didn't inform me of the reason for the session. *Just to talk about your behavior... a different doctor this time.*

I don't know if I should tell you this. It might give the wrong impression of Ruth… but OK, here goes:

After breakfast I dressed in my only business outfit at that time; a skirt and blouse, drank two cups of coffee, and waited for Mom. Ruth finally returned from her shopping expedition and tooted her horn impatiently at the gate of Grandma Stephanie's house. The passenger door of her Mercedes was wide open. I stepped into the bright sunlight with a forced jaunt. The sight of me seemed to cause Ruth's eyes to snap shut. It was the first time Ruth had seen me wear something that wasn't long, black and baggy. Her face looked tired. She drove slowly, and limped like she had a sore back as we walked into the therapist's office.

There were names of three therapists on the door now. This place was the sanctuary that Ruth had been visiting for two years to help her deal with the controlling behavior of Grandma.

I sat on the red couch, and took my mom's cold hand. I sensed the sickness behind Mother's panic, there in the caramel color of the walls. Her sickness was confirmed by the nervous way Doctor Levi's hand trembled when he greeted her. I came to the realization that Ruth would never escape her own mother; never stop hearing the judgment around choosing a violent drunk for a husband, a man that Stephanie had warned her about, warned her that he was evil.

Ruth got to the point without a preamble. *I think they are having sex*, she said, *my husband and my daughter.*

The doctor turned to me, his eyebrows raised. There was a silence that I filled hurriedly. *It just looks bad to Mom, with her insecurities,* I told him. *I know she must be worried, but all that is happening is the occasional flirt… It's just that…* I purposely faltered. *See, I never knew my father. It isn't John's fault. He likes being teased... that's all. We have never even kissed, or anything.*

I paused at exactly the right moments. I looked back at the therapist, consciously breathing through my nostrils, slowly, gently. *I like John a lot, but it... I'm not... I'd never... I wouldn't do that.*

The doctor looked at me as I sat before him in my cream blouse and green skirt. I looked him in the eye, brushed a loose hair off the side of my face. *Of course I wouldn't do such a thing.*

Doctor Levi believed me. I knew without a doubt that he believed me.

Ruth shrieked. *My daughter has taken my husband's sexual interest away from me, and now she has taken you, Dr. Levi, my only ally, the one person I thought I could trust to share my secrets.*

Doctor Levi clenched his fists. *It's not a crisis, Ruth. She didn't do it. See you at the regular time next week.*

I jumped in. *Isn't it my mother's job to protect me from perverted family members, from my Uncle Ray, a dirty old man, and to protect me from a violent father that Mom chose to marry, despite warnings from those who love her, like her own mother...*

Dr. Levi interrupted me. *You are not my client, Lillian. But call me and I can refer you to another therapist.*

I felt the self-destructive insanity of attacking the person I needed the most. I saw the consequences loud on Mom's face, the abandonment of any hope that there might have been for Mom to trust me, to respect me, to give me the benefit of the doubt under future accusations. I felt my shoulders shudder. My chest and my throat throbbed in time with Mom's circling ankle.

Ruth stood up, wrenched open the door and marched toward her car. With a dramatic gesture of the remote control, Mom unlocked the car doors.

When we got home, I expected to cry, but I didn't. Ruth walked into my room. She shut the door silently. *We'll be civil to each other. I'm sorry you have seen fit to play games with me. My life is too busy for such crass behavior. My assets now include a half share of fifteen million dollars. If you treat me well I will leave my estate to you, in my will. But you must not marry a man of whom I disapprove.*

I wanted to scream and slap my mom. Instead, I put on my poker face and pulled a book from the shelf.

Two days later, I called my family insurance provider, Kaiser Health Insurance, who offered ten miserly hours of therapy. The therapist to whom I was assigned put a box of tissues on the coffee table beside my lap and began: *I understand that something is wrong. You're upset, obviously. But I can't help you if you won't talk to me.*

I nodded, tears washing down my face, then down my neck.

So, he said. *Perhaps you'd like to wait for a couple of weeks? Maybe it would be better for you to come back when you feel like you can talk.*

I nodded vaguely. I didn't intend to go back.

That evening, I lay in bed and wondered what I could possibly have said to that gawky graduate therapist at Kaiser Health--with his pink face, his manicured nails, the squeaky clean vision imparted by his virgin eyes? What pearl of wisdom or insight could I possibly have gathered from that junior doctor? How could this bionic shrink possibly have helped me to deal with my aching shoulders, hunched with the burden of carrying my mom? How could this wet noodle help me deal with teeth grinding all through the night and another Gorgon nightmare, with snakes jumping from my mom's hair to my own?

I am not sure why Ruth had imagined that I was having an affair with John. It had to be more than her insecurity. It might have been when Ruth came home unexpectedly, early one evening, and found John and I both laughing hilariously, mercilessly high on pot. I had discovered that the painful feelings simply vanish when I am high, high on anything. It didn't matter what the cause of the pain was, drugs always worked to numb it.

Ruth didn't broach the subject of sexual infidelity again, not with me… or evidently with John! I didn't discuss it with him either. Ruth now carried the righteous attitude of a victim. I felt like a beaten dog for a long time. I suffered because I was more honest than Mom or Grandma could handle. They seemed to suspect that I was in the devil's camp, a hedonist, out of control. And all I have ever wanted is to be with my soul mate.

CHAPTER 16, DYLAN:

Lunch is a cold tuna sandwich, and Greg looks as if Lucifer has got to him: All his flesh is sagging on his sweating face. He looks up from the Chronicle, orders a vanilla milkshake, and turns back to the previous page: "The world is on the edge of an abyss. At home here, in Europe, in Asia, the environmental and terrorist problems are impossible. It's bad, bad, bad! And the Asian economies are too expansionist. The world is a teeming cauldron of insecurities."

"Come over for a BBQ this evening. There will just be Lil and I, and my daughter," I say. "We can talk."

A BBQ is often the best thing when something like this happens to a friend.

The evening is pretty, as usual—a clear blue sky with a fringe of orange around the horizon. The freeway hum can sound comforting some days. Lil and I meet Greg at the transit station, and then we continue on to pick up Kathy from Angela's home up in the hills on the opposite side of the valley.

Kathy is waiting in the driveway—to avoid the need for me knock on her mother's door. God bless her! Kathy is slender and tall for a nine-year-old. Her bony arms and legs look tan against her white dress.

"What do you want for your birthday, Kathy?"

Kathy is bouncing on the back seat.

"That depends," Kathy says.

"Depends on what?"

She doesn't answer, and sits still, looking at the fields sliding by the window.

"Depends on what?" I ask again.

"On whether you might be saving up to get me a pony."

Oh, shit! I can imagine what Angela would say to that. "Do you want a pony?" I ask.

"Yes, I do." Her eyes are moist and shining, all that enthusiasm.

"It's a lot of responsibility."

"I know. But I could keep it at the Pony Club. My friend's dad will exchange horse poop for hay. He cuts the grass at the flood-control reserve, and they just dump the cut stuff."

"Will you come in with me when I ask Mom?" pleads Kathy.

"Yes, but we have to pick the right time. Not this evening."

"OK."

We are home and Kathy, as anticipated, rushes to take Lil's dog for a walk.

"Are you OK?" Lil asks Greg.

"Yes," Greg says, looking away.

"Come, sit here," she pats the space next to her on the patio sofa.

For a moment it seems as if he might refuse, as if he can't be bothered moving for the sake of being close to her warmth. But then he stands, heaving with one hand on the arm of his chair while the other hand balances his martini. Lil rubs her hand rapidly over his shoulder blades.

"You look tired," she says.

"Not tired. Just run around."

"Who's running you around?"

"My boyfriend."

"Oh?" Lil says.

I cook the lamb while Lil slices vegetables for the grill.

Greg begins pouring his heart out. "My boyfriend has joined up with the Church of Scientology… quit his job."

"I'm sorry. Those people are control freaks," Lil says.

"That Church's power is worrying me. Especially considering the incidents of recent mass killings and stand-offs in other weird sects," Greg says.

"I had a brief encounter with Scientology but didn't like the mind control," Lil says.

"Why is that?" Greg asks.

"As far as I can tell, Scientology is about a group of supposed Aliens, who come to planet Earth to release evil spirits," Lil says.

Greg sobs louder, about how he misses his boyfriend… I call a taxi. Kathy returns from walking Sheba in time for the three of us to walk Greg to the gate.

It has been a silent meal up until now. I'm not sure how to broach the distance between Kathy and I, fueled by Greg's drama… Angela doesn't like Greg, so naturally Kathy is suspicious. I try to prompt Kathy with a new subject. "Do you like playing with Lil's old dog?"

"Yes, but I especially like wild animals, like rabbits and birds--and I like horses of course," Kathy says.

"So, you prefer to watch blue jays rather than birds in a cage like my finches and cockatiel?" Lil asks.

"Yes, free birds are much more interesting than your caged birds."

"I like to hear my birds singing in the house… cheerful. What fascinates you about wild birds?" Lil asks.

"Why do you ask?"

"I've seen you checking out that hawk that lives up in the redwood," Lil says.

"See how the hawk is always looking around? They don't like being still. I wouldn't either if I could fly. I wish I could just spread my arms out like that and take off… and feel the wind in my face when I swoop down towards the ground, seeing everything from above."

"Do you have flying dreams, like your Dad?" Lil asks.

"Sometimes in my dreams I can fly. I don't have to move my arms or anything. I just think of a place and I'm flying towards it. It feels so lovely and free. Waking up is a disappointment after flying dreams. Then I feel heavy and clumsy."

I join in. "When you are asleep and flying high and the fear of falling comes into your mind, do you have to work at relaxing, letting go of the doubts about staying aloft?"

"Yes. Rabbits could never fly because they are riddled with caution. So is my mom."

"What is your mom cautious about?" Lil asks, too quickly.

"She gets terrified before she goes on a date. It's funny how birds don't have to do any work. I suppose it seems like work to them, out looking for crumbs and worms."

"Birds are always working," I say absently.

"But they don't have to go to school or do boring chores. And they always find enough food."

"It seems that birds are free compared to humans, but aren't they busy while they're playing all day?" Lil asks.

"I love the way birds build simple nests for their little babies. Do you think the baby birds feel lonely when they get left on their own? Or when their mommy wants a new boyfriend?"

Lil puts her hand on Kathy's for a moment. "I hope you don't feel too lonely? It's important that your mommy is free to date with men. Otherwise she would be unhappy and that would be no fun."

"I hadn't thought of it that way. Dad has a girlfriend, so why shouldn't Mom have a boyfriend? As long as I can have pets at home." Kathy is on a roll now. "I'd like to stay over here some weekends, especially if I can take Sheba for walks and swim in the pool."

"OK," I say. "We can work that out later."

I drop Kathy off at her home and then Lil and I have a bath and go to bed early. We are almost asleep when Ruth calls. Lil's response is terse. "I'll think about it. No promises."

Then she turns to me; "Sweetheart, would you mind attending a mediated meeting that Ruth wants to organize, a family discussion about Ruth's concerns regarding you?"

"No, why not?" Anything that will help Ruth to chill out is worth a try. "Who's going to do the mediation?" I ask.

"A psychiatrist."

"Hmm. That should be interesting."

Lil picks up her book, reads a few lines, and drops it again. She leans back into her pillows, her face fresh and pink from her bath, and smiles, wanting to talk more.

Lil and I can talk for hours in the twilight. We don't bog down in current stuff like pollution, global warming, terrorism, or war. We are more interested in building something special between us. No matter if Lil is talking or listening, her jade eyes are attentive and steady, her head still. She talks with a confident voice. "We could move to our own ranch in five years, a ranch that is self-sufficiently growing bio-fuel, vegetables, and firewood." She has thought about our freedom, freedom from the agenda of the corporate world, and she is ready to take action. When she falls asleep with her arm around me, I smell the natural scent of her body, subtle, difficult to recreate the next day, but the impact of her scent lingers permanently in my memory like a crossroads dream, a scent that smells as Heaven must smell... a little stronger than spring water, not as strong as vanilla.

I don't need to change anything in my world. I find the remote control from the rare clutter on Lil's bedside cabinet, push the dimmer switch, one setting lower every minute, creating a second sunset. The colors of the bedroom furnishings dim, then the photograph of Bill is no longer visible… the Bill who betrayed her. He died. The light dims until people like uncle Ray are from another world, long ago.

I continue to push the remote button until nothing remains of the past but lighter and darker shades of gray. Lil's immaculate breath is a frictionless perpetual motion, the most powerful Earthly manifestation of God that awareness offers. Sleep lazily rolls over to visit my own breathing, easy, smooth. Love has proffered paradise: resting anonymously around us, granting us by grace, a precious hope.

CHAPTER 17:

Lil has taken the entire day off work. Ruth and John pull into our driveway at 10am. I watch them drink coffee. Lil is still up in her bathroom. The house is silent. Even the finches sense it. The 11am appointment is clearly a bigger deal than I had anticipated.

Lil and I follow Ruth's yellow Mercedes through the hilly suburban streets of San Gabriel to the meeting place. Ruth walks ahead and Lil, John, and I follow in single file down the ivy-lined path. The psychiatrist's office is adjacent to that of Lil's lawyer, Mr. Holdall, who is trying to resolve the dispute over the estate of Lil's deceased boyfriend.

The red door has a lock box. Ruth punches in numbers and opens the door. The tall clock chimes the hour. We are on time, but the clock is an hour slow. There is no receptionist. Ruth leads us across the reception area to the entrance of an office similar to that of Lil's lawyer: It has two plush red leather chairs, two cherry wood bookcases, and an empty cherry wood desk, with shiny brass ornaments and hunter green accessories. The lawyer's office has a conference table against the near wall, but the psychiatrist has a couch there.

The doctor comes through a different door than I had anticipated. He is a slender pinstriped gentleman with slick black hair and comfortable eye contact. He seats us on four hard chairs in a row, John, Ruth, Lil, and me. I sit confidently in this situation that Greg insists will be demeaning: *It's a no-win situation for you. You cannot prove your integrity in a psychiatrist's office; only disprove it.*

My brother has also counseled me not to attend this meeting. The purpose of a psychiatric test of your health is to determine any eccentricity or neurosis that you may have, but it cannot affirm good health.

I could not justify avoiding this meeting. Lil had passed on her mom's desire for the meeting in a way that was both apologetic, and insistent; *Ruth promised me that she will welcome any reassurance of your health, and that such reassurance will usher in a new era of goodwill.* Lil further reasoned that any chance of clearing my conflict with her mom was worth a try.

"Are we ready to begin?" asks Dr. Schick, the most expensive psychiatrist in San Gabriel.

"Yes," says Lil, touching my arm.

I jump in before the meeting gets underway. "There is something that needs to be said. My friends consider Ruth and John's action in bringing me here to be outrageous, an interfering action. But Lil and I prefer to interpret their calling of this meeting as a demonstration of their parental concern for Lil's welfare, and therefore Lil and I wish to co-operate in this endeavor. We wish to co-operate so as to reassure Ruth and John, as far as possible, of my health, and to demonstrate goodwill."

Doctor Schick has ready eye contact and nods approvingly. Ruth flashes a contemptuous look at me and turns to John--who tries to smile at her comfortingly. Ruth clears her throat; "Lil has let me read a book of poetry that Dylan has written. I have copied a number of pages that alarmed John and me, particularly where he says, *Lovers are born to heal, to kneed the clay; We thirst to heal our lover-self, to heal our God, our Self; To look in the mirror, for the untroubled Face.*

We would like to hear your professional evaluation of this self-obsession."

The interview goes on for an hour, and then a lunch adjournment is taken.

Ruth, John and I lunch uncomfortably together at a diner in San Gabriel. We three order steamed spinach on liver and bacon… Lil is attending a business meeting.

After lunch we meet Lil in the parking lot and return to the afternoon session. Ruth draws Doctor Schick's attention to a poem from my book that is about an event in a psychiatric hospital. "This poem demonstrates Dylan's familiarity with the psychiatric patient experience," Ruth says.

"How do you know that?" interrupts the doctor.

"Because I was a nurse, the sister in charge of a ward," Ruth says. "I have concluded professionally that Dylan must be demented, and is certainly not marriage material."

The doctor cuts her short. "We are here to talk about Dylan's current health. Any history of seeking psychiatric health care is irrelevant."

Ruth is aghast, feigning betrayal and a pending seizure, until I look at her in an extended and neutral way. I have a sense that reason may prevail here despite the doctor being hand-picked by Ruth for her specific purpose.

At the end of the second hour of our scheduled time, Ruth asks the psychiatrist, "Would you let your daughter marry this man?"

The doctor seems to deliberately avoid any hint of hesitation. "I have no concerns about Dylan's mental health," he gushes.

Ruth puts on her coat with an effort at dignity, but her animosity stretches the seams and distorts the shape away from any prior resemblance to elegance.

Lil and I follow Ruth and John back to the mansion.

Lil replays the messages from her answering machine as she exchanges small talk with her mom in the kitchen. Then a cultured voice of an adult woman cuts through their banter: "Lillian Halifax, you are nothing but a slut and a whore. Better keep your hand on your sleazy pussy so you don't need to spend so much time sharing it around."

Ruth jerks around, hoping I am not within hearing distance, but the three of us are at the kitchen counter, frozen as if the music has suddenly stopped. John is the only one who hasn't heard.

"Who's that?" Ruth demands, "That voice sounds familiar!"

"Tracy, Big Bill's daughter. She's upset about my lawsuit," Lil says.

"Sounds demented to me!" Ruth says.

I go up to our bedroom.

Lil follows. "That call was about a naked photograph that my ex, Larry, took of me while lying on the bed. Larry was going to do a close-up so I used my hand to cover my nakedness. But in the photograph it appears that I am playing with myself. Tracy must have found a copy of the photo among Bill's things."

Dinner this evening is subdued. Ruth slams a plate on the dining table. "We're off to bed, we'll be leaving early in the morning. Don't get up for us!"

Shortly after sunrise, I bump into Ruth behind the laundry door. "Why don't you like me? What have I done wrong?" I sound like a twat in the context, but we need to talk.

Ruth squeezes herself around to turn her back further away from me, clutching a bundle of wrinkled clothes to her chest, "I'm not happy. Why don't you just go away, stop perverting my family with your mad ideas about marriage and babies? Grow up!"

Lil yells down the laundry chute; "I heard that, Mom. Get out of my house now and don't come back!"

Ruth slams the door, leaving behind a forgotten pile of her laundry and a suitcase. I hear the Mercedes start, then squealing tires.

The next day, I drive over to pick Kathy up after school. "Is this a good time to talk with your mom?"

"Yes," Kathy nods, smiling. Hopeful. Lifting her hand and pushing the loose strands of hair back behind her ear in the way I have always adored.

"I'll go get Mom."

Angela walks down the stairs slowly, glaring at me.

"Did you promise Kathy a horse?"

Angela's voice is calm, too calm. I know it well enough to sense the threat beneath it. Do I fight… or let her have her way? Do I apologize… or agree with her?

"No, I did not promise her a pony."

"Where did she get the idea from, then. She forgets to feed Fluffy sometimes. If Kathy can't take care of a cat, how can she possibly take care of a horse?"

"Kathy asked me and I said we would discuss it with you."

Why do I feel tense, guilty?

"Kathy, is this true?"

"Yes, Mom."

"OK Dylan, and will you pay for the saddle and vet bills and food bills as well as buy the horse?"

"Yes."

"OK. But you'll have to wait until her next birthday, until she's older and had a chance to read up on the caring."

"No! She's old enough now."

"If you'll wait another year I'll work with you and share some of the costs. But if you charge in at this, then I'll have nothing to do with it!"

Kathy interrupts; "That's fine, Mom. I don't want a pony if you are going to make a thing about it."

"Don't be petulant, Kathy. You're behaving like your father!"

"Come on, Dad. Let's go."

The sense of disappointment I feel is softened by the fact that I had not rolled over and completely given into Angela's demands. I will get Kathy a pony somehow, but not this birthday.

Kathy and I take Lil's lame dog, Sheba, for a walk, and Kathy asks me about Greg, about something that has been puzzling her: "Why is Greg so interested in astrology? Mommy says astrology is a hoax, entirely unscientific."

I try to tease her, "You misheard. He must have meant astronomy. I must get you a new battery for your hearing aid!"

"No, Daddy! He definitely said astrology."

"Greg's real interest lies in artificial intelligence. That's why he has developed our chess program."

"Yeah, so?"

"Greg is trying to simulate the emotional world on a computer, similar to what has been done in the intellectual world of chess. So he has purchased the best astrology program available and is studying it scientifically."

"But that doesn't feel right. People are not that simple," Kathy says.

"Of course not. Greg wants to prove that astrology is wrong. That's why he has an interest in Lil and me. We are astrological twins, almost… on the cusp between two star signs, with dual personalities and internal conflict."

"That is crap, Dad! You and Lil may be twisted, but not split."

I marvel at my daughter's newly found maturity. Kathy has grown tall and thin-legged, with tiny wrists and shoulder blades that protrude, and yet when she tenses, you see that her muscles are well developed. And it comforts me to know that her speech impediment has been almost eliminated with the help of a therapist and her new high-tech hearing aid.

Sheba cannot walk much further because her arthritis is bothering her hips. We take her home, feed her and wrap her in a blanket.

Lil is working late so Kathy and I order sushi in and spend the evening studying the photo albums from my office while we play a complex game of chess. It is Kathy's turn to play white and I choose a little-known version of the Indian defense. Kathy finds a picture of her mom, taken when Angela was a nurse.

"Doesn't Mom look like an angel in her white uniform?"

"She must be an angel to have a lovely daughter like you."

"And doesn't Mommy look smart and capable… like she could manage an entire hospital all by herself."

"Hmmm. I had never thought of Angela like that. I suppose she is a managerial sort of a person."

"I'm glad that you don't hate Mom. That would be impossible. You know how I want to be a professional chess player?"

"Yeah."

"Well it's not that I like you better than Mom. It's more that nursing is a lot of physical work, according to Mom. Lifting heavy people, machinery, and bedpans. Mommy advised me that nursing isn't as glamorous as the uniform looks."

"You have a good head on you. Must get it from your mother's side of the family."

"Daddy, is Greg gay?"

"I never think about it. But yes, he is."

"And that doesn't bother you?"

"No, thank goodness. It doesn't. But then I don't meet his gay friends."

"That's nice."

"It is nice."

"That's what I said. I wasn't being sarcastic."

I can see a staunch suffering of pain within Kathy, pain from the divorce and subsequent craziness. And perhaps it is a foolish deception for me to hold a secret from my family, about working for Greg--for the CIA. Perhaps Angela and I were foolish not to have stuck it out. That's probably why Angela is so angry. She knows that our marriage should have worked.

What can I do for Kathy now? She needs my reassurance that our divorce was not her fault. That's why I try to be convivial around Angela.

How sweet is Kathy's smile, the reflection of the window scene in her eyes, her milky breath, her bony wrists, and her long fingers. I kiss her fingertips and say a silent prayer. I'm certain that she understands a lot more than I give her credit for.

Kathy leans forward, charging her white bishop to d7 with a loud crash.

"Checkmate!"

CHAPTER 18:

My task of repairing the pump in the pool house has no guarantee of an ending, especially with my limited mechanical skills. But the process of eliminating the possible causes of failure is pleasant enough—until I see Ruth stepping down toward me. She has arrived unannounced and sits beside me while I attempt to release an air lock from the pump system.

"Don't worry. I'm only staying one night."

"Oh?" She must sense my apprehension.

"Are you on medication?" Ruth asks.

"No." What an absurd question.

"Are your parents still alive?"

"Yes." Where is this leading?

"Are they well?"

"Yes, they are well and happy. I hope they'll come over for our wedding."

"I understand you have a daughter. Where does she live?" Ruth asks.

"Kathy lives in Yucca with her mom, except for every other weekend and Wednesday evenings."

"What is your wife's maiden name?" Ruth asks.

"My ex-wife's name is Angela Pratt."

"Yes, an uncouth family. But I can see why you would be attracted to her type," Ruth says, and walks back up to the house.

Later, I press Lil for an explanation for Ruth's behavior.

"My mother is afraid that you will divorce me in a few years and hire some lawyers to get your hands on her money," Lil speculates.

"Never crossed my mind. Anyway, there are legal ways for Ruth to protect her assets."

"But you might hire a better lawyer than her," Lil says.

"This is bullshit! How can we put a stop to this paranoia?"

"If only we had decided to move to New Zealand, eloped, never let on to Ruth that we are together, and then I would be happy. Paul would be contentedly smoking homegrown pot, and Barbara would be at college in Hollywood. We'd all be fine."

I say nothing. I will not condone young Paul using illegal drugs around my home, around my parents and around the Powers family.

Lil turns back to me. "Ruth wrote a letter to the medical association about our meeting with the psychiatrist, a letter demanding that Dr. Schick be de-registered on the grounds of incompetence.

"Ruth's leaving tomorrow," says Lil. "I've made it clear that I don't want her interfering in our family."

I am hiding from Ruth down in the pool house, working on the heater controls--trying to survive one more night with Ruth in the house. I move on to cleaning the valves on the chlorinator. I really don't know what's up with Ruth, and she's driving me bonkers.

Oh, shit! I can hear Ruth and Lil talking in the spa behind me…

"Not a good match Lil, you will be stuck with changing his diapers in ten years. I have read his poetry. The guy has spent forty-eight hours in a psychiatric hospital. You read that poem again. The third verse says, *manic as a dog with a bone.* Get real, Lil! That sort of person can never be healed. It lasts a lifetime."

"He's not sick, Mom, just a little different. You've got to give him credit. Look at how he outwitted you in the psychiatrist's office," Lil says.

"Bullshit! Dylan and those sick bastards like him always have a story. Surely you are past the bleeding-heart stage."

"Oh, stop it Mom! That was a poem about an old girlfriend whom he lost because she was sick and he lost her because someone interfered in the relationship. That someone was a male family member... It was about me, when I had that breakdown."

"Whatever are you talking about? You never had a breakdown!"

"Is it any wonder I didn't tell you? I spent two days in a mental hospital, twice, after suicidal thoughts, because of abuse by Uncle Ray! Just like you. Don't be a hypocrite, Mom!"

"Oh really? I remember you saying, wisely--that you'd never again have a boyfriend who wasn't wealthy. And what about the drinking? You were knocking it back after Bill passed on."

"It's OK, Mother. My grief has passed. Anyway, I want to have a healthy baby."

"That involves a future I prefer not to think about," Ruth says.

"I won't discuss Dylan with you ever again! Hear me, Mom!"

Ruth drives off in a huff. What a relief, we can spend a weekend at home alone. Lil and I have decided to get married in July, and the date is getting close. The midday sun has made the tiles around the pool uncomfortable to walk upon. There is no breeze, and the rattle of the cicadas is intensifying. I stretch and watch Lil as she settles back into the reclining chair beside the pool. We can enjoy a weekend of domestic bliss… more relaxed now that our living-arrangement options are resolved, now that it is clear that Big Bill's daughters won't sell the mansion to us no matter how much money we offer.

Lil swims a lap in the pool, then sits back in her reclining chair and takes her gin martini from the shade of the orange tree. The naked sky is boasting and hot air wraps lazily around San Gabriel.

"I've invited some people over for a party next Saturday to celebrate our engagement," Lil says. "Why don't you invite Kathy and some of your friends?"

"OK."

We are taking care of Fluffy while Kathy is on a school trip. I hoist the shade umbrella. Fluffy jumps from under the table onto Lil's knee. She slides her hand around his ribcage and lifts him to her face, buries her nose into Fluffy's soft fur. Fluffy gives a twitch, wriggles, and then lies down in Lil's shaded lap. Lil reaches for her martini, but Fluffy's claws needle. Lil strokes him and he settles.

Lil's friends are charming. When I look across the crowd attending our party, Lil's face stands out. Her head is motionless, serene, with thick wet hair swept back. She looks directly at the person she is listening to. Lil speaks with direct eye contact, enunciation precise and enquiries insightful. Then she smiles and I love her.

We are content to stay at home again the following weekend, where the pool, spa, gym, tennis court and entertainment center keep us engaged. Kathy and I fit in a chess lesson, and study the recorded games of her next opponent on the ladder. Kathy has studied and learned this scientific language without difficulty, because she has already learned sign language and that enables her to be more open to abstract concepts than most.

I wake up in the sky above San Gabriel Airport, returning from a mission for Greg, reporting on an explosion in the basement of a large apartment complex in Tijuana, Mexico. The drug lab had been detonated by a rival gang. The local newspapers claimed that this rival gang was the CIA.

During the landing, the plane swerves in a gust of crosswind just a few feet above the ground. It is scary. My life rushes before my eyes and I am overtaken with clarity of purpose. This moment cures any need I may have to be mega-successful at business. Domestic harmony is much more important.

It is 10pm. Lil's front door is unlocked, so I whisper her name into the darkness.

She shoots out of the lounge and leaps onto me, wrapping both her arms and legs around me.

"Where have you been all my life, Dylan?"

"I missed you. Finished the project early, so I just flew in to surprise you."

She drops off me as quickly as she latched onto me, and walks back to the sofa.

"Dylan, my future impregnator," Lil says in a little girl's voice.

"You OK, Lil?"

"Mmm-hmm."

"You sound... different," I say.

"Can we get married? A happy marriage?" asks Lil.

"Yes, we can, it's all planned, In July, with a simple reception. But I'd rather not have it at your mom's ranch."

"But we must do it there. The landscape is perfect! We'll pretend that Ruth doesn't exist. Of course, I'll arrange it. Be a good sport and run down to the store and get two bottles of white wine or champagne. It's time to celebrate."

"Are you sure that's what you want?" I ask.

"After July I'm going to be your wife," she says.

"OK. Back in ten minutes."

There is only cheap wine in the one store open in San Gabriel at this time of night. When I return there are candles burning in the bedroom. Lil calls out. "I'm going to be your perfect wife starting tomorrow." She sounds stoned.

"Yeah, well what is this? Cocaine?"

"Do you want me to be your dirty little whore tonight?"

"What?"

Lil turns over on her stomach and pulls her underwear down around her knees.

"Do you want to fuck me in the ass, Dylan?" She crouches on her knees and pushes her ass up into the air.

"What?"

"I know you do," she giggles. "We've never done this before, but I know that you want to. I look back sometimes, when you're fucking me from behind, and I see you looking at my ass. I see your eyes. You want my ass, don't you Dylan?" She presses her face into the pillow, her words becoming muffled. "I want to make you happy, Dylan. I want to be your little whore tonight. I know you want to. Make it hurt, I can take it. I want to be dirty."

"Lil… "

She reaches across to the nightstand and pulls a mirror towards her. "I want you to get high with me, and then I want you to stick your cock up my ass and give it to me. Give me what I deserve."

I walk to the nightstand. There are four lines of cocaine spread across her mirror. I put my hand on Lil's hip and push her onto her side.

"You're a bloody fool, Lil."

"What are you mad about, big boy?"

"You said you were done with this shit. You promised me."

"Snort it with me this one time, then we'll be equal and I won't feel like you are looking down on me. It makes me happy."

"Love is supposed to make you happy! Love! Not some white powder you stick up your nose!"

"Oh, shut up, Dylan. You're such a prude. Just fuck me in the ass! I know you want a clean little wife. I know you won't be able to fuck me in the ass after we're married. Last chance."

"How could you do this to yourself?"

"Stop it, Dylan. Starting tomorrow everything will be perfect. Now, snort some coke and fuck me in the ass!"

"I prefer to make love sober."

She reaches out with her hand and grabs the erection underneath my pants.

"You don't feel sober, more like jacked up."

I slap her hand off me.

"Fine, be that way." She leans past me and snorts two lines of coke. After a few seconds, she collapses back onto the bed and speaks to me through a rubbery smile.

"Come to bed, Dylan." Her underwear is still tangled around her knees.

My erection won't go away.

"Come, come, come to bed with me," she sings.

I stand over her. I do want to fuck her. But the cocaine bothers me. I want a stable marriage.

I stagger into the bathroom and scrub my face. I stare into the mirror and then back down at the erection that refuses to go away.

"My shiny Bishop," Lil says quietly, as she drifts into sleep. "We're going to be married. And I'm going to be your wife and everything's going to be good. Right, Dylan?"

"Right." I walk over to the side of the bed, kiss her forehead, and pull the covers over her.

"I love you, Dylan."

"I love you too, Lillian Bjorn."

She smiles and looks as innocent as a child.

I turn away and walk out to the patio, not returning until she's asleep.

CHAPTER 19:

I get home about 7pm and hear hip-hop music from the patio. Lil is out there relaxing after a hard day at the office. It seems like a good time to ask where we are going to live after we're evicted from the mansion.

"We'll just move into that rental condo down the hill that Bill gave me. Bill's daughters will have to agree to that," Lil says.

"I'd prefer to live in my Victorian, or to take out a mortgage and buy the mansion from Bill's estate through a third party."

"Not a good idea," Lil says.

"Oh. Why not?"

"The condo will be perfect for us. Low maintenance. I've dreamed of getting married at Mom's ranch, perhaps under a pagoda by the lake, with white swans. Perfect!" Lil says.

Not a good idea. Those words felt like a dismissal! "I like your idea of an outdoors wedding--beside the water, but not on Ruth's property, not by the lake in front of Ruth's ranch house."

"Please, Honey. The bride's prerogative! Your home is lovely… but not the neighborhood. Too much crime! Bill's daughters would find some way to sabotage us if they knew we were married in their dad's home," Lil says.

"OK," I say. What a spineless idiot I can be.

Lil is making a list in her wedding planner. And now she's on the phone, while applying pearl-colored nail polish… I watch Lil's face go white, and then flood with tears. She slams the receiver down. "Ruth says she will only allow us to marry at her ranch if… if I will acknowledge her disapproval of our marriage--acknowledge it publicly at the ceremony!"

"That's her issue."

"Ruth also requires that a prenuptial agreement be hammered out now--so you don't get any of her money… or get custody of any child we may have, and cheat Ruth out of the joy of her own grandchild."

Lil doesn't wait for my response. She calls Ruth back, yells that we are not interested in conforming to Ruth's conditions. "In fact, I don't ever want to talk to you again!" Lil slams the receiver down… and squeezes a watery smile. "Ruth's a control freak. She is never going to approve of us."

Lil has seen a nice church in New Zealand--at Warrington, near Dunedin, while she was traveling with Big Bill. "That would be perfect for us. Would you please arrange it, and a honeymoon hiking in the rainforests of Fiordland."

"It will be winter in New Zealand. I don't want a winter wedding, or the fuss of traveling so far. And I am not keen on simply bypassing the conflict with Ruth."

But Lil will not be moved.

We are to be married in the Episcopal Church at Warrington. Episcopal is the same denomination as my parents, but they call it Anglican back there.

We are qualified for marriage without the usual time-consuming reading of bans because of the recommendation from my rector at the St. John's Diocese in San Gabriel, Father Chester.

I don't want my brother, Selwyn, to marry us. He has shown a conservative inclination from early in life and is too traditional for us. Starting from childhood, he joined successively the Boy Scouts, Navigators, Militia for Christ, Pro-life, the Catholic Church, and the Priesthood.

Lil insists that I call my parents right now. "Are they happy that we are getting married over there?"

"Helen and Hotty are thrilled. Although they want to know why you agreed to marry away from your family. I had to explain it all."

"No! Don't you ever discuss my family circumstances with anyone! That is my business and nobody else's!" Lil is shouting.

The phone interrupts my report writing after breakfast. It is the school secretary. I explain that Lil is at work. The secretary exhales loudly; "Paul must enroll in a drug rehabilitation program, or be expelled from school."

Jeez! And Paul is only twelve years old!

"The cops picked Paul up at 2am in downtown San Francisco early Sunday morning, intoxicated, and zonked out on mind-altering drugs, of the type druggies can purchase from hardened criminals on dark street corners." The school secretary should have verified that I was Paul's father before she blurted private information out like that.

Lil throws a dish when I tell her about Paul's problem--and immediately calls Ruth. They talk for an hour and Lil sounds defensive, then she goes to bed without dinner.

Lil sleeps late, before calling the school to object regarding the propriety of school procedures for parental notification. The school secretary complains to her that the administrators at the school can never reach her during school hours; *So what do you expect?*

She enrolls Paul in a recovery program at Kaiser Health, which requires all of us, including Paul's dad, to attend three program sessions each week. Larry is contacted and agrees. Barbara is the only one of us to refuse attendance.

While all this is developing, the recommendation for marriage is mailed, along with confirmation of the required counseling on the letterhead from St. John's, even though we haven't finished our series of prerequisite marriage counseling sessions with Father Chester. The rector was skeptical of our proposed marriage at first because we were a new couple by church standards... but not now.

Our final session is in the choir room. The rector asks us to share our most significant experience with the church. Lil is unusually keen to respond:

"In preparation for our first communion, Pastor Phil examined me. I only got one question wrong in the exam: *What did Jesus turn the water into at the wedding? The first miracle?* Pastor Phil wanted to know.

Imitation wine. Probably grape concentrate in water, I said.

You are leading with a jab? The pastor looked at me across the top of his horn rim glasses.

Alcohol is a poison. So, why would Jesus turn nice pure water into poisonous wine, especially at a wedding? I asked.

He looked me in the eye.

I feel like Mary sometimes. Trapped. She was very smart though, I said.

Oh? Pastor Phil removed his glasses, looking at his desk.

What was the poor girl to do, preggers to a man the family didn't like? Mary claimed a virgin birth, mothering the Messiah. Abortion wasn't a simple option in those days, I said.

Careful. What do you think happened?

Phil moved his head close to mine so I stood up before responding. *The Virgin waited till everyone was drunk and the wine ran out. Mary did the 'bait and switch'; she planted the grape concentrate in the jugs of water. Jesus was too smashed to notice. A martyr was born. Jeez Phil, read between the lines.*

And where did you hear this? Phil asked, his eyes fierce.

Jeez, Father Chester… That ended the conversation. I didn't want to talk to the point where the pastor would feel obliged to save me. Pastors may know what's wrong, but I have never seen them do a miracle yet... and Lord knows there was a need for a miracle in my family."

Father Chester has been attentive during Lil's venting, and surprisingly, pauses for a considerable time before responding to Lil. "For your final homework assignment I would like you both to write down any occasion or situation in which you can imagine yourself being unfaithful to your new marriage partner."

"When do we hand it in? This is our final session isn't it?" asks Lil.

"Yes, and you both have passing grades. Wouldn't do for only one of you to pass. So, please do the exercise and share it with each other. You don't need to hand it in."

Outside, Lil says that she has changed her mind and likes Father Chester, "He comes across as open minded and a good listener."

Something that Father Chester said apparently challenged Lil because she tosses and turns in her sleep all night. It is only two weeks before we are to be married.

Lying in bed on the Monday morning, Lil holds my hand and kisses my fingertips. "I'm going to spend the day with you, at your work." Then she calls her office to tell the receptionist that she won't be in.

Lil and I drive down the coast road to Monterey, holding hands and taking in the majesty of the coastline. We are on our way to investigate a gasoline explosion at a tank storage depot.

I am glad to finally exit the confinement of my car. Outside it's humid and the heat is discouraging. I squint against the glitter of the mangled steel. The building is out in the country, next to the Monterey Naval Station where Lil's father was once based. I am forbidden from touching the twisted steel, the sheared bolts or the curious welds. I inspect the welds at the base of the shiny new tanks. After I review the installation procedures for the tank and copy the specifications, we order our lunch at the restaurant on the end of the wharf at Monterey. Lil says; "This is a good time to talk about the homework Father Chester gave us regarding fidelity."

I am puzzled, and then it comes back to me. Father Chester said, I want each of you to share any situation where you could be unfaithful to your future partner.

"Shall I start?" Lil asks.

"Well, OK, but I hardly think it necessary."

"I was sort of unfaithful to my first husband, Larry. Larry and I were out drinking heavily with friends at a Chipmunk bar, then dancing separately, he with a slut and me with one of the male strippers. I followed the male stripper into his dressing room, while Larry was still dancing with the slut. But the stripper called a security guard, who hauled me out of the room before anything happened. And then someone called the police because I had broken a beer pitcher."

The restaurant suddenly feels cold. Before I can swallow, Lil goes on:

"On another occasion I kissed my dentist, as best I could while under the influence of a dental drug, as I sat in his chair. The dentist resisted."

There is a silence as I struggle with my composure.

Lil speaks first. "OK, now it's your turn." She has a nervous tic, and looks away.

"The priest asked us a specific question; *Tell each other any situation that you could be unfaithful to each other during your future marriage.* I take it that that you are now telling me that you can be unfaithful to our marriage when you consume too much alcohol or drugs."

"No, I'm just telling you the truth, what has happened to me in the past."

My bottom lip is twitching and my gut is screaming *danger--run.* Lil doesn't seem to understand why I am upset. It is too uncomfortable to sit here and freak any longer so I pay the check immediately.

As I drive us back toward home on the coast highway I am not able to replay her entire story, not even once, despite my dredging for good will and acceptance, because of a sinking fear and an ominous foreboding.

I have to stop. I leave Lil in the car and walk the beach. The wind is firing bullets off the ocean and cold blasts whip sand into my eyes. I huddle on the lee of a log and try to imagine calling off the wedding. It would kill my mother--and me. No! I am going to marry this woman--who I evidently should not trust to be faithful. But no! Could she possibly do such a thing? No! It cannot happen.

Larry arrives to pick up Paul after school. Paul's father has returned to the district for the sake of Paul's recovery program. I explain that Paul has gone to an Alcoholics Anonymous meeting and won't be home for an hour or more.

"How are things going with you and Lil?" Larry asks.

I feel I should be cautious with him. "Fine."

Larry settles into the living room sofa. "You'll have to watch that one. She's trouble." He takes his shoes off. "Let me tell you a few things. I was in a covert war before I met Lil. Did she tell you about that?"

I shake my head and refuse Larry's offer for me to sit in Lil's living room chair.

He shrugs, and wipes his wild hair back. "When I came home everybody said I wasn't the same person. I came back across the border after fighting for Uncle Sam and not only was I not appreciated; I was scorned as a drug dealer. I wasn't expecting the hero treatment because it was a war no one knew about. I was the boy from San Gabriel who didn't feel inferior to anyone before the war, happy Larry with lots of friends, a convertible and all that stuff.

Then, one day I'm door gunning, seeing choppers explode, flying down so low I smell cocoa fields burning, hear the sobs of children, see whole families destroyed, and the next month I'm back in San Gabriel with a drug habit. And now I really don't belong, and I've got fears about people talking behind my back. I don't want to be around other people, I can't laugh or joke.

Then my first wife got killed in a car accident. Too much! I stayed at home with baby Barbara and dealt drugs. But when I try the Veterans Administration, they tell me that I'm just there for the money. Early on I tried to get government help and all they gave me was some Valium, put me to sleep, so fuck the government! They treated me like shit.

It was after this that I met Lil. It was like she had experienced it all. Unfortunately, I adored the bitch."

Larry helps himself to cheese and roast beef from the refrigerator and then goes on. "Now I've got the prize, the pretty wife, the home, the kids, and the fucking mother-in-law from hell… But Ruth is blackmailing me cause she has known from the start about my drug business, caught me out one night in Mexico while I was doing a big transaction. So I paid for her ranch and god knows what else. Fuck her too!

I wanted to be alone after that, but Lil wanted to be social as well as settle down. So we did some partying. She waited until I was a crank addict to get my kids away from me. She tricked me. I should have known never to let her go off with Barbara and Paul! I'm the father!

So Barbara's become high maintenance and my son Paul is an addict.

Lillian has ruined the kids; it's her neglect. She was too busy screwing Big Bill. Obsessed with money. She never could be trusted. Never! She turned her back on me and she turned her back on my kids. Now, I'm fine. I hope you guys make it. Good luck with the wedding. New Zealand, eh? At least the kids are grown up now.

The front door opens.

"Come on, Paul. We gotta go. See you around, Dylan."

Did the cold way I dumped Lil when we were teenagers, did that coldness drive her to Larry? Did I drive her over the top? Or is Lil attracted to guys who are troubled--another product of her molestation. Whatever, I'm committed and afraid.

CHAPTER 20:

Lil and I watch movies and sleep on the plane to New Zealand, holding hands all the way, always holding hands.

We settle into our hotel suite, appreciating the elegant drapes, a huge vase of complimentary flowers and the acceptably firm bed.

Lil and I can talk for hours in the twilight, lying in bed. No matter if Lil is talking or listening, her luminous eyes are attentive and steady, her head still. She talks again of her dream; "We could move to our own ranch in five years, a ranch that is self-sufficiently growing bio-fuel, vegetables, and firewood."

When she falls asleep with her arm around me I listen to her breathing, a soft perpetual motion.

We drive our cream Holden rental car to Elsinore, detouring on the way at the Otakou Marae to check in with my cousin Witi, who walks out to greet us; "You want me to be the star of the show eh?"—He is to have several major roles in the wedding…

My family ranch has a unique front gate with an address plate, *1 Upland Rd,* above the mail slot. It swings beautifully when I nudge it open with the bumper of the rental car. It is good to be home and nothing has changed except the kitchen counter is clear of dirty dishes, wiped clean of crumbs and the coffee table is new. My parents are delighted that we are getting married at home. Dr. and Mrs. Powers come over before the second cup of tea and join in the joviality.

Just before sunset, Lil is staring vacantly out the window, and when interrupted remarks on how the Powers cows have come across to the orchard.

"Oooh! I forgot to shut the orchard gate," Jean Powers says.

"Don't worry," Lil says, "Let me do them, please, I want to."

"Stay there, you're on vacation."

"That's good, perfect, I must milk the cows, I insist!"

The rest of us look at each other as Lil hurries to the back door and starts putting on dad's overalls to cover her city clothes. "Come back here, Sweetheart. The cows don't have milk at the moment, they're dry in August," Jean says.

Jean Powers is rocking in her chair, laughing. "God love you, Lil! What a lucky man our Dylan is. Eh, Richard, don't you think?"

Richard Powers clears his throat, "Yes! Lil, I persuaded Dylan to disconnect from you when you were here before. I'm sorry, I was wrong. Obviously you have not had any further health episodes, so I wish you two the very best and I know you can make it work."

It is our wedding day and I'm going to play nine holes of golf with Dad and then have breakfast with my parents. Lil wants to stay in our hotel room and get ready, alone with her thoughts, biding her time until 3pm.

When I return to our hotel suite, Lil pokes her head round the door of her bathroom, surprised that I am back so soon. The light sparkles on her hair. She's wearing a slip and has a bobby pin in the corner of her mouth. Her hands are behind her head, pulling her hair back in preparation. "Fabulous," I say. She ducks her head back into the steamy interior.

I shower and begin to dress. I'm buttoning my shirt when Lil pokes her grinning face around the door, then prances a few steps of the wedding march, wearing white satin underwear and a blue garter. It's really going to happen, an August wedding in the middle of winter in Dunedin.

It is the grayest sky that Lil has ever seen and it will probably stay that way all day, although there is a faint thinning of clouds to the east. The northeast wind gusts rattle the windows and chills Lil's bare arms. She puts on her thermal undergarments and then takes them off. "I can't wear such practical stuff on our wedding day. Better to freeze than to look frumpy."

Witi calls us from reception office. "Hey Dylan, my black ass is at your service."

Lil and I climb into the back seat. The sight of my old buddy's face brings me back to a different time, reminds me of how much I have changed… how I am more responsible and more burdened now.

"How's the music business going, mate?" I ask.

"Sweet, but I'm not my own boss yet," Witi says.

"Well, you are today; chauffer and musician extraordinaire," I say.

"What sort of music do you play now?" Lil asks.

"Learnt some new ones. From the Stones second LP. Ha ha! Hey, girl! Lighten up. How come you didn't let me take Dylan out on a stag night?"

"Can't trust him. You know how he is," she says.

"Yeah, I know the miserable bastard. Get a ring on his finger and lock him away quick before he joins a band again. Make us all deaf!"

"Hey, Witi. Did I tell you that my new computer can write music?"

"Yeah, a couple of emails ago. Sex makes you lose your memory, eh? As well as striking you blind," Witi says.

"Don't remember. But my computer's got a long memory, like you, eh, Boy?"

"Yeah Dylan, you owe me fifty bucks from that time you stopped at the fish and chip shop in Taihape, eh, Bro?"

"Where's Taihape?" I ask.

"Where the fish and chip shop is. Where I loaned you fifty bucks," Witi says.

"Bugger! I don't remember." I laugh.

"No wonder you need a new computer."

Lil looks at me sideways, and then hands Witi a hundred dollar note.

"Na, Girl. I don't do it with married women."

Witi drives us slowly on the Port Chalmers road toward Warrington, on the scenic route around the high road. From here we can see Elsinore across the narrow mouth of the harbor, Aramoana this side, across a two-mile wide range of hills to Purakaunui, and then along a stretch of virgin white sand to Warrington.

"Hey, Lil, I'm just pulling your tit. Your old man would never borrow $50. He'd rob the joint first. Besides, where was a flat-nose like me gonna get fifty bucks at that time of night?"

Warrington is another village like Elsinore, and I wonder about the odds of Lil and I marrying at such a remote place as this. I have sailed my boat among the seals and under the Albatrosses, from Elsinore to the bleached powdery beach of Warrington.

Lil is looking out the window as we travel and doesn't seem nervous.

Neighborhood children are waiting for us in front of the Warrington church, curious to see the rare occurrence in this village of man marrying woman in fearless union. The children, Lil and I, are all fresh-faced and beaming. There is a piper dressed in a Scottish kilt playing the wedding march on the bagpipes.

We approach reverently and enter the old wooden church, which is painted antique green with plum-colored edging glass in the stained windows.

The sanctuary is warm, despite the high cathedral ceiling and open vestibule. Mom and dad are sitting in the front row with the Powers family. Mat is sitting with his wife, both dressed to the nines. Mom smiles. Witi's family is behind them. Selwyn and Kathy haven't arrived yet. Trust my brother to be late.

The vicar is standing up front, a large ruddy fellow, and I am happier than any day in my memory. The vicar's white robes reflect a mosaic of color as the sun glimpses through the stained-glass windows for just a few seconds. Pungent incense melds with the softer fragrance of freshly cut flowers. Life is as it should be.

Lil and I stand in front of the vicar, Father Michael Riddell, famous in these parts for being controversial—as he starts the ceremony.

"The conjunction of eternity and human transience steeped in the wisdom of the Church… a joining of man and woman, of God and humanity, of purpose and chance, of commitment and love. The binding with ancient symbols, full of mystery and grace: the ring, the cup, the promise, the blessing." There is a transcending dignity to the ceremony.

We hold hands as we prepare to say our vows. Lil ignores the prayer book and repeats the vows that she had written during our first week together.

"I, Lillian Bjorn, do solemnly declare that I will stay with this man forever, whatever may happen. I acknowledge that Dylan is my soul mate, a man I will adore, love, and cherish for the rest of my days. I will always celebrate the soulful purpose of our marriage, to complete the journey of our individual and married souls."

And now it is my turn. "I commit to accepting Lil unconditionally, to enduring what ever obstacles might come our way, to be in love, now and forever."

We grin at each other, through joyful tears. We feel as innocent as we have ever been, as uplifted as any couple has ever felt in the history of the planet.

Vicar Riddell insists that we listen to a homily. He pauses for a moment before beginning, presumably to allow the gospel reading to sink in, or is it to build anticipation before he begins to sermonize?

I stand sideways so I can look out over the faces of the congregation. I recognize every single person of the forty that are gathered here and can sense their uncertainty over what to expect. I smile at our captured guests to reassure them.

"Here we are in God's house!" Vicar Riddell is enjoying a long moment as his first words reverberate. He pauses again, enjoying the uplifted eyes, the waiting ears. The silence stretches like the echoes after a clap of thunder...

"Love is much misunderstood."

Another theatrical pause that probably sounds eloquent to the Vicar, as he allows his melodic voice to expand due to the amplifying influence of the Holy Spirit and the Church acoustics.

"We imagine it as something over which we have no power."

Lil squeezes my hands and smiles into my eyes.

"Love is a force which seizes us, a wave which sweeps us over, a state like drunkenness which we may fall into. Love, as it were, lies in wait for us. When we stumble upon it, we are helpless to save ourselves. Love is the emotional equivalent of gravity. We fall, brothers and sisters, do we not? We fall."

The Vicar is pleased with his elocution and his choice of words, as I am pleased with my choice of bride.

"Lillian and Dylan are here because they have fallen in love. When they look at one another, they feel that they are caught up in something greater than themselves."

Vicar Riddell directs a smile toward us, bestowing approval with those wrinkles around his eyes.

"This is as it should be. They are young, full of life, and they have fallen in love. Why should they not imagine that this state lasts for ever?"

He glances around the congregation before changing his oratory tone.

"Sadly, my friends... and I say sadly with all the grief of one who works amidst the chaos of relationships--that which is fallen into can just as easily be fallen out of. Scandalous as it may be to speak of such a thing on a wedding day; those who have been carried along by a wave of love can sober up to find themselves washed up on the shores of disillusionment.

Love never ends, says the Apostle Paul. Is he unaware of the way that domesticity and commerce erode passion, until all that's left is resentment and apathy? Paul understands that it is at the point when the romance fades and the devotion wilts, precisely at that point in a marriage is the willful choice to love called upon.

Dylan and Lillian know nothing of successful marriage as yet. But when that crossroad comes... as it will, as it surely will... then they will need to look back on this day, not as the day on which they felt like soul mates, but as the day on which they decided to commit, despite the drudgery.

These two have just promised to each other that they will stay together whatever may come. Whatever may come! And we who witness are upholders of such a promise. Let us believe in and act out a love that never ends. And in so doing, add our blessing to Lillian and Dylan."

Vicar Riddell, orator extraordinaire, is pleased with the resonance of his final paragraph. But his wife, seated behind him at the organ, has a frown and a cynical look in her eye, as if she knows differently.

Lil and I serve the bread and communion wine, firstly to the choir, then to Mom and Dad. Our guests and family line up in silence, mostly avoiding the radiance of our shiny eye contact as we feed them. Our guests seem to have reached a limit as to how much hope they dare behold.

The Vicar wishes us luck and gives us a gift, a novel he has written titled *Masks and Shadows*, which he promises will fortify us on cold winter nights before going to bed.

The reception is at 5pm in the conference room of our hotel. We enter to find Witi has arranged for his band to be playing in full swing, as is the local tradition, on a stage made from sheets of plywood on empty beer crates, playing a Maori love song about Maui and Hine.

I am relieved when Selwyn shows up with Kathy just in time for dinner. They missed the plane in Wellington because they were playing a tense game of chess in the airport cafeteria… Selwyn does not like losing.

Gone is the woozy feeling in my stomach about Lil and the horrid subject of infidelity. Father Chester had been of no help when I asked him: *What was the purpose of your final homework assignment?* Father Chester just shrugged his shoulders.

I sink a large shot of Scotch, and then propose a few too many toasts. Lil doesn't mind my extravagance, but I can tell that Mom is getting a little anxious so we dance, laugh and dance. Mom and Dad are thrilled that I have finally married my teenage sweetheart--and they tell anyone who will listen.

The memory of Lil's casual attitude toward infidelity sneaks up on me again, two days since the last time, as I am walking around the ranch with Selwyn before the honeymoon in Fiordland. I am about to ask Selwyn if I may talk with him. Then I change my mind because I don't want to bother him and can't imagine what he could possibly say.

I adore Lil and have no regrets about us getting married, but I can't hide my gnawing fear--and my stomach knows that its enemy is at the door. I gag as a slug-like texture swells in my throat. My stomach heaves! I jam my mouth shut, let the putrid slime bounce off the roof of my mouth, and stuff it back down to my stomach.

Lil and I drive off on our honeymoon, cruise the four hours over to Lake Wakatipu, and stop at Glenorchy for an early dinner. We have rented the Philip Temple Cabin on the Dart River.

The next morning we load our packs and start down a track through the Teasel, Tussock and Spanish to the shore of the river. Watercress and mint run along the edge of the gravelly shore, holding aloft branches of driftwood, signs of a recent flood. We hike on to a small valley flat through which the river runs to Lake Wakatipu. A tributary channel has cut across the foreshore, and the floods have backed up the river sand which crunches under our feet. The channel bed gleams with runs of gray and silver sand, blue stones and several massive boulders, reminding us to keep to high ground should it start to rain up in the head waters.

There are three sturdy Kanuka trees on the sandy foreshore, and from here the valley of beech trees and Totara rise into the hills. We climb up the east bank of the Dart River, floundering through gullies of Fern and Punga and teetering across stony streams. We hear a rumbling up ahead; water funneled to falls and rapids. It's another hour before we close with the source of the sound. The forest is cooler, moist with fine mists of spray, and the tumult is now deafening. I part last leaves and look out on a wide waterfall. The water billows, creating fine and transparent mist, frilled thinly with foam, to crash and crackle on rocks forty feet below. There are silver Ferns, giant Beech, red Rata, mossy Totara and palm-like Pungas framing the falls at its foot. We swim in the lake below and experience nature's massage by sitting directly under the fall, with our backs exposed to the surging rhythms of the waterfall.

The steep trail through the forest is indistinct, dank, and cluttered with fallen trees; it crosses hiccupping streams and surging rivers and takes insane twists among clustered stands of rain forest with outrageous moss colors: lime, orange, lemon, brown and plum on the tree trunks. There are psychedelic colors and patterns on the mushrooms: red with white dots, lemon with orange dots, and lime with green leopard pattern. Undergrowth and drapes of creeper close in; fat trees escape skyward, leaving murky cascades of leaf and lichen behind. Even at noon light flickers only weakly on the forest floor. The exotically colored and abundant mosses shine iridescently--even in the shade. Forest clearings with sharp light become more frequent, until finally we glimpse the Southern Alps beyond giant greenery, punching skyward above a clearing mist.

Now the track becomes more distinct, mountains move apart, and we have the view of a reflective lake. We loiter, and then slowly return to our cabin--armed with a new serenity, soothed by nature.

We stay a night at the family cabin at Purakaunui on the way home, strolling on the vacant beach on an unusually warm winter's day. Kathy has flown back to California with Selwyn. I am concerned that she may feel neglected, so I call her.

Angela answers the phone. "Kathy is out at the chess club." Angela then takes a snipe at me; "Shame on you for forcing Kathy to attend the pre-divorce hearing of her father's sick affair with the snobby bimbo!"

I am still laughing when we take a run along the beach. Then we shower under soft reticulated rainwater collected in tanks off the cabin roof. Our hair is shiny from the pure water, and our skin soapy to touch.

"Let's have dinner at the Alphar Ranch--it has huge windows overlooking the sea." The owners join our table, reveling in the ambiance of our happiness and the view of one of the many pristine white beaches circling Dunedin city.

Later, we talk alone over coffee.

"I want to continue with my career as a financial advisor for another four years, mixing it with the big boys to prove my mettle in the business world," Lil says.

"Sounds good to me."

"In four years, Paul will be finished at high school and he plans to leave home for a career in the music industry, like his dad, but smarter. Then you and I will be free to relocate to a ranch, either in California or here in New Zealand—to enjoy the sophisticated luxury that we deserve."

CHAPTER 21:

Lil and I are still holding hands as we return to San Francisco Airport from our honeymoon, and still again as we drive up to our San Gabriel mansion in a taxi. She kisses me at the threshold and leaps into my arms. We kiss in the hallway again. She sucks my upper lip into her mouth and undoes my zipper. We smooch our way upstairs to the bedroom. But a blip appears on our previously clear radar screen: The bed is without duvet or sheets and the naked royal mattress is mottled with stains.

Lil stabs Larry's phone number into her portable. "What the fuck has been going on?"

She walks back down the stairs with the portable to her ear. Doors are banging. She returns with a note and a scowl, amidst another phone conversation, this time with her son, Paul.

She turns to me with a hint of a grin--overlaying a frazzle of exasperation.

"Larry has been house-sitting, adulterating in our marriage bed with a married woman, and Paul busted his dad last week for showing up to Paul's drug rehab meeting at the Kaiser *D-Tox* center high on cocaine."

"Holy shit!"

"Larry is now attending Narcotics Anonymous meetings for himself, as well as going to his son's meetings. Larry has become born-again from the experience. What an idiot!" Lil says.

The house is in chaos, with dog shit accumulated on the entrance carpet and the family room overrun with dirty dishes. Barbara's car broke down just after we left, so being an enterprising daughter she found the keys to my car. However, she cannot conceive of a plan to return my car for a week or two, certainly not until her car is either replaced or repaired.

"Oh, my God! I need my car."

"Tell Barbara about it. There's nothing I can do."

Lil calls her Mexican maid to come over early to clean up the mess. We, the newly married couple, get to return home to sleep on our soiled bed. I gather the smelly bed clothing from the floor and dump it in the washing machine, gather clean sheets and make the bed around Lil, who has fallen asleep on the bare soiled mattress.

The dog shit is professionally cleaned from the carpet, and although the stain is still visible to the discerning eye, the smell is altered so the teenage wing of the mansion now has the aroma of a methamphetamine lab. My car is eventually returned, after which time I discover my home has been the site of numerous Barbara parties, and is now the talked-about scene among high school seniors.

Poor Lil. She now has two rehab zealots, converts to clean living, within her family: Larry and me. In addition, Paul is showing signs of being ready to burst through to the other side, an advocate for sobriety and the twelve-step revolution of forgiveness and ruthless self-honesty.

Larry zealously takes this opportunity to make his eighth-step programmed amends to Lil. "Sorry Lillian, I've been too busy with my recovery program to do any dishwashing or housework, too busy to clean up dog shit, mind Paul, or make the bed. Isn't the twelve-step program great?"

"Brainwashing bullshit!" Lil says.

Lil and I are enjoying a quiet dinner at home, celebrating our four-month anniversary, which therefore may not be a good time to bring up something that is bothering me; "I'm worried about all the booze in our bar, with alcohol being a temptation for Paul… like the program teaches."

"Why should that be a problem?" Lil asks.

"You know how kids can drink off the top third of an opened bottle and replace the booze with water."

Lil grimaces.

"I'm also concerned that you are drinking too much while we are hoping to get pregnant," I say.

"I'll give the entire contents of the bar to Greg! Will that satisfy you?" yells Lil, turning away.

"Yes."

"Fuck!" Lil throws a series of china dishes at the fireplace. "I won't stop drinking just because you want the perfect wife! This marriage is supposed to be about accepting each other as we are! Right?"

"Right."

"Well, you are not right! I can't handle this."

"What's the trouble?"

"I can't see you changing. You've become a twelve-step rehab fanatic!"

"Sorry. Just trying to do what's best for Paul."

"Well, you are not!"

"Sorry."

"I want you to move out of my home!"

"You've got to be kidding!"

"No! Move out of my home now… before your self-righteous fears spread any further!"

Shit! Is she really serious? "My next appointment is not for an hour, can I wait here until then?"

"If you keep out of my way."

"You bitch!" I say, and grab her, pushing up against her skirt, focusing where her skirt is pressed against her swelling crotch. "I love you so much," I whisper.

"Well, fuck me then," she says.

I slip my warm hand inside her panties and stroke her wetness. "I love you." My thumbs slip her black panties from her thighs; I kiss them as I go down. I push her onto the huge living room sofa. She falls across sideways, letting herself bounce on the cool leather upholstery.

"Hold on," I say. I loosen my zipper and kick off my trousers, shoes, and socks. I kneel beside her. She reaches her hand out for revenge, cupping me, taunting me. She throws the remainder of her clothes across the room. I grab the small of her back and pull her close. Our lips and tongues dance like waves. I force myself inside her as she makes a token protest. The waves of pleasure begin even before she begins to thrust back at me, as I angle myself inside her deeper, the tip of my penis stroking her white hot spot. My rhythm becomes more furious, sending silver lines of ecstasy running between us, as I reach behind her to grab her butt, stroking it, toying with it, using it to pull her deeper against me, until all she can do is to gasp my name and clutch me. The bright wall of pressure inside her explodes as her body cascades into another orgasm, and everything but; "Dylan, you still have to move out," falls away.

"Can we talk now?" I ask.

"What about?"

"About why you are upset," I say.

"What do you want to say about it?"

"I just thought you'd want to say something."

"No! Nobody can reason with a diehard do-gooder!" Lil says.

"You just want to leave it at that?"

"I don't want to leave it at anything, I know you'll be moving out in ten minutes!"

There is something calmer about Lillian now. I was certain that she would immediately go on a binge and lose the plot--which could involve a lot of ranting, and an awful lot of contempt directed at me. But there is nothing like that. She seems so sure of herself.

"Is our marriage over?" I ask, even though I know it is not.

"I don't know."

"Please talk to me?"

"OK… Go!" she snaps.

Lillian is banging doors downstairs and playing *Korn* music loudly while I pack. I purposely leave many of my clothes, tools, and some work files in the house. I make a simple exit to my former home, to my sleeping bag.

Lillian calls two days later. "Let's go to Raffles Comedy and Dance Club on Friday night for a date."

"OK."

"I'll be taking both my kids up to Ruth's ranch for the weekend, but Ruth doesn't want you to visit the ranch, not ever again."

Ruth is outrageous. And Lil must be feeding her information for Ruth's animosity to be growing. I agree to go on the date, but I'm loaded with resentment.

Raffles Comedy Club is full at 8pm on a Friday evening so we are seated in the vulnerable front row. Lillian is not wearing her wedding ring. That pisses me off! The lights go down as the first act begins; we order drinks, a beer for me and a highball for Lillian. The comedian picks on us: "Are you two married?"

I jump into the challenge. "I'm married, but she's not!"

The audience laughs, a laughter that expands as various connotations are absorbed. Lillian is embarrassed.

A second comedian replaces the first, is slicker, and talks faster.

"Are you two married?" The second comedian asks the same question!

"Yes," we reply in unison.

"Are you two mad?" The comedian asks.

"I am, but she is not!" I say.

"Then you two would be crazy to be together!" The gleeful comedian jokes... "Marriage would be better if you both were mad."

After the comedy show is over, Lil talks to the younger people sitting behind us, then we go out onto the balcony for a cigarette. Lil is annoyed when the shaven headed doorman grabs our drinks. "You guys can't take alcohol outside." The night is warm and San Gabriel is buzzing. The music comes up loud and we go back inside. The huge skinhead doorman has saved our drinks, covered them with a paper napkin, what a lovely man.

Lillian hangs out beside the dance floor with the group from behind us. We finish our drinks. I am feeling disorientated. The first comedian tries to make conversation--but my mouth won't move. Lillian grabs my elbow and we stroll onto the dance floor. She doesn't stop in the middle of the floor. She walks all the way to the other side and dances with a man, a stranger. I stand alone, in the middle of an almost-empty dance floor, feeling woozy. I rush outside to walk off the nausea. Fifteen minutes later, Lillian comes outdoors looking for me.

"Would you like to go home now?" she asks.

"No! I want to have a dance with my wife before we go."

We attempt to dance in the exhibitionist's cage, mounted like a chandelier above the dance floor. But I feel clumsy and something isn't right. Lillian excuses herself and climbs back down the metal stairs from the cage. Again I am stranded on a dance floor. Strangely, I find myself dancing alone in the cage, then I have difficulty negotiating myself down the steep stairs… need to sober up.

I wander toward Lillian at her table. "It's time we got back to living together."

"It's time you changed your attitude!"

"That's bullshit!"

I nod to the approaching skinhead guard and ascend the two exit steps lightly, knowing I needed to make this a peaceful protest. I walk in circles outside, for twenty minutes. I go back into the nightclub. Lillian is dancing with the second comedian, trying to put her arm around his neck.

I run outside, barely able to avoid vomiting, but don't barf.

Did what I thought I saw really happen? I swallow my emotional nausea and then go back… to observe Lillian objectively, with no panic. There are only about thirty people in the club now. I order a glass of water. Holy Shit! There is Lillian, on the dance floor with the two women friends. They scream when they see Lillian marching across the dance floor toward another stranger. A rush of adrenalin tweaks me. I hide behind a column. Lillian continues to walk across the dance floor, to walk at the stranger. She grabs his shirt and pulls him to her. I feel sick again and slink outside. I walk the block many times.

It's getting late, almost midnight. I order a taxi and go back inside to find Lillian. But the skinhead doorman confronts me at the entrance. "Raffles Club is closing soon and no one can get back in."

"But my wife is in there, I've got a taxi for her!"

"I don't care if the Queen of Sheba is in there; you're not going back in."

The doorman is huge, domineering.

"In that case, will you call inside and have the staff let my wife know that I am here with a taxi for her? Lillian, the woman with the striped sweater."

"That is not going to happen. Go home."

This guy gives me the creeps. Weird!

The taxi driver calls. "Come on! I haven't got all night."

I explain the situation to the driver, and that I feel jilted. "I don't want to make a scene, but Lil might be trapped."

"No use calling the cops. They are always busy and only respond if a crime has occurred… and a serious one at that."

I ride to my home and walk in small circles. I consider going back to Raffles, but instead I stagger in larger circles for an hour, panicked--and finally I collapse, exhausted.

CHAPTER 22:

The manic voice jack-hammers my brain. *This is Lillian here, your wife. Where are you? I want to see you.* She sounds worse than loaded... Smashed! My answering machine announces a recording time of 5.30am. It is 9am now--Saturday morning. Lillian was planning to go to her parent's ranch for the weekend. The message was recorded by my cellular phone... forwarded from the intercom located outside my front door. I call her condo. No answer, she must have gone.

I can't think! The damn phone is ringing. But it's not Lillian, it's Angela. "Will you please take care of Kathy today because I have to go out of town?"

"No! Don't ask me! Lil was out of control last night, was out all night."

"Get your sorry ass over here now and pick up Kathy! It'll do you good to get your mind off protecting that slut's reputation."

"That's cold, Angela!"

"Sorry. Just trying to shake you out of it. OK. I'll cancel my class."

"No. You're right. I'll pick up Kathy. Be there in thirty minutes."

It's Sunday night, and I've still got a headache. The 6pm news isn't making it better. Jeez, another hurricane! I don't know what this world is coming to.

The phone rings. "Hi. It's Lillian here."

"What in hell do you want? You're not going to fuck with my head! Shit! Drunk at 5 o'clock on a Saturday morning! Keep away from me!"

"I'm calling from the Sierra branch of Kaiser hospital. Did you know I was drug raped on Friday evening?"

"Are you OK? Oh, my God!"

"What do *you* think! Can I come over to your house and sleep when I get back tonight?"

"Yes, of course you can."

"Why did you go home early Friday night? Why did you abandon me!"

"Of course I didn't."

"I don't trust you. You put speed and Rohypnol in my drink!"

"That's ridiculous! What's Rohypnol anyway?"

"A date rape drug. You had the opportunity, Dylan," she stabs.

"But not the motive."

"Are you sure?" Lillian asks.

"Of course I fucking am! You can come over tonight, but don't blame me for what happened."

"They have tested me here in the hospital. They found three different drugs in my system: amphetamine, opium and rohypnol."

"Can I help, Lil?"

"Just be there for me, Dylan."

"OK."

Lillian hangs up.

I make up a bed for us, with clean sheets, and wait.

When I think about it, Friday night had been a truly bizarre night; I must have been drugged also. Lillian will be suffering terribly, but why did she attack me, trying to make me feel guilty for going home? She has succeeded.

I wait up until very late, but Lillian doesn't show.

I call Lillian mid-morning.

"I went to Raffles Comedy Club last night to do some detective work," she says.

"What did you find out?"

"Nothing! They were of no help."

"Can we meet, talk about it?" I ask.

"Fine, as long as we meet at a public place. I don't trust men now, and that includes you, Dylan! Barbara is taking me to the police station this afternoon to make a statement."

"I would like to come with you."

"My daughter insists that you don't. Ruth says you're responsible."

"That's fucking crazy!"

"Dylan, is Ruth correct? Did you hire guys to rape me? To punish me because I told you honestly about my previous infidelities?"

"That's outrageous, Lillian!"

"I'll meet you at Kaiser. I have to go there for an abortion pill and STD medication... outside the pharmacy."

There is a roaring in my brain--a massive adrenalin flow. Colors, noises, smells, fear--everything has intensified. Time slows to a flickering progression of horrid images, of my wife being subjected to hell. Grief and anger turn inside my galled stomach.

Lillian and I walk slowly towards each other in the pharmacy hallway. She has blue and yellow bruises, fat, all around the edges of her lips. We hug, tight, wounded, stand in line for her prescription, and then sit outside the café across the street, not saying much. We smoke cigarettes in the cold afternoon, and look at three dogs eating scraps at a restaurant backdoor. The wind races down the alley so fast it sleeks the fur of the dogs.

In the early evening I listen to Lillian talk on the phone. "I wouldn't have reported the rape to the cops because they're insensitive… but I'm concerned for Paul and you, so I'm going through with prosecution."

"How can I help?"

"You can't. Just carry on with your life as normal, and I'll try and pick up the pieces as best I can."

"Can I see you tonight?"

"No! Get some sleep," she says.

"I haven't slept for days! That's out of the question."

"You don't sound well. Go down to Kaiser hospital and get some counseling and sleeping pills," she says.

"Maybe I will. I'll call you tomorrow."

Lillian is the victim here, not me. But I will go to Kaiser Health anyway. At least she's talking to me, and doesn't seem to believe Ruth's crazy speculation. It must be so humiliating and dehumanizing to be the victim—and then to have male cops interrogating you about the rape.

The Kaiser emergency room is quiet at 9pm on a Monday evening and a nurse soon calls me into the triage room. "What's the problem?"

I describe the rape. I explain that I am not coping well.

"Please wait in this office here. We'll have to call a psychiatrist in."

I wait ninety minutes before the psychiatrist arrives from her home. We sit opposite each other at a small desk in a cubicle.

The psychiatrist is a tall woman and she looks down on me intensely, making the small space seem claustrophobic. "Tell me about the rape, please?"

I describe the events at Raffles Club and tell about Lil's phone calls Then I conclude; "Kaiser in Sierra has measured rohypnol, speed and opium in Lillian's system, and I'm not coping. A bit jittery."

The psychiatrist nods. She has already heard this, from the admitting nurse.

"I've done some research and your information is… dubious. The Kaiser file indicates that Lillian could not have been drug raped with the drugs that were in her system, I think she may have lied to you. One of the drugs in her system cannot be dissolved in liquid--or covertly imposed upon Lillian in any way."

"What does that mean? I can't understand this!"

"I'm sorry we don't have time to go over this now. Please take these valium--and you should call Kaiser Health tomorrow for an emergency therapy appointment."

At least the valium puts me to sleep.

I make an appointment for emergency therapy the following day.

Lillian calls in the afternoon; "Things did not go well with the police."

"Why, what happened?"

"The cops have contacted the rapist. His name is Michael; I found his phone number in my pocket. My memory is coming back slowly, partially. Witnesses say they saw Michael and me dancing for hours, and Michael was buying me drinks."

"Not Michael from your office?"

"No. A stranger. Then we got a taxi to the Radisson Hotel."

It is difficult to breath and an awful nausea fills my stomach. This is hard to believe. And there is more…

"All I remember is waking up fully dressed in a hotel room. Michael gave me $20 for a taxi. I rode a taxi to your house. There was no answer. So I walked home, walked for miles, crying all the way."

"Shit! What went wrong with the police?"

"Michael had called me the next day. He left a message on my answering machine Saturday. When the police interviewed Michael he claimed that I asked him for sex last Friday night. Clever bastard! The police told me that they are closing the file. Bastards!"

"Oh, no! That's not good!"

"Assholes! Michael has a police record of crimes against women, of physical violence to his wife. And the police didn't suspect a crime, despite their acknowledgment that there has been a high incidence of reported drug rapes out of Raffles Comedy Club recently."

"Oh, hell!"

"I was further embarrassed because I had to admit to previous cocaine use, had no option but to confess in front of Barbara or risk being exposed as dishonest."

Lillian is sucking air. Thank God that I have a therapy session coming up.

"I wish I could go to the police station with you."

"Well, you can't!"

I wonder if she is hiding something that the police know? I wish she would apologize for wrongfully accusing me.

In the morning, I visit the police station anyway, alone. The police have no questions for me, and they have no answers or information for me. They cannot discuss the nature of the consumed drugs, claiming *confidential information.* When I express concern for Lillian's welfare the police detective fires a parting shot. "I hope you're not planning to see her again. Don't be an idiot. Divorce her!"

I do not like the police. Why do they believe that they have a better understanding than the rest of us? It seems that the frequent exposure of the police to the criminal class has caused a bias. How dare they assume that Lillian is the sort of person who can be dismissed like that. And to say that I should divorce her based on their prejudice. How dare they judge Lillian! She and I are good people, in most ways. But I'm beginning to think that being a good person in most ways doesn't count for anything very much, if you're a bad person in just one way. Am I bad because I abandoned Lillian at Raffles Club? Am I bad because I am starting to doubt elements of Lillian's integrity?

Most people are good people, aren't they? Most people want to help others, and if their job doesn't allow them to help others then they do it however they can--by serving food at a homeless shelter, giving to charity, wanting to love Jesus or raise good children. But I am bad because I don't give a shit about the homeless, charity, or little baby Jesus right now! I am so angry!

CHAPTER 23:

Chris Else opens her door cautiously. She is an angular woman. The step up to her Kaiser office makes her seem taller than I. She watches me from her height, a moment's hesitation as she weighs up my sideways glance. I smile but it is only with a wince of my eyes. My eyes are darting over her. Her brown tweed skirt to her calves and matching jacket with a red lapel pin over a floral blouse are from my mom's generation, smart but old. She has gray-brown hair, parted, and a touch of black lipstick, a dab of powder pack. Her eyes are dull with no luminescence, make-up or mascara.

"Come in, please." I trip on the step and enter her cold office. She takes my jacket in her bony hand—a hand devoid of adornment except for a plain gold wedding band. My shirt reeks of cologne, an effort to mask my sweaty anticipation of this meeting. She hangs my jacket on the coat rack beside the flowerpot, and offers one of the two chrome chairs in front of her tidy desk.

"Sit down," she says. "Please."

I pull the chair beside her desk to the back of my knees, but I don't sink back into the curved back, instead I perch on the edge of it with my hands in my lap and my legs stretched out and crossed at the ankle.

Ms. Else sits opposite me on the other wooden chair. A cardboard box sits on the comfortable stuffed chair behind her desk.

"Welcome." She smiles to help me feel at ease. When people are nervous, I get nervous too.

Immediately, Ms. Else leans forward, drawing her feet back towards the chair, her elbow on her desk.

"Hi," I say.

She lets the pause lengthen. I can feel her resistance, her uncertainty beneath the parting of her lips.

"I'm here to listen," she tells me, "and to support you. This single emergency session is to see if we can identify the issue for you. Shall we go on?"

How do we start?" I ask, my voice deeper than usual. I am quite skeptical of a desirable resolution ever being possible.

"Perhaps you could tell me a little about yourself?" Ms. Else asks.

"What do you want to know?"

"Whatever seems appropriate," she says.

"My name is Dylan Hotta. You know that. I'm thirty-four years old. I own my own consulting company, doing forensics on industrial accidents." I hesitate, turn my head and look out of the grimy window into the hydrangea bush that presses close up against it. "You know the practical details of my wife's rape, from the file. Today… I've had a lot of doubts about my capacity to understand my wife."

She shows a hint of recognition… and then waits.

"That's mostly why I am here," I say.

A pause.

"Mostly?" she asks.

"My wife, Lillian, says I'm not coping with things well. She thinks I need help to come to terms with her rape."

"What do you feel about that?" Ms. Else asks.

"Me? I just want to know why it happened. Not in the philosophical sense. That's bullshit! I want to know in a practical way."

A pause. She is very still.

"How old was Lillian when you first met her?" she asks.

"Seventeen."

"And now?"

"Thirty four."

"How is your wife coping?"

"She's angry, grief stricken of course, but doing OK," I say.

I look out the window again.

"It's different for me. People expect Lillian to be broken--and rush to comfort her, but they are just stiff with me, like I am some freak who failed to protect his wife."

Ms. Else watches me, sees the signs of guilt, the sour turn to my mouth, the shame. I am sure she will now announce that I have a deeper level of responsibility for the rape of my wife. But instead she seems to bide her time. Perhaps she is letting me try to find my own way out of this maze for a few more minutes, until I get to trust her a little her for some emotional support.

But I snap out of it and realize that I no longer need carry this burden. Michael did it… my innocence has been established by Lillian.

"I'm not really answering your questions, am I?" I say.

"What question?" she asks.

"About how I'm feeling."

"Do you have an answer?" she asks.

"Mistrusted, violated." She looks me dully in the eye then looks down at her feet.

I pause for several gulps of air and a dry swallow. "Lil's mother is no longer accusing me, because they know Michael did it. But there is a suspicion that I hired Michael to punish Lil."

"That is absurd, ignorant and crazy. It's just noise," Ms. Else says.

"Thank you. I suppose the guts of it is…" I look up at her.

"I guess… I don't know… The other Kaiser psychiatrist seems to think there is something odd about Lillian's recollection of the events."

Ms. Else's eyes alight and dart around the floor, then focus on the light fixture, waiting for the right words.

"Tell me more about that," she says.

"You know the story about the drugs Lillian claimed to have in her system. The doubts mostly happened because of what your Kaiser Psychiatrist said… and the police, to an extent. I don't know why. And I don't seem to be able to stop doubting my wife!"

"Do you want to stop it?" she asks.

"I don't know. There doesn't seem to be any emergency--the doubts will probably pass with time. But when I'm struggling, it feels like Hell."

"And this is Hell, right? Do you want that feeling to stop?" She asks.

"Yes. I mean, it's normal to be upset. The difference is that I need to get a resolution before I can sleep again, and to feel that I'm connected again in some spiritual way to Lillian."

"That's what troubles you? The alienation?"

"Yes. I don't think it's necessary," I say.

"For Lillian to suffer more?"

"Yes. She doesn't need any further grief, not from me," I say.

"Tell me again what happened?" Ms. Else asks.

I tell her all the details that I know of regarding the incident, including the Kaiser psychiatrist's statement about a drug in Lillian's system that isn't soluble--which I assume means that the drug must be snorted, smoked or injected.

Ms. Else leans back with a stern look.

"Lillian is angry at men, angry because a male family member sexually abused her… this may even have been her father rather than her uncle--and you know intuitively that's relevant. That anger is understandable. But now she behaves promiscuously, like a lady of the night--to try and hurt men. You saw her stalking men last Friday, before you went home."

I can't believe that Ms. Else is saying this.

"Her behavior is more than counterproductive. As a therapist for Kaiser, I know that Lillian wasn't raped. She has lied to you about the drugs, and at the bottom of your heart, you know that it wasn't rape. She is out of control. Lillian-of-the-Night is purposely hurting you, because she sees you as a surrogate of the male family member who abused her in the past, a surrogate for her anger. And that's not fair on you, Dylan."

"Thank you, but… How can you be so sure it wasn't drug rape? You aren't telling me everything. And it's unfair to judge Lillian!"

"I'm sorry, Dylan. But I believe you need this information. And I'm also sorry, but our time is up."

As I drive home, I am plagued by questions. How can Ms. Else be so sure?

Does she know enough to be sure? She must have extended herself beyond professional boundaries to look up my wife's medical file—even though I know it was out of compassion for me. But she hasn't told me everything, so I must question her conclusions. Anyway, I cannot just walk away from Lillian; I need to confront the situation, to find a resolution. So I call her.

"Hello, Sweetheart. How are you?" I ask.

"Struggling. I called my lawyer. The police are insistent they have closed the file, but they may still want to talk with you. You are under suspicion. How did your therapy session go?"

"Difficult. And confusing. How was your session?"

"OK. But my therapist asked me not to discuss it."

I decide to share what Ms. Else said earlier today; Lillian's behavior is counterproductive. As a therapist for Kaiser I know that Lillian wasn't raped, she has lied to you about the drugs. She is out of control. Lillian is hurting you, because she sees you as a surrogate of the men who have abused her in the past, a surrogate for her anger. That's not right.

Lillian spews at me; "What bullshit! I'm so angry, I'm furious... You will get divorce papers served tomorrow!"

"I'm only repeating the words of the therapist, Lillian! Let me give you her phone number, she is at your branch of Kaiser in San Gabriel. I will let her know that you may wish to discuss this with her."

She hangs up.

This is crazy! God give me some mercy! The nightmare of pending divorce sits cold on my chest. I sit here thinking, blood pulsing through my temples. What a fool I've been!

Two days later I am served divorce papers, including instructions not to contact Lillian--and that any further correspondence must be made through Lillian's attorney, Mr. Holdall.

CHAPTER 24:

What do I do with divorce papers? Absolutely bloody nothing! I put them into a drawer I never use. But I do take Kathy back to New Zealand to stay with Grandma and Grandpa for a week.

"Where's Kathy?" It's evening and I've been sleeping.

"Down at the School Beach Park, talking to the rabbits," Dad says. "I told her I would come down and push her on the swing, when I'm finished with sharpening the carving knives."

"I'm not sure about letting her go down there on her own."

"Relax, Son. This is a different country," Dad says.

"I'd feel terrible if anything happened."

"You have to let her be a kid sometimes Dylan," he says. "She can't come to much harm at School Beach."

"I'm being neurotic, I know. What happened to Lil has changed me."

"I'll go down to the park now, OK?"

"No. I can go down."

"I see little enough of my granddaughter. Let me have this time with her."

I go down to the pier and wash the bird shit off dad's boat. This is strangely enjoyable. It is good to be able to clean something up—and get a resolution.

On the way home I stop at School Beach. Dad is sitting on the swing. Kathy is over against the fence by Upland Road, where the wild rabbits live, where it is almost dark. Kathy with her dark hair and black blouse over green jeans is just a shadow. She seems to be talking to the rabbits. I stroll closer.

"Come on, Furball... I've another carrot for you. Nothing to be scared of. And for you too, Bobtail. Don't bite my finger. Mommy might let me have a rabbit of my own. And maybe Grandpa will get a rabbit, so we can come down here and visit you. I hope you won't be jealous of the pet rabbits. I won't love you less. But it'd be so much fun to have a baby bunny to take care of."

"Its OK, Bobtail, I've got more for you. Give me time."

I have to turn away. Tears pour down my face. Kathy's fun reminds of what it was like to have a carefree childhood… and that is comforting.

The morning before Kathy and I fly back to San Francisco, Mom gives Kathy a riding lesson, which reminds me, I must get her a pony. The sky is hinting of infinity, and I feel a clarity again—that is the antithesis of Raffles, a clarity that is the antithesis of being drugged.

I remember how drugged I was. How did it happen? Who drugged me? And who drugged Lillian? I only had a couple of drinks, but I was nauseous and out of it. Those drugs could only have been planted in our drinks by the Sheba man, the hairless doorman--planted when he took the drinks from Lil and me. And why else would he refuse me re-entry to the club? Why else would he not agree for me to collect my wife? And the police said that there was a rape from Raffles Comedy Club just about every week.

This explains it all: Sheba spikes the drink of the selected victim, and then informs his fellow predator, Michael, of his choice. Then the Sheba man drugs the victim's partner, and evicts him. Now the stage is set--and the Sheba bouncer joins Michael in the appointed hotel room. They cover their tracks by injecting an opiate into their victim's semi-conscious arm… So bloody obvious, why didn't I think of it before? Because the therapists and police led me up a blind alley!

Oh my God! Poor Lil. Goddamn! She has been screwed. And why didn't the police think of it? All they had to do was look at the video surveillance camera at the hotel entrance, like I suggested to them. I wonder if they checked to see when the bastards reserved the hotel room. What do I do now? Lil doesn't want me to contact her. I could call the police detective, tell him what really happened, but that bastard is so closed minded, so cold!

CHAPTER 25:

Despite the unbearable uncertainty, I dump the proposed divorce papers, unread, on a lawyer's desk--and instruct the lawyer to stall. I worry about Lil and I want to end this standoff--so I leave a gift at her door.

Lil calls me the next week, on Monday evening, thanks me for the gift and invites me over. "Paul is away until tomorrow, why don't you come by?"

"OK. In an hour." I dress in my baggy white shirt, her favorite.

Lil has lit some candles out on the patio. I can smell cigarette smoke in her hair. "How are you?" I ask, and sit at the patio table.

There is uncomfortable small talk, and then Lil asks me again if I would like a drink.

"What the hell. Why not?"

Lil pours herself another also. "I don't want to be at work, at home, anywhere. My mind is numb. I've forgiven my rapist. I don't hate him. I could kill him, or myself, as easily as not."

The tone of her voice is too soft. And I don't like the suicide inference. Maybe she is suicidal. But I'm not going to call the cops. Not them.

Lil takes another sip and sets down her glass. "I'm going to a therapist. We'll talk about it. And we'll talk about our dreams."

"You want my dreams? They have not changed. I want a happy marriage," I say.

If you knew my dreams and ghosts--would it make a difference? I want to yell this at her. But that would sound like anger... And anger is a bad thing--would get me in trouble. "I just want to be normal," I say.

She sits on the chair adjacent to mine--not opposite, and doesn't sit all the way back. She perches on the front edge, leaning forward, with her hands flat on the table. Her legs are crossed at the ankle. She throws a word back at me; "Normal?" She looks away. If I were any kind of right-thinking man I'd explain that husbands get all sorts of strange fears and nightmares, but at this moment, I can't.

Lillian gives me a long wet stare, and then slumps in her chair. "I feel dirty," she says. "I want to regain some self-respect."

"I want to help you, Lil."

"How? What do you have in mind?" She smiles stiffly. Her ankles entwine the chair legs, her elbows rest on the table and her hands reach up to cover her mouth. I let the pause lengthen. I can feel her uncertainty, her discouragement. "I want to see if we can work through our past," she adds.

"You know me." I say this even though I know that she almost certainly doesn't.

"Why don't you think I am capable of being unfaithful? Don't you remember? We talked about it?" Lil asks.

"I remember."

Lil stands. "You always… you always used to tell me that you liked snuggling with me more than you liked sex."

"Yeah."

"I always thought you were lying," she says.

"Maybe the truth is that I like both?"

"I know that your truth is negotiable!" she stabs.

Lil is humming, softly, an old hymn.

I cannot forget why we are here like this. Bloody hell! I was there in Raffles that night. I can still taste the bile from that evening as I watched my wife preying on men, out of control. How can I ever adapt to living with something as hideous as rape or betrayal?

"Why did Raffles and the rape happen?" she asks. "To us, of all people. Why is it that we, the victims, are the only people who suffer?"

Lil's humming grows louder. She starts to twirl her hips a little, and then steps into the dark garden. Lil takes off her boots and sweater. She tells me that she needs to feel with her hands and feet as she twirls barefoot on the lawn. Her shirt goes next.

"I need to have my skin open to the world."

She reaches for the sky, arches, walks toward me, eyeball to eyeball.

I stare at her beauty.

Lil tops my glass, lights another cigarette, powerful despite her nakedness. She lifts her hand to my face.

"Why don't we go to bed and slit our throats? The world has been so cruel to us. Let's show them!"

"Why don't we? Because it's the most fucked up thing I have ever heard! Because we have children who would be forever scarred! Because we have family and friends who love us! Because it is wrong! Because I have absolutely no interest in missing out on one single minute of this life!"

"A fucking survivalist," she says.

I don't acknowledge her game. "Do you think we should get a therapist?"

"Who, for god's sake? You and I have tried every damn therapist in the county. Do you want to try your writer friends next? How about Nick Hornby or Owen Marshall? What about Drew Stepek or Brian Caldwell? No! Therapists do not heal addicts or marriages," she says.

I go to the bathroom, and as I pee, I rededicate myself to loving this damaged and dangerous woman as best I can—but maybe from a safe distance.

I return, and there is Lillian. We are at the patio door. She walks toward me and stands very close. I put my arms around her and sense her holding her breath. I suspect that she is going to reject my affection. Then she lets go of her breath and her tongue darts out, I see it coming. Her tongue is now flickering across the electric skin on the side of my neck. Her fingers brush across my shoulder. "It wasn't your fault, Dylan." Her hand presses down onto my shoulder and I touch the skin on her wrist, hesitantly, as if I'm afraid of her. She slides close to me, and I push my face into her shoulder. She wraps her hand around my shoulders, and rocks me back and forth. I raise my face. She looks at me, her breath pressing warm against my face.

The wet smile disappears, and her face becomes frozen as she leans over and kisses me. She pulls her hand away from my face and slides it down my chest, undoing shirt buttons on the way, finally resting it on my groin.

"Lil…" I pull away from her mouth.

"Dylan," she whispers, and bites into my nipple.

"Lil, can't we talk…"

She tugs at my belt, skillfully yanking it open.

"Lil…"

The buckle flips open and she unzips my fly.

"Lil, don't!" I grab her wrist.

"I want to suck your cock, Dylan," she whispers with a throaty voice, before sliding her tongue into my ear.

I pull her hand away.

"Please, Dylan, please let me suck your cock. I want you to cum in my mouth!"

"No! Not like this, Lil."

"Please, Dylan."

She tries pulling my hand free. "Please. I need to suck your cock. She shifts her body and drops her free hand onto my lap.

"No, Lil. No!" I grab her shoulder and push her away.

"Well, to hell with you then!" She pulls out of my grasp and slaps me across the face before standing up. "What do you want you tightwad? What do you want?"

"I want to help you."

"FUCK YOU!" She slaps me again. Where were you when there was still something left to save?"

"I'm sorry."

"Those words don't change anything!"

"I know. But I'm still sorry. I love you."

"I HATE YOU!" she curls her open hand into a fist and punches me hard in the face.

I fall back.

"I still love you," I say, and wipe the blood away from my split lip.

"You fucking asshole!" She runs towards me and pummels my chest and face.

"I wrap my arms around her legs and she falls down on top of me, her arms swinging wildly. I grab her arms and hold them at her side.

"It's too late! There's nothing left!" She spits in my face. "There's nothing left!" She stops fighting my hold and begins sobbing. "There's nothing left, Dylan.

Where were you when they were raping me, raping me the first time, and raping me again?"

"I'm sorry."

"I hate you," she cries and falls onto my chest, wrapping her arms around me.

"It's OK."

"No it's not!" She rubs her face back and forth across my chest. "It's not OK. They did things to me, they… They made me do things. They… Oh my God, Dylan, they hurt me so much." She claws at my chest as though she is trying to climb inside me. "Why did they do those things? Why would they do that? I never… they did things, Dylan. There's nothing left. It's all gone. I'm lost! God save me, please."

"They hurt you. But they didn't kill your spirit, they didn't beat you down."

"I'm so dirty, Dylan."

"Lil, you're the cleanest person on this whole miserable planet." I wrap my jacket around her naked body and smile. "It doesn't matter what they did to your body, you never let them get near the place that really matters. Your spirit's good and beautiful and clean and perfect. They couldn't touch that. You didn't let them."

"I love you, Dylan," she says, so quietly that I barely hear it.

"I love you too, Lil." I press my lips to her cheek.

"Dylan, will you... will you please fuck me?"

"No. But I'll crawl under the covers with you and snuggle your butt. How about that? I'll wrap my arms around you and we'll close our eyes and pretend that we're at home permanently, living together."

We wend our way to the candlelit bedroom. Lil is so high. There are no inhibitions. Her body gets long and taut like a diving board. She is turned all the way on. Then I scream. Lil has bit my nipple so hard that I cannot hold back tears. I am so angry. We continue fucking, all night, waking over and over again--with a lust that is way beyond normal.

In the morning, while we are having our shower together, Lil sinks to the floor of the stall and sobs for ten minutes… and can't be comforted. "The memories are coming back. There was more than one guy fucking me that night."

Lil calls her office, and tells the secretary that she is having flashbacks from the rape and won't be into work for a few days. She then suggests that I move back in with her.

"But please go back to your place for today. I'm hung over."

My room stinks of cheap bleach. But the impact of Lil's scent still lingers in my memory like a sensuous dream… as does my memory of cowering below Lil's fury and scorn; *You're just a memory, Dylan, a vague memory too stupid to stay that way. It strikes me that I've heard all of this shit before.* I'll protect you. I'll save you. *Grow up.*

The following day, my real estate agent calls. "Will you accept a full price offer from an Architect to buy your Victorian—to use for his office? It's conditional upon city approval of parking expansion."

"Parking approval is outside my control. But yes. I accept."

Then I call my divorce lawyer. "Mail me the refund of my deposit fee because Lil's divorce filing is cancelled."

My lawyer says, "Lillian's divorce filing has not been cancelled. Lillian and you are still, officially, legally separated."

That night I decide to get down to the tough business with Lil. "I would like to go back to being a married couple. I suggest that you cancel the divorce proceedings," I say. "My lawyer won't refund my deposit fee until the case is closed."

After a pause Lil reacts; "*My* lawyer says that would be a waste of time, considering our history."

I say nothing and move back in.

CHAPTER 26:

We are sort of together, on our way later to a dance club in the city, to celebrate Cinqo de Mayo—but first we visit Greg's large high-rise apartment on the Embarcadero. The evening is cooler in San Francisco. After an unusually hot spring day the fog has rolled in, so Lil and Greg have put their coats on before going outside for a smoke. I watch them through the balcony window. Lil is leaning into the conversation.

Greg can't smoke pot indoors because the cleaning staff might report him. Even though Lil and I have only been married for a few months, Greg is already into our bank account for four hundred bucks--to pay for Lil's astrological chart.

Lil doesn't know about Greg's work with the CIA. To Lillian, Greg is just another retired guy with a nice apartment… who is into that astrology bullshit—a bonus to Lil because she has developed an interest in predicting our future.

Greg has been a good friend to me, but once in a while he has a rough day, when he gets carried away with the secrecy of his job and his creeping age.

Greg is lighting up--smoking Lil's stash… actually he is smoking big Bill's stash that was left behind in the safe of the Mansion.

Did she just give Greg another check? It's difficult to be sure because Greg's windows haven't been washed for a long time.

I step over and sit in the cane chair--just a few feet from the half-opened sliding door. I can hear Lil talking…

"Greg, I realized yesterday, I've found my perfect man…"

"Don't bullshit me, Lil! Dylan's not the perfect man for you. No one is! You're a Capricorn, on the cusp, and therefore with major Sagittarian traits; you have a dual personality, you'll have as many bad days as good days, and Dylan may not be able to handle that."

Why does Greg have to burst everyone's bubble? And, to rub it in, he's charging us a fee for printing out a programmed astrology chart. Lil is taking all this stuff in like it's direct from God. It's like she still needs some affirmation that we are perfect for each other.

"But, Greg. It doesn't matter what difficulties you predict, I could live with Dylan in a tree house. He is so accepting of me, he understands me more than I understand myself. He's my soul-mate!"

Then the cynical buzzard butts in; "Wait another couple of months. And if Dylan really was committed to your relationship, he would pay me the extra bucks for an astrological chart of him."

"Bullshit! Anyway, Dylan and I were born at about the same Greenwich time on the same month of the same year. So we don't need a second astrological chart." Lil says.

Greg takes a toke on the pipe.

"So, what interested you in Dylan initially?"

"His speech about the incarnation of the soul. It really got to me."

"Oh really! All men become boring once you get them talking!"

Asshole! I can't believe what Greg is saying.

Lil goes back at him; "But Dylan said those magic words... Our soul incarnates, it entered the universe to complete an ancient purpose--it hungers. His words took me to that place where I know that I have a purpose and am unique."

"And how were you seduced?" Greg asks.

"Dylan invited me to a party. I found in him more than just an intellect."

"You got sucked in by that chemistry, attraction to a mysterious man."

"No. It was the sculpting of his lips. He talked, and then asked me to dance. A lot of men were looking at me. He danced with rhythm, in touch with his soul. And I was glad of his attention. Why do so many men avoid me, and those that don't become obsessed? After one dance I had to go to the bathroom because I felt the room spin. Dylan had intoxicated me."

"Yeah but... "

"Yeah but nothing! The next morning, I woke feeling that I had been delayed on a long journey with a purpose forgotten until yesterday. I felt the connection that Dylan talks about, with the one who loves unconditionally... "

"What's Dylan done for you?" interrupts Greg.

"I believe that Dylan's spirit possessed me. I know that when I look out to the bay he is with me. And that's a good feeling."

"That's a nice story, but I still reckon you guys won't last," Greg says.

"Whatever you think is your business," Lil says, with a carefree wave of dismissal. "The question is, Greg, why would you want to tell me how to feel?"

Greg shrinks visibly. Lil and Greg do another round with her pipe.

The city is moist, with lights reflecting on the dew. I slide the balcony door open further and step outdoors.

"Time for me to join you guys." I reach for Greg's pack of cigarettes. Lil slaps my hand away.

"No!"

Then she grabs half a burning cigarette from Greg's mouth and tosses it carelessly into the night air, sparking toward Jackson Street far below. Before returning inside she does her post-cannabis routine: a whiff of breath freshener, a squirt of perfume on the right hand, another to the hair. She beckons me to follow her into Greg's living room.

"You guys were having an argument?" I ask.

"No. I was just telling him how perfect you and I are for each other..."

Greg interrupts; "Women more than thirty years old inevitably become cynical about love—they just use the sizzle to get what they want... Power! Personally, I'd be more convinced of this soul-mate stuff if you purchased my astrological chart of you two as a couple."

"How much does that cost?" I ask.

Lil sighs loudly. "Oh shit, I'm only thirty-four!"

After an uncomfortable silence Lil laughs. "We're not going to pay you another dime. Give it to us? Then, if the chart really helps us I'll give you the fucking money!"

Greg and I look at Lil. She shrugs, "What's a few dollars between friends?"

Greg joins us dancing at Romero's club. It is 4am before we take a taxi back to Greg's place. This is the first night I have slept under the same roof as Greg.

CHAPTER 27:

"Kathy will not sleep under the same roof as that Bjorn harlot… my daughter is an innocent ten-year old! Bring her back tonight!"

"Don't talk like that, please--and especially not in front of Kathy."

I close my car window and drive away from Angela's wretched house with Kathy—feeling like I have stolen her from her mother.

Escrow is about to close on the Victorian. It is empty, not a suitable place for me to host Kathy either. Kathy and I are having day visits only now… still at Lil's home, usually just the two of us.

Kathy insists that I follow her and stand outside the door when she goes to the bathroom in Lil's guestroom. She likes the comfort of conversation while she does goodness knows what in there. She likes to have these long chats through the door, which is OK as long as there is no one else around. We are chatting about nothing in particular, and then out of the blue she asks me where the sky ends.

"I don't know," I say. "It doesn't really have an end. Just becomes outer space." I remember my math classes: A straight line is a segment of a circle that passes through infinity. Kathy is too young for that leap.

"Where is heaven then?" she asks.

"It isn't a place at all, not like the library or the chess club, so it doesn't have an address."

After a pause she asks, "Do you think there really is a Heaven?"

"Yes," I say, and there is a longer pause, with shuffling behind the door.

"It must be peaceful," she says.

"What do you mean?"

"Peaceful isn't a place. It's just something that you are. Maybe Heaven is a bit like that?" Kathy asks.

"Maybe," I say, not sure how far to take this.

"Maybe Heaven's a place where you feel good rather than a place where you get some thing you want," she adds.

"That's a good understanding," I tell her. "Heaven is a feeling that we are in tune with God's will rather than stuck in trying to do our own will."

"Right now is Heaven for me," she says.

"Good, so what are you doing in there to take so long?"

"I'm flying again. Down below me the ocean is warm and blue, and there are whales spouting. I dive down and swim with them. Then I'm soaring up into the sky again, and the sun is warming my back. I fly over land, and there are green fields with zebras, and all the zebras are looking up at me and admiring how well God has taught me to fly. I'm as peaceful as can be, and the wind is blowing the hairs on my arm. I'm happy."

It is the following day and Lil is buoyant. "You and Kathy must come to Ruth's sixtieth birthday party."

Ruth's birthday celebration is at the Lutheran Church Hall on Saturday evening. I know that Ruth doesn't want me here, but Lil has declared this to be an occasion to mark the turning of a new leaf.

We are seated at the head table. Ruth's husband, John, steps up to the rostrum and speaks in a dignified voice before a crowd of more than fifty formally dressed guests. He says thank you to just about everyone in the room, starting with Grandma Stephanie, who is sitting to my left, sitting beside Ruth. Grandma Stephanie doesn't look well. Suddenly the room shrinks into darkness. There is an electricity failure.

When the lights come back up Ruth is at the rostrum. She takes another sip from her wine and clears her throat.

"I'll tell you about my man--John is a sex addict... "

John is uncomfortable when everyone laughs. He waves for Ruth to sit down. Grandma Stephanie stamps her foot, but Ruth insists upon continuing.

"I want to tell you about my first real date with John. We were lounging after an exotic dinner in the Tonga room, talking over a glass of fine wine… as is my custom. I felt at my best that night, perhaps because I had cut back on my partying, and lost weight over recent months. I didn't want an innocent fling, or another one-night-stand. I wanted a meaningful connection with an interesting, sensitive, healthy, intelligent man..."

Ruth pauses, sips from her wine, and then continues.

"John said to me when I first met him, *I am not intimidated by extreme beauty*. Now, I am not immune to flattery, and I know John will always be different, sort of pure, and yet earthy. I'm not attracted to insecure men. John seemed entirely secure, with the confidence that comes from a good noble family."

John looks skyward and signals for Ruth to stop.

"I remember that John's eyes moistened. John leaned across the table and I kissed him. He received this gift as if he deserved such special treatment. I liked his confidence, secure that he didn't need to rush us.

And then he asked me to dance. And was he hot!"

The laughter is spirited… until the people see John's flushed face. The laughter fades rapidly.

"We were following the music's pulse. It felt to us, and surely to the members of the band and to the other dancers--that we looked like an attractive couple with an intimacy of many years… having a special night out.

Afterwards, John leaned over the table and kissed me. It felt too good to stop. The people at the next table were watching us. It was time to go home…"

Lil grimaces a smile toward Kathy. "I'd better rescue Grandma Ruth. Too much wine." Lil steps onto the rostrum, puts an arm around Ruth, passes her the largest of the wrapped presents, and announces a toast; "To my dear mother, to Ruth on this happy day. May she live forever!"

"You could have parked your car in the garage," Lil says, as I come up the stairs after dropping Kathy off.

"Fuck the car!" I say. I want to get to bed and think to myself, think about that damn photograph that Grandma Stephanie gave Ruth for a birthday present.

"OK. Out with it. What's upset you?"

"Who's the stranger in that photograph?"

"A distant relative from Canada, Tor. I hate that Stephanie kept that photo. But Grandma says that it's the only family picture with everyone, and without my dad and Larry."

"And that relative with the crinkle in his eyes stayed in your home?"

"No. He's long dead. Do you recognize Tor from somewhere?"

"Please, can we drop it!"

"You have to trust me. I'm your wife. I know this must be difficult… I'm sorry." Lil puts an arm around my shoulder and squeezes. She lets her head touch my chest, standing still, not breathing.

"It's so horrible! We should drop it."

There are trees still visible outside in the low light, the branches sagging under their own weight.

"You've worked hard trying to come to terms with something." Lil closes her eyes.

I pull away from her, and tell her briefly about Lomas.

Lil hugs me. "Tor isn't Lomas."

"But he has the same face!"

Lil whispers in my ear, arms around my shoulders, "It's difficult to forget, I know. But Tor died when I was twenty three."

There is a long silence, and she hugs me.

"Let's go out next weekend. Did you realize we have been married a whole year? And we still have the spark! Let's have some fun," Lil whispers.

"OK. Remember we have seats to that new play? Right after that, we can go away," I say.

"Perfect. I'll book us into a nice hotel for the night."

Lil takes a deep breath, and then exhales slowly. It is all there with us, everything. Not just the lust of the moment, but our whole life together: all our loving from the past, the nights when the wanting wouldn't let us sleep, the fights we had, our plans, the kids and all their problems too, the future. Our plans to go to the theater next week add a flavor of domesticity and therefore hope for our relationship.

Lil is wearing a dress that is red and backless. She has an attractive tan for this time of the year. We walk up the three marble steps to the theater. She has painted a tiny mole above the right corner of her lips, and is admiring her creation in the foyer mirror.

"I want to thank you for agreeing to come," I joke with Lil in front of the theater.

Lil smiles over her possum-fur scarf. "First time I have seen you in a tux. You look good, Dylan."

I think now, briefly, that our marriage could have been more normal, in other circumstances.

"If I look this good, why didn't I get invited to Barbara's graduation?"

"Think yourself lucky to have got snuck into Mom's birthday party," Lil whispers in my ear.

"I'm sorry. What can I do to make up for my short-comings?"

"Drink nitric acid, very very slowly," Lil says.

"You ask a lot... come on. It's time for the theater."

I love every second of the play. I drink it, like someone with dehydration might drink a glass of beer. I love being made to think about something other than our past. I love its wit and its seriousness. I promise to improve myself by reading more literature.

I spend almost as much time trying to snatch glimpses of Lil's profile as I do watching the stage. Sometimes she almost looks relaxed, but sometimes a scene in the play provokes a pained grimace. But soon after, it's as if an overriding satisfaction takes over, and a delighted scrutiny anchors on Lil's face all through to the final act.

"But you have always avoided the theater," Lil says.

"I think… I thought I hated the inflated egos of the actors. It was, it was a judgment I hadn't examined properly."

"You want to watch yourself," Lil says.

"Why?"

"If you start editing your judgments there'll be nothing left of you."

I laugh and we saunter on.

We register at the Summit Hotel near Santa Cruz to celebrate our anniversary. Our late dinner consists of crab cakes with champagne--in our ground floor room beside the pool.

Lil wants to sit sidesaddle on my knee. She asks me nicely, and gives me a kiss… So I grant her wish. She opens my trousers and plays with my penis. I like that. Lil puts her arms around my neck, reaching up. I feel the fabric of my lungs stiffen, as I hold my breath. Then I let go. I brush her nipples, lightly, tormenting, the way I know drives her crazy, forestalling any further conversation. She gasps for air. Her bra is black silk, and it surely must caress her breasts when they swell like this. I brush her dress half off her shoulder, freeing her breasts from the bra, dropping it to the ground. I bend my head so my nose touches her neck, then her throat. I waft my warm breath onto her nipples until she aches for me.

"God, you're beautiful," I say.

She tugs off my shirt, looking at my tanned shoulders. I close the door to the patio. She rakes her nails down my back.

In the morning, we gorge on egg-benedict and champagne. I have creamed spinach on the side. Back in our room, we do it again. I take her confidently on the table. By the stage when it is too late to take it slowly any longer, her sex takes over. I pause to savor her textures and tastes. Then she wants me to do it harder, and I do. Her sex begins to surge and vibrate, like she is about to cum. I can tell. It lasts a long time. Then we move along the wall to the bed, and I pause again, kissing her and licking the salt off her skin. Perhaps she wants me to do something different, because I do. Her head is banging into the wall. Then she gets a lot louder, and calls out. Screaming! I am embarrassed when a young man taps on the window and applauds. But Lil doesn't seem to care. Her whole body begins to throb and vibrate. She seems to be going into another world. Then she pushes me away and waves to the man at the window.

CHAPTER 28:

From my office window I see Lil arriving for our lunch date. She waves. Then the phone rings. The piercing voice of my ex-wife, Angela, informs me that Kathy has volunteered to join the Red Cross… merely to enable Kathy to be eligible to take in a refugee from China.

Angela imitates Kathy's voice: *We have the spare bedroom where the little refugee could sleep. I'll make sure that no one will be allowed to harm the poor little girl.*

"Madness, out of the question," Angela says.

Angela is entitled to her opinions, but madness? No! Just the idealism of youth!

When I pick Kathy up after school she is crying. "I had to resign from the Red Cross today. I'm so disappointed."

"Do you want to talk about it?"

"No! I can't talk. It was such a mad idea."

"Not mad, Sweetheart! But kind-hearted! However, a suffering refugee is a bit too much to add to your mom's plate, eh?"

"I suppose so," she says.

When we get back to the mansion Kathy surprises me by pinning her Red Cross badge to the front of her overalls with a smile. She takes my hand and walks me to the neighbor's house.

Kathy knocks and is careful to make a special effort to be cheerful when the door opens.

"Hi there, Irene and Edna, I'm collecting for the Red Cross. We've an emergency with lots of refugees coming over from China this week."

The elderly sisters smile at Kathy demurely and leave the front door ajar. Finally Edna returns to the door and hands Kathy a bunch of spinach wrapped in old newspaper.

"This should keep the wolf from someone's door."

Kathy thanks the ladies as kindly as she can.

"What do we do with spinach, Dad?"

"It won't make it as far as China, but could be good in tonight's dinner."

CHAPTER 29:

The morning begins with a red sky above the mountains and tints of purple and yellow in the east. The western view is mostly blocked by a pot plant that Lillian purchased yesterday--a spiked cactus, devoid of leaves or nourishment.

Lil wakes and hugs me. "Honey, there is something I really want."

"What's that, Sweetheart?"

"A son!"

"We'd better say some prayers then … or call the stork."

The early morning sun filters through the blinds beside us, transforming our bedroom into a world of shadow and light. I lie in bed watching as she studies her belly in the mirror.

"My nipples feel tender. It may be time for a pregnancy test," she says.

She removes the pregnancy test kit from its package…

She rushes back from the bathroom and holds up the test strip. "Dylan, we're having a baby!"

We dance and hug, hug and dance.

Lil gets on the phone to Ruth.

"A grandchild! A grandchild for me, a February baby!"

Ruth wants to talk to me also, and even congratulates me.

"Thank you," I say.

"You must agree to have the baby aborted if he has Down's syndrome or brain damage."

"The nice Ruth didn't last very long," I say.

"And Lil must get tested for Down's syndrome… because of all the drinking, and her age! Help us all to be more anxiety free. OK?"

Paul comes into our room and is unrestrained, laughing and bouncing. "Awesome, Mom, way to go!"

Then Lil calls Barbara. I can hear Barbara's voice from the receiver on the pillow beside me, abrupt, hoarse.

"You don't sound like yourself," Lil says.

"I'm fine," Barbara says.

"Is something wrong, Sweetheart?"

"I'm fine."

"How's school? How's graduation planning?"

"Fine."

"And Alex?" The current boyfriend is a football player.

"Fine."

"How is your girlfriend? The one who fell in the pool?"

"Everything's fine!"

Lil then asks lightly, "Would you care to know how I am?"

"I know how you are!"

I can hear Barbara slam the phone down.

Lil turn turns to me, pale. "How did Barbara know I was pregnant?"

"No idea."

"Ruth's doing," Lil says. "It has to be." Lil sticks her chin out, hugs me tightly and then quickly falls asleep.

Lil still looks tired when we meet at Kaiser Hospital. The nurse leads us to a tiny room, does the prep and picks up a cold instrument. Lil holds my hand loosely while her nubile belly is being ultrasonically scanned. We are given a copy of the first image of our baby, our love child.

"The examination hasn't found any abnormalities. A healthy baby," the nurse says.

"But what gender?" Lil asks.

"A lovely girl."

I see Lil holding herself in, trying hard not to cry out loud.

I lead her to a chair in the waiting room.

"I had my heart set on a son."

Lil can't look me in the eye.

The astute nurse leads Lil to her office for a chat. "Alone, just the two of us. We can review all your options privately."

When Lil comes out she seems distant, distracted.

"Let's call the baby *Natalie*," Lil suggests.

"OK with me. Are you sure? What about *Sarah*?" I ask.

"I prefer *Natalie*."

"Great. *Natalie* it is."

Ruth objects. "I don't want my granddaughter to remind me of the death of that Hollywood star, *Natalie Wood*."

"Face your demons!" Lil yells.

We return three weeks later--to the same nurse in the same cubicle for the Downs Syndrome test, involving a big needle being stuck into Lil's belly--to sample the amniotic fluids surrounding Natalie. She also tests Lil's blood. The results reinforce the good news that our baby girl is developing normally, and there is no brain damage evident, or Downs Syndrome. It is now early August, and Natalie is due in February. I had never feared Downs Syndrome, but bring on February!

CHAPTER 30:

My happiness about Natalie is interrupted: Lillian's lawyer has called on the weekend—Lil's reward for being a nuisance to Bill's estate is merely title to the condo. And there is a substantial penalty if we do not move out of the mansion by Saturday next week. Kathy is here so the day still flaunts itself over San Gabriel this Saturday morning, hanging lazily, waiting for something to happen. I raise the patio umbrella for shade. Lillian brushes her hair off her face, even though it's not there. The hint of a frown hovers on her brow—then dominates it as if her patience with the world has suddenly been stretched to the limit.

We have to move out of Bill's mansion in a week, so I repeat my proposal. "Why don't we move into my home? It hasn't sold yet."

"Your house is too close to downtown," Lil says. "I want maid service and a nurse now. Let's move to New Zealand, we've talked about it, let's take the plunge."

"And what about Kathy?"

"Do you think we should call Kathy to join us now?" Lil asks, as her eyes veer toward my daughter who is playing down by the pool.

"She's OK."

"It's time for lunch. I'll start getting it organized."

Lil comes back with a pair of alcohol-free margaritas, and juice for Kathy.

There's not much of a breeze, just an occasional stirring of thistledown.

I lay out the condiments. Kathy is still down by the pool, busy writing in her book. I call her. She wanders up absently, and sits with us around the patio table, her book open.

"Is that poetry you're writing?" Lil asks.

Kathy self-consciously covers the book with her hand.

"I liked your poem about the rabbits and birds," Lil says. "Do you write a lot of poems, Kathy?"

"Sometimes," Kathy admits.

Lil stands, holding her empty glass. A pause twists as the desire for alcohol pulls at her. She looks at me. "Can I get you another drink?"

"No, thank you. I'm only halfway through this one."

"What are you writing about now, Kathy, or is it a secret?" Lil asks.

"Of course not," Kathy smiles. "It's about tigers. I watched a program on TV about tigers with Dad. I've never seen a real one, though. Have you?"

"Only in a zoo. Tigers are my favorite animals," Lil says.

"They're terribly proud. Beautiful coloring. But I wouldn't want one as a pet. I'd rather have a rabbit," Kathy says.

Lil seizes the moment: "I'd get a pet if I wasn't having a baby."

"It must be exciting having a baby, even better than having a pet," Kathy says.

Now I seize my opportunity: "Lil and I have been talking. We could have a pet rabbit in the new condo we are moving into next week. Lil says it's OK with her. What do you think?"

"Really, Lil? You'd let me do that?" Kathy asks.

"Yes, Sweetheart," Lil says with a distracted smile.

"I'll take good care of it. I'll be as good a mom as you," Kathy says.

Lil brings out ingredients for sandwiches, and spreads a cover on the patio table. "I'll get some more drinks and bring out a damp cloth for hands. Cranberry or margarita?" Lil's gaze is fixed upon me.

"Cranberry juice, please." I lean across and wipe a crumb from the side of Kathy's mouth.

Lil returns with a pitcher of margarita. It is too full. She is gripping it in both hands, her attention on the brimming rim. "Don't worry; It's a special occasion and I've made it without too much alcohol."

Ruth and John call Lillian to say they are going to stay with us for our final week in the mansion.

Lil is insistent. "It's the only way. They are going to help us by packing, ready for the move to the condo next week."

"Do they have to stay that long?"

"Yes, it's the only way. I'm pregnant, remember! My parents are going to leave here the day before the removal truck arrives."

On the first day of the visit Ruth flounces into my office and offers me a wine, which I decline. "Do you realize yet that Lillian drinks a lot?"

"She does like a drink after work, but nothing unusual."

"She'll drink anything but vodka and sherry."

"Oh?"

"Anytime, anywhere!"

"Do you think she's an alcoholic?" I ask.

Ruth pauses and looks out the window. "Yes, yes! I do think she is."

Her voice chills me. Ruth moves to the window and stares down at me.

"I hardly think so." I say.

"You think you know better than I! The arrogance of the foreigner… Let me tell you straight! An alcoholic is anyone who drinks for the sole purpose of getting high. Can you deny that Lil fits the definition?"

"Sometimes... I wonder if it may be better to relax, let go of fear and join the party."

"Drink every day, match her drink for drink? That is the height of craziness!"

"No need to drink if it's not enjoyable. Lil doesn't drink all that much. I'll just be there with her, no judgment. She has a lot on her plate. And I love her."

"Never! Never drink with her! That is the worst thing you can do. I have driven all the way down here to ask you to get yourself together… My grandchildren are caught up in this chaos. Paul aspires to be a disc jockey. Barbara wants to be an actress… God forbid! And show some leadership. Get them into regular study habits and eating proper food. Tidy their rooms up! This is important to me. Surely you can do that much!" Ruth says.

I don't believe that Lil is an alcoholic. Ruth is just trying to create another drama. I research the Kaiser Health definition of alcoholic… "An alcoholic is anyone who drinks enough to exceed the legal driving limit for blood alcohol more than once or twice a year… alcoholics will find this definition absurd!"

I find this definition difficult to accept, but in moments of clarity I get glimpses of just how insidious the disease of alcoholism establishes itself through the denial of the host—and how this Kaiser definition of alcoholism enables the Kaiser Recovery Program to establish a confrontation with drinkers who refuse to admit to their disease. "If you are *not* a victim of the disease of alcoholism, as you say, then demonstrate it so by quitting alcohol!"

I am committed to accepting Lil just as she is… but what about the impact of alcohol poisoning on our baby?

Tonight we plan to sleep early, but Lil is restless--says her nipples feel electric, her breasts heavy. I put my ear to Lil's stomach as she focuses hard. Natalie should be able to communicate with us by now, participate in some way in all of this. Natalie kicks. Lil and I grin.

CHAPTER 31:

"I'll settle for a beer," I say as I pry open Selwyn's fridge. "Think I need a drink after that move from hell. Lil has so much stuff."

Selwyn gives me a squeeze as we stand there in his new kitchen. My brother has settled into the manse of Saint Mary's parish church in Yucca, only four miles from our new home.

Selwyn says that leaving New Zealand at this time has been a big breakthrough for him--that the priesthood has offered him an opportunity to do a global ministry for the less fortunate.

"Why come to California for that?" I ask him.

"To acclimatize. I will be transferring to Mexico soon, to Tijuana."

"That's not too far away, I suppose."

Having a brother with clear boundaries can be a bonus… I feel safer in my marriage now that my brother is here.

"You look tired," Selwyn says.

"I'm exhausted from heaving heavy furniture up stairs into Lil's condo with only a little help from the stoned furniture removal company employees. We didn't finish moving until 5am."

"You also look pissed! What's the problem now?"

"Lil is angry because the big TV screen got ripped during the move. I'm mad because Paul got ripped last night, and didn't carry one single item from his old room to the new. I even had to carry his tennis shoes and school books."

"I gather you don't like the condo. Why?"

"The sound of fucking polka music comes from the neighbor's condo all night! I can hear their boy yelling through the walls. I don't like the crassness of the tiny patio, the steep narrow stairs or the crammed rooms. It's bullshit!"

"Well, move out if your physical environment is so important."

"It's not that… It's just that I'm trying to make my marriage work."

"Some say that fulfilling desires is the path to happiness. Mind you, some Eastern religions teach that having no desires is the better path," Selwyn says.

"Anyway, I'm worried about Lil drinking so much alcohol. Lil is four months pregnant."

Selwyn's silence fills the room, as do his bookcases stuffed with old books and stale air. I am trying to discuss my anxiety around Lil's apparent ignorance of the games that Ruth is playing, and the resentful way Paul turns his music up full volume after school. Perhaps I don't want to bring Selwyn into my chaos.

"What do you want to happen?" Selwyn finally asks.

"I want a therapist, a professional third party to counsel us."

"What else is going on?"

"Lil has lost enthusiasm for our baby—she doesn't want a daughter, but a son… and I don't know what to do about it."

"How is Lil doing with Paul?" Selwyn asks.

"Paul is clean. He and I are going to the Kaiser Rehab program at *D-Tox* regularly. Lil is too busy so only attends *D-Tox* one evening per week.

"Good for Paul! Your leader, Frank Gunter, is a good man. But do you think Lil is able to keep up with Paul's problems?"

"Lil's love for Paul never waivers, but she is reluctant to hold him to firm boundaries, such as a curfew--perhaps for fear of losing him entirely."

"Why don't you see Kaiser about getting some family therapy," Selwyn asks. "I'll talk to Frank. He'd be great."

"Good idea. I'll talk with Lil… and you must come over for dinner tonight, Selwyn—meet the family."

Selwyn drives up later in his convertible, with the top down. He looks gay wearing a cowboy hat and boots. "Sorry I'm late, Lil. The traffic was a nightmare. You'd think that five-dollar a gallon gasoline would have encouraged a little more carpooling."

"Who did you carpool over with? Or did you ride your horse today? Nice outfit, Selwyn," Lil says mischievously.

Selwyn laughs. "Okay. Point taken. Anyway, I picked up a pizza on the way, and a salad to go with it."

"Would you like a glass of wine?" I say.

"A beer, please." Selwyn opens Lil's fridge. "I need a cold one."

Lil gives my brother a hug as they stand there in the kitchen. Everyone goes to the lounge to watch the *Face the Nation* program on TV. Both of them love politics, almost as much as I… They stand united in their antagonism of the "soft-centred" Al Gore--who is surely the front-running Democrat for the next presidential election campaign. The fuss over Bill Clinton's alleged infidelities has strained my relationship with Lil. I have become an avid Democrat—opposing the Republican Party position that Lil and Greg support because of its anti-abortion and pro-gun position.

Lil leans forward. "Well, Selwyn. What did you think about the TV program tonight? Do Bill Clinton and Al Gore's new programs for the poor live up to your negative expectations of the Democrats?" Lil scans the television to off, and kicks back in her recliner.

"I don't know anymore, Lil. I'm wondering if Al Gore may be too weak… or not following his heart," Selwyn says.

"The Democrat's ability to polarize has hit a little too close to home for me. I am not up to any more intense debating about what's moral," Lil says.

"Perhaps Al Gore was born to do something more creative than merely be the President of the United States," I say.

Selwyn leans toward her. "My father said, *Michelangelo never considered the size of the ceiling, just the corner to be painted that day.*"

Lil walks toward the dining room. "I'm tired of waiting for those boys, let's sit down to dinner. Come on Barbara—sit up. Selwyn, would you please say grace?"

I cannot wait any longer and crunch into my bread. Lil is already halfway through her steak when Paul and his guest, James, clamber to the table, eyes glistening and blotchy--as if they have been laughing heartily.

Paul is on his best behavior. "Uncle Selwyn, please pass the mushrooms, chives, cheese, and more steak. No! Not the fucking broccoli. Sorry... is that Coke or Pepsi?"

Barbara giggles. James laughs. Then Paul scrunches a potato on top of James' head.

"Keep the food on the table please," Lil says.

Paul pushes his dinner plate down hard upon James' dinner, squelching his food. They both laugh. Barbara raises her dull eyes with a faint smile. Selwyn is gob smacked. I look to Lil as she angrily stares at Paul. "Paul, please." The boys ignore her. James pours Pepsi on Paul's steak.

By the time the boys leave the table, a riot of stains and wet patches decorate the tablecloth, and food is scattered over the floor and on the dishes.

"Thanks for cooking dinner, Honey," Lil says. "I'm sorry the boys were so stoned. I've grounded Paul for two weeks… Oh, and Selwyn, you'll be pleased to know that Dylan and I have an appointment for counseling with Frank Gunter at Kaiser."

"Great!"

CHAPTER 32:

Frank Gunter seats us in his tiny booth and asks a series of routine questions. Then Frank looks directly at Lil.

"I'm sorry that Paul couldn't get his ninety-day pin. Paul was not doing well. He *was* awarded his sixty-day pin for being clean of drugs, but that milestone was a probably a lie. Paul finally did a urine test before the program meeting, and failed… after three months of avoidance and denial. I know that Ruth and you two were looking forward to Paul's milestone with birthday cake and laughs."

"Paul was gutted," Lil says. What can we do for him?"

Gunter looks out the window. "I have been trying to figure out what went wrong. Ever since your mother spoke at our session the other week I have been puzzling. It is natural for you to be loyal to your mom, Lillian. Especially when she depends on you… but why does Ruth depend on you?"

Lil's answer shocks me. "I have saved Mom's life, several times, rescued her from my violent father, and lately, saved her marriage to John. That changed everything. I am no longer her daughter; I am her guardian angel. Some people see my mom as a bitch. I cannot see that side of her. I only see the person who I have the power to help!"

Frank turns on her. "That is co-dependency. But much worse, I have been studying you and conclude that you are psychotic! If your doctor saw you now, she would not let you carry the baby to term… even though you are six months pregnant. You are not well!"

Despite my shock, I almost want to cheer. At last one other person can see that we have a family problem. But how could Frank Gunter make such a radical diagnosis--by observing Lil sit, mostly silently, in the corner of his office? It is the end of October and the baby is due in early February. What is Gunter thinking? He seems to imply that a doctor could intervene in the pregnancy at this late stage. Surely not?

Lil walks out of Gunter's office in tears and calls Paul from the library. While we are out of range of Paul, Lillian begs me. "What are we going to do? Should we send the kid to a military academy?"

"Maybe, but only if he refuses to accept boundaries and curfews."

"Bullshit! Your fanatical ideals only work for therapists! In the real world we support our children. I want you to move out! By tomorrow!"

CHAPTER 33:

I am homeless… I knew that Lil couldn't conceive of kicking Paul out of her home just because he failed a drug test, but how was I to know she would turn on me?

As I sit on the end of my bed in this motel I try to piece together recent events, to work out what I have done wrong. This first morning alone, I sit in the motel chair and pull off yesterday's socks. *Should I stay with her? Shit! Forget about it all for the moment. Get some sleep!*

After almost a week in this bloody motel, I find a one-bedroom apartment—and sign up to a twelve-month lease!

Lil drops into my new apartment almost every evening now.

"How are you feeling?" I ask lamely.

"Fine."

"Do you still feel OK about Natalie living here?"

"Yeah."

"Would you rather I had a bigger apartment?"

"That's your choice."

"How are you dealing with being pregnant?"

"Fine."

"Is there anything more that I can do to help?"

"Just relax."

"Should we have more pre-natal tests done?"

"No. I'm fine. Natalie's fine."

I am hurting, what more can I say? I take her to my bed, knowing that she won't mind that I have forgotten how desire works, so that which leaps to the eye is merely a place to lie down. We cuddle for an hour.

Lil prepares to leave, reluctantly, to pick up Paul from a recovery meeting, stalling as if waiting for something undefined to happen.

The following Tuesday, I move my bed to the living room, and work at furnishing Natalie's room in my one-bedroom apartment. I visit a baby store and purchase a crib, bedding, pharmaceuticals, bottles and clothes. I make up the crib and put the little woolen booties that my mother has knitted at the foot of Natalie's bed.

After lunch I climb the stairs to the manager's apartment. She is middle aged, and doesn't allow pets. "I am going to have a roommate. A newborn. Natalie Hotta. Lillian cannot have our baby at her condo. Do you mind awfully?"

"How lovely! OK, as long as I can come visit the baby."

I don't like shopping at the busy Macys, but do so anyway, selecting about twenty items of maternity clothes--while Lil sits splayed in the changing rooms on a chair that is too small, picking through my selections. Lil chooses one smock and a pair of pants with a pop-top belly. I go to a different row of racks and repeat the process. Lil's grim expression tells me that she is disappointed about how ugly the stock of maternity clothing is… even at the most popular store in San Gabriel.

Why does Lil want Natalie to live at my apartment, rather than at her condo? She is not behaving normally and this is eating me up. Is she pulling away? I hope that after Natalie is born and we leave the maternity hospital Lil will not be able to say goodbye to Natalie--will not be able to simply walk out the door of my apartment and leave us behind!

"I hope that's not a vibrator in your pocket," Lil says.

"My body knows what it wants."

She throws her arms around my thighs and sways into me, "Hey you, you sexy bugger," she whispers, her breath blowing soft below my ear.

"Yes?"

"I'm going to be away visiting Ruth for a few days, so I think you'd better lie down now."

Afterwards, I walk Lil out to her Jeep. She is seven months pregnant. She staggers a little before stepping up. I look at her and kiss the little grin on her lips.

Back inside my apartment, the phone rings. It's Jean and Richard Powers. They are over to attend a conference on midwifery in Los Angeles. They will visit in three days, but can only stay one night in San Gabriel.

Three days later my doorbell rings. "Merry Christmas," I say, pleased to see Richard and Jean, who have driven down after visiting Ruth's ranch.

"We've picked up Selwyn. He's just behind us, carrying some gifts," Jean says.

I settle them and pour the tea.

"We have spent the day with Ruth and Lil up at the ranch, renewing our exchange student connection with Lil," Jean Powers says.

We discuss the conference, their travels, and finally, Ruth.

"I've already told this to Selwyn… Our visit to Ruth's ranch was friendly enough but…" Jean frowns.

"Oh! What happened?"

"There's something I have to tell you Dylan… I couldn't help but overhear a conversation between Ruth and Lillian while I was reading in the lounge…"

"Go ahead," I say.

"Ruth was in the kitchen, and accused Lillian of using drugs! Ruth accused Lil of using more cocaine than with her previous pregnancy. Ruth made it clear that she didn't want a granddaughter with brain damage. Ruth went on to ask Lil to agree to an abortion!"

"Surely that's not possible!"

"Lillian ridiculed her mother's proposal, and denied using cocaine."

"Thank God for that!"

"It was strange… almost as if Ruth provoked the conversation—knowing that I would overhear it from the next room," Jean says.

"Of course not," Selwyn says. "I will not allow an abortion to happen! It is illegal and immoral… anyway, got to go. Goodnight everyone."

"OK. Bedtime. I'll sleep in Natalie's room so Jean and Richard can have my bed in the living room."

It is uncomfortable for me that Selwyn is such a fanatic. I don't know which is more straight-laced: Paul's twelve-step program, or the Catholic Church on contraception and abortion. Selwyn is always trying to create an opportunity to weave another of his beloved religious dramas. Fuck! I wish my brother would just butt out.

CHAPTER 34:

A lone gull is surfing the morning wind gusts, escaped from his brothers, flying beyond an oak tree as the sun peaks beyond a lone cloud. A shadow crosses behind me. It is Sunday and I am alone… I telephone Lil's mom and am relieved when her stepfather answers.

"Hello?"

"Hi John, I hope I'm not disturbing you. But I haven't heard from Lil. Is she OK?"

"I can assure you that… Lil is… OK." John's apologizes but says he must go.

Something is not right.

It is 11am. I take a seat near the back of the sparse crowd at the St. John's church--in a pew where the sun is shining through stained glass windows, bathing my seat in amber light. I haven't heard from Lil since Christmas day. Nor has there been any answer to my calls.

Father Chester's sermon is over--and I can't recall a word of it.

Lil calls my phone during prayers. "If you want to know how Natalie is, then call Mr. Holdall, my lawyer."

Hell's teeth! I am already on my knees. Prayer comes easily.

I call Holdall, but he isn't in, not on a Sunday.

What the fuck is going on!

My next Al-Anon meeting is at the same church, midmorning on Monday, New Year's Eve. The meeting is tense. Perhaps some of the wives are developing tension at the prospect of another New Year Eve of betrayal, of their husbands cheating with the bottle. A bird crashes into the front window. A number of people jump. My mouth is dry.

I rush outside to call the lawyer. His secretary transfers me through.

"Sorry Mr. Hotta. Lillian should not have asked you to call us. She must talk with you in person. I'll call her now."

Mr. Holdall's secretary calls back and promises me that Lil will call within half an hour.

I wait, trying to fight back nausea, but fail and vomit on the pavement.

I pace the parking lot, alone, cold. A large seagull, a Molly Mawk, flies in from the ocean, flies directly overhead and circles me. As I look up, I hear a voice inside me whisper, *Can you hear me, I am safe.* Is it Natalie speaking to me? I feel comforted by this. *You are both responsible.* I get the impression that Natalie is judging Lil and me. However she said she was OK didn't she? I guess this means that Natalie is in Heaven, transported from fetus to spirit. But perhaps my nature is to respond to grief with wishful thinking, with denial? Who knows? But I wasn't looking for this. This is not real. I've got to find Lil…

She calls me twenty minutes later, while I am driving home on the freeway. "I'm calling to tell you that Natalie is gone... I can't help you Dylan, you'll have to deal with it by yourself."

My head screams with every heartbeat! Cars rush at me like missiles. How could she do that? There is a mechanical clicking behind my ear. *Get off this murderous freeway!* There is a buzzing somewhere lower in my body. *Get home!* I am afraid, afraid of what? That I have lost everything? *Get inside your apartment!* I am afraid this won't stop, that this will become my permanent reality.

The first light is filtering through the dark curtains. I am in Natalie's room, asleep on the floor. My mind is washed clean by sleep so my thoughts are still dream-like, abstract and clean. And then I remember. Something terrible has happened. This moment is the most unbearable.

I slip Natalie's photograph from the frame on my desk… the sonar image from the hospital shows the shape of her large head with perfectly spaced eyes, shows her beautiful forehead and mouth. I look out the window and scan the children's park next door. There is a shadow that makes everything look bleak.

Then I am sinking again, not resisting the unconscious world.

A ceiling fan creaks and flutters the curtains as it whirls overhead. The window blows open. I stir, shiver, grab a pillow and hug it just as the eerie cry of a baby caws in the distance. A gust of wind tosses the curtains up and about. A flickering moon's light suddenly shines through the window.

Where am I?

I go outdoors in bare feet. A surreal landscape of misty forest drips beyond the narrow clearing after a gush of rain. I search the perimeter. There I see an image of my Lillian in a white silk nightgown, walking on a lonely road flanked with gnarled trees and withered mangroves. Distant parrots caw. A breeze ruffles her transparent nightgown. A peal of thunder echoes as flashes of lightning illuminate the road. The vision of Lillian seems to fuse with reality. Lil cups her mouth with a palm. Our naked child, Natalie, crawls toward her, crying. Lil stifles a scream, hugs herself and shivers. Her eyes dart left and right. A distant eagle dives. Lil bites her lower lip and walks on. Natalie's haunting shrieks grow louder, demanding my protection. Lillian fidgets with her nightgown, panics, and runs away into the darkness of the steaming forest.

I sit up and looked around. I am alone, on the floor, holding Natalie's sonogram.

Jean Powers calls and says that her flight back to New Zealand has been delayed. I am relieved to be able to talk for a few minutes--to talk with her especially. Jean reminds me that we know dreadful things happen all the time, and that when it happens to us, we mustn't allow it to shake our confidence, because the world is still the same place… We are just beginning to understand it better.

I sleep for another day, and then finally call Kathy. She can't understand why I still love Lillian.

"It is simply destiny… The nature of love is to always support the ones we care about," I say.

I love Lil for reasons that Kathy cannot understand.

"I'm so sorry, Dad."

I don't want to hurt Kathy either, so I try to be strong for her, bury my thoughts in memories of the hills of Elsinore--the vacant white beaches, the Otakou Marae where the Maori ancestors might parade after death… and the dripping afternoon bush of home. I run through a litany of regrets. *What if? What could I have done differently? It doesn't help. I've got to find Natalie.*

I have to do something. I crawl to the phone again and ask Father Chester to come over and help me organize a memorial ceremony for Natalie.

Then I sleep again, for a long time.

When Father Chester opens my door, I expect to cry, but I don't expect to scream and pull my hair out. Chester hugs me. We go to Natalie's room. We are quiet for a long time.

Chester asks if he can take the crib for the church fundraiser, and her blankets, and her little booties.

"No!" It comes out harshly.

I am cold!

Chester shuts the door silently and sits again. "I'm sorry you are suffering."

Chester asks if he may read from the Bible, and pray. I am glad to hear his voice as he reads from the book of Job. The reading starts slowly, punctuated by Chester's rasping breath.

He embraces my account of the bird crashing into the window at the Al-Anon meeting, and of the circling Molly Mawk outside, and of the echoless voice of Natalie from beyond the grave.

"What a miracle that you received signs from God during your time of testing."

"It doesn't feel like a miracle to me. More like hell." I say.

"Of course! A prophet is never appreciated in his own home. You are called to be a witness for God, to demonstrate the victory of Christ over death."

"What? You want me to be a preacher? No way!"

"Let's not get ahead of ourselves. I'm thinking of the memorial service. Imagine all your family and friends gathered, who might otherwise have come to express grief for your loss of Natalie. But when they see your victory, your countenance will radiate the victory of Christ over Natalie's death! Through the resurrection of our Lord Jesus!"

"I'm not fully with the program here, Chester. Why don't you read from the gospels, and let me grieve?"

"Would you rather spend your time in eternity with Jesus, or without Him?" Father Chester asks.

"With Jesus."

I am tired.

"Jesus changes us from the inside out. The world tries to change us from the outside in. Jesus wants to save you and cleanse your heart, change your desires, now and forever," Father Chester says.

Chester leans forward and reaches out his hand. "Dylan, I want to pray with you."

"I'd like that," I say, reluctantly.

Chester has a firm but tender grip. He prays for me, that I might know and become a true follower of Jesus from this day forth. Then he asks me to pray with him by repeating a prayer he has typed out--and to consider each word to make it my own. Chester's grip tightens and we pray, one phrase at a time.

"Dear God, I believe in you and I need you in my life. Have mercy on me, a sinner. Lord Jesus died for my sins—for my wasting guilt. Cleanse and heal me from my sins and come into my life, Dear God—I ask this in the name of my Savior and Lord, Jesus Christ. I believe that Christ lived without sin, died on the cross for my sins and arose again on the third day, and has now ascended unto you, the Father."

"Where is Natalie?"

"Hang in there, Dylan. Hold tight."

We continue reciting together…

"I love you God, take control of my life, and take care of your child, Natalie. I believe you hear my prayer. I welcome the Holy Spirit of God to lead me in Your way. I forgive everyone and ask You to fill me with Your Holy Spirit and give me love for all people. Lead me to care for the needs of others. I accept the Lord Jesus Christ as my Savior, and desire to be a true believer in and follower of Jesus. Thank you, God, for hearing my prayer. In Jesus name, I pray."

I feel my pain burrow and then bury. I don't know why but I need this. I snap. It is an awesome and glorious moment! We are two brothers rejoicing in Christ.

"There is rejoicing in Heaven now! You are saved! I pray for rapid healing of your troubled heart."

Chester opens his bible to a marked passage.

"There is joy in the presence of the angels of God over one sinner who repents. Luke 15:10."

I am smiling and Chester is still reading…

"Jesus has come to live within your heart. Behold, I stand at the door and knock. If anyone hears My voice and opens the door, I will come in to him and dine with him, and he with Me. Revelation 3:20. …When you open the door Jesus comes into your heart to stay… to replace your ego-will. This is a personal relationship with God. You can come to Him with every need and receive certain victory. The One who has made us now comes to live within us.

Your sins are forgiven.

But the fruit of the Spirit is love, joy, peace, long suffering, kindness, goodness, faithfulness, gentleness, and self-control. Against such, there is no law. Galatians 5:22-23

Our life becomes different. God's Spirit lives and abides within us. Your relationship with other people is changed. We forgive others as we expect God to forgive us. Walk in a forgiving relationship to others.

Forgiveness is a mark of a true follower of Jesus.

And whenever you stand praying, if you have anything against anyone, forgive him or her. Forgive them, and yourself. Forgive so that your Father in heaven may also forgive you your trespasses… But if you do not forgive, neither will your Father in heaven forgive your trespasses. Matthew 11:25- 26"

"So, I must forgive Lil for what has happened to Natalie?"

"Yes, voluntarily. The radiance glowing from your face indicates that you have already started this journey. Pray for Lil every day, for her health and peace. And ask for a forgiving heart, ask for that every day."

"Does that mean there is more than one level of forgiveness?" I ask.

"When we are saved, the Holy Spirit comes to live within us--yet we are not fully in control of God's Spirit, so that we are often only capable of a lesser and more clinical type of forgiveness at first. To be filled with the Holy Spirit is a moment-by-moment walk. When you realize that any of your attitudes or actions are not of God, then at that moment, repent, ask God's cleansing and have Him refill you with the fullness of His Spirit."

Chester says a benediction, and asks me to call and invite my family and friends to Natalie's memorial service.

I call Lil first. "Hi, Sweetheart. We are organizing a memorial service for Natalie on Saturday. I hope you'll come."

"No. Thanks, Dylan. I won't be able to make it." She sounds lethargic.

The next call is to Selwyn. He is in Tijuana, at a meeting with the Archdeacon, and can't fly in until the morning just before the memorial. Selwyn will pick up Kathy on his way in from the airport.

The rest of my calls are productive… and I am comforted to hear so many pledges of attendance.

On the morning of the service, Father Chester and I say a prayer in the Church anteroom, and then he briefs me in preparation for Natalie's memorial service. "Dylan, my brother in Christ, I want you to come into the Sanctuary last, after everyone else has arrived, and I want you to walk down the aisle a saved man, radiating your liberation from the fear of death, rejoicing in the victory of Christ over Natalie's death."

The organ breathes a soft and steady tone. As I walk down the aisle toward the wall of flowers, I can feel my spirit shining. People turn to look. Then Selwyn arrives, and sits in the front row beside me, with Kathy and Greg... and Frank Gunter is here.

I serve the communion cup, following Chester's robes along the lines of people. Selwyn and Kathy are glowing, so I look deep into their liquid eyes as I feed them from the golden goblet of red wine. "The blood of Christ, keep you in eternal life." I wink at Kathy. She smiles through her tears. The ritual of the ceremony feels cleansing and hopeful. Selwyn is watching out for my daughter, arm around her, he passes her a tissue. I would need a box of tissues if I were not in this unreal state, if I dared think about what this ritual is really about.

CHAPTER 35:

I am alone. I call my brother and plan to stay overnight at Selwyn's apartment. Selwyn opens a bottle of wine. We have to use teacups and the wine is average, but it doesn't matter.

"Hey, Dylan. You did well today. Where did you get your serenity? You were glowing."

"A gift of the Holy Spirit, Brother Dear. Ask and you shall receive."

"I wish you wouldn't be so flippant, Dylan."

"No. I'm full on for the Lord, in my own way. A student of forgiveness."

Selwyn pours me a second cup of wine and clears his throat. "I knew the time and place where Lil planned to have the abortion—in advance. I got a phone call two weeks ago… from someone whom Lillian had approached."

"Jeez Boss, not now. I can't keep my eyes open." I take my shoes off and lie down, closing my eyes.

Selwyn goes on in a monotone; "Lil and Ruth were planning a trip down to Tijuana. I pulled into the Kaiser parking lot after I spotted Lillian's wagon. The back was loaded with blankets and bags, confirming my worst fears. I slunk down in my car and waited.

Thirty minutes later Lillian came out from Frank Gunter's therapy office and got into her Jeep.

I followed.

She picked up her mom from her condo, and headed to the interstate.

I followed.

They entered the interstate near Stockton.

I dialed to Tijuana; *Is the Archdeacon in?*

I need to leave a longish message please; 'Call Selwyn Hotta urgently. Mission is on, and Selwyn driving to Tijuana now. Request that Archdeacon clear his calendar for the next two days…'

Yes, I know it's still the Christmas season. Busy. We all have to sacrifice for this matter. Call me, 925-332762 as soon as he returns, please…

Yes, thank you. Bye.

And that set the ball rolling."

"Bloody hell, Selwyn! I can't handle much more of this cloak and dagger crap. I'm tired!"

"Humberto, that's the Archdeacon's name. Humberto Contreras, he called back within the hour. Every day, I thank God for that…"

I interrupt. "Thank God for small mercies! Sometimes, Brother Dear, you don't have a flaming clue about the real world. I'll take one more cup of wine and another piece of Christmas cake before I go to bed."

I close my eyes again and try to listen.

Selwyn's voice continues droning, but it's too faint to comprehend; "I followed Lil and her mom all the way to the abortion clinic in Tijuana. The Archdeacon joined me. We got out of our car and said a prayer for a victory for God, and for everyone's safety… "

My brother is trying to wake me up. "Leave me alone. I'm tired."

"This is important, Dylan. Wake up."

"What did you say? I'm tired."

The next morning I rush home before Selwyn rises. My sense of a spiritual victory beyond Natalie's death is put into a more somber perspective when I try to write the report about my forensic investigation of a plane crash… My head and my stomach both refuse.

I go back to bed.

CHAPTER 36:

I get up before bedsores develop and choose a time when Kathy is in school to meet with her mom. This will not be a conversation that I want Kathy to hear.

"I know it's not the school holidays yet… but I'm going to take Kathy back to New Zealand anyway!" I yell.

Angela is frozen in the headlamps of my fury. She doesn't resist this time, just grimaces with trembling lips.

"This will be the last time you'll have visitation with my daughter if Kathy is traumatized in any way!" Angela says.

"Agreed."

Airborne again, Kathy and I are carried west to New Zealand. The intercom clicks; *Please do not move about the cabin or congregate in the aisles.* Kathy watches a movie about super-bugs that are invading the planet. The sealed cabin around me has grown septic with life. Everything is green and growing. Dozens of millions of species seethe around me, few of them visible. I stare at my shaking hands while whole rainforests of bacteria and insects burrow deep inside the plane's electrical and ventilation systems. I sleep all the way… thanks to my meds.

Kathy and I stay two nights with Mom and Dad, while I prepare for our three-day hike into the wilderness.

Mom is discouraging. "At least leave Kathy behind, if you must lose yourself in the outback!" Dad doesn't like it either, but he understands why I have to do this.

I get a phone call from California, from my real estate agent, "Your Victorian has finally sold, to that architect."

I have definitely lost my home now! My life is going down the tubes. All I have left is Kathy. But I'll have to leave her and move back to the family ranch now, claim it as my home, and claim the wilderness beyond, available to any New Zealander who has the boots to walk it. How very sick and bitter I have become! My self-destructive bitterness might be purged by the wilderness—and my doctor agrees.

Kathy and I take a bus on the four-hour trip to the hinterland, to Lindis, and then we start hiking. I plan for us to be out in the wilds for three days. We have artic sleeping bags. At Dad's insistence, we also have a CB radio and flares.

We hike rapidly through the clumps of Teasel and Lupin to the summit of a series of mound-like hills. From here we look out to the space and the height of the big country. We walk compulsively through uninhibited miles of Tussock and littered schist rock, dodging the sheen of Speargrass, the black spindles of Irishman Thistle and the unburned damp gullies. Further we tramp, to the high edges of the new world: black and brown uneven mountains, shaped and mantled by ice sheet and snow, half disguised by clouds which motor from the unknown western country beyond.

I walk these hills to observe and reassure myself of the difference, not the difference of tussock and glacier, but the difference of boundaries. There is no longer fence or road; there is only boundary of river and mountain, and the limits of the strength of our legs, our boots, and the limits of my own mind--when I have to carry Kathy on my shoulders.

I sing loudly, my eyes half-closed so that the ocean of tussock and the vast sky are formless brown and gray.

We reach the ridge and the land falls away. Kathy and I have a great viewing platform… a wide valley sweeps away from us westward, thirty miles into the mountains.

"Do you see it Kathy?" The wind is stronger now and my eyes water, so the mud cottage located high on our lee becomes a small blur in the expanse of rock and sky, and the Tussocks dulled brown by the failing light. Then I see a new valley across the river, and decide this will be a good place for Kathy and me to find a cave and spend the night.

I can feel the atmospheric pressure drop suddenly. The new darker clouds break. Rain starts slowly, in huge sparse drops, then accelerates, hammers us. The river is low and the water comes no higher than my knees. But it is ice-cold, and Kathy is heavy on my shoulders. I am concerned that a flash flood from the heavy rain might isolate us, so I turn around and march back over the stony flats toward the mud cottage located on higher ground.

No need to be cautious, the cottage is vacant… with a sign saying *Philip Temple restored this shelter for all.* But I feel guilty about something. Thank God that Kathy is such a good sport. It is not right for me to burden her with my need for relief. She could turn out like Ruth's children, having to rescue a parent from self-destruction, and later become harnessed to my search for compensation. I am finally able to grin at Kathy, and our wild surroundings. She brushes the rain from her nose and grins back.

Inside the dim cottage, I take off my coat, shake off the raindrops on the hard earthen floor, and stand by the cold fireplace. The cottage only has one room, and is entirely vacant, ours for the night, for two nights. I look at the far wall and am frozen in place, mesmerized by the grainy strokes of Irises by Vincent van Gogh. Incongruously, a print of my favorite painting--the original located in New York City's Metropolitan Museum of Art--is little more than a bouquet of flowers, but the colors are hypnotic. Violet irises on a backdrop of faded pink. The colors contrast profoundly, the one making the other more brilliantly shine. I remember viewing the original; the swirls of Van Gogh's brush were so thick it looked like he had just then laid the paint to the canvas. This is a print of Van Gogh's great work *Irises*, one of many painted while he was interned at the insane asylum in Saint-Rémy.

I lose track of time staring at this print … the world melting away around me. Kathy has become cold inside the hut. There is firewood from the valley willows resting on the stone hearth. A black pot hangs from a nail in the wall. I light the fire. Kathy crouches to warm her hands. I soon have a hock of lamb simmering.

The small fixed windows let in a weak light and my eyes have grown accustomed to the shadows, but I have neither felt nor heard the wind and rain that I now see blustering outside. I push back the damp rings of my hair and listen to the silence and feel the warmth between the thick walls. I run my hands over the plaster wall lining and over the rough shelves and press down on the table, which stretches half the length of the room.

There are pots and crockery, and playing cards, but no clock or books. There is a rustle from a bird above the ceiling, among the rafters and in the tussock thatch. A spade and an axe are behind the door, and rusty rabbit traps are beside the hearth. The bed fills the space behind the door hinge and the far wall, hard up against the sidewall. There is a newspaper, and the mattress is stuffed with dry tussock. I read the date on the newspaper, *December 7*. The cottage has been vacant since the early-summer muster.

Kathy can enjoy the luxury of a sleep in a dry bed and my home cooking. I shake and roll out a mat on the dirt floor for myself. We start a game of chess but I cannot relax. I have to talk. "Kathy, this is a difficult time for me and I want you to understand."

"Of course Daddy, I'm here for you."

"I'm thinking of moving back to New Zealand for a while, to try and get my thoughts organized."

"For how long?"

Oh, shit! Do I have to do this? "Until I'm recovered from Lil. It shouldn't take more than a year. I know that seems like a long time."

"So you're messed up?"

"Yeah but… who knows what may happen in a few months. But I have to close the business down. I cannot concentrate on all the myriad of things like invoices and tax returns. It just goes on and on."

"Get a grip, Dad. Sounds like you're feeling sorry for yourself."

"My doctor advised me to move over here and take a complete break."

"What about me?" Kathy asks.

"I'll come over and visit. You can come over for holidays."

"What is the doctor saying will happen to you if you don't go away?"

"Maybe a nervous breakdown. He has diagnosed me as having curable manic depression," I say.

"That serious? Well, you stay here in New Zealand, and I'll be OK going home by myself. I wouldn't want you to end up in a lunatic asylum, Dad."

"No, I'll fly back with you and stay for a month or two. OK?"

"OK. But I'm just joking, Dad. Lighten up!"

I sleep better than I have for a while. The rain has stopped. We leave early, stomping to get our feet warm.

"We'll come back here tonight, before hiking back to Lindis." I leave my backpack in the cottage and just carry the picnic lunch, first aid, CB radio, and sunscreen. A tuneless drone rises in my throat and I am on the move again, almost happy.

The warmth of the sun comes between the mountains, reflecting a snowy glare that makes me smile. I brush my stubble of a beard, sticky from the lamb hock from the night before, and smell the wild Thyme and Rosemary that grows in abundance. A warm wind is coming off the mountain. Half an hour of scrambling up through bluffs and gullies, through the Tussock, Rosehip and rocks, dodging bog holes, Speargrass, and Foxglove that missed the burning--and our limbs are warm.

Kathy is lagging so I carry her for a while on my back, and she sings in my ear. There is shade in the gullies that are now below us, breaking a thousand feet to the valley floor. The warm wind gets up, and by noon is strong in our faces.

The weather forecast has been accurate and my fury is melting. I produce a cake of Kiwi chocolate after our sandwiches are digested.

Kathy doesn't say a word when I pull a terrified rabbit from its freshly dug burrow. I know from childhood that old burrows are long and have rear exits. Shiny droppings and fresh diggings give away the new shallow burrow that is not yet complete, and therefore an obvious choice for digging out our dinner.

We see black stilts around the bogs, wild pigs and mountain goats in the high country, before we return to the cottage for a dinner of beans and stewed rabbit.

The mud cottage is not so comfortable tonight, and Kathy complains about our lack of amenities and the abundance of spiders. We play poker in the candlelight, I give her the last of the chocolate and fill a bottle with heated water to warm her sleeping bag. I do not try to explain to her that providing for her in these rough circumstances warms me--warms a heart that was in danger of going cold and bitter if I were to sit around mourning and regretting. My mom was correct; this hike was a stupid idea… but only good has come from it.

We reach the little town of Lindis an hour before the 3pm bus leaves for Dunedin. We have time to buy a steak pie and an ice cream, and then browse the second hand shop. I buy a bow and four arrows, another fly rod, and a riding helmet and saddle for Kathy. We carry our ice cream cones onto the bus.

CHAPTER 37:

It is time to empty my freezer: icecream, peas, lamb chops, bread… I have been back in my little apartment in San Gabriel for a week, packing up and closing down my business, preparing to go home to live in New Zealand for a while. I get a call from Greg. "I've talked with Lil. She's struggling emotionally, and has feelings of regret."

"How can you be sure there is a change? Because it would be crazy for me to have anything to do with her otherwise."

"She said that she likes to sleep naked with the green angora scarf that you gave her, giving her the only real comfort possible," Greg says.

"That doesn't mean she's changed! How is she?" I already know the answer.

Greg lets out a long breath. "The first week back at work after the holiday was a challenge for her; it was especially challenging to hold it together after holidaying at the ranch with her mom. It is hard for her to do holidays while you are angry with her. She sounded truly sorry."

"I wish I could believe her. And what else have you got?" I ask.

"She told me that she got home from work last Friday night, cleaned up, and then drove around to visit you at your apartment. Right?"

"Right," I admit.

"Lil got no immediate answer from your intercom at the front gate but it rang through to your cellular phone. Tell me straight Dylan, what do you remember from last Friday night?" Greg asks.

"I remember… everything. It went like this:

Hi, Dylan Hotta here, I answered.

This is Lil. I am at your front door, at the apartment. Thought I'd come and visit you.

I'm sorry. I'm just about to walk into a movie theater. Can I meet up with you in two hours, when the movie is finished? I asked.

It'll be too late by then. Bye, Lil said.

I wasn't sure that I ever wanted to see Lil again…"

Greg interrupts, "I know what happened after that. Lillian went home, did a line or two of cocaine, and then wrote a letter to you. She didn't even read it back. She didn't tell me what was in it, except that it was exactly what she needed to say. Then she tuned into the metal music that was belting out as she rolled around her bedroom floor. Her mind still was not numb enough. She assumed you were out with another woman.

Lillian did another line of cocaine and then went to the Black Mountain Nightclub, a short walk down the road from her condo. She danced and grooved without leaving her chair near the bar. And while all this was going on, what were you doing, Dylan? You watched a movie." Greg chuckles down the phone line, "I'll tell you what you did after that, Dylan Hotta! According to Lillian, you walked in to the bar around ten o'clock, two hours later, as you had promised. Lillian wondered if she was so obvious that you were able to guess where she was hanging out.

You didn't have a girlfriend with you, just walked up to her face and asked her if she wanted to talk. She said nothing--she couldn't move her rubbery lips. She tried to gaze into your fierce eyes. You asked her if she wanted to dance.

Lillian nodded yes, and you took her hand. You two danced until the band took a break. You were drinking water, and she was freshly high on coke. Her buddies were waving to her from across the dance floor, but Lillian didn't want to introduce you to them, so she sent you on an errand to your new apartment, to read her emailed letter off your computer. You sat down in that mix of dread and buzz that comes from opening the inbox after too long."

"You've got to understand, Greg. I felt relieved to have Lil back in my arms. I had no idea why we both sought to get back together that night. Love is so outrageous."

"When you returned, she asked if you had got her email.

No. It wasn't there, you said.

Too bad! You might not have wanted to come back here if you had read what I had to say, Lillian said.

It was time to go home. You drove Lillian back to your apartment. But Dylan, you didn't take her clothes off. You just talked about sensible stuff till 6am, " Greg says.

"I did the right thing. I remember her saying over and over, *I'm lost, totally lost.* It was best for me to just listen."

"Lillian wishes that you two could have sex one night while you are both high on coke," Greg says. "She's paddling with a broken oar. She didn't cheat on you this time, or have another abortion. It's just a tough decision. See you at the regular time next week," Greg says, and hangs up.

I call Greg back. "She didn't cheat on me. She was raped! By the doorman and his accomplice!"

Greg says nothing. I hang up and pull out Lillian's letter, the letter that arrived by snail-mail… the letter I don't want to share with Greg.

Dear Dylan,

I now realize that I cannot be a friend of yours. The thought of you out on a date leaves me paralyzed. I cannot be your friend if I cannot handle another woman in your life… That is the feeling I got when I went to your apartment tonight.

Not only that, but the pain that accompanies loving you is unbearable. I don't understand. How could I have fallen so deeply in love with you? How could I, after all of the pain and conflict I have experienced with you, still feel so deeply in love with you? Did you brainwash me? Did you hypnotize me? What happened?

How could I be so together in the other areas of my life and just fall apart when it comes to you? How did you destroy me so thoroughly? I fell in love with you again during our first hours of intimate conversation in California. Were you just telling me what I wanted to hear? Were you picking up on what I wanted and feeding it back to me? Were you pretending to be what I wanted in a man, long enough to bear a child?

Please help me understand, I don't think I am going to make it this time. How could I have let this happen?

I know I cannot stay married to you. My parents think you are evil, and mentally ill to boot. They give me books about your personality type. My children think you are evil too. They felt it from the beginning.

God, I feel so sick. I've never felt this sick before. Am I losing my sanity? How did it happen so fast?

I cannot stay married to you because my association with you has made me insane and you are too willing, as my husband, to commit me to an asylum. I have to take that power away from you. I had to abort our child because I knew you would go to lengths to declare me an unfit mother. I couldn't bear the thought of a child growing up with an evil caretaker, alone.

Dylan, I am afraid of you. Why do I feel so afraid? Did I fall into your trap?

Please, please tell me.

God, help me.

Lil

CHAPTER 38:

"I'm here to help you, Dylan." Greg insists that I join him on a vacation at the Bohemian Grove retreat on the Russian River in Northern California. The accommodations appear modest, until we go indoors. The interior décor is theatric, with fabric hanging on the walls. As Greg's guest I am automatically included in his house-group, *Cedar*… whose turn it is to team up and do an entertaining skit for the variety concert tonight. I recognize two reported leaders of the powerful Masonic-type society, Illuminati, in our group.

Greg takes me aside after the concert. "Your wife wasn't raped. I promise you that, she cheated on you, a lost cause now. Lillian should be dealt with by the law for the murder of Natalie."

"Don't call it murder! That's an ugly word!"

"OK. But an abortion at seven months is immoral and illegal. It must have been done in Mexico," Greg says.

"Back off!"

"OK. Look, just stay here at the Grove for a week then go to your ranch in New Zealand. We've added to your bank account. There will be a lot more projects coming up, but not until you're ready. This is a critical time!" Greg says.

"A big project come up, huh?"

"Yes, and no questions tonight! We're going for drinks at the clubhouse across the river. A hundred of the most attractive escorts are coming up from the city to entertain us."

"There's something about Lil that doesn't add up," I say.

"Must be hell for you. Want me to put a tab on her?"

"Shit no! That would just lead to further anxiety."

The next day we have lunch back across the river, at Northwood. Greg's friends were excellent tennis players and the escorts made intelligent and humorous conversation last night… but I have to leave the Grove… I am anxious to finish packing for my return to New Zealand.

On the ride with Greg to the San Francisco airport, I remember to give him my apartment key, and to file a change of address notice at the post office. I haven't terminated my lease at my apartment in San Gabriel. I'll wait for a few months in case there is a turn-around.

I call Lil from the airport. "I'm going back to New Zealand for a while."

"I won't ever see you again?"

"I'll be back," I say.

"I'll miss you terribly."

"Goodbye!"

CHAPTER 39:

I am alone at the San Francisco airport. The flight back to New Zealand is turbulent, and my parents are not expecting me. They know about my mental illness so they could be afraid of me. So… I am stranded at the tiny Dunedin airport.

I end up behind the wheel of a rental truck. The key turns the ignition easily now that I have the right music. I bounce a little to the internal music before driving off enthusiastically. It's hard to keep the music going sometimes after the engine starts; I like to restart until the engine is on the beat. I turn off Upland Road, down the hay field behind the dam, across the bridge, around a thin strip of road bulldozed into the hillside with an incorrect camber, my eyes watering. On the rear-view mirror hangs a little white fluffy ornament. My baggage bounces on the deck at the rear of the truck. My eyes become blind from tears and anger as I press the accelerator. The ornament shakes harder and harder. Clouds of dust and hay drift behind me. Greenery and trees surround the thin trail. I come into a tight curve blocked by sheep and cows drinking from a puddle in the road. This takes me by surprise. Startled, I wrench the wheel, spin, and over-correct the steering. The truck flies off the ranch road. Panic-stricken I heave the wheel in an effort to regain control, but to no avail. I slam into a tree and my shoulder crashes into the steering wheel.

Excruciating pain passes from my neck to my heels. God, I cannot believe my luck! First, my marriage breaks up, and now the truck.

The pain suddenly leaves my body and I feel relief. It was all just a nightmare. But just as I start to believe that it isn't so bad—and turn the starter motor, I hear steel battling steel. The noise concerns me and I go to see the cause. "Wow!" The damage takes me by surprise. But it's not so bad really. I'm alive and only suffer from a curable case of mental illness. To hell with the truck!

I decide to cross the fields to Upland Road and walk home. I'll worry about the truck tomorrow. I begin waving wildly, but no one comes to my rescue—of course... I'm out in the country. I continue walking down Upland Road. A piercing siren echoes in the distance. I begin running towards the sound, but suddenly the siren stops. To my surprise I realize that an ambulance has driven through the upper gate onto the Hotta ranch, driven across the dam, and is stopped near my accident. Oddly enough a small crowd has gathered… three spectators are watching something. I raise my hand and begin to shout from a distance; "Hello! I am right here! Don't worry. Thank God, I'm fine!"

I receive no reply. Two people in white overalls push through the onlookers. "Where did you come from?" I ask. "My insurance and rental information are in the glove compartment."

They check my vitals, and observe me in the ambulance for half an hour—then drive me home.

Mom and Dad are away camping. I call Kathy; "Hi, Sweetheart. I flew to New Zealand today."

"For how long?" Kathy asks.

How can I possibly explain to her? It is impossible to be near Lillian. I can't even be in the same country as her. "It's going to take a while to recover… the doctor estimates five years. But I'll visit you often. And you can come over here whenever you want, on all the school vacations, and my share of the holidays."

"Yes, I'll do that. But what about my chess coaching?" she asks.

"Easy," I say. "We'll play every day, correspondence chess the way you play your championship games. We can talk on the phone to discuss tactics and strategies."

"I need a new battery for my hearing aid. And, Daddy… they reckon I need a professional coach if I'm going to excel in the Youth Chess Olympics."

"You find a coach that you like at the club and give him my phone number. We'll get just the right person. OK?"

"OK. How are Grandma and Grandpa?" Kathy asks.

"Just got home… Happy to see me, and sorry that we're separated," I say.

"Who? You and Lil, or you and I?" she asks.

"Us, Honey, you and I. I'm going to get a new house built, over the ocean on the plateau above where you like to ride."

"Send me lots of pictures. And I'm coming over for my birthday."

"I'm going to start planning now. And we'll get you a horse."

"How will you make money?"

"Don't worry. I have savings. And I'm growing ten thousand head of flowers, hydrangeas. And there's the sheep of course." And income from Greg…

"OK. Well, be careful. Remember that you are a bit sick at the moment."

"Yes, I know. I love you too."

I definitely will have a house built near here. It will have tall windows with low sills, so the living room carpet will feel like it extends to the edge of the cliff over the ocean. Some days I stare out at the horizon from the building site, stare like my dad did after he got back from the war, after he got released from the hospital. I am sure that my dad came back home with a mental illness, probably similar to what I have… that depression that requires me to hire a carpenter and a farm hand because my attention span is often only twenty minutes on menial jobs—yet funnily enough, I can play chess and concentrate on a good movie or book.

Once a week, I call Selwyn long distance, just to rant for half an hour. He has changed—he listens a lot better. I remind him to call Kathy--especially today because she has just won a big game. It was against last year's youth champion and she played the Sicilian defense, reputed to be her opponent's strongest game. Kathy and I have studied almost every possible variation of the Sicilian defense, and tested them against the computer. The name "Kathy Hotta" will make the newspapers soon. And she won't just be a flash in the pan. She has the courage to play to her opponent's strength and then quickly twist their head with an unexpected move. Kathy is always clinical about pressing home this advantage.

I've slept till 10am and yesterday's attack of depression has gone, replaced with an energetic mania. The voices from the hayfield seem to be coming from beneath my bedroom window. The shadows of clouds motor across the hills. A shimmer reflects from the harbor, cast from the sun breaking through a clearing in the clouds, and everything--the voices, the light, and shapes, the bony hills and the barking of my distant dog--have about it a whisper of hope.

It is Kathy's birthday today. Mom and I are to pick up Kathy and Selwyn from the airport at midday—I'm not allowed to drive.

Kathy and Selwyn are strolling across the tarmac. They see us and wave. Kathy holds my hand and doesn't let go until we get to the car. She sits close to me when we get home. Kathy admires the full-height windows in my lounge and her bedroom with the elegant bathroom.

Selwyn steers me to the spare bedroom. "Call me sentimental or what. But I have saved something for you." He shows me Natalie's wool blankets and booties that he folds into an empty drawer.

"Thank you, Selwyn. But I was trying to forget."

"You'll understand when you get better. You've got a lot of healing to do."

"Are you sure?"

"Yes. And I've copied your childhood and family photographs from the family albums. You can always be proud of who you are."

Selwyn is hanging a selection of framed photographs in the entrance of my home. The photographs that he does not hang in the entrance hallway he puts in albums for me, along with photographs of friends from California, and wedding photographs.

Kathy holds the tank of sheep medicine, while I squeeze the jaws of the sheep and squirt the drench-gun into their mouths. The sheep roll their tongues in a neutral way so we cannot decide if they like the taste or not. It's a job that has to be done several times a year, not too strenuous, but invariably involves getting sheep shit over my trousers, and often down my Wellington boots. A pleasant job often leads to pleasant thoughts.

We play a game of chess in the sheep pens, without a board, imagining the pieces, barking out our moves aggressively: "... nc6."

"Got you, Bf5, check."

I resign before my mind explodes. Kathy squirts sheep-medicine at me.

We gather for the evening birthday dinner and a tour of my new house. Richard and Jean Powers, and my buddy Witi are here now. The south wing has only got the foundations down, but the rest of the house is finished, although sparsely furnished. The layout is similar to that of Lil's former mansion, except that it has only one living room, but will have more bedrooms, only two bathrooms, but will have a sauna and a Jacuzzi room when it is finished.

Dad pours the wine and Mom helps me serve the meal. Mom has cooked the celebration dinner on my behalf because I cannot manage the tedious things like chopping lots of vegetables and peeling potatoes.

After dinner, we gather outside for a surprise… Kathy gets a white pony--twelve hands, and she is over the moon. "Grandma will help me take care of Jasper while you're away," I say. Kathy has Jasper saddled up already and persuades me to ride with her.

She should be tired after our ride and the long flight, but insists that we replay the start of the only chess game that she lost this year. We talk and joke as we pause before each move. Kathy had played white and her opponent played an opening that is so unorthodox that Kathy evidently underestimated his guile. "An important lesson," I tell her.

I wonder if I have made a mistake with Kathy, encouraging her to compete like this. Maybe I'm too ambitious.

Jean and Greg have just returned from a walk. It is bedtime. I look at the photographs on the hallway wall: my baby and childhood photos, some photos with Mom and Dad, and some with Selwyn. There are also photographs of Kathy, even some with Lillian included. It surprises me that Selwyn would be so insensitive. I say nothing, but am drawn to Lil's face when I walk the hallway to my bedroom.

I take Lillian's photos down from the hallway in the morning. I tell myself that I am going to have a good day.

The days have rolled by lazily. Kathy rides her pony and I walk beside her down to the pond in the stream by Mom and Dad's house. The pond is stocked with salmon. There are two hammock-chairs slung from a tree that overlooks the pond. Kathy and I spend the day reading, horseback riding and fishing… releasing the young fish back into the pond. Dad comes over with his rod in the late afternoon and we share a peaceful couple of hours, broken only by the drama of the catch.

Kathy has to go back to California. I have set my alarm for 9am to prepare for the early flight. Kathy doesn't like getting up early either, and I don't like the petty arguments that arise if I try to herd her into compliance with a timetable.

I am ready at 11am, with Kathy's two suitcases in the car. I lean against the rear of the Jeep and look out over the harbor. Finally, Kathy tumbles out the front door with a pillow and handbag cradled in her arms, and rushes me to open the car door. Kathy assures me. "I am so comfortable with flying that I want to visit next month." I dwell on the realization that Kathy will soon be in the same country as Lillian. It would be impossible for me to go to California and not drop in on Lil.

It is a huge but necessary exertion for me to joke with Kathy at the airport. There is the final boarding announcement. Kathy kisses me, walks to the gate, turns and waves cheerfully. I will her to hurry to the jet way… so she will not see my tears. I love my Kathy. She is brilliant.

CHAPTER 40:

I feel like shit! It's a half-mile from my home down to my mailbox. I'm hoping for a letter from Kathy--and I'm still wearing my slippers.

I remember back to this morning, when the hairdresser joked about me wearing my slippers to his salon. I fell asleep while waiting my turn. I hate that drugged feeling of waking from a deep sleep. I know Mom doesn't like me wearing my hair so short—but Kathy does. It's been two long months since her school vacation here, and there was a long wait for the Christmas visit before that.

Now I am thinking about something Richard Powers said on the phone this morning, just before he hung up, almost as an afterthought. *There is a way to fix it for good.*

A memory of Lil's voice whispers in my head: *We have a chance at something special.*

The postman has finally come and the mailbox is jammed.

But it looks like junk mail. Ah! I extract a blue envelope. It has a New Zealand stamp. No letter from Kathy. Bugger!

There is smoke coming up from Aramoana, wafting across the harbor. Lomas worked on the Aramoana project… It is terrible that a madman shot fourteen people dead over there. A cop was killed. Crazy stuff. *Worst ever shoot-out in New Zealand*, they say. Richard said he heard nothing but gunshots and sirens across the water for twenty-four hours. Horrific!

The courier truck churns up a cloud of dust along Upland Road. That'll be the letter from Kathy. Everything is done first class with her.

There's an aerogramme and a large legal-sized envelope, courtesy of Federal Express.

I won't open it till I get to the kitchen and boil up a cuppa.

Through the kitchen window I can smell herbs from the garden below. The heat of the day opens a seedpod on the Kowhai tree with a crack.

Holy shit! The letter is from Lil, it reads:

Dear Dylan:

We had it all, everything. Not just the sexual connection, but also our common history, our children, our plans for living together on a ranch. It has been hard to let that go. That was real life…

The aerogramme goes on to say that Lil is recovering from hypothermia and from a broken ankle she suffered while climbing on Mount Shasta last week.

I now realize how much you meant to me.

Damn! The envelope contains a Dissolution of Marriage notice. I don't want a divorce. OK, I know part of me did, when and I didn't know what I felt and how much I loved Lil... but now I don't want a divorce!

I read the next page. This is different, a long letter from Lil. I scan it and choke.

Now you have got what you want.... What is she saying? Surely she is not inviting a dialogue over my feelings about divorce? No. If that was the case there are more timely ways to achieve such a discussion. She has signed the letter Lillian Halifax, but Lillian Hotta is the name listed on the divorce papers. Why did she go back to using Larry's name? Could it be to piss off Ruth? Or me?

I search through the register of Certified Financial Advisors in California. There she is, but her name is now Lillian Bjorn. Her address is 131 Sierra Lake Road, Sierra. That address is near her mom's house. Her work address is still in Yucca, but at Sidney Farry's house. I know Sidney Farry, from a family of property developers I worked with on an arson case back in San Gabriel. Sidney may not be as smart as his younger brothers, but he's a wealthy codger.

Lil's initial decision to file for divorce seemed reactionary. I didn't show up in the Californian court for the divorce hearing because of my depression. I hardly care what she has changed her name to. I step outside for some air. The herons are active, swooping from one Macrocarpa tree to another, landing with their gangly legs reaching below for a high branch.

I can visualize Lil sitting at her desk writing this letter. Her office desk is clear, except for her writing pad. Family photographs and framed qualifications with the wax seal line the wall with precise alignment.

I go back inside to read the entire letter. It is written on onion paper, wrapped inside the dissolution document with the Seal of the State of California.

Dear Dylan,

Now that you have got what you want, I expect you are wondering what will happen to me. There is no salvation, and there never can be. I will be happy to be divorced. But not from you personally, just from men in general, and the whole men's world of duty, pressure, and betrayal.

Once I even tried to... Sometimes I can see you, smell you and feel you inside me.

You would always come to me whenever I was angry or desperate about something. You really listened. Secretly, I still wish you would come and take me away. And now I feel more disconsolate, and will continue to do so until I say it out loud; "I shall never see you again."

I loved my job. But it was almost impossible for me to stay at work the day you flew back. My throat tried to turn inside out, and tears dammed up at the brim of my eyelids. But I stayed at work. That was important. I got desperate that first night after you went abroad… I got laid by a boy not much more than half my age. He was fun for a few weeks, and then he got serious, so I had to dump him.

Then I started to get these illnesses. First, the skin on my neck broke out with blisters, each the size of a match head and clustered in patches of twenty or more that opened to form raw sores. Then the lesions, as my doctor called them, spread over my shoulders and back. It was horrid. The doctor said I was suffering from stress, physical and emotional stress, and wanted to know what was happening in my life.

I told him that I was divorcing you, and was struggling at work. Then I got an ulcer. Then I got fired. After a while, I got tired of partying. The lesions finally cleared up. Hardly a day went by without thinking of you. I was overwhelmed with the sense of losing you, emotions that caused the veins in my wrist to ache for the relief of a cold sharp blade.

I started another job in a small financial consulting practice in San Gabriel. It was horrible. The boss was always checking on me. Then I found a wealthy boyfriend, Sidney Farry, but Paul started to kick up opposition to Sidney staying over in the condominium, and opposition to us ultimately moving into Sidney's home.

Paul was just as negative as he had been with you. You were right when you told me that you could see, from Paul's behavior, those times when he was relapsing into alcohol or drugs. Jeez, Paul is fifteen years old now. No other option was viable. I arranged to have Paul kidnapped and put in a strict Drug Recovery Center in Mexico, out in the desert somewhere. They said: Don't try and contact him until we inform you that he has made it to a recovery attitude, and is ready to deal with you.

You and I had a real chance at making something work. Damn. Now you have gone. It brings a dry burn to my throat at unexpected times. I hate it when tears fall down my face while I am talking with a client.

I wonder if I have just wanted to win a power game… to be part of the movement to punish men for torment and grief, generation after miserable generation. Am I ready to sacrifice my chance at happiness for a political victory?

I recognize that you would have sacrificed anything--almost anything, to go for domestic bliss. But, you had a line in the sand, and the line seemed to me to be a straight line, a rigid judgment about sloppy drinking and monogamy, traditional values that were impossible to live with. Rampant divorce speaks to the irrelevance of traditional values.

The premature sound of Christmas music invades from the neighbor's yard… still seven weeks to go. And I can hear their boy whining. No wonder you didn't like it here. My home sucks, the condo sucked! The crassness of toilet freshener, the plastic chairs around the communal pool, which reek of cheap. My boredom and discontent are dominating the pleasures of Christmas and friendship... and sometimes the possibility of salvation for Paul, for myself, for anything in this world. I pray for Paul.

You were still holding onto the obsolete dream, weren't you? You argued against me, about some statistic that you got from a family court judge; that 85 percent of all divorces are caused by alcohol or drug abuse issues. How can you have a life with that sort of perspective? Jeez!

I started working harder at my own business as a financial advisor, but it was difficult to focus. Then I got a melanoma cancer growth on my leg… All those years lying on beaches... The growth was removed and the doctor sounded confident he had got it all.

Why does it make me so sad when I think back to our time? Is it yearning for past happiness? I was happy in those times with you, and we loved each other. I was confident that nothing could come between us, or have any interest in damaging us further.

I have a cold now, so severe that my sinuses throb painfully, throbbing at the same pace as your heart when it lay across my arm after we made love.

Why did what was beautiful suddenly shatter? Did it shatter because what was beautiful concealed dark truths? Were you freaking about my assumed addictions, were you judging me? I could never ask you for an explanation because you could respond with words and feelings that would destroy me.

I talked about my secrets in therapy until the need to talk anonymously got less and less. But sometimes, I wondered if you were real, like I was possessed or something. And I got so scared you might come back and find where I am hiding from you. Find me fallen... Find me in a relationship with Sydney Farry that is only medicinal, for my survival, survival from the grasping of Ruth. I must avoid her. She wants my children to live with her, on the ranch. That may be good for Paul. But I shall live a separate life from Ruth. I can let my children be with her if they wish. But Ruth is poison for me.

It is dark, too dark. I can't sleep when it is dark like this. I switch the light on, Please, for the love of God I need to sleep.

Dear Dylan, I want you to not contact me again. I am asking you not to disturb me.

Lil

She has finally recognized the need to disconnect from Ruth. But she doesn't mention the loss of Natalie.

The sky is an impossible blue today. I get mushroom gatherers up here occasionally, riding by the ranch, mostly on long weekends. The older hunters like riding on Upland Road because there are no boundary fences along either side of the road, just cattle stops at each end made up from a bridge of railway tracks. The mushroom gatherers can search trails through the bush, and follow sheep tracks up to the top of the cliffs above the ocean.

The accompaniment of Lil to my dreams is only occasional now, and different: After a few drinks she throws her head back, laughs, carefree, and so seductive. She shines under the influence without losing any of her wit.

The sky above Upland Road hints of infinity beyond the massive deep. The phone rings. I throw it through the kitchen window.

CHAPTER 41:

I get a call from Mom before dinner-on my new phone. "I've got some bad news, Son. Your Grandma Olive died this afternoon. The funeral's to be at the Otakou Marae in three days."

"Oh, Mom, I'm sorry. This is shattering. How are you doing?"

"I'm OK, but will you please call Selwyn, let him know?"

"Yes, of course. How did she die?"

"A nurse found her in the hospital lounge before dinner. The nurse telephoned me, said Grandma died very peacefully. Tell Selwyn that, will you, …died peacefully."

"Are you OK, Mom? What a shock."

"Yes, I'm just a bit short of breath."

I can tell my mom is struggling, probably regretting not having visited her mother Olive for a while, all that sort of stuff you go through. Mom and Dad are getting older. They have worked hard clearing the land, building the fences around the ranch, fertilizing, and planting the flowerbeds and trees. They are a treasure to me, and have been a rock during my recent years of insecurity.

"I'll be over soon, Mom."

I call Selwyn. "I'm glad that you are better anyway," he says. "I'm catching the next plane home. See you soon."

My phone rings again, just as I'm starting on a list of people to call with the bad news.

"Hello, can you hear me? This is Mom here, have you called Selwyn yet?"

"Yes, Mom. He's catching the next flight."

"Call him back, please. The hospital just called me to say Grandma's still alive! Perky. Just sat up and stretched. Must have been coming out of a sleep."

"Thank goodness. Are you going to visit her tonight, Mom?"

"No. I am a bit flustered. I'll visit tomorrow."

I call Selwyn back.

"I'm coming home anyway. Had a wake-up call. Tell Jean Powers, tell Jean that Grandma Olive had a resurrection, please," Selwyn says.

When I tell Jean and Richard about Grandma's reincarnation, Jean cries and laughs at the same time, "A beautiful portent," she says. "It is time for Selwyn to come home, for some good news." Jean asks me for Selwyn's phone number, and tells me she has been writing to him.

In the morning, I walk down toward School Beach. It is low tide. I follow the road, and then cross down a track through the native grass to the shore. Stringy ice plant forms a lawn, strewn with pieces of driftwood, kelp and feathers that have been left by a stormy high tide.

The sand bank is out there, a wide white carcass. There is a tidal channel across it where the best shellfish, flounder, and crab are found. The sea is green and clear close in, with empty shells catching the sun. I look away out where the sea and sky are purple and blue.

In the afternoon, I get a phone call from Greg--I have lost interest in his covert operations, but listen to him politely. "The Mexican Government not only have survived our attempt to undermine their currency, but they're calling our bluff now. Are you ready for a new project?"

"Please, not at this time, Greg. There is a crisis in the family. Grandma is not well."

"So, you're still not over Lil. That's what's weighing you down. She should be prosecuted, and you're up to your armpits in self-doubt. Lillian Bjorn is not from your world. What you suffered because of how she treated your Natalie was cruel, and horrendous as that was, it is what her type feel every minute of every hour of…"

"That's enough!"

Greg knows that it is time to shut up. He finishes the conversation in his soft voice. "Take your time. I'm always here for you. You have become a dear friend, Dylan. Trust me. It's going to get better."

The phone rings again. It is Angela. Kathy's grades have deteriorated and Angela is blaming me. "Kathy knows enough of what has gone on with Lil to confuse her. Your daughter might benefit from having the details brought out from the closet."

Angela might be right this time? And what about Lil's children? They must be as confused as Kathy. Maybe more so. I wonder how Lil can possibly console her children with a minimal explanation.

PART V:

CHAPTER 42:

I can hear bellbirds feeding in the Fuchsias. I lean over the packing room sink as I trim the stems off the Hydrangeas, saving the flowers in a bucket of fertilized water. I can hear seedpods from the Kowhai tree exploding in the sun. The flower-packing room is cool, and as colorful as Gauguin's Tahiti: fuchsia, plum, feijoa, cream, and avocado. The blooms are the size of dinner plates, and stiff. The stoutest cuttings off the stems are to be planted out beside one of the orchard ponds after rooting. It's been a good season, ten thousand head. It gives me pleasure that I, and anyone driving along Upland Road, can enjoy this exotic palette for five months before we sell the flowers for Easter weddings in New York and Tokyo.

I hear a car pull off Upland Road onto my driveway, half a mile away. A visitor drops in about once a week, usually Richard Powers. It will be a few minutes before the visitor climbs the driveway, parks, and walks to the front door. I switch the hot water jug on, anticipating a cuppa. The front door bell rings… Funny, Richard would have walked in without ringing. Must be a real visitor? Knocking at the side door now… probably an impatient salesperson.

I open the kitchen door to a slender bearded man wearing a priest's collar and a black silk shirt with short sleeves.

"Selwyn! What a surprise! I didn't expect you so soon." I haven't seen my brother since Christmas. Jean Powers has arrived with him.

"Good to see you, Dylan," Selwyn says, pumping my hand.

"It was strange, the nurse thinking that Grandma was dead."

"Yes. Could be a portent," Jean says.

"A bloody relief for me. Mom and Dad visit her almost everyday now. Are you in Mexico for a while longer?"

"Yes," he says abruptly. "Can we talk?"

I remove the wine bottle that the flower merchant and I emptied last night. My brother is a perfectionist around domestic details. The kitchen is almost tidy, except for an overflowing carton of books on the floor. The lounge is closer to acceptable.

"Yes, of course, let's sit in the lounge."

But first I insist that Selwyn refreshes himself with the view from the picture window. It is a pretty day, a good day for company. The tide is out, the beach bright in the foreground, the shimmering heat reflects in waves from the sand. The deep water in the center of the harbor is green and gray. Just off the point in the foreground the water is turbulent where it runs into the channel with a blistered texture.

Selwyn's knees click as he sits. My half-scale bronze statue of Romeo, arms stretched upward, stands to the side of my new fireplace. Romeo looks effeminate by himself, missing the Juliet piece that is on the other side of the world, with Lil.

I settle my guests and pour the tea.

Selwyn gets up and studies the photograph of him on my wall—of my radical brother protesting with some nuns outside an abortion clinic in Nicaragua, just before they were arrested.

Selwyn has never had a girlfriend that I know of… yet Lil and he looked good dancing together at our wedding. Selwyn had the same dance lessons as me, with the French teacher that Mom was so keen about. Mom also keeps that photograph of Selwyn and the three pretty nuns on her living room wall. She spends a lot of time reading love stories and has definite ideas about what a happy marriage should look like for both of her sons. Mom still holds hope for her boys, even though one has been divorced, and the other is a fanatical priest.

"You got a busy year ahead, Dylan?" Selwyn asks.

"Not bad."

Across the other side of the harbor a pallet knife stroke of silver and blue water mimics the ribbon of foreshore. There are stabs of colored light as the breeze blows up sea spray and sand. I lay out my best china teacups.

"It can get a bit hectic when Kathy's here. She starts high school this year. I've only got a few planting-out projects to do over the next season, and I want to rebuild the sheep pens. I'd like to get Kathy doing some more home schooling, but her mom objects."

Selwyn turns away and back, then seeks eye contact. "I knew about Lil's abortion plans in advance…"

"Everyone knows the details of our private lives, everyone except me."

"I knew that Lil was going to Tijuana for an abortion, on December 28th, immediately after your final counseling session with Frank Gunter," Selwyn whispers.

"Why didn't you tell me?" I am walking in circles.

"I did tell you about this the night of Natalie's memorial service. Your mental health was not stable… and hasn't been good until very recently. Anyway, you cut me off that night before I could tell you the full story," Selwyn says.

"I have thought a lot about that final counseling session with Frank," I say, continuing to walk in circles. "Frank took me aside afterwards, told me that I did well by making it clear that I wanted a healthy marriage. He didn't mention a bloody thing about Lil planning an abortion to me."

"He probably didn't know. And couldn't tell you anyway." Selwyn shrugs.

"Selwyn's right, it's their professional code of ethics," Jean says.

"What's this, a conspiracy? I remember it too bloody well!" I wince and sit down. "Frank's morale boosting chat outside the women's bathrooms while I waited and waited for Lil to come out… Fucking Hell! Frank was purposefully distracting me so Lil could make an escape—he was aiding her to get away from me!"

"Stop it, Dylan! Lil's plan was already in place by then. She'd asked her midwife nurse at Kaiser for an abortion--but the nurse wouldn't do it. Lil was beyond reason. Nothing anyone said would have made any difference. Lillian had lost it!" Selwyn says.

"That was six years ago. Why not talk before now?"

"Ruth and Lil drove off to Tijuana while I was on the phone." Selwyn's pale eyes are bulging.

"What! Jeez, little brother, you're sounding weird."

"I knew! And I did what I thought God was calling me to do. I know I did the right thing, Natalie was saved, Dylan."

"Don't you mess with me, little brother!" I stand up and want to hurt him. "Your little Catholic cartel is in danger of believing you have some power to change things."

Just look at him, the Reverend Selwyn Bloody Hotta! He's got that serious look, like during a sermon, or before he goes to his pro-life gig with his placards on Saturday mornings.

"Dylan, She's alive!"

"Don't try and bullshit me with theological double-talk! I'm a rancher. I see death eyeball to eyeball!"

"Have you finished already?" Jean asks.

"No! It'll never be finished."

"Natalie is waiting in the car parked in your driveway," Jean says.

I run.

Selwyn tries to stop me. "Wait, let me finish," he says, making a grab for me.

"No way." I sidestep past him and I see the car. A child is sitting in the back seat, with a nun. I stumble to the car, and kneel on the ground.

"Natalie..."

The girl leans away and buries her head into the nun's arm.

"Hi Dylan, my name is Ginny. I've been caring for Natalie since last week."

They tumble out of the car. The girl has Lil's luminescent jade eyes… and the Hotta big lips and teeth. But it is too unreal. I walk behind them, never taking my eyes off Natalie. She has blonde hair like Lillian. Skinny. I feel a manic burst of energy, like I could run to the top of Upland Road and back before the hot water jug boils. My Natalie is home!

I walk them indoors. "Here Ginny, you and Natalie sit on the sofa. I'll sit beside you."

Ginny steps back. "It will be better if you take it slowly, it may be the end of the day before your daughter knows you well enough to sit with you."

Selwyn is behind us. "Ginny is right. Why don't we let her and Natalie stretch their legs, get familiar with the terrain, and we'll chat?"

We watch my daughter descend the patio steps hesitantly, like a newborn foal, then run with more confident legs across the lawn toward the ducks and lambs.

"Thank you. I'm glad she was named Natalie. That was our choice."

"I know. I was there, remember?"

I feel tears… let them roll. "Is this for real? It's hard to believe."

"Yes."

"Is it certain she's my daughter?" I look into my brother's pale watery eyes.

"Yes. And the DNA tests have been saved for you. Lil knew nothing. She was unconscious."

"Why have Natalie and I had to wait all these years?"

"Your daughter weighed 657 grams. Premature. She's always been a wonderful child, but was very sick at first. She was tiny and had low blood-sugar. She needed nasal feeding and growth hormone treatment."

Selwyn looks away. "Natalie has bad asthma. And she gets pneumonia regularly. She could easily have died. That would have upset you further at the time. I decided to wait until we were certain that she was OK. Then I wasn't sure if you could deal with it, so I waited until I thought you were better. I'm sorry, I know it's not fair, but I did my best."

"Is Natalie going to live with me now?" I can dare hope.

"Yes, that's possible, if you're ready. But it's a tricky legal situation. Your child was brought into this world against her mother's will," Selwyn says.

"What are the legal problems?" I walk in circles.

Jean explains, "Abortion is illegal in the third trimester. But in Mexico it's an underground industry. The Archdeacon bribed the clinic administrator to look the other way. Then he logged Lil into the abortion clinic. He was wearing a doctor's gown. A hired doctor was waiting in the clinic-come-delivery room. The church doesn't officially know about the rescue."

"And what is your role?" I ask Jean.

"Selwyn has called me periodically to check on your mental health. But he only explained about Natalie's rescue last week," Jean says.

"Why not minister to Lil before she lost the plot?"

Selwyn has a grin now, all tension gone. Or is it guilt he's let go of? "You'll want to know how they did it. In order to induce the birth Lil was anesthetized and then injected with the drug Oxytocin. The abortion clinic doctor would have followed the same inducement procedure. The only deviation from their standard abortion procedure was that *our* doctor's name was on the roster, so when Natalie arrived, instead of being strangled with forceps as she approached the birth canal exit, and being sucked out by a vacuum machine, she was delivered by our doctor in the same way as you and I. Natalie was allowed to travel the last few centimeters alive. Lil slept through it all, under sedation."

"Hell's teeth! What a brutal world! How come you haven't talked to me about this before?" I ask.

"I had to wait, to wait until she was healthy, and wait until you were ready," Selwyn says.

Lil and I had never really talked about the abortion. You cannot talk about something as hideous as the death of an infant, because denial kills conversation. There are words I wanted to say, but thought better of it. Just as well I hadn't. I have lived with that hell so long that it became a dull underwater sound in my head. Now, all that has suddenly gone… it is like the relief after getting the news that Grandma Olive was resurrected.

"And what about Lil?" She told me she almost died down in Mexico."

"Lil was rested for twenty-four hours. Then her mother drove her back to California," Selwyn says. "We instructed the doctor to watch her closely, like I have been doing for you these last five years…"

Jean interrupts. "I can see there were definite risks."

"Risks for whom?" I ask

"More for the doctor than the clinic. But he's a professional. It's our job to save lives when we have the opportunity," Selwyn says.

"I can't believe you didn't tell me!"

"Lil was lost. Natalie's life was on the brink for a long time. We didn't tell you earlier because you were too stressed. I've been keeping an eye on you, calling Jean or Richard every week. Glad to see you're back to your old self," Selwyn says.

"That bad, eh? Lil needed help! We both needed help! All this drama could have been prevented if just one of the many people that I had asked for help had been able to hear and respond…"

Selwyn jumps in. "Humberto Contreras arranged to get Natalie a passport from Vatican City. But she doesn't have a birth certificate."

"How am I supposed to comprehend all the ramifications of no birth certificate! Natalie and I are now set up to rely on the church for the rest of our lives for our security, and our very identity."

"Delicate ethical issues arise here. There's a risk of scandal," Selwyn says.

"Yes. But I have to let Lil know. It's only right!"

"I beg you not to communicate with Lil. She could enforce DNA testing, and hound you to the grave," Selwyn says.

"She has a right to know. Natalie has a right to know!" I drink my cold tea with one gulp.

"I agree that Natalie has a right to know. You could tell her some of the details when you feel it appropriate, when she's old enough. But do not tell Lil. May

I suggest that you rely, for the moment, on the collective wisdom of those who have worked on this over six years," Selwyn says.

The phone rings. "It is a Father Contreras for Selwyn," Jean says.

"Good morning Humberto. How are you? …Excellent."

I gaze past Selwyn, avoiding eye contact as my brother talks, then places the receiver back on the cradle. "Humberto is now the Bishop of Tijuana," Selwyn says.

I see Natalie walking through the orchard. You can't argue with success. A sparrow crashes into the living room window, startling me. "Hell's bells! What is it with birds? They seem to sense things in the ether, like a portent."

"It is important that we get you prepared to raise this daughter," Selwyn says, "I have packed clothes, a toothbrush, the teddy, dolls, and books."

"Thank you, I'm lucky to have a brother like you."

"Quickly, they're coming back. Natalie will ask you about her mom when she gets older. I told her that Lil was very sick, too sick to even know she had given birth. Be careful what you say around Natalie, she can understand more than you think."

The room becomes brighter as the door from the patio is opened. Natalie and Ginny return with a collection of flowers; blue Irises and plum-colored Dahlias.

"Would you guys like a cup of tea, and milk for Natalie?"

"Yes, please, that would be lovely," Ginny says.

"Actually, we'd better be going. We'll drop in before bedtime, and we'll be down again tomorrow morning. OK?" Selwyn asks.

"Yeah, we'll be fine. But I don't have much food suitable for a young child."

"We brought some food with us, and I'll go over the details tomorrow," Selwyn says.

"And if you need anything give me a call," Jean says.

"Thank you. Thanks Ginny. OK, Natalie. Let's get you some milk, and take you to your room, eh? Tomorrow we'll shop for food and furniture… and toys. After inspecting your room, we'll get some dinner cooking. See you guys later."

Selwyn takes my elbow and steers me aside, saying, "Do it strictly by the book. No creative parenting ideas like exploring the outback, building hang gliders, or sailing the Pacific with this one. "Jean and I will be back about 7.30pm, and remember, her six years in a church orphanage was different from our childhood. Ginny will write to her, but Natalie has no familial bond to Ginny or anyone else."

Natalie and I select a room for her… with its own bathroom. Her baby booties are still in the top drawer. Natalie's bedroom has a door leading to a safe balcony, which looks out across the ranch and the lambs. Her bed has brass ends and a raspberry-colored duvet with cream pillowcases. She likes her room.

A cabbage tree rattles outside the window as a sea breeze takes the heat off the evening. We look over the sea together, as I talk to her about my boat. Natalie is quiet for a while, and then she asks me where the other kids in my home are today.

I tell her that I can show her pictures of her brother, her two sisters, and her mom. "Your half-sister's room is just down the hallway. Look, that's her in this album, the girl on the left. Her name is Kathy. She'll be here for Christmas."

"How old is Kathy?"

"She's thirteen. And she's lovely. And that's your mom with her. Not a very good photo of her. I've got lots more."

Natalie follows me up the library stairs. We drag the heaviest album from the bookcase and lay it out on the desk. "Here's a baby picture of you—before you were born, and that's Lil, that's your mom, with her son Paul, and her step-daughter Barbara. Lil's handwriting is on the back." Natalie turns the photo over, and back again.

"This is a group of us at a party beside the pool. That's your sister Kathy in front. She's eight years older than you. The two horses down below the orchard are hers. She'll stay for a couple of weeks over Christmas."

"I have my own private sister then?" Natalie asks.

"Yeah. She's your half-sister. She has a different mom than you. You both have me for your father. Kathy is a sweetheart. You'll like her. She's a bit of a tomboy though, she would rather wear boots around the ranch than dress up and go to town."

"That's OK, I can dress myself. I'm glad she knows about horses. Do you have any more photos of Mom?"

"Yeah, there's a bunch of wedding photos."

"That's so special. OK, do we have prayers before dinner?"

"You bet we do. At least from now on."

Lying in bed, I am still anxious—Someone, such as Ruth, might tell Natalie about Lillian's attempted abortion. How am I ever going to respond to that inevitable question from my daughter about what happened?

CHAPTER 43:

Six years have passed since Natalie arrived. These years has passed amidst a fog, not in regard to Natalie, but in regard to Lil. Natalie is my anchor. Lillian has been a dark secret dream. But then, at times I have found myself laughing hilariously—and grinning inside as I observed a new bloom in the flowerbeds, and felt the impact of Natalie or Kathy starting another project. I have at last digested the knowledge that we can go on living when we are wounded, and that we keep feeling around until we find ourselves living with a softer touch.

School is almost out for the summer holidays and the lambing season is done. Good time for a break. I get a call from Richard--and then return to preparing breakfast. "Hey, Natalie. Richard wants to give his top paddock to us."

"The Powers family likes us. There'll be room for another horse and jumps now," Natalie says.

I had admired Richard's top paddock only last week, when I climbed the boundary fence to recover an adventurous ram. The sheep seek out those very first and last rays of the sun that light up the top paddock.

I serve up breakfast of muesli, yogurt and fruit. Natalie pours her freshly squeezed orange juice and we sit at the kitchen table.

"I'm almost twelve now… and I want to know why Mommy doesn't visit me!" Natalie sticks her chin out; stretching her skin over her jaw, the same way Lillian did when she was debating something important.

I pace around the kitchen, scratching my head. I knew this question would come up. I have tried to prepare an answer… but nothing has prepared me for this! Natalie is so lovely and I hate to see her suffer.

"I'll try to explain," I say. "Your mother was sick when you were born. She lives in California and has had a difficult life. Her name is Lillian Bjorn. Let me show you the photos of her again, quickly, before school." Natalie follows me to the library and sits beside me at the Kauri desk. "Here's a photo of your mom when she was pregnant with you, showing off her belly, and if you smell that pillowcase inside the plastic bag it's exactly the way she smells. You have to hold it close, and you won't notice her perfume for a few moments, until just after you put it away. Some people are like that, have impact after they have left the room."

"She looks so pretty. Where'd you get married, in New Zealand or California?"

"In the church at Warrington, just over the bay and up the coast."

"When will I finally meet her?"

"I don't know, Sweetheart, that's beyond my control."

Tears well up in her eyes and overflow. I brush her cheeks. "I'm sorry," I say. "She doesn't know about you. She was sick and didn't realize she had given birth." A burst of pain twists my liver around my spleen. I double up and wince.

"What's wrong?" Natalie asks.

"It's nothing."

"Bullshit! What are you going to do about it?"

I reassure Natalie that I will see Dr. Powers. "Right now. And I'll discuss my health problems as well as what to do about trying to contact Lillian."

"I'm going to take the afternoon off school and come with you to Richard's house," Natalie says.

"No, that's not wise, you taking time off school. But *I'll* take the afternoon off and I'll let *you* cook dinner. Then we can talk more about your mom while we eat. Is that a plan?"

"As long as you are OK. Imagine if you got sick too."

Natalie bikes to school and I limp over to visit my neighbor. One look is enough. "Come in, Son. Let's take a look at what's up." I follow Richard into his study where he keeps his old medical equipment. He does a thorough exam and takes a blood sample. Finally he folds the deflated ball with its black tube back into the Velcro armband, and stands, turning to gaze out the window framing the water beyond. After a stretched silence he turns back, sets the blood pressure gauge onto his desk, and paces the room. I can hear the clock ticking.

"We're going to have a heart to heart," the doctor says.

Richard's eyeballs sit comfortably in their eyeglass frames of brown tortoiseshell—frames that amplify the red veins in his cornea, and the old skin below.

"Blood pressure is 190 over 125. That's high, and you've always been so good. You must change if you're going to live long enough to raise Natalie."

"I eat well, and exercise. I'm not a bloody fool!" I say.

"No! This is stress. You're going to have to change! Ready for it?"

"I'll try anything."

"OK, here's the deal. There's no decision that will help Natalie!"

"What? That doesn't sound right!"

"If you told Natalie what you know she'd be too young to handle it. If you flew Lillian here tonight, it wouldn't work!"

"How can you be so sure?" I might have called Lil already, in a rash moment, but she clearly doesn't want to communicate.

"You're not God!" Richard says. "Natalie has to make her own decision about what she wants!"

"OK! Natalie has been upset about not knowing her mother. She wants to go shopping for a few days, in Wellington. It's Natalie's twelfth birthday and she spent hours crying in her room last night!"

"Take her… But isn't her birthday after Christmas?"

"Selwyn set her official birthday for December 18, to muddy any possible trail back to that day in Tijuana."

"But what's upsetting her this time?" Richard asks.

"The birthday season without a mom is a time that Natalie has struggled most with, especially this year. I wonder if it was such a good idea to have booked our vacation at this time?"

"You're doing fine," Richard says.

"Natalie is much more emotional than previous birthdays... but then she's older now. She still meets with a child psychologist every month, yet she rarely talks about what is happening inside. And I'm not surprised that Natalie continues to ask questions about Witi's provocative creation story regarding the native Maori ancestors. I guess the Christian and Jewish creation story was also propagated by incest after Adam and Eve... similar to Tane and Hine nui te Po. But the abortion reference is close to the bone."

"Yes. She's a smart girl, Dylan."

"Natalie has changed me. Now I'm more into gardening but far from an ideal parent. It hit Natalie hard when she realized that she's the only kid in her school with a flat-breasted rancher for a mom.

She gets embarrassed when I yell too loud at her hockey games, or buy her pretty pink dresses. Then she lets me have it. *You're trying too hard, Dad. It's simple to be a mom. Just put your brain into gear before you get out of bed, Silly.*"

Natalie is relieved to see me looking healthier when she gets home, but that doesn't last long.

"I feel weird," Natalie says. "It's like I was born without arms."

"I'm so proud of you."

For the birthday dinner, I serve up homegrown lamb shanks with new potatoes, peas and carrots from my garden.

"There must be something I can do about finding Mom," Natalie says, sticking out her chin.

I look out the window, fighting to recover from some vague inadequacy. I turn back and seek eye contact with Natalie. "What do you want to happen?"

"I'd like to write Mom a letter. But I wonder if it would be better if you wrote it," Natalie says. "But first, tell me what you think is the cause of Mom's sickness."

"It's an unusual problem... and what would you like the letter to say?

"Tell her I hope she's better now, and I want to meet her, in a safe way for both of us."

"And what would be safe?" I ask, knowing that predictability is not possible.

"For her to fly over to here, and meet with me."

Natalie is biting her lower lip. I am not sure what to say, so I try to give her a hug... but she pushes my arm away.

"Don't be so cheesy Dad," she says, and juts her chin out, just the way that Lillian used to do.

I pace around the kitchen. "Lil must still be sick. She would have called if she had got better." It is uncomfortable not being able to tell my daughter the entire story. Jean has assured me that I'm doing fine with this delicate situation.

"Don't be silly Dad, she'd be too busy to call you," says Natalie, wiping tears with her sleeve.

Natalie would have to believe that.

"Are you sure that's what you want me to do?"

"Yes please, Daddy."

"OK, we'll work on it."

"Let's look at her photos again?"

I pull out the album and open it on the kitchen table.

"She looks so confident, who would guess she is ill," I say.

Natalie looks up at me. "A big part of me is scared of her."

"Well, let's say that in the letter."

"How will that make Mom want to be with me now?" Natalie asks.

"Is that the purpose of your letter?"

"Yeah."

"OK."

We sit together for an hour, working on the letter:

Dear Lillian:

I have decided that I need to break our silence because of special circumstances. Please be assured that I would not have taken this step without due consideration of your request for solitude.

I am healthy at this time and trust that you are also.

Please sit down.

A miracle has happened. Our daughter Natalie is alive… She was rescued down in Tijuana and has been returned to me following the death of her institution-appointed Nanny.

Natalie is a little scared of the unknown, but is very keen to make loving contact with you. What do you say?

Regards, Dylan

"Do you still love my mom?"

"Yes, once you really love someone you don't stop, not because they get sick, or anything else."

"That's the way I feel too," Natalie says.

We edit the letter, and send it to Lillian's address in Sierra.

Sleep doesn't come easily for me tonight. I am as excited as Natalie about the letter, and nervous. The letter felt hopeful and scary, then downright uncomfortable. It isn't just that Lil has asked me not to contact her; after all, this is a special circumstance. But introducing her to Natalie is such a gamble, and to set it up by choosing a few words to set out on a piece of paper feels risky. I don't doubt that Lil will want to see Natalie… as long as she doesn't freak.

Natalie is the one who has made the decision to contact Lillian. And that is what Dr. Powers recommended: *Let her be the one to decide.* Natalie is turning twelve, and this is the time she has chosen to open the door to who knows what possibilities. I know that a part of me would commit to a relationship with Lil again, if she took just half a step towards rebuilding her life.

I have set my alarm for 4am to prepare for the early flight to Wellington for our shopping trip, Natalie doesn't like getting up early, and I don't like the petty arguments that arise if I try to herd her into compliance with a timetable.

I am ready at 5am, with suitcases in the car. I lean against the rear of the Jeep and look out over the harbor. The perimeter of the sky is powder blue now, back lit. The sunrise changes the color of everything. I put this realization down to the vacation spirit, to that time which is perhaps the most opportune time to sense everything afresh.

Natalie tumbles out the front door with a blanket, pillow, teddy bear and handbag cradled in her arms, and rushes me to open the car door. We are off on vacation and the eastern half of the sky is turning pink.

Natalie assures me. "I am so comfortable with flying that I want to fly with you when you go over to visit Kathy next month, in California."

But that will not be wise. I cannot imagine Natalie being in the same country as Lillian and not demanding to see her mom. It is difficult enough for me to go there and not drop in on Lil.

Damn! I must not go over to California at this time… I call Kathy and try to explain. "I'll send you tickets so you can come over here."

CHAPTER 44:

It's Saturday evening. The telephone rings as I finally get home for dinner.

"Hi, Dylan. It's Lil here. Did Natalie tell you I called?"

"No! I've just got in the door. Jeez, I wish I'd been here. How are you?"

"I got the letter about Natalie," Lil says.

"This is so difficult…"

"I don't need this drama. Fuck you, Dylan!"

"I knew nothing about her survival either, not until Natalie was six years old."

"Someone knew about Natalie, so why didn't I!"

"You are probably confused and scared, so am I, confused as hell."

"You always throw chaos at me. Fuck you!"

"Bloody hell! What was I supposed to do? I'm just reacting to circumstances you have created. I know this is a shock for you."

"How dare you be so righteous! So now you've got what you want, you'd better not mess her up--like you messed me up."

"Bullshit! You'd have called me before now if you had a bloody clue about what you are doing with your life."

"So you wrote because you needed my help!"

"No! Natalie needs help from both of us."

"I've been trying to clean up. I haven't had a boyfriend for three years. I regret what I've put you through."

"So how come you are so mad at me now?"

"I haven't been well. I rent a tiny apartment in Sierra now, only six miles from my mom's house. My son is living with Ruth, and doing well. I only see my mom when I visit Paul."

"So, what have you been doing?" I ask.

"As little as possible… At Christmas time I tried some meds for my depression. Legal meds. It wasn't so much what I didn't achieve last year that bothered me, but the things that I had done badly."

"Like what?"

"Prozac pills. They kicked in two weeks ago. It isn't that they make me feel on top of everything, not brilliant like coke or ecstasy. No, the antidepressants seem to put me in a space where the winter grime on the windows doesn't bother me, and it is no trouble for me to take the garbage out or do the ironing. It's not that life is entirely pleasant or the chores satisfying, but that the chores get done."

"Why did you talk to Natalie first, before me! It could stress her!"

"I was calling *you*. I thought it was your girlfriend who answered … I was feeling my head above water for the first time in years. It's winter here. The garden has snowflakes on the leaves. Pretty. That injected enough courage for me to dial your number—and did I get a shock!

Hello, are you there? A woman's voice answered.

May I speak to Dylan please? I asked.

I was shocked at how young your new girlfriend sounded.

Sorry, he's over visiting the neighbor; can I give him a message?

Please tell him that Lil called. No. Never mind… When do you expect him back?"

Lil! Are you the Lil that used to be married to Dylan?

Yes, and none of your business.

I'm Natalie, the daughter of you and Dylan. Did you get Dylan's letter?

The letter… where were you born?

Mexico, you were unwell. We mailed the letter last week. I know you've been in a coma, and didn't know that I survived, she said. *The letter asked you to phone Dylan if you had recovered from your coma.*

This has got to be bullshit. You tramp! Just because you're Dylan's latest squeeze doesn't give you the right to fuck with me like this!

Natalie screamed at me like a little girl. No, Mommy! It's really me, Natalie. Don't be cruel!

Only then did I know that it was Natalie. What a disaster! I hung up on her. I was so furious with you that I hurled my phone through the kitchen window.

Fuck you! I turned the stereo up full blast and started thinking about drugs. But I called Natalie back before it was too late. Natalie was sobbing when she picked up the receiver.

Sorry I hung up. This is a shock... Could you ask Dylan to call me? And… I'm sorry. I said.

Does Daddy have your phone number? Natalie asked.

No. I've moved to Sierra. My new number is 8427669. He'll know the area code. Are you OK, otherwise, apart from my tantrum? I asked.

Yes, fine. This isn't my fault, so I hope you'll calm down.

I'm sorry. It's a shock. I'll call Dylan back in an hour or two. Don't tell him I called. OK? I asked.

OK. Please, try and understand that we meant well with the letter, Dad and I spent a lot of time on it. I hope to see you soon. Bye, Natalie said."

Before I can get a word in, Lil continues; "Fuck! I talked to my daughter like that. The first words she's ever heard out of my mouth, apart from the lullabies we sang to her before she was born. I thought that you'd set me up for some kind of revenge; a revenge I had almost been looking forward to."

I take a deep breath, knowing I must somehow contribute. "No, revenge doesn't work. I had better check on Natalie, just a minute."

Natalie is in her room, with the phone to her ear. I take the phone from her and she grins.

"Hello, are you there? It's OK. Natalie's in her room. She's OK."

Then Lil goes at me again. "What in hell is happening! I have to pour another cup of coffee and light a cigarette, now, right now! The fucking adrenalin is overwhelming me! This is too far out, way beyond rage, fucking outrageous… Natalie sounds sweet, and smart. Got your brains eh?"

"Could be a handicap..."

"Let me think about this."

I put the phone down. My knuckles ache from squeezing the receiver. Lil hasn't asked much about Natalie. The rural silence sounds like distant applause, until broken by the bleating of a goat up on the rim of the valley. I need to think. I find myself walking, past the upper pond and along Upland Road. Dust covers the lower leaves of the purple foxgloves. A gust of wind rattles the Macrocarpa trees, wafting tree-oil scent on the warm salty air. A few rabbits start to come out in the late afternoon, so it is well after dark now in California, Friday night rather than Saturday evening.

CHAPTER 45:

It's Sunday, a month since Lil's last call, and the ringing of the phone breaks through the friendly chatter of a passing rainstorm pelting the iron roof of my workshop.

"Hello, Dylan. It's Lil. How are you?"

"Fine, and yourself?"

"I'm getting better, slowly adapting."

The ocean surf sound from the telephone line fills the silence…

"I've booked a flight over. How is she?"

Lil's voice sounds hoarse but confident. My throat constricts, fear and hope facing off.

"Not eating much. It's a lot of trauma for Natalie."

"Probably just coming out of the spin cycle. I've sensed something about Natalie ever since that day down in Tijuana."

"Shall I arrange for the first meeting to be in Doctor Powers' office… in case we need help from a professional?"

"That may not be comfortable for Natalie. What about at the local park?"

"Great idea, do it on her territory."

"Who rescued Natalie down in Tijuana?"

"Selwyn's friends from the church. Frank Gunter overheard you talking to your mom on the phone—and that set them off."

"Who got Frank into this?" Lil asks.

"My brother. Frank and he are buddies."

"Hmmm. The priest who likes to dance," Lil says. "Was Greg involved?"

"No! We can talk details at Richard and Jean's home, then you could meet with Natalie in the park, without me in the way. Will that work for you?"

"Thanks. But I'd like you to be there."

"OK..." The silence drives me to distraction. "Warwick Powers died last year, a brain tumor," I thrust into the void.

Lil makes no comment. The conversation is almost over. We haven't talked about what really happened, about apology or mistrust… Nothing of what I had anticipated.

The path of our connection heaves and subsides with each sentence, like kelp riding the surf, elusive, but attached to something buried on the ocean floor.

"You can stay at my parent's house if you want. They're away."

Love diesels on, a commitment never quite letting go, no matter what is lost to sickness, to disappointment, to years apart. And when I ask her again, "How are you doing?" her reply sounds rehearsed.

"The past must be allowed to go where it will; otherwise the feelings can tear out our roots. All my friends are moving away, trying to escape the past. I count you in that category."

"What does that mean?" I ask.

“Think about it for a few days. My life has always been in California. Paul lives here. You left--ran away!”

“Yes. I escaped. But Lil, what can be done now?”

“I can’t afford plane trips every week; Bill’s money is all gone.”

“I’ll help.”

After the essence of the conversation is replayed, the feelings drift. The sun is sinking into the hinterland. Gulls are gloating as they fly in from the ocean. The township of Carey’s Bay winks and glimmers across the water. The several dockside cranes at Port Chalmers chirp in the still air, feeding among the racks of logs on the dock like a family of giant grasshoppers. A warm breeze comes in from the west, off the hot earth of the hinterland.

The Tuesday morning of Lil’s arrival begins with a purple sky in the east, and hints of blue and red in the clouds on the western horizon. This is the dawning of the day that has been long coming.

It is time to pick up Lil from the airport. Alone, my contentment is related to the welfare of Natalie--who is safely at school. I have grown past feeling like an inadequate parent. I can be as territorial as any mother. However, parenting has become a partnership between our community and me. My parents, despite their reduced capacity, have been a dream.

Lil finally strides into the airport terminal--alone. Her face is blotchy red from stress. She doesn’t seem to care how she looks at this moment. She has put on weight, and her hug is warm.

“Jeez, I’ve been feeling weird. Like an addict stuck on a plane for twelve hours without a fix,” she says.

“Good to see you.” I have waited so eagerly for this worn woman. This is about Natalie, not me. Or is it? Lil pokes that dart of her tongue and I feel the old fizz ignite… for a moment. I follow Lil into the familiar territory, around the corner to the same baggage claim lounge where we gathered that Easter--more than twenty years ago. I am less nervous now. Now that she has come this far, all the way to Dunedin, she must be committed to achieving some sort of progress. She looks tired, of course, but well enough, with a blonde rinse streaking her hair. She still has that glorious laugh, the laugh that I used to search for, in many streets and many dreams. I am a generation older than these young Dunedin students who are at the airport to welcome their girlfriends back for the new semester.

On the drive home the landscape looks brighter than I remember. Pristine white beaches are surrounded by sensuous lean hills that lie low like lovers, hemmed by sandy skirts that swirl around the purple ocean margins. We sit comfortably in silence during the remainder of the journey to Elsinore.

Lil holds my arm as we walk through the back entrance to be greeted by Jean and Richard Powers. We all shuffle through the familiar basement band room where

Lil and I first met, up the squeaky stairs, into the doctor's office. We collapse into leather chairs. I haven't told my parent's that Lil is coming. I want to wait and see that it goes smoothly before exciting them. Maybe I have made a mistake in trying to protect them from our craziness.

"Lil, I'm sorry. It might have been better to let you rest for a day before meeting Natalie," I say.

"No. I wouldn't have been able to wait… Thank you Jean. Your home hasn't lost any of its charm," Lil says.

Richard, as usual, is the social lubricator. "We almost sold the place after Warwick died..."

"Sorry. Sorry for your loss. A terrible blow," Lil says.

Richard continues, "I kept on hearing Warwick's ghost for a while. The ghost always made a noise before dropping in."

I get Richard and Jean another cup of tea while Lil and they talk about Warwick. After a silence I continue; "We've got a little time to iron out any details if you want?"

"You have a special daughter," Jean says.

Lil sits down again; "You should all know that Ruth opened my mail and read Natalie's letter."

"How did Ruth take it?" Jean asks.

"Vindictively… Dylan, I'm sorry, so sorry it's taken so long to finally see Ruth in perspective. I'm sorry you got hurt."

"This is the first time you've apologized to me, about anything." She can see that her apology hits me, was too long in coming. My lips quiver. My eyes water. She's always avoided any admission of a mistake.

"How has Natalie been?" Lil asks.

"She was very independent when she arrived from the orphanage. But she has bonded with me. It took many six months. Now she is changing from being a tomboy. She studies your photographs and wants to dress like you and smile like you."

"How's your son doing, Lillian?" Jean asks.

"Paul is clean and sober. I'm proud to say that he finally graduated from High School and has been accepted into the Navy. Goes to boot camp after Christmas," Lil says.

"Awesome. I'm thrilled for you both," I say. "Natalie's good at sports, and likes to read. But she has days where she gets down. She's in therapy."

"Is she able to deal with it?" Lil cringes.

"She's doing OK. I told her that you've been too ill to even know that she exists, that you've been in a coma."

"Sweet Jesus! I suppose that's true in a sense." Lil grimaces. "I'm so nervous. I'm sorry, Dylan. Thanks."

"Oh, and Lillian. We want you to have Warwick's car… His yellow Toyota is parked in Dylan's driveway. The key is in it," Richard says.

"I couldn't."

"At least keep the key in your bag—in case of emergency."

We drop Lillian and Jean off at the School Beach Park while Richard and I drive over to collect Natalie from her school.

I regret that Natalie wasn't present through the beginning of this meeting; she could have benefited from seeing her Mom dealing with adults like this. Lil has the most nervous stage still to endure… Now!

Lillian has her shoulders hunched forward as she sits at the picnic bench by School Beach. The three of us wade through the long grass across the park. The wild rabbits are still here. My boat swivels at its mooring in the next bay under a gust of wind. Lil stands up. A smile visits her tight face, only briefly. She extends her right hand to Natalie with a slight dip of her knees.

Natalie stops, freezes, steps back, staring at Lil.

"I'm pleased to meet you at last," Lil says.

Natalie looks away for a second.

Jean invites us all to sit down.

Lil continues, "I'm sorry that I've been so sick."

Natalie's eyes moisten. She shudders. "Why did it take you so long?"

Lil looks like she is going to reach out and hug Natalie, but that shudder must have warned her, taught her to pull her arms back and take it slow.

"My sickness was one that didn't get better until it burnt itself out, like a fever. I'm better now," Lil says.

Natalie leans into me. "Were you very sick?"

Lil reaches for her nose, patting the red end with a tissue. "Yes, I'm afraid so." Her jade eyes are wet and bloodshot, desperate. She looks as if she's aching for a fix.

Natalie wants her mom to be comfortable. "Did you and my dad play tennis together?"

I feel so proud of Natalie.

Lil is having trouble getting her breath. "I used to step outside about now for a puff of a cigarette, always missed the center of things."

"You're very brave to fly all this way," Natalie says.

"I'm your mom. I'd have climbed a mountain to find you."

Jean places the picnic basket on the table and pours drinks.

CHAPTER 46:

Natalie reluctantly rides her bike back to school at my insistence because Lil is exhausted and needs to take an afternoon nap. The sight of Lil, asleep on the sofa, a book in her lap, hair across the headrest and eyelashes closed like butterfly-wings… fills me with regret. I wish I could trust her enough to be lovers again.

The following week, I withdraw to my study before opening the letter that has arrived from Greg. It contains a serious allegation against Lil. I call Greg. "What in hell are you doing with that woman in your house!" he says.

"Trust me. I'm going to confront her," I promise.

"I've proved to you that she lied about her rape claim. Why don't you dump her? Now!"

"Fax me her medical record, the part about the drugs, and the post-rape examination," I say.

"Gladly. I figured that you'd come to your senses one day," Greg says.

"It's time to plan a confrontation."

Two days have passed since the fax arrived from Greg. I must drench the lambs before I take time out to confront Lil this afternoon. Natalie doesn't come home from school for lunch on Thursdays; she goes to the chess club. This evening, Witi and the other men from the local sailing club will drop in for a barbecue… Lil may leave when I confront her, so those crusty men will be company to help me endure the separation.

The effort of drenching the sheep is minimized by herding just fifteen sheep into the pen at a time; too many and I cannot move among them, too few and they have space to duck away from me. My hands are soft from handling the wool. It only takes two hours to drench the sheep… Just a touch of the gun barrel to the side of the jaw is enough to encourage most of them to docilely let me slide the gun barrel between their gums, then a squeeze of the trigger and on to the next one. A breeze lifts and a fat cloud crosses the sun. The lunch bell rings. Lillian is calling me in.

"Would you like a hot drink?" Lil says. I step through the kitchen door into the aroma of coffee and fresh scones. "Thank you." The kitchen counter has fresh fruit and damp trails from being wiped clean.

I look over the fields with shadows of racing clouds to the left, and the bruised ocean to the right. The new kitchen table is freshly polished. I sit beside the larger plate of scones with raspberry jam.

There are three bowls; one with guacamole, another with corn chips, and the other with bean dip. Lil's bean dip! I dip a scoop of chip into the reddish paste of beans and coriander, then lifting to my mouth; I experience the scrunch, the cold, the texture of pinto beans, the scent of garlic, the sharpness of lime juice. Then another taste, maybe the musty flick of oregano on the end of a sweet bite of diced onion.

"Don't eat it all, it's for your barbecue tonight," Lil sits at the table.

"Thank you, and for the cleaning. Did you have a good nap?" I ask.

"Strange dreams. I'm sorry about what I've put Natalie through... I made a horrible mistake."

"I take it you're volunteering to turn a new leaf?"

She blinks, three times, quickly. "Yes, I'm punished by my dreams. I intend to make it up to you both." She sits on the chair adjacent to mine, not opposite, and doesn't sit all the way back. She perches on the front edge, leaning forward, with her hands flat on the table. Her legs are bent at the knee and crossed at the ankle. Her boots are shiny black with small heels and chisel toes.

I decide this is definitely the time to confront her. I unfold the fax from my pocket.

"How do you see that working?" I ask.

She smiles stiffly. Lil moves, leaning forward, drawing her feet back towards the chair, and then her ankles entwine the chair legs, her forearms are on the table, and her hands flat, facing upwards.

I let the pause lengthen. I can feel her uncertainty beneath the mask of her social competence.

"I'm just here to listen," she says.

"You used and abused me."

"And you used me." She sips from her coffee. "And, that's what people do in relationships. Right?"

"What about empathy and trust?"

She looks at me without the slightest flinch of discomfort, takes another sip of her coffee, but then looks down.

"In what way did I use you?" she asks softly.

I look out the window again.

"Maybe understanding it, or trying to, is a means of working through it," I say.

Lillian nods, allowing the moment.

I watch her; see the uplifted nose, a pained grimace to her mouth, and the shame, at last the shame.

"Where to start?" she asks.

"I have tried to avoid judgment. But there was no rohypnol. There was no rape."

She stares at the back of her hand, no diamond ring, just wrinkles and broken nails.

"There was! ...But Dylan, you're looking at a rare case of a bad girl who wishes to turn good."

Lil smiles brightly, but freezes when she sees I am waiting for more. She picks up her coffee and looks away.

Fuck this! I can't hold it in.

"Here's the deal! You cheated on me! You filed a false rape claim! Think about it! The doctors from Kaiser said that you lied.... there was no rohypnol in your system!"

"That's a lie!"

"It wouldn't have mattered to the doctors what drugs were in your system..."

"You're not making sense."

"The reason that Kaiser didn't believe you is because of the one drug that wasn't in your system. Rohypnol! They both knew then that your rape claim was a lie."

Lil takes another sip of coffee and slowly stands up. She looks as if she might hit me. Suddenly her expression is twisting up, the tears threatening. "The lab did find rohypnol, asshole! I was raped and now you are putting me through this! For God's sake!"

I can't let this go! "Both of the Kaiser doctors called you a liar because there was no fucking rohypnol in your system!"

"Maybe I got the names of one of the drugs wrong, so soon after the rape?"

She gives a little sigh while she is conquering her emotions. Watching her fight back the tears is more distressing than to see the tears themselves. But I can't stop now.

"Manipulation and bullshit are your tools of trade, Lillian. Why did the police drop your rape case after only one day of investigation? I'll tell you why! Because they also know you lied!"

"No! That was because... I can't believe you are doing this!"

I see her fold over, collapse on the sofa, crying--but am unmoved.

"Damn it, Lil! You cheated on me, faked a rape, accused me of planning your rape, tried to abort Natalie... never tried to make amends. I call that out-of-control behavior!"

"You are vicious!" She spits her words. "And it wasn't an abortion. It was an adoption!" I look her down. She almost grins, knowing that I cannot counter that.

"Keep your voice down, Natalie will be coming home from school soon."

"Oh, shit! Lil's hands cover her mouth as her head bows. She peers between her fingers. I've got a confession... The cat got Natalie's pet lizard."

"How?"

"She was playing with it on her bed. Then I opened the door to her room and the cat pounced in."

"How'd Natalie take it?"

"She said, I've told you before to knock before you come into my room! Why does life always have to be tragic around you?"

"Oh dear, then what?"

"I apologized."

"But you haven't apologized to me about the lie," I say.

"…OK. I want to finish this before Natalie comes home," Lil says.

"A further reason the police don't believe you, is that your medical records report that you had no bruising to your body apart from the usual vaginal abrasions that come with normal sexual encounters, and except for the love bites around your mouth."

"Are you finished yet?"

"No! And, furthermore, your vaginal abrasions were at twelve o'clock, indicating consensual sex. Not at the six o'clock position on the lower vaginal wall as always occurs with non-cooperative or forced sex."

"Have you spied on my Kaiser records, you bastard?"

"Here's a copy of your medical record. For God's sake, listen to yourself, why don't you try dealing with the truth!"

She scans the records. "Oh, shit!"

"I assume this is an acknowledgement that you have lied, lied through your fucking teeth!"

"Fuck off!" she says.

"Do you have any idea how difficult it has been for Kathy and me to deal with Natalie's tragedy, with your so-called rape and our divorce… to deal with so many lies?"

"It's not just about you, Dylan. Get off your high horse!" Lil dashes out of the house, slamming the door. I hear her Toyota start. She spins off down the road leaving a cloud of dust.

Desperate for something to do, I wrap the uneaten food in plastic, and then sink back into my chair… There is a bang on the outside wall and the cooking utensils hanging on the kitchen wall move and rattle. Natalie's bike has landed after school.

Natalie's thin flushed face moons around the door, framed by a creation of straight, mostly reddish hair.

"Hi," Natalie says, shuffling to the kitchen table.

"Hello, Sweetheart, how's it going?" I look at her, the way she has changed. I'm overwhelmed. I try to take comfort in the things that haven't changed… but it's difficult.

"Is Lil here?"

"No, we're having a fight. She'll be back later."

"It's my fault; I yelled at her this morning."

"Why is that?"

"It doesn't matter, Dad."

"No. The fight isn't your fault. We're just clearing the air."

"Sometimes I want to push Lil away."

"Give her time. She and I have a lot to work out."

"Good luck with that job. You should feed your cat better!"

"How was school?' I ask.

"OK."

Natalie is sitting at the kitchen table in her navy blue school uniform with a cream blouse. She is eating cereal, her bony wrist shoveling. Head bowed, not looking at me.

"Natalie, I need you to stay with Grandma for a few days, starting tonight… while Lil and I work out our stuff. Here, take the spare phone with you. Please?"

"If that will help," Natalie says, "As long as I can take my CD's and lizard with me, and be back on Saturday morning."

"OK. Of course."

I drive Natalie over to the old homestead to settle her in. We have a cuppa with Mom and Dad, but I do not tell them that the big confrontation has finally started. Maybe I am being too aggressive with Lil, but too bloody bad!

It is evening by the time I get back home, and Lillian still has not returned. I go out to weed the vegetable garden… my knees on an old sack--digging with a hand fork, tossing the clumps of green vegetation into a bucket. The stillness of the evening ocean reflects the clouds with a blue-gray wash, but it feels like a storm is on the way.

The next morning Lil's Toyota is back, parked out front, and Lillian is in the kitchen and greets me without turning. "Hi."

I ignore her peace offering. "So, you were raped were you? Bullshit! Liar!"

Lil turns to me with a sheet of tears, thick like snot across her blotchy face, "I'm sorry I hurt you. It was wrong. Why did what was beautiful suddenly shatter? Did it shatter just because I had a meaningless sexual encounter?"

"Wipe your face. *Meaningless*! This is not about sex, it's about trust!"

Lil walks toward me, eyes softening. "Listen to me, Dylan! You and I had a real chance at making something work. Damn! Even if I was to admit to the world my obsession with self-destruction, what good would that do? You once talked about learning to forgive our abusers. I didn't understand that then, but I have always loved you... and what about you?"

"Me? I just want to know why it happened. Why do you have a compulsion to fuck strange men?"

Lillian smoothes her skirt over her hips. "If you suspected that I had been unfaithful all that time… why wait? Why take it so personally?"

"I didn't know… It affects me—very deeply," I say.

"But you were terrified of infidelity even before we were married! I made up the rape story because I knew you couldn't deal with my sex addiction. Dylan, I want to work it out, I want to be with you and Natalie now."

"I've no idea what to say."

"Well, you'll have to make some changes also!"

"I suppose the thing that bothers me…" I look across at her… "I guess-- I'm hurt."

Her gaze flicks to the right and she sits there, very still, waiting for my judgment, the moral judgment. I have none to make. Judgment is a self-demeaning instinct. Like revenge.

"I know, Dylan. Can we talk about it?"

"Too soon. I need some time."

I hear Natalie's bike scrunching on the driveway, then vibrating against the outside wall.

"Natalie! You're supposed to be staying with Grandma."

"Oh! I forgot. Sorry, Dad."

I call Grandma to let her know what has happened, and prepare our lunch.

Natalie turns on the radio and watches us.

The news comes on; "The case for the defense started today in the trial of the rape of Megan Jones. The prosecution will examine Megan's state of mind, her injuries, and the lack of DNA evidence."

"What an awful thing it would be to get raped," Natalie says.

"What made you say that?"

Natalie is oblivious to Lil's discomfort. "Rape is a violation of a woman's soul."

"Yes. I hope that it never happens to you or I." Lil murmurs her response, looking away.

Natalie has the last word as lunch is served, "Of course it won't." Natalie looks at Lil, calm and reasonable. Then begins shoveling omelet.

My black cat smooches Natalie's leg, back and forth. Sometimes I suspect that I have a clever witch for a daughter.

"That cat should starve for eating my lizard. Lousy bastard!"

"The cat didn't eat it," Lil says. "Just played with it. The lizard died of fear."

"The bitch of a cat killed it. Destroyed my pet," Natalie insists.

"I intend to knock at your door in future. I'm Sorry. What did you do with your pet?"

"Buried her in the pet cemetery."

Lil smiles sympathetically; "You are such a direct young woman; you make it very clear where you stand."

Natalie smooches Lil and I, and then rides off on her bike, back to school.

"We have an amazing daughter, she blows me away," I say, turning to Lil.

She gathers up dishes from the table, avoiding eye contact. I remain seated.

"I assume it is just coincidence that Natalie has hit every one of my raw nerves." Lil says.

"That's crazy, Lil. Do you want to stop the crazy stuff?""

"Yes. Do you?"

"No!"

"Why?"

"I guess I don't know how it can work," I say.

"You've lost interest in our relationship?"

"No! How can it work when I can't trust you. Why do you have to fuck strangers!"

Lil sits. "When I'm with someone I find attractive I hope it will drown out the bad memories from my past."

Lil is so obvious, I want to ask, *And do you tell these strangers of your purpose*? But I can't ask Lil that, it isn't meaningful just yet. Instead I ask, "And does it ever work?"

"Yes, it did with you, until you started to remind me of my past."

"I want to be accepting of you, but you're out of control."

"Yes, I know. So, you're saying you can't change until I accept you as you are, right now?" Lil asks.

"I'm not sure. How can I trust you?"

"It'll take a while. Test me," she says.

"I need some space."

"Take all the space you want."

"I'm going for a drive. I have to think about this, will be a day or two. I'll call Natalie and tell her where I'm going."

I drive to the family cabin at Purakaunui – at the ancient fishing village laid out around the leeward side of a lagoon--warm in the late morning sun. I turn down the single-lane road that leads to the ocean, where as kids we vacationed, living off the land: clams, flounder, rabbits, and watercress. I smell again cut grass and seaweed and glimpse the pier where the dinghy is moored. The wood shed is packed to the ceiling, and the rain gutters have filled up the water tank.

Resentment toward Lillian is eating me, loving and hating her at the same time, afraid of failing to heal her, losing her forever. I am only going to stay here for one night. I wish I had brought some scotch; a shot might have helped loosen my resentment… I remember how drugged I was that night at Raffles Comedy Club. The police told Lil that there was a rape from Raffles Comedy Club just about every week. The bouncer, Skinhead Sheeba, definitely spiked our drinks at the door so surely he was the rapist. The therapists and the police led me up a false trail--trying to convince me that Lil had been a willing participant… that it wasn't rape. Oh, my God, poor Lil!

The cabin has three comfortable bedrooms, and is entirely vacant, mine for the night. In the lounge there is a big-screen TV beside the stone hearth. I light the fire for ambience--even though it is the beginning of summer. I will soon have a plate of mushrooms and clams simmering.

I listen to the silence and feel the warmth. There is a rustle of a bird among the rafters below the corrugated iron roofing. A spider hangs down from the light fixture—and repeatedly exerts itself in an attempt to climb up the side of the bulb and liberate itself to the rafters. After many efforts it succeeds. An old newspaper has turned brown under the coffee table. I read the date on the newspaper, *October 7, 2009*. The cabin has been vacant for more than two months.

I read in this newspaper about some research they were doing at my old university, about alcoholism and other addictions being caused by a genetic propensity combined with childhood trauma. They suspected the same conditions were the trigger of mental illness; *An accumulation of traumatic experiences overloads the system. The overload builds up until there it is, the final straw that breaks the system, and any long-term semblance to dignity.*

Whatever! I must accept what I cannot change… you have to keep calm and clear at these moments, no matter what.

I wake to the sound of rain dripping from the trees but walk to the beach anyway. A variety of shells litter the foreshore and I look for one worthy of giving to Natalie. A bird's body lies in my path and as I draw nearer I see it is a Molly Mawk, its fading plumage split by maggot-infested flesh. Am I a desperate romantic, robbed of my true love? Or am I just another angry man, afraid to let my shield of pride fall?

I search further and discover a tiny iridescent Abalone shell, no bigger than my thumbnail. Perfect. I take it back to the cabin and wrap it in tissue.

What am I really afraid of? What has happened is intractable, but the idea of losing Lil once more makes me sick. Yet I'm afraid to trust her, afraid she'll take my heart away and leave me to rot. I know she doesn't belong to me, but doesn't she owe me some piece of herself? What part of me does Lil want? I don't want to think of us in pieces.

I want to go home, so walk to my car and reach for my keys. Bugger! There is a hole in my pocket. I return and search the cabin methodically. No luck! So I search in the long grass around the car park. Nothing! I search again… until a Molly Mawk, circles above and lands behind my car—disturbs something shiny. It is my car keys!

A flock of gulls gather above me, swirling and squawking. Waves of echoes bounce off the cliff beyond, then silence. This silence reminds me of the time when

I shot the seagulls that were shitting on my dad's boat. Maybe I haven't had a bloody clue as to what forgiveness is really about, nor my failure to let go. What are my options? Forgiveness is the only known antidote to resentment. My experience has been that forgiveness has a delayed effect… and requires an effort deeper than I have exerted to date—but that exertion is my only option if I wish release from a future of bitterness.

I start my car engine and head back along the foreshore, avoiding the rabbit darting across the road. I drive back toward Lil, simply following emotion… scared. I turn on the radio, set to my program of current affairs and debate. How do I feel about Lillian now? Maybe I am the one who needs help. My mind comes back to driving over the mountain toward home and I listen to the radio program.

There are flashing lights around the corner, an ambulance. A yellow Toyota Corolla has rolled into the gutter on the opposite side of the road. Oh, my God! Is it Lil? Damn! Further along the road a St. John's paramedic is about to put a gray sheet over a dead woman lying on her back on the side of the road. I am shaking. I walk over to the body, purposely not looking at the paramedic. Three spectators are watching.

The paramedic walks toward me. He must have grabbed my arm. I push him into the gutter. I am staggering now, not daring to think or feel, holding on before another breathe. Praying, I grab for the sheet before the paramedic gets back to his feet... It is not Lil!

I am so relieved that I cry.

Lil is waiting at the door when I get home. I run and grin. She runs up to me and hugs me. I step back and look closely at her eagerness; feel the stir of her strong smooth-skinned body. Her jade eyes flick over me then away. They are restless and very bright.

"You like trouble?" she asks.

"No, but it's happened so often it can't be an accident."

"I'm not scared of you," she says.

"Good," I say.

"In that case..."

She starts to wriggle out of her jeans. The tops of her buttocks gleam as she shakes her hair free and I know I am being tempted. The timer on the microwave rings and she hesitates. Then, with her back to me, she releases her bra under her sweater.

"I want to touch you," I say. "But I can't."

"Of course," she says, throwing me down. Then she is holding me, rising over me like an old dream, her face burning and staring with open mouth, desperate lips, staring into my eyes. I gently push her away.

She shrinks, embarrassed. I hug her. "I know you want to move forward. But this isn't the way."

I see the shimmer of her necklace turn my way, then the flicker of her eyes.

I hug her again. Lil stands and talks as she tightens the belt of her jeans: "I guess that would have been too easy."

"I want more than that," I say.

"And I do too." Lil says. "Maybe we can have it when I return from California with Kathy."

"In the meantime, let's try and take it easy," I say, "talk as we go."

Then she grins and starts crying at the same time. She excuses herself and goes outside, turns, waves, and jauntily rakes my straw hat over her head.

By the time Natalie comes home from Grandma's house it is bedtime. Lillian has weeded the cornfield, helped me cook dinner, and there have been tears on both sides. What has been denied is not our passion, or even our connection through experiencing similar histories of abuse, but the deep-seated sadness that follows vulnerability revealed, insecurities exposed. Natalie will ask more difficult questions about the details of her birth as she gets older. What does she really make of Witi's creation story? Maybe I will have to tell her some details about her birth drama… but better if Lillian does that. Shit! Forget about all that anxiety for the moment.

It is difficult for me to cry in front of anyone, even myself. Now, I am awash.

Natalie has fallen asleep, slumped on my lap with her head on my shoulder and an arm across me. A couple of oystercatchers rasp optimistic notes down on the foreshore; a yellow light blinks on in the gathering dusk. That is what Elsinore is like; it sets no agenda or timetable.

Two weeks later, Natalie and I rush to the airport and hug Lil and Kathy. We can't let go. Everyone is watching us as we laugh excitedly.

Kathy wants to drive the car home. "Not after a long flight, Honey, tomorrow."

Lil tells us that her trip went well—she got Paul settled into his first job and attended Barbara's graduation ceremony.

"What is Paul's job?" Natalie asks.

"A trainee chef in the Navy, after he finishes boot camp."

When we get home, Natalie takes Lil over to the Powers' barn to show her mom that she has learned to milk cows. Kathy takes the dog out to round up the stragglers. There are eighty cows now and four milking bays. Neither Lil nor I let on that Lil knows her way around and under a cow. Lil helps out; milks half the herd. The girls come home laughing with dirty faces and arms laden with duck eggs, eager to tell me about their adventures.

"Forgiveness," Lil quotes from the book she is reading; "Can be hard to come by. You carry a wrong around with you for years and years, and then one day you look around and find you've put it down somewhere and didn't even notice."

That I can relate to.

I have never given up on Lil. I understand now that my persistence was a good instinct. I make her a cup of tea. Kathy, Natalie, and Lil are finishing a long game of scrabble. It is midnight on December 23rd, and we have birthdays starting. I put my gifts under the birthday tree, opposite the Christmas tree--I cut both trees this morning, just branches off the pine tree behind the tool shed.

I depart for bed early because, in the morning, Greg will telephone from San Francisco, and my parents, Selwyn, the Powers, Witi and his family will join us for dinner. I am grateful that I have discovered a new life to share, a life of pillow pampering and good honest sweat, coming home and making home.

Gazing into the bedroom mirror I see that my eyes are red. Natalie and Lil are still up, laughing. The phone rings and Natalie answers the call. *Could it be Ruth?*

I look deeper into the mirror and see the reflection of the moon, mercurial on the sea. Upland Road follows the contour of the hill—the hill that reflects the faint sound of a stream that ripples down to the sea. Through the open window I smell herbs from the garden. The residual heat of the day drives one more crackle from a Kowhai seedpod. As I drift off, I see myself plowing up a new field, while Natalie and Kathy ride through pastures of blue irises.

EPILOGUE

It was Witi who said that all families are somewhat like jungles… I think Lillian would have to agree with this. Lil is sitting with Natalie and I on the highest terrace of the old Pa, the ancient hill above the village of Elsinore. The three of us admire the gigantic crescent staircase of eleven terraces, like the Poutama pattern described in the novel *Matriarch* as the wondrous Stairway to Heaven.

Down below is our village and beyond is the next village, Otakou… with its fisheries and sandy beaches--and a few widespread country towns afar.

Natalie tells Lillian the ancient Maori creation story that Witi first shared with her years ago. Lillian's beauty shines out with a gleaming light that Natalie might almost touch and feel; it vibrates and electrifies the air. Natalie's voice thrills with excitement. "…None of the Maori ancestors, the offspring of the gods, knew death. Among them was Maui, who was aborted by his mother and cast into the sea."

Natalie pauses. "Oh, Mom. Pay attention." Then she looks deep within Lillian. "I have much in common with the brave Maui…"

Natalie looks far out to the east, across the Pacific Ocean, tears welling.

"Maui set off toward the red flashing light…" Natalie finishes the story with a broken voice.

"That's a very nice fable," Lil says.

"What do you mean, Mom! It *isn't* a fable. The creation story is about me!"

"What do *you* mean?" Lillian asks.

"You tell me!" Natalie is gasping for air.

"How do you *feel* about that creation story?" Lil asks.

"I want to know exactly what happened to me."

A pause. Lillian is very still while she looks out to the horizon. "I'm not some freak who coldly failed her daughter," Lillian says. "Your father and I both suffered horrid childhood abuse that would have left most people in prison by the time they were adults—check the statistics…at least I am not a criminal."

Natalie watches Lillian, sees the signs of guilt, the sour turn to her mouth, the shame… she gives Lil more time try to find her way out of this maze.

"I'm not really answering your question, am I?" Lil says.

"What question?" Natalie asks.

"About how exactly it happened."

"If I had died then you could have been a criminal!"

"It happened because of mistrust." Lil looks Natalie hesitantly in the eye then looks down at her feet. "It is difficult for people like your father and I to truly trust other people when we are vulnerable."

Lillian pauses for several gulps of air and a dry swallow. "My behavior was ignorant and sick!"

"Tell me about that," Natalie says.

"The mistrust mostly happened…" Lillian turns to Natalie with a sheet of tears, "I'm sorry I hurt you. I want to be with you and Dylan. I don't know what else to say at this moment…"

BIBLIOGRAPHY:

Contributions to this novel by the following authors are acknowledged:

Philip Roth, Toni Morrison, Michael Riddell, Ben Olson, Philip Temple, Brian Caldwell, Chuck Polahniuk, Drew Stepek, Nick Hornby, Chris Else, Owen Marshall, Henry Miller, Richard Powers, Chris Abani, Elizabeth Moon, Lloyd Jones, Witi Ihimaera, Vanessa de Oliveira, Arthur Blessitt, Curtis Sittenfeld, Janna Levin, Marianne Williamson, Ezeibieli Kingsley Chidi and Anne Desclos.

This bibliography contains title details, in chronological order of appearance, of the paragraphs and smaller exerts of sampled literature from outstanding authors displayed in this novel:

Witi Ihimaera: "The Matriarch," Raupo Publishing (New Zealand) Ltd. 1996, See Prologue (larger exert comprising the creation story) and Epilogue.

Lloyd Jones: "Choo Woo," Victoria University Press (NZ), 1998. See Chapter One.

Janna Levin: "A Madman Dreams of Turing Machines," Random House, 2007. See Chapter One.

Richard Powers: "The Echo Maker," Farrar, Straus and Giroux. (New York), 2006. See Chapters 2, 3, 5, 36.

Owen Marshall: "Harlequin Rex," Random House (NZ), 1998. Chapters 3,7,10,12, 25.

Chris Else: "On River Road," Random House (NZ), 2004. See Chapters 3, 10, 12, 15, 18, 23, 25.

Vanessa de Oliveira: "The Diary of Marise," Matrix Editora, Brazil, 2001. See Chapter Seven.

Ezeibieli Kingsley Chidi: "Limbus Infantum" Unpublished screenplay, 2007. See Chapter Nine.

Philip Roth: "The Professor of Desire," Vintage, 1977. See Chapters 9,10,13.

Chuck Polahniuk: "Fight Club," Henry Holt (NY), 1997. See Chapter Ten.

Philip Roth: "The Human Stain," Vintage, 1999. See Chapters 10, 13, 19.

Marianne Williamson: "Return to Love: reflection on the principles in A Course in Miracles" Library of Congress # 299.93 Published 1992. See Chapters 10, 13.

Brian Caldwell: "We All Fall Down," Alphar Publishing, 2006. See Chapters 18, 25.

Michael Riddell: "Masks and Shadows," Flamingo (NZ), 2000. See Chapter Twenty.

Philip Temple: "Stations," Collins (NZ), 1979. See Chapters 20, 36.

Nick Hornby: "How to be Good," Penguin Group, 2002. See Chapters 20, 22, 27.

Arthur Blessitt: "Praying with George W, Bush," www.blessitt.com, 1984. See chapter Thirty Four.

Elizabeth Moon: "The Speed of Dark," Ballantine, 2002. See Chapter Forty.

Toni Morrison: "The Bluest Eye," Vintage at Random House, 1999. See Chapter Forty-Four.

Toni Morrison: "Beloved," Vintage at Random House, 1979.

Henry Miller: "Tropic of Capricorn," Grove Press (New York), 1961.

Anne Desclos/Pauline Reage: "The Story of O" Jean-Jacques Pauvert (Paris), 1954.

www.ingramcontent.com/pod-product-compliance
Lightning Source LLC
Chambersburg PA
CBHW020611310726
48979CB00008B/1432/J
* 9 7 8 0 9 7 8 6 0 2 4 2 0 *